Aida conce ___ tic crackled around her ___ , Aida knew the ghost was gone.

She considered pretending to faint, but that seemed excessive. She did, however, let her shoulders sag dramatically, as if it would take her days to recover. A little labored breathing was icing on the cake.

"Your breath is gone."

She cracked open one eye to find the giant's vest in front of her. When she straightened to full height, she saw more vest, miles of it, before her gaze settled on the knot of his necktie. It was a little annoying to be forced to tilt her face up to view his. But up close, she spotted an anomaly she hadn't noticed from a distance: something different about the eye with the scar. Best to find out who the hell this man was before she asked him about it.

"Aida Palmer," she said, extending a hand.

He stared down at it for a moment, gaze shifting up her arm and over her face, as if he were trying to decide whether he'd catch the plague if they touched. Then his big, gloved hand swallowed hers, warm and firm. Through the fine black leather, she felt a pleasant tingle prickle her skin—an unexpected sensation far more foreign than any ghostly static.

# BITTER SPIRITS

## JENN BENNETT

BERKLEY SENSATION, NEW YORK

**THE BERKLEY PUBLISHING GROUP**
Published by the Penguin Group
**Penguin Group (USA) LLC**
375 Hudson Street, New York, New York 10014

USA • Canada • UK • Ireland • Australia • New Zealand • India • South Africa • China

penguin.com

A Penguin Random House Company

BITTER SPIRITS

A Berkley Sensation Book / published by arrangement with the author

Berkley Sensation Books are published by The Berkley Publishing Group.
BERKLEY SENSATION® is a registered trademark of Penguin Group (USA) LLC.
The "B" design is a trademark of Penguin Group (USA) LLC.

For information, address: The Berkley Publishing Group,
a division of Penguin Group (USA) LLC,
375 Hudson Street, New York, New York 10014.

ISBN: 978-0-425-26957-2

PUBLISHING HISTORY
Berkley Sensation mass-market edition / January 2014

PRINTED IN THE UNITED STATES OF AMERICA

10  9  8  7  6  5  4  3  2  1

Cover art by Aleta Rafton.
Cover design by Lesley Worrell.
Interior text design by Kelly Lipovich.

*To the ghost of Mary Ellen Pleasant*

# ACKNOWLEDGMENTS

I couldn't do this without my extraordinary agent, Laura Bradford, who never blinks or loses patience with me when I hurl my (often) madcap book ideas her way. And I'm so thankful for my lovely new editor, Leis Pederson, who not only "gets" my voice but also champions it with grace and positivity. Many thanks to the talented Aleta Rafton for her gorgeous cover art, and to everyone at Penguin who works tirelessly behind the scenes.

Thanks to: Ashley Diestel at the Palace Hotel for her archival assistance, the *San Francisco Chronicle*, The Bancroft Library at Berkeley, the Swedish Club of San Francisco, and the numerous people who answered my questions about the (often painful) history of Chinatown, especially Philip Choy. Hat tip to Stacey Luce for the 1920s map of San Francisco.

Much love to the fab Sandy Williams and my wonderful beta readers: Miriam Blackmon, Cat Lauria, and Katie Morley. Special shout-outs to: Annika Einarsson (who corrected my wobbly Swedish) and Daphne Yeung (who made me fall in love with Hong Kong and taught me how to swear, toast, and give thanks in Cantonese). And I'll never be able to thank my (massively creative) husband enough; his ideas for fixing plot problems are always better than mine. Always. Lastly, my unwavering gratitude goes out to: all the booksellers and librarians who carry my books, the bloggers who write about them, and to the readers who read them.

# ONE

JUNE 2, 1927—NORTH BEACH, SAN FRANCISCO

AIDA PALMER'S TENSE FINGERS GRIPPED THE GOLD LOCKET around her neck as the streetcar came to a stop near Gris-Gris. It was almost midnight, and Velma had summoned her to the North Beach speakeasy on her night off—no explanation, just told her to come immediately. A thousand reasons why swirled inside Aida's head. None of them were positive.

"Well, Sam," she muttered to the locket, "I think I might've made a mistake. If you were here, you'd probably tell me to face up to it, so here goes nothing." She gave the locket a quick kiss and stepped out onto the sidewalk.

The alley entrance was blocked by a fancy dark limousine and several Model Ts surrounded by men, so Aida headed to the side.

Gossip and cigarette smoke wafted under streetlights shrouded with cool summer fog. She endured curious stares of nighttime revelers and hiked the nightclub's sloping sidewalk past a long line of people waiting to get inside. Hidden from the street, three signs lined the brick wall corridor leading to the entrance, each one lit by a border of round bulbs. The first two signs announced a hot jazz quartet and a troupe of Chinese acrobats. The third featured a painting of a brunette surrounded by ghostly specters:

WITNESS CHILLING SPIRIT MYSTERIES LIVE IN PERSON!
FAMED TRANCE MEDIUM MADAME AIDA PALMER
CALLS FORTH SPIRITS FROM BEYOND,
REUNITING AUDIENCE MEMBERS WITH
DEPARTED LOVED ONES.
—PATRONS WISHING TO PARTICIPATE SHOULD
BRING MEMENTO MORI—

One of the men standing next to the sign looked up at her when she passed by, a fuzzy recognition clouding his eyes. Maybe he'd seen her show . . . Maybe he'd been too drunk to remember. She gave him a tight smile and approached the club's gated entrance.

"Pardon me," she said to the couple at the head of the line, then stood on tiptoes and peeked through a small window.

One of the club's doormen stared back at her. "Evening, Miss Palmer."

"Evening. Velma called me in."

Warm, brassy light and a chorus of greetings beckoned her inside.

"The alley's blocked," she noted when the door closed behind her. "Any idea what's going on?"

"Don't know. Could be trouble," said the first doorman.

A second doorman started to elaborate until he noticed the club manager, Daniels, shooting them a warning look as he spoke to a couple of rough-looking men. His gaze connected with Aida's; he motioned with his head: *upstairs*.

Wonderful. Trouble indeed.

Aida left the doormen and marched through the crowded lobby. At the far end, a yawning arched entry led into the main floor of the club. The house orchestra warmed up behind buzzing conversations and clinking glasses as Aida headed toward a second guarded door that bypassed the crowds.

Gris-Gris was one of the largest black-and-tan speakeasies in the city. Social rules concerning race and class went unheeded here. Anyone who bought a membership card was welcome, and patrons dined and danced with whomever they pleased. Like many of the other acts appearing onstage, Aida was only booked through early July. She'd been working here a month now and couldn't complain. It was much nicer than most of the dives she'd worked out East, and to say the owner was sympathetic to her skills was an understatement.

Velma Toussaint certainly stirred up chatter among her employees. People said she was a witch or a sorceress—she was—and that she practiced hoodoo, which she did. But the driving force of the gossip was a simpler truth: polite society just didn't know how to handle a woman who single-handedly ran a prosperous, if not illicit, business. Still, she played the role to the hilt, and Aida admired any woman who wasn't afraid to defy convention.

Though it was a relief to work for someone who actually believed in her own talents, all that really mattered was Aida was working. She needed this job. And right now she was crossing her fingers that the "trouble" was not big enough to get her fired. A particular unhappy patron from last night's show was her biggest worry. It wasn't her fault that he didn't like the message his dead sister brought over from the beyond, and how was she supposed to have known the man was a state senator? If someone had told her he preferred a charlatan's act to the truth, she would've happily complied.

Grumbling under her breath, Aida climbed the side stairs and sailed through a narrow hallway to the club's administrative offices. The front room, where a young girl who handled Velma's paperwork usually sat, was dark and empty. As she passed through the room, her breath rushed out in a wintery white puff.

Ghost.

She cautiously approached the main office. The door was cracked. She hesitated and listened to a low jumble of foreign words streaming from the room, spoken in a deep, male voice. Beyond the cloud of cold breath, she saw a woman with traditional Chinese combs in her hair, on which strings of red beads dangled. Bare feet peeked beneath her sheer sleeping gown. She stood behind a very large, dark-headed man wearing a long coat, who stared out a long window that looked down over the main floor of the club.

Aida's cold breath indicated that one of them was a ghost. This realization alone was remarkable, as Aida had only encountered one ghost in the club since she'd arrived—a carpenter who'd suffered a heart attack while building the stage and died several years before Velma came into possession of Gris-Gris—and Aida had exorcised it immediately.

In her experience, ghosts did not move around—they remained tethered to the scene of their death. So unless someone died in Velma's office tonight, a ghost shouldn't be here.

Shouldn't be, but was.

Strong ghosts looked as real as anyone walking around with a heartbeat. But even if the woman with the red combs hadn't been dressed for bed, Aida would've known the man was alive. He was speaking to himself in a low rumble, a repeating string of inaudible words that sounded much like a prayer.

Ghosts don't talk.

"Is she your dance partner?" Aida said.

The man jerked around. *My.* He was enormous—several inches over six feet and with shoulders broad enough to topple small buildings as he passed. Brown hair, so dark it was almost black, was brilliantined back with a perfect part. Expensive clothes. A long, serious face, one side of which bore a large, curving scar. He blinked at Aida for a moment, gaze zipping up and down the length of her in hurried assessment, then spoke in low voice. "You can see her?"

"Oh yes." The ghost turned to focus on the man, giving Aida a new, gorier view of the side of her head. "Ah, there's the death wound. Did you kill her?"

"What? No, of course not. Are you the spirit medium?"

"My name's on the sign outside."

"Velma said you can make her . . . go away."

"Ah." Aida was barely able to concentrate on what the man was saying. His words were wrapped inside a deep, grand voice—the voice of a stage actor, dramatic and big and velvety. It was a voice that could probably talk you into doing anything. A siren's call, rich as the low notes of a perfectly tuned cello.

And maybe there really was some magic in it, because all she could think about, as he stood there in his fine gray suit with his fancy silk necktie and a long black jacket that probably cost more than her entire wardrobe, was pressing her face into his crisply pressed shirt.

What a perverse thought. And one that was making her neck warm.

"Can you?"

"Pardon?"

"Get rid of her. She followed me across town." He swept a hand through the woman's body. "She's not corporeal."

"They usually aren't." The ghost had followed him? Highly unusual. And yet, the giant man acted as if the ghost was merely a nuisance. Most men didn't have the good sense to be afraid when they should.

"Your breath is . . ." he started.

Yes, she knew: shocking to witness up close rather than from the safe distance of the audience when she was performing onstage. "Do you know what an aura is?"

"No clue."

"It's an emanation around humans—an effusion of energy. Everyone has one. Mine turns cold when a spirit or ghost is nearby. When my warm breath crosses my aura, it becomes visible—same as going outside on a cold day."

"That's fascinating, but can you get rid of her first and talk later?"

"No need to get snippy."

He looked at her like she was a blasphemer who'd just disrupted church service, fire and brimstone blazing behind his eyes. "Please," he said in a tone that was anything but polite.

Aida stared at him for a long moment, a petty but sweet revenge. Then she inhaled and shook out her hands . . . closed her eyes, pretending to concentrate. Let him think she was doing him some big favor. Well, she *was*, frankly. If he searched the entire city, he'd be lucky to find another person with the gift to do what she did. But it wasn't difficult. The only effort it required was the same concentration it took to solve a quick math problem and the touch of her hand.

Pushing them over the veil was simple; calling them back took considerably more effort.

After she'd tortured the man enough, she reached out for the Chinese woman, feeling the marked change in temperature inside the phantom's body. Aida concentrated and willed her to leave. Static crackled around her fingertips. When the chill left the air, Aida knew the ghost was gone.

She considered pretending to faint, but that seemed excessive. She did, however, let her shoulders sag dramatically, as if it would take her days to recover. A little labored breathing was icing on the cake.

"Your breath is gone."

She cracked open one eye to find the giant's vest in front of her. When she straightened to full height, she saw more vest, miles of it, before her gaze settled on the knot of his necktie. It was a little annoying to be forced to tilt her face up to view his. But up close, she spotted an anomaly she hadn't noticed from a distance: something different about the eye with the scar. Best to find out who the hell this man was before she asked him about it.

"Aida Palmer," she said, extending a hand.

He stared down at it for a moment, gaze shifting up her arm and over her face, as if he were trying to decide whether he'd catch the plague if they touched. Then his big, gloved hand swallowed hers, warm and firm. Through the fine black leather, she felt a pleasant tingle prickle her skin—an unexpected sensation far more foreign than any ghostly static.

# TWO

---

WINTER MAGNUSSON WASN'T SUPERSTITIOUS. IF ANYONE would've asked if he believed in ghosts a week ago, he might've laughed. He wasn't laughing now. And after a lousy week marred by one bizarre event after another, he frankly wasn't sure what he believed anymore.

First, a crazy old woman had accosted him on the street and shouted some hocus-pocus curse at him. After that, a specter began appearing in his study every afternoon—something no one in his household could see but him. Then, during a business meeting tonight at a bar in Chinatown, someone spiked his drink with a foul-tasting green concoction. And before he could spit it out, a prostitute with a gaping hole in her head walked right through a wall from the brothel next door.

Like the specter in his study, no one but Winter saw the dead prostitute, but she'd damn sure followed him from Chinatown to North Beach. All she did was stare at him, but until the spirit medium walked in the room, he'd been questioning his sanity.

Now he was too unsettled to question much of anything.

After the medium's breath returned to normal, the first thing Winter noticed about her was her breasts, which were respectable. Much like looking into the sun during an eclipse, staring at her breasts would only lead to harm, so he quickly shifted his gaze upward. Slender fingers combed through blunt caramel brown bangs covering her forehead. Straight as a ruler, her sleek hair was styled into a short French bob that fell to her chin in the front and tapered to the nape of her neck. When she introduced herself and extended her hand to shake, it drew his attention to her skin, which was pale as milk and densely covered in bronze freckles. Not the kind you'd see smattered on the sun-kissed face of a child.

Freckles *everywhere*.

They began in a sliver of pale forehead above arched brows, gathered tightly across her nose and cheeks, lightened around her neck, then disappeared into the dipping neckline of her dress.

Winter's gaze raked over her breasts again—still respectable—down her dress to the jagged handkerchief hem below her knees. He followed the path of the spotted skin around her calves, half hidden by pale stockings, to the T-bar heels on her feet. Freckles on her *legs*—how about that? For some reason, he found this wildly exciting. Increasingly lurid thoughts ballooned inside his head after he wondered *exactly* what percentage of her skin was speckled. Did freckles cover her arms? The curving creases where her backside ended and her legs began? Her nipples?

He pushed away the enticing reverie, shook her hand, and successfully remembered his own name. "Winter Magnusson."

Her enormous brown eyes were ringed in kohl like some exotic Nile princess. A strange heat washed over him as their gazes connected.

"Good grief, you're a big one, aren't you?"

He stilled, rooted to the floor, unable to think of a response to that.

If he was big—and at four inches over six feet, he definitely was—then Miss Palmer was *very* small. Average height for a woman, legs on the long side, but there was something petite and slender about her frame. Graceful. She was also unusually pretty—far more attractive than the sketch of her on the poster outside Gris-Gris's entrance.

"I suppose everyone jumps when you snap your fingers." The way she said this, in a calm manner, almost smiling, made him think it wasn't a criticism as much as an honest assessment. Maybe even a compliment.

"They jump when I snap my fingers because without me, they have no income."

"*Aha!* I knew I'd heard your name around here. You're Velma's bootlegger."

She had such a disarming, casual way about her. Very straightforward, which was off-putting and exciting at the same time. Women didn't speak to him this way—hell, most *men* didn't speak to him this way.

"Not Velma's alone," he said. "And on the record, I'm in the fish business."

And he was: fish during the day, liquor at night. Both were considered some of the best in the city. Quality is an unusual thing to specialize in when your enterprise is illegal, but that was his niche. Winter's father owned boats before Volstead and fished up and down the coast, from San Francisco to Vancouver. His old routes and the contacts he'd collected made it easy to set up bootlegging from Canada. And like his father, Winter sold no bathtub gin—nothing cut, nothing fake—which allowed him to cater to the best restaurants, clubs, and hotels.

It also earned him the status of being one of the Big Three bootleggers in San Francisco.

Aida nodded as if it were of no consequence, then said, "They're different colors."

"What's that?"

"Your eyes."

Strangers never had the nerve to comment on his maimed eye or the hooked scar that extended from brow to cheekbone. Either they'd already heard the story behind it, or they were too intimidated to inquire. He wasn't used to explaining, and even considered ignoring the medium's questioning tone altogether, but her curious face swayed him.

Or maybe it was the freckled ankles . . . and what he'd like to do with those ankles, which started with licking and ended with them propped on his shoulders.

He cleared his throat. "One pupil is permanently dilated."

"Oh?" She stepped closer and craned her neck to inspect his eyes. The sweet scent of violet wafted from her hair, disorienting him far more than the foul drink and the damned ghost already had. "I see," she murmured. "They're both blue. The big pupil makes the left eye look darker. Is that genetic?"

"An injury," he said. "I was in an auto accident a couple of years ago."

God, how he detested the disfigurement. Every time he looked in the mirror, there they were, wounded eye and scar, reminding him of the one night he wanted more than anything to forget: when his family was brutally snatched away from him, crushed by the oncoming streetcar. Dumb luck that he survived, but some days he truly believed his continued existence was really a curse in disguise.

The medium made no comment about the scar; though, to her credit, she didn't appear to be revolted or frightened by its presence, nor did she politely pretend it wasn't there. "Can you see out of the wounded eye, or does the dilation affect your vision?"

He smelled violets again. Christ alive. She was intoxicating, standing so close. A pleasurable heat gathered in his groin. Any more pleasurable and he'd be forced to hide a rampant erection. He pulled his coat closed, just in case.

"My vision is perfect," he answered gruffly. "Right now, for instance, I see a tiny freckled woman in front of me, asking a lot of questions."

She laughed, and the sound did something funny to Winter's chest. Maybe he was getting ill. Having a heart attack at the age of thirty. He hoped to hell not. He'd rather be burned alive than tolerate another wretched doctor's so-called assistance. Between the parade of psychiatrists who treated his father's illness before the accident and the overpriced surgeons who sewed up his own eye after it, he'd seen enough doctors to last a lifetime, no matter how short.

When the medium finally turned away, he let out a long breath and watched the spellbinding sway of her ass with great interest as she strolled toward Velma's desk to set down her handbag and the cloche she'd been gripping in her hand. The view only got better when she shucked off her coat: freckles covered every inch of her slender arms.

He might pass out from excitement. His legs were definitely feeling unsteady. Wobbly, even. He felt high as a kite. Feverish. But when the room started to spin, he had the sinking feeling Miss Palmer's freckles weren't the cause.

After Aida set her things down, the bootlegger silently stared at her for several beats, an unnerving intimidation that chilled the sweat prickling the back of her neck. And because she was clearly depraved, a thrill shot through her.

God above, he was well built. Like an enormous bull. Just how tall was he, exactly? Her gaze stuttered over the solid bulk of his upper arms, which stretched the wool of his expensive coat, then ran down the rather distracting length of his meaty legs.

This was a body built for conquering. For smiting enemies. Ransacking villages.

Ravaging innocent women.

Maybe even some not-so-innocent women.

He wasn't pretty or conventionally good-looking. More savagely handsome, she decided. Rough-hewn and dark and intense. A barbarian stuffed inside a rich man's suit. Not her usual taste in men, but for some reason, she found his big body rousing.

"So tell me," Aida said, attempting to get her mind refocused on the reason she was called here. "How long was that ghost following you, Mr. Magnusson?" His name sounded Scandinavian. He looked it. Something about the combination of those ridiculously high, flat cheekbones and the long face . . . his reserved, intense nature. No accent, so she assumed he wasn't fresh off the boat.

"A couple of hours."

"Any idea why?"

He made an affirmative noise. His mouth didn't seem to know how to smile—it just stretched into a taut line as he stared at her with those strange, otherworldly eyes. Eyes that fluttered shut momentarily. When they reopened, he looked dazed.

"Are you all right?" she asked.

"I . . ."

He never finished. One second he appeared cognizant; the next, he was swaying on his feet. Before she had time to react, he was leaning toward her like a felled giant sequoia. Instinct opened her arms—as if she could catch someone his size. But she did . . . rather, he crashed into her, a dead weight that overtook hers.

"H-help!" she cried out as his big body took hers down in a series of awkward, slow motions that had her bending backward, dropping to one knee—"Oh, God . . . dammit, Mr. Magnusson . . ."—then finally crumbling beneath him.

Her mind made great, panicked leaps between the mundane—*He smells pleasantly of soap and witch hazel*—and the practical: *How could another human being weigh so much? Is he filled with rocks?*

A thunder of footfalls shook the floorboards, and before she could fully wonder if it was possible to experience death by crushing, the impossibly titanic weight of Giant was lifted from her. Sweet relief! While two club workers lifted Mr. Magnusson, Aida's boss helped her to her feet.

"You hurt?" Velma Toussaint's briar rose dress had a softly sweeping neck that revealed sharp collarbones and pale nutmeg skin of indeterminable ancestry. Her shiny brown hair was sculpted into a short Eton crop, with slicked-back finger waves molded close to the head.

"Fine . . . fine," Aida replied between breaths.

Velma was a former dancer in her mid-thirties who

moved to San Francisco from Louisiana a few years back and began running the club after her wayward cheat of a husband—the original owner of Gris-Gris—died of an aneurism. Rumor had it that his untimely death came after Velma used a pair of scissors to cut his photo in half during some midnight ritual. Aida didn't know if this was true, but if it *was*, no doubt the man deserved what he got.

"The poison's settling in," Velma said.

"You poisoned him?"

Velma made an impatient face. "He *came here* poisoned. Hexed. Someone sneaked poison in his drink and left a written spell on the table. Appears to be some sort of Chinese magic that acts like a supernatural magnet. Draws ghosts."

"Like the one that was in here."

"So you got rid of it? Thank you," Velma said. "I've got a friend in Louisiana who might know an antidote. Called the operator to set up a long-distance call a quarter hour ago. Should be coming through the line any minute now, but he's getting worse."

Everyone gathered around the downed bootlegger. With disheveled hair falling across his forehead, Mr. Magnusson lay on the floor with his eyes shut, groaning. Looking down at him, Aida thought he really did look like a giant, and that she wouldn't be surprised to see an army of tiny men scurry over him to tie him down with ropes.

Hurried footfalls drew Aida's attention to the doorway as a slender Chinese boy burst into the room. Dressed in a well-tailored cedar green suit and a newsboy cap, he couldn't have been a day over twenty, twenty-one. His face was pleasant, his body sinewy and strung tighter than a guitar, bouncing with energy.

"Aida, meet Bo Yeung," Velma said. "Bo, this is Miss Palmer."

Bo turned a friendly face her way and touched the brim of his cap in greeting, then tilted his head as if he'd just worked out a crossword puzzle answer. "Oh, the spirit medium," he said, looking her up and down with a quirky smile. "I'm Mr. Magnusson's assistant."

"A pleasure."

"Bo," Winter mumbled from the floor, attempting to prop himself up on one elbow and failing. "Did you get a chance to have the symbols on the paper deciphered?"

"Yes, boss," Bo said coolly. "Unfortunately, it seems you've been poisoned with *Gu*."

# THREE

---

AIDA HAD NEVER HEARD OF SUCH A THING. "GOO?"

"*Gu*. Black magic," Bo elaborated. "Old Chinese myths say sorcerers can make a magical poison to manipulate a man. Different kinds of *Gu* for different things."

Velma waved a small circle of paper filled with green symbols. "This particular magic is drawing ghosts to you, Winter. If we don't get rid of it, you'll be the Pied Piper with a herd of ghosts following you around." She turned to Bo. "You sure you don't know anyone around town who could do this kind of magic, Bo?"

The bootlegger's assistant scrunched up his nose in irritation. "Only magic worker I know is you, conjurer. And it seems to me that you're the one with the reputation for curses that kill. Maybe *you* want to hex Winter."

"Why in God's name would I want to hex my own supplier?"

Winter grunted from the floor. "If you ever want to kill me, Velma, do it to my face—no riddles or hexes. And give me fair warning."

"Believe me, Winter, if I'm gonna kill you, you'll be the first to know."

Merriment danced behind Winter's dazed eyes as Bo laughed.

Velma frowned. "I don't specialize in Chinese curses, but if you can think of anyone who might, Bo, you need to tell us now."

"You think I know every Chinaman in the city?"

She put a hand on her hip. "I think you know a little about everyone. Why else would Winter pay a scrawny, orphaned thief a better salary than my own manager makes?"

"I can't help it if you're miserly," Bo deadpanned. When Velma shot him a murderous look, Bo winked at her. "Look, I really don't know anyone other than the person who interpreted the *Gu* symbols. I can ask around. I've heard rumors about restaurant owners cursing one another—maybe they learned tricks from someone. But it might take me a few hours to get a name. Maybe longer."

"My source will be quicker." She stared down at Winter. "You came to me for advice, so I'm going to give it to you. Best I can piece together, that old woman you claimed accosted you in the street? She was a witch sent to lay a spell on you that opened your eyes to ghosts, and the *Gu* poison was administered tonight to draw them to you. Sounds to me like someone is trying to frighten you."

"Who?"

"You'd know better than me. Let's just hope my source can help me with a cure. In the meantime, I can do something to help ease the jinx. Why don't we get you upstairs to my apartment. Aida, you might as well stick around and help, just in case he attracts more ghosts."

Aida briefly wondered if she was going to receive extra pay for all this.

Two bouncers peeled Winter off the floor. Velma led them all down a short passage to a locked stairwell. Up a short flight of stairs, they entered Velma's private living quarters through a warm yellow hallway. She pointed her men into a room halfway down the hall, swinging the door open wide to reveal a spacious bathroom, where a black-and-white checkerboard pattern covered the floor and an enormous claw-foot tub sat in the back.

"Boys, you manage Winter." She turned to Bo. "And you, run a bath. Cold water only."

"A bath?" Bo shot her a bewildered look.

"Not for cleaning. For unhexing. Don't put him in until I come back. I need to mix something up first." She crooked a finger at Aida. "Come with me."

Aida followed her boss's rapid path through the apartment to a bright sitting area filled with dark wood and buttery chintz silk. Next to a fireplace, Velma unlocked a nondescript narrow door and beckoned her inside.

The scents of spice and wax filled Aida's nostrils. A single bulb hung from the rafters of a tiny square room with no furniture other than a long table butted up against one wall. The walls were lined with shelves from floor to ceiling, crammed with books and candles and bottles of every size, shape, and color—a few of them old liquor bottles with the labels torn off. Bundles of dried herbs dangled from long nails that had been hammered into the sides of the shelves.

"This is my workroom," Velma announced casually. She scoured the shelves for several minutes and began pulling down jars. A couple were filled with tinted powders: one with a mixture of dried herbs, and another, unidentifiable. She set them all on the worktable with a dinged metal bowl, measuring cup, and spoon. While Aida inspected them, she retrieved a worn book with a broken spine, which was littered with scraps of paper serving as bookmarks, and opened to a page that said: UNCROSSING BATH TO REMOVE CURSES. A list of ingredients followed. Scribbled pencil notes filled the margins.

A muffled *brring-brring* rang through the walls. Velma quickly tapped her fingers on the tops of the jars she'd collected. "Rue, hyssop, dried okra, and the two compound mixtures needed. Stir all of these together. Follow the recipe. Don't touch anything else," she added, and then left the room in a flurry.

Aida stood still for several moments, looking around at the assortment of oddities crowding the shelves. As if she'd *want* to touch some of these things. Velma wasn't the first person Aida had known to possess a talent for spellwork or to dabble in mysteries. Aida had stumbled upon witches, psychics, cartomancers, and other assorted characters with unexplainable skills, as they all seemed to be drawn to one another as iron is to a magnet. Like speaks to like. Aida's own abilities often seemed tame by comparison.

It didn't take much time to mix up the ingredients for the spiritual bath. As she finished, Velma raced back into the room, mumbling to herself, and dragged a wooden stool to a bay of shelves. She stood on tiptoes to retrieve a jam jar filled with what appeared to be evenly cut sticks with thorns—only, when Velma dumped out several of them inside a large mortar and pestle, Aida realized that she was wrong.

"Dried centipedes," Velma said blithely when Aida stared. "My associate claims that *Gu* poison is venom magic. The sorcerer will put all kinds of creepy-crawlies inside a spelled jar—snakes, scorpions, frogs." Velma pounded the dried centipedes with alarming gusto; the shells made a horrible crunching noise beneath her pestle. "Then it's a fight to the death. The venomous insects and reptiles battle it out, eating one another. A spell is cast upon the last one standing. That's what they use to brew the poison."

*Crunch, crunch, crunch.*

Velma stopped to retrieve two more jars. From the first, she used tongs to retrieve two frail, perfectly preserved scorpions, their curled tails stretched out and feet shriveled against their abdomens. She dumped them in the mortar with a sprinkling of some dark red powder and began grinding them up with the centipedes.

"The remedy for the hex is to fight like with like—the centipedes and scorpions will eat the *Gu* inside him. Let's go ahead and do the unhexing bath. It should help weaken the spell and give the remedy a better chance to take hold. Here, give me your bowl." Velma bowed her head as if praying and spoke a few mumbled words over the bath mixture. When finished, she let out a deep breath and handed it back to Aida. "Take this to the bathroom. Dump it in the bath water and mix it up."

"Me?"

"It won't harm you. I called downstairs and asked someone to bring ice from the bar. We want the water as cold as possible to shake the curse loose. Once you get the powder mixed up in the water, get them to put Winter inside. I'll be in shortly with the antidote."

Hugging the bowl against her middle, Aida hurried to the bathroom and nearly stumbled into a girl exiting with two empty ice buckets. Then she nearly stumbled again when she stepped into the bathroom and set her eyes on Winter. He was naked. Very naked.

"I swear to Buddha, Osiris, *and* your Christian God—"

"Who clearly hates me," Winter said, interrupting Bo.

Velma's man held one of Winter's shoulders, Bo the other, and Aida stood, gawking at the bootlegger's bare body. He was pale and more finely shaped than she'd imagined when she'd been eyeing him earlier: broad chested, upper arms thick with muscle, his stomach a brick wall. Dark hair peppered the center of his torso, from his breastbone to his solid, blocky legs. But it was the thicket below his rippled stomach that drew her attention. And the substantial length that hung under it.

Dear God.

She wasn't exactly an expert on men's naked bodies, but she'd seen a couple, and neither possessed anything between their legs quite like *that*, and definitely not in a state of rest. She could only guess what it looked like when it woke up.

She forced herself to look elsewhere. Twice.

Her gaze zigzagged everywhere, up and down, back and forth. No, Aida had definitely never seen a body like this, like a statue in a museum—not the athletic, trim David, but a meatier Zeus or Poseidon. As if one extra sandwich a day might take him across the line from stocky to stout. He was big and mighty and intimidating.

A mythological-sized beast.

She couldn't stop staring. Her face warmed, not with embarrassment over seeing him naked, exactly—well, maybe a little—but mainly because of the raw lust he stirred up.

Oblivious to her entry, Bo flung Winter's trousers onto the floor with malice and continued ranting. "This is the worst thing you've ever asked me to do. And I'm including the spy job in the hull of that steamer with all that rotting fish."

Winter laughed and nearly toppled over, face-first.

"Whoa, now." One of Velma's men pressed a firm hand in the middle of Winter's chest to hold him up against the tiled wall. He couldn't stand on his own, but he was conscious.

Mostly.

"It's not funny," Bo said. "Did you hear what Velma said? You're hexed. You're probably going to die, and I'll be out of work."

"Where is she?" Winter complained, almost sounding drunk. The poison appeared to be pushing his mental state into boozy territory.

Aida's elbow bumped against the doorframe. Everyone looked up. She was sure her face was reddening, and it would be best if she'd just avert her gaze and head to the bathtub. She didn't understand why her feet weren't moving—or why she was still gawking. *Move, feet, move!*

Winter's mismatched eyes met hers. His lower face melted into a lazy smile—he actually *could* smile, imagine that—which sent an intense fluttering through her stomach. Good grief. She was acting like a daydreaming schoolgirl.

"Hello, cheetah," he said to her.

She lifted her chin and tamped down the chaos burning through her mind and body. "Mr. Magnusson—"

"No need for formalities when someone in the room is naked."

"Mr. Bootlegger, then."

He chuckled, low and deep. "You can call me Winter."

"Oh, may I? Now that you've nearly crushed me to death and exposed me to sights I don't care to see."

"Keep staring like that and I might think you're lying."

Aida's already-warm cheeks combusted with mortification. She quickly shifted her gaze to the bathtub and made her way across the room.

"Where's Velma?" Bo asked Aida.

"Brewing his remedy."

"Isn't the bath the remedy?"

"I think the bath is an insurance policy." The bathtub was half filled with water; chipped ice floated on the surface. She dumped the contents of the bowl and watched them sink, wishing she'd thought to bring a spoon or a long stick. Then again, Velma said the mixture wouldn't hurt.

Sighing, she pushed up a sleeve and plunged her arm in the icy mixture. It was shockingly cold. She winced as she used her arm to swirl the frozen water.

Winter's voice rumbled from across the room. "You bathing with me?"

Now *that* was a picture. But never in a million years would she give him the satisfaction of knowing his comments about her staring were on the mark. Bootleggers were notorious womanizers, or so the gossip rags would have one believe. A man who looked like that probably bedded every flapper in the city. "I'd rather be horsewhipped."

Both Bo and Velma's men laughed.

When the bath turned pink and the herbs and okra seeds floated to the top, she hastily withdrew her arm and shivered, flinging drops of water away. "Okay, get him inside."

The men grunted in unison as they half dragged, half shoved Winter toward the tub. Aida snatched a towel off an étagère to dry her arm, sneaking a look at Winter's backside as they passed. A majestic sight. When he tried to take a step on his own, his buttocks rippled with muscle, deepening the clefts on either side and indenting two succulent dimples on his lower back.

He twisted in their grip and caught her staring again. "Go on. Look," he encouraged with a grin. "I'm not ashamed."

"Can you not get him in there faster?" she asked the men in exasperation.

They hauled one long leg over the side of the bathtub.

"Cold!" Winter shouted, suddenly energized. He attempted to bolt.

"Oh no you don't!" Bo said, giving him a shove.

The giant cried out as he crashed in the tub. A tidal wave of pink water surged over the rim. His great body shivered as water and ice clinked against the sides of the tub.

"Don't drown the man," Velma said from the doorway. Her dress fluttered around her calves as she strode past Aida with a steaming cup of tea on a saucer. The scent wafting from the liquid was nothing short of repulsive. "You gotta drink this, Winter," she said, hooking her foot around a three-legged stool to shift it next to the tub. "You gonna go quietly, or am I gonna have to have Manny and Clyde hold you down?"

"Holy shit," Bo murmured, jerking his head away from the potion.

"I won't lie—it'll taste terrible," Velma said to Winter in a calm voice as she sat on the stool. "But it will remove your hex."

"Want . . . doctor," he answered between shivers.

"No regular doctor can save you now, you understand?" Velma said firmly, snatching his chin between her fingers and turning his face toward hers. "*I* am your doctor—you are my patient. I will heal you. Drink."

Winter hesitated, his face pinching from the ghastly scent of the tea, teeth clicking together from the cold. "Iffit kills me—"

"Then I'll get Miss Palmer to bring you back from the beyond to chat as often as you like. Now, open up and drink."

He obeyed. His face was rigid as she held the cup for him, chanting a prayer. Brown rivulets leaked from the corners of his lips. Aida thought of the crunch from the mortar and pestle and couldn't bear to watch him drink. She clamped a hand over her mouth.

He gasped in pain—he was trying to keep it down, gagging. Bo turned around, hands on his knees, breathing heavily.

"There you go," Velma praised.

Winter stilled. His eyes rolled back into his head, but instead of white, they were swarming with black lines, moving and vibrating like a spiderweb being shaken by a fly. He looked possessed. Aida had never witnessed anything like this—and she'd seen a lot of strange things in her line of work.

Bo gaped at Winter with horror-stricken eyes. "He's not breathing. What have you done, witch?"

"He's really not breathing," Aida seconded.

"Wait!" Velma shouted.

They all stood stock-still. Watched. Waited. Winter wasn't moving, but the water was. It bubbled up, the pink hue turning darker . . . blackening. Something moved within it, shifting and stirring.

Suddenly the surface rose like boiling water inside a pot. It churned and roiled, and up from the depths, tiny black shadows wriggled and danced, thousands and thousands of them.

Everyone jumped back. Disjointed shrieks of terror reverberated through the bathroom.

Winter's body sagged into the mass of black shadows as if he were melting. His limp arms hung over the sides. Velma called his name, but he was unresponsive.

As his head sank below the surface, the shadows rose until they spilled over the sides of the tub. But when they hit the black-and-white checkerboard of Velma's floor, they just . . . disappeared. As if the entire gruesome spectacle was a mirage. Might've been; magic often was.

Winter remained underwater, unmoving.

Aida's heart drummed a crazed rhythm. A silent scream welled up inside her.

The foamy bathwater calmed and lightened to pink. Then, like a submarine surfacing, Winter's head shot out above the water. Eyes wide and clear, he gulped air and began coughing.

"You see?" Velma said triumphantly as Bo and her men

rushed to pull him out of the water. "I told you I was a doctor."

Aida exhaled a long-held breath as the men hauled Winter onto his feet and covered his shaking body in towels. He looked exhausted and defeated, but he could stand. He gave Velma a pitiful, grateful look, as if that was all he could manage.

"My pleasure," Velma said as she turned to exit the room. "Get him dressed and leave the bathwater alone. I'll need to throw it away at a crossroads and cleanse this room later."

Aida stepped in the hallway with Velma and shut the bathroom door with a shaking hand. "Is he really going to be okay?"

Velma nodded. "He'll feel better after a good rest. Hopefully he won't be drawing any more ghosts . . . though I can't do anything about him seeing them if he stumbles on any around the city. His eyes are open now—no fixing that."

Tough break, but Aida had little sympathy. She'd been able to see ghosts since she was a small child. If she could live with it, surely a big, tough man like him could do the same.

The conjurer stared at the empty cup in her hands. Traces of antidote ringed the bottom. She turned it upside down on the saucer. "Once he's back to normal, he'll need to track down the person responsible. Looks to me like he's got some enemies in your neighborhood."

# FOUR

———✦———

A FEW HOURS AFTER LEAVING GRIS-GRIS, WINTER SAT IN A leather armchair in his study, staring out a long set of windows that overlooked twinkling city lights ending at the bay. A splendid view. One of the best in the city. He never grew tired of it, and right now it was a small comfort he needed in order to ground himself after the evening's unsettling events.

The hot tea his housekeeper, Greta, had brought up was doing little to take the chill off his bones. He was slowly feeling normal again, but he couldn't get the taste of Velma's satanic brew out of his mouth.

Once he got his hands around the party responsible for what happened tonight, he was going to choke the life out of them or break their neck trying. But he had his work cut out to find the culprit: all they had was the chop mark of the sorcerer who'd issued the spell, scribbled among the arcane symbols on the paper left on the table when he was poisoned.

Black Star.

Bo had never heard the name; maybe someone around Chinatown would know it.

In the meantime, Winter wouldn't be imbibing any more strange drinks. And there was still the matter of the resident ghost inside his study. "Maybe she can get rid of it, too," Winter said, but he didn't really have the ghost at the top of his mind. He was thinking of the way the spirit medium had looked at him in Velma's bathroom. That look was telling. Maybe she didn't find his scarred face attractive, but she was interested on some sort of base level. No virgin blush on that curious face of hers. No one had looked at him like that in years. Perhaps he'd been hallucinating under the poison's dank influence.

Leaning against the window frame nearby, Bo stuffed his hands in his pockets and said nothing for several moments. "She's witty."

"She's got a sharp tongue. That's always trouble."

"Trouble's better than demure and boring. And I've never seen someone with so many freckles. Kind of exotic, don't you think? Looks a bit like Louise Brooks."

"Far better-looking than Brooks."

"Same big brown eyes," Bo argued.

"Mmm. Bigger, I think. Should probably ask her to come up here."

"You mentioned that already. Are you sure you're all right?"

Winter felt himself becoming irritated. "Considering what I've been through tonight, I think I'm feeling pretty damn good. I won't pretend to understand what happened to me tonight, but somebody's screwing with me, and I don't want to see another damn ghost again if I can help it. Miss Palmer is an expert on spiritual matters, and I want her to come out here and get rid of it. What's wrong with that?"

"Nothing."

"That's right, nothing."

Bo gazed out the window. "She should come out here because she's an expert."

"Exactly."

"And her eyes are bigger than Louise Brooks's, as well as her breasts."

Damn that impudent kid and his smart mouth. But he'd made his point, and now Winter was angry at himself for saying too much, maybe a little embarrassed as well. He also didn't like Bo noticing her. At all.

"Might take some convincing to get her out here," Bo said. "Maybe *you* should go call on *her.* Apologize for flaunting your balls in her face and nearly smashing her to death."

He hazily remembered her last words to him—*I'd rather be horsewhipped*—and wondered if she'd already had her fill of him. She'd not only seen him naked; she'd seen him weak and sick and delusional. God only knew what she must think of him. His mood blackened.

"I'm sure Miss Palmer—" Bo started.

"Enough!" Winter snapped. "I've changed my mind. I don't want to hear her name again. *You* just concentrate on finding someone in Chinatown who knows the hellish name on that cursed piece of paper."

Winter fully expected the matter would be solved. People were always trying to muscle him out of business, and they always failed. But after a couple of days had passed, Bo hadn't tracked down the name and the ghost in his study appeared like clockwork every afternoon at a quarter past two, sticking around for a minute before it disappeared. And this was probably the only reason why Winter still found himself thinking about the spirit medium. The deviant fantasies his mind had been conjuring of the two of them together weren't unusual; after all, she was a pretty girl, and he was a healthy man.

But with those fantasies haunting him before bed and the damned ghost in his study haunting him by day, he got fed up. Three nights after the hexing, on his way to a midnight meeting with a bootlegging client, he stopped by Gris-Gris. He told himself it was merely a business transaction: he'd ask the spirit medium to get rid of the ghost in his study, she'd do just that, he'd pay her. End of story.

But he arrived too late to speak to her in person. Miss Palmer's show was already starting. Since he'd gone to the trouble of coming out here, he might as well see what she did.

So he stood at the back of the club, hat in hand, and watched from the shadows.

Faces turned to the stage and scattered applause broke out as the house lights dimmed. A dark-skinned middle-aged man in a top hat and tails strode to a standing microphone—Hezekiah. The smiling compere's good humor and witty commentary between scheduled acts was legendary. In one hand, Hezekiah carried a small, three-legged table, and in the other, a glass bowl filled with the torn halves of the lottery tickets that they'd been passing out in the lobby.

"Good evening," Hezekiah said in welcoming voice. "Please take your seats and locate your tickets. Mrs. Monroe, my dear, I think yours has fallen into the front of your gown, but I'm sure that young man at your side will be happy to retrieve it for you."

A booming chorus of laughter followed the master of ceremonies as he placed the table near a secondary microphone to the right of the spotlight and set the glass bowl on top. "Ladies and gentlemen, it's my pleasure to welcome the famous spirit medium from the East Coast, recently transplanted to our fine city. Please give a warm Gris-Gris Club welcome to Madame Palmer."

Velvet curtains parted. A burst of applause filled the room as the medium made her way across the stage. All of his muscles tensed at once as she stepped into the spotlight. Some childish part of him hoped that he wouldn't find her as attractive onstage as he had the night of his poisoning.

No such luck.

His attention roamed the length of her champagne-colored gown, tracking floral beading that ran down her stomach and arched over gently curving hips. Elbow-length gloves hid half her arms, and her golden stockings were opaque—a pity to cover up all that freckled skin, but it made what skin he *could* see that much more enticing.

She was stunning.

"Good evening," she said into the tinny-sounding microphone after the applause died down. "To those of you who are new to my show, I am a trance medium. Tonight I will call forth spirits of your loved ones from the beyond, temporarily welcoming them inside me so that they may use me to converse with you. They will speak with my voice. I am fully aware during this experience. I do not lose consciousness or forget what's happened."

The reverent quiet gripping the club was only punctured by the occasional tinkle of glass at the back bar or a single sneeze from someone in the audience; she had them all in her sway. How different she was onstage, so serious and reserved. But the confidence was still there. He remembered how she'd boldly spoken to him in Velma's office and smiled to himself.

"Before we start, I'll mention one last thing concerning memento mori," she continued. "As it states in the program, I need to touch an object owned by the deceased in order to establish a connection, preferably something beloved that was handled frequently. I see that many of you have come prepared, so shall we proceed with the first participant?" She nodded at Hezekiah. "We will call as many numbers as we can during the next hour. Please be patient. If your number is called, please walk to the front with your memento and hand your ticket to Hezekiah."

Hezekiah retrieved the first lottery number. "Number one-five-eight."

A man in a green suit near the stage raised his hand and stood. His table clapped as he proceeded up a small set of stairs at the front of the stage and handed his ticket to Hezekiah.

"What is your name, sir?" the medium asked.

"Hannity." He nervously thrust a pocket watch in her direction.

"Who does this belong to, Mr. Hannity?"

"My brother, Lenny. He was killed in the war and—"

Miss Palmer held up a gloved hand. "Don't tell me anything more. Please give me a second to prepare myself. If I am able to summon your brother, you will only have a minute or so to speak with him once he enters my body. I cannot hold on to him indefinitely. So I will advise you to keep your wits and don't waste time. To ensure you're speaking to the right person, I'd suggest you immediately question him about something only the two of you would know. Do you understand?"

"Yes," Mr. Hannity said.

The club waited with bated breath like children around a campfire listening to stories. Even the balconies above the sides of the stage were filled with spectators hanging over the railing. The medium placed her left hand over Mr. Hannity's pocket watch and balled up the other against her thigh. Winter watched, curious. She closed her eyes. After a few seconds, she inhaled sharply and her right leg twitched as if someone had kicked her. Her eyes flew open.

She exhaled.

Her breath floated out in a cloud of mist . . . just as it had the night they'd met.

Goose bumps pricked the back of Winter's neck.

"Go on, Mr. Hannity," Hezekiah encouraged from the stage. "Ask your question."

The lottery winner hesitated, wringing his hands. "Uh, Lenny? If it's really you, can you tell me where we buried the dead cat we found in the street on my sixteenth birthday?"

Miss Palmer looked down at him. Her manner didn't change. Ghostly breath continued to flow from her mouth as she spoke. "In Old Man Henry's field."

Mr. Hannity gasped.

"Hello, Michael," she said. "Happy to see you're finally going bald."

Her voice was unaffected. And even though Winter had already witnessed what she could do to an existing ghost, it was startling to see her possessed—if that's what this was called. A couple of weeks ago, he wouldn't have believed it was possible, but now . . .

What was that thing she'd done with her hand when she was calling the spirit? Winter tuned out the conversation between her and Mr. Hannity and concentrated on figuring out her process. It was almost as though she were holding something, but what?

After a few exchanges between Miss Palmer and Mr. Hannity, Winter gave up cracking her method. His eyes roved over her sleek caramel bob and the freckled neck and shoulders below. He found himself desperately wishing he could set fire to her long gloves.

Then her gown.

His cock pulsed appreciatively at this thought. Christ, he needed air. Seeing her again had been a mistake. If he'd already had trouble tamping down fantasies of her in his bed, then watching her perform onstage, radiating poise and confidence . . . It wasn't something he'd soon forget. After taking one last look at her, he slipped away and—quietly pocketing a program with her photograph printed on the inside—headed back through the lobby to his waiting car.

Aida rented a room in a five-story building in Chinatown over Golden Lotus Dim Sum, at the northern end of tourist-laden Grant Avenue. All the residents were single working women like her. Cable cars clanged down the street during the day, and local streetcars ran until midnight, so she usually didn't have to pay for a taxi after work or worry about straining her calf muscles hiking up and down the hilly streets alone, which made the six-block walk from Gris-Gris seem twice as long. Weekly room and board included free dim sum—as the proprietors owned both the apartments and the restaurant—and her room contained a Murphy bed that folded up into a closet, an armchair, a desk, a telephone, and a private bath.

But the best part was the black iron fire escape that stretched outside her window. It doubled as a meager balcony, upon which she sometimes sat at night to stare out over pagoda roofs lined with swaying paper lanterns and the gold dragons entwined around Chinatown's lampposts.

Four days after the incident with Winter Magnusson, when Aida rose at her usual late-morning hour, she rubbed goose bumps on her arms and pulled back curtains from her window to peek outside past the fire escape. Nothing but gray skies and drizzle. Mark Twain supposedly once joked that a summer in San Francisco was the coldest winter he'd ever spent, and from what Aida had experienced since she'd arrived, this wasn't an exaggeration, especially at night when the fog rolled in.

"Better than the blistering heat out East," she said to the small oval photo inside her gold locket. "And cold weather just means more customers stopping by the club tonight to warm up with a drink. See, Sam? I'm still thinking positive." She snapped the locket closed and headed to her humble bathroom.

As she bathed, her mind wandered to Winter Magnusson. She'd dreamed about him twice—unsurprising, considering what she'd seen that night. But in her latest dream, instead of him being naked, it had been *her*, and he'd taken on the persona of some tabloid gangster, fighting rival bootleggers with machine guns and sawed-off shotguns.

She wondered if he'd ever been involved in anything like that in real life. Perhaps it was better if she never found out. He was likely wishing he never saw a ghost again. Maybe he'd already forgotten her. She certainly wished she'd forgotten the melodic rumble of his voice, the two dimples in the small of his back, and other notable parts of him . . .

Shaking that thought away, she dressed in bright clothing to fortify her mood: a lapis blue dress with long, sheer sleeves and knife pleats that fell just below her knees, and a pair of matching Bakelite drop earrings. After donning her gray coat and cloche, she grabbed her handbag and headed out the door. Four flights of stairs later, she stepped through a side door into the ground-level restaurant.

Golden Lotus was in the middle of a brisk lunchtime rush, and its ostentatious red and gold decor greeted her as she wound her way past dark wood tables and velvet-cushioned chairs, inhaling the enticing aromas of ginger and garlic. Customers who dined here were a mix of locals, tourists, businessmen entertaining out-of-town clients, and young working girls—typists and switchboard operators. Servers in smart red *tangzhuang* jackets with mandarin collars wheeled wooden pushcarts brimming with tiny plates of pungent bites: slender spring rolls, buns filled with Cantonese-style pork, and bamboo trays of steamed shrimp dumplings.

She headed to the restaurant's main entrance. Near the door, a counter held a rosewood Buddha statue on one side, and on the other, display boxes filled with Wrigley's gum and cigarettes sat next to a cash register. Day or night, one of the owners stood behind the counter—usually this was Mrs. Lin, as it was today.

Aida waited for a customer to pay his check, then stepped up to the register and rubbed the potbellied Buddha for luck. "Afternoon."

"Miss Palmer," Mrs. Lin replied cheerfully. The kindly Chinese businesswoman was petite in height and round in girth, with pretty plump cheeks and loops of black hair pinned tightly above the nape of her neck.

"Any mail for me today?"

"Mail and more." Mrs. Lin lifted a small key that hung on a long chain around her neck and opened a lacquered red cabinet behind the counter, which housed tenant mail and packages. She retrieved two pieces of mail. The first was from a woman in Philadelphia; Aida had performed regular séances for her when she'd worked at a club there last year, and they'd since maintained a correspondence.

The second envelope was from an address in New Orleans. The Limbo Room, a new speakeasy. The owner, a Mr. Bradley Bix, was interested in booking her later this summer. He would be in San Francisco visiting his cousin at the end of June and proposed to call on her after taking in one of her performances at Gris-Gris. If he was satisfied by what he saw, he would offer her a booking. He included a brochure printed with photographs of the club, intended for potential members; their annual fees were much higher than Gris-Gris and the photographs made it look nice. It was a good prospect, and she was happy to receive it, but part of her was growing weary of planning her next move when she was barely situated at her current job.

Or maybe she was being too sentimental about San Francisco.

A group of noisy customers approached the counter. Aida moved out of their way and turned to find herself face-to-face with someone familiar.

"I said you had mail and more," Mrs. Lin explained. "Mr. Yeung is 'more.' Been waiting for you the last half hour. I was going to send Mr. Lin to fetch you, but the kitchen is backed up."

"Bo," Aida said in surprise, greeting Magnusson's assistant, who was dressed in another smart suit and brown argyle newsboy cap. "Mr. Yeung, I mean. What a pleasant surprise."

He politely canted his head. "Either is fine. And it's nice to see you again."

"How's your boss doing?" she asked in a low voice, glancing over her shoulder at Mrs. Lin. The restaurant owner was making small talk with the customers at the counter.

"Much better. And no ghosts," Bo reported. "Or at least, none following him. He sent me here to inquire if you'd be willing to get rid of the ghost in his study."

Aida's pulse quickened as adrenaline zipped through her. "Oh?"

"It shows up mid-afternoon, so that's why he sent me to fetch you now. If it's not too inconvenient, I've got the car outside."

"Right now?"

"Yes."

"So he just assumed I would drop what I was doing and rush over there?"

"To be honest, people usually do," Bo said with a sly smile. "He wants to hire your services this time. For payment."

Aida almost laughed. "I'm very expensive."

"He's very rich."

"I expect he is."

"He's impatient as a boy on Christmas and never invites people up to the house, so you should probably come. Let's get going before everyone finishes their lunch and jams the roads."

Calling on a man in his home? Surely wasn't a sensible thing to do, especially a man like *that*. But when did she ever shy away from a novel experience? And it certainly would be interesting to find out where a rich bootlegger lived.

Besides, she could always use the cash, so she should probably go. The dimples in the small of his back had absolutely, positively nothing to do with it.

"I can't stay long," she told Bo. Then she slipped her mail into her handbag and waved at Mrs. Lin, whose keen look of curiosity followed her out the door into light gray drizzle.

Aida's first lesson in a bootlegger's personal life loomed at the curb near the neighboring sidewalk newsstand. There was a dark red Pierce-Arrow limousine with a polished black top—like something the Prince of Darkness would drive out of the gates of hell. And even with the nefarious coloring, it was an insanely well-bred automobile with whitewall tires, glinting windows, and gleaming chrome. Its enormous chassis looked like a steamer ship on roller skates, led by a silver archer ornament on the hood. Showy luxury. Hollywood stars owned these cars. Aida had only seen them in magazines. She dumbly stared along with the tourists passing by.

"A beauty, yes?" Bo said. "She's brand-new. Custom-built." He held open the back door for her while she slid inside. The interior was a dream: polished wood steering wheel, chrome reading lights, crystal pulls on the window shades. It was all Aida could do not to whistle in appreciation as she settled into the leather backseat, propping her heels on the footrest below.

A long window, rolled down halfway, served as a privacy divider between the front and the back. A small handheld motor phone made it possible to talk with the driver. Bo saw her eyeing it as he started the car. "You want the divider all the way up?"

"So that I can talk to myself back here?"

He grinned in response and pulled out into traffic.

Aida stared out the window through lengthening rain-drops. Stores selling silk slippers and Oriental rugs blurred as they headed west. A few more blocks and she'd be headed into parts of the city where she'd never been.

Her hands didn't know where to settle. She raised her voice to be heard over the rumbling engine. "How long have you worked for Mr. Magnusson?"

"Seven years, thereabouts. He hired me when he started helping his father with the family business—after he left Berkeley."

Berkeley educated? Surprising. "How old were you when you started working for him?"

"Fourteen."

Good grief. He was running around doing illegal things when he was still a child? She supposed she shouldn't feel too sorry for him. He was obviously doing well now, and she certainly knew what it was like to be hungry for money.

"At first he just called on me now and then to run errands for him," Bo explained. "Then I started working for him every day after school. After the accident—"

"The one that caused his eye injury? What happened, exactly?"

"You don't know?"

"He didn't say."

"I'm surprised you haven't heard talk around the club."

"I'm all ears now."

"He'll have to be the one to tell the story, and I wouldn't recommend asking until he's warmed up to you. Touchy subject. Anyway, as I was saying, after the accident, he took over his father's business full-time, and when he moved back into the family house, I came with him. I've got a room there."

So Winter's *father* was the original bootlegger, which meant he must've died in the accident, Aida reasoned. How terrible. She wondered if the mother was still alive, but it unearthed memories of her own parents that she didn't care to think about, so she shifted the conversation back to

Bo. "What exactly do you do for him, if you don't mind me asking?"

"This and that. Communicating instructions, scouting, relaying information . . . driving spirit mediums around." Brown eyes met hers in the rearview mirror, sparkling with humor. "And I guess you can add 'personal valet' to that list after that night at Velma's."

She laughed to cover up the unwanted picture of Naked Man floating inside her head. "I imagined the life of a bootlegger being a series of gunfights in dark alleys."

"There's a little of that. Winter's definitely more comfortable with guns than ghosts, but you shouldn't be afraid to call on him. He's had additional security at the house since the supernatural business started up, and no one working for him has ever been killed . . . at least, not on purpose."

She almost choked. "That's, uh, helpful to know."

He steered the car down a side street. "Honestly, I'm surprised you agreed to come today, after everything at Velma's."

"Guess I'm a glutton for punishment."

"He might seem irritable at times, but he's been through a lot, so I guess you could say he's a little mad at the world. You just have to grow a thick skin around him when he's in one of his moods. He's not a bad person, despite what you might think."

"I didn't think he was. Maybe a little demanding."

Bo grinned at her in the mirror. "You fight your way up to a certain level of success after being nothing but an immigrant fisherman's son, you'd be demanding, too. Can't command respect unless you act like you deserve it."

In their line of business, she didn't doubt it.

Houses began to increase in both size and grandeur as Bo turned onto a street with a steep incline. The Pierce-Arrow's engine protested as it turned faster to make the climb past an eclectic mix of grand homes. "Where are we?" she asked.

"Pacific Heights. Never stepped foot here until I started working for Winter. It's swanky—where all the Nob Hill millionaires built after the quake and the Great Fire. Everyone here pays for that." He pointed toward a spectacular view of the bay and the rocky cliffs beyond, now shrouded in quiet rain and light fog. All the homes sat shoulder-to-shoulder, cramped on horizontal streets that lined the hill in tiers like movie theater seats, where everyone gets a good view of the screen.

Bo slowed the car as they passed through an intersection. Aida read the street sign here: BROADWAY. Her nerves twanged as she looked at a beautiful beast of a home on the corner. Bo parked the car at the curb.

"Welcome to the Magnusson house," he announced.

# FIVE

———◆———

AIDA STEPPED OUT OF THE PIERCE-ARROW IN FRONT OF A GRAY
green Queen Anne mansion. Four stories high, it was twice
as big as the neighboring houses and looked like something
out of a fantasy tale, with steeply gabled roofs, fish-scale
shingles, bay windows, and a round, turreted tower. Like
the other homes in this area, it had no yard to speak of—only
a short iron fence and a shallow border of grass separating
its massive girth from the public street. And like virtually
everything else in this city, it was built on a steep slant with
half the bottom floor disappearing into the hill.

"Goodness, it's grand," she murmured to herself, craning
her neck to take it all in. She spotted two men stationed at
either fence corner—security, she supposed. "He lives in
this big house all by himself?"

"His younger sister, too. The help. His brother, when he
comes home on holidays."

Ah, no mother, then. Maybe she died in the accident, too.
No wonder he didn't like talking about it.

Bo led her down a narrow sidewalk in front of the house,

up a short flight of steps to a covered portico that harbored a wide green door. As he reached for the handle, the door swung inward to a tall, pale, silver-haired woman. She wore an apron tied around her middle and a look of aloofness that was only slightly warmed by the pink of her cheeks. She studied Aida critically from head to foot for a moment too long while Bo removed his cap.

"Greta, this is Miss Aida Palmer."

The woman gave her a funny smile that Aida couldn't make heads or tails of. "Miss Palmer," she said in a birdlike voice with a heavy Scandinavian lilt. "Mr. Magnusson is waiting for you in his study. Come. I will take you."

Aida stepped into a spacious entry, bigger than her entire apartment, with a high ceiling that opened up to the second floor and dark wood floors below her feet. A labyrinth of rooms sprouted in every direction.

"I'll be eating lunch down here in the kitchen," Bo said. "When you're ready to go, Winter will call me and I'll drive you back home. I've got business in Chinatown later."

She thanked him before he headed down a hallway and disappeared.

Aida followed Greta's impressively fast strides through the entry. At first she thought they were headed up the massive staircase, but Greta veered to the side and stopped in front of a black elevator, a small rectangular contraption that looked like an Art Nouveau metal birdcage, with scrolling whiplash curves.

"I've never seen an elevator inside a private home," Aida remarked upon entering.

Greta shut the scissor gate, then the cage door, and operated a lever. "The Magnussons are fond of wasting monies."

Well. Aida didn't know what to say to that. The rickety elevator groaned and whined as it made a shaky ascent to a highly polished dark hallway on the fourth floor.

Greta led her to a set of carved doors, guarded by a man sitting in a chair, playing solitaire on a folding wooden tray table; he doffed his cap when they passed by. A wide room lay beyond, filled with standing bookshelves, a large desk, and a billiards table. Several windows on the far wall offered an expansive view of the city and the foggy bay.

A cozy sitting area surrounded an oversized fireplace. The fire was lit, and sitting on a brown leather couch reading the *San Francisco Chronicle* was Winter Magnusson.

Surely he heard the elevator or their steps echoing down the hallway, but he remained engrossed in his reading, legs crossed, lounging in his shirtsleeves. His suit jacket lay folded on the back of the couch.

"Winter." Greta's singsong accent made his name sound more like *"Veen-*ter."

He glanced up from the paper and looked straight at Aida. His eyes narrowed slowly, like someone playing blackjack who'd just been dealt a ten and an ace.

And Aida felt like she'd just lost all her chips along with the shirt off her back.

"You came," he said in his low cello-note voice.

"I hope you won't find a way to make me regret that."

He looked amused but didn't smile. "I'll try to keep my clothes on this time."

If he was trying to embarrass her in front of his house-keeper, he'd have to try harder. "I'm only here because you're paying me an exorbitant fee for a house call."

"Worth every cent." He folded up his newspaper. "Hungry?"

"Not sure," she replied honestly. She had been, but now her brain was sending some confused signal to her body, preparing her to either become sick or run for her life. Why was her heart beating so fast? She could feel her blood pulsing at her temples.

"Greta, leave us. I'll call when we're ready for a tray," Winter said, prompting the housekeeper to exit the room as he tossed the folded newspaper aside and stood.

Aida suddenly remembered just how big he was, and took him in from head to foot as he approached: crisp white linen shirt, black necktie with horizontal bands of silver, pin-striped gray vest anchored by the gold chain of his pocket watch, black wing tips. His flat-front charcoal trousers were so accurately tailored, they hugged the muscle of his thighs in an almost obscene manner. She liked this.

"You're looking . . ." *Enormous. Handsome. Intimidating.* "Recovered," she said.

"I'm feeling a hell of a lot better. Are you planning on dashing right back out? Or did you not trust Greta with your coat?"

"She didn't offer to take it."

"Since she's failed at her duties, allow me." He said this as if it were some great chore and made an impatient gesture for her to comply, but she caught a curious gaze flicking toward her under the false front of seemingly bored, hooded eyes.

She set down her handbag on a small table by the door and unbuttoned her coat. As she was shrugging it off her shoulders, Mr. Magnusson stepped closer. Several things cluttered her mind at once: That he smelled of laundry starch. That the gold bar connecting his collar points beneath the striped knot of his necktie was engraved with tiny nautical compasses. And that she was almost positive he was looking down her dress.

That realization did something strange to her stomach. She knew she wasn't unattractive—at least, she didn't think so. Not anymore. When she was a child, she was teased about her heavily freckled skin. Even now, most men only looked at her with mild interest before setting their sights on other women with flawless complexions. But every once in a while she ran across a man who actually *liked* freckles.

Maybe Winter was one of them.

Did he see her as a sideshow curiosity, or something more? Perhaps he was merely a man, and breasts were breasts were breasts. She held up her coat between them. "How's the view from up there?"

"Not as clear as your view of me the other night."

"To be fair, I don't believe *that* could've been any clearer."

He plucked the coat from her fingers. "You sure didn't act like you minded."

"I didn't." She meant that to be a question, but it came

out wrong. Winter seemed as surprised by it as she was, but he didn't comment. Surely he was aware how nicely his body was put together; he probably heard it all the time. He hung up her coat, then, without touching, extended his hand behind her back, urging her to accompany him farther into the study.

They skirted around a bank of standing bookshelves in the middle of the room and came face-to-face with the head of a dragon—or the neck and head of one, to be exact. Openmouthed and baring sharp teeth, the wooden carving was about her height, on display in a glass case.

"That's Drake," Winter said, stuffing his hands in his pockets. "The bow off a Viking longship from the twelfth century."

"You *are* Scandinavian, then?"

"Swedish. My parents immigrated here when my mother was pregnant with me."

"An arduous journey for a pregnant woman."

Something in his brow shifted. A wistfulness. Or guilt, perhaps. "She insisted on coming to give me a better life. My siblings were born here."

She walked around the dragon, peering through the glass. The carving was crude, the wood cracked and splintered. "Shouldn't this be in a museum?"

"Probably. If we ever need money, we can sell him. He's worth more than the whole damn house. It was one of the first things my father had imported after the bootlegging money started flowing. I've got an uncle who's an archaeologist. My younger brother is on a dig with him out in Cairo right now."

"Really? How exciting. Hope he's not opening up any cursed tombs."

"My brother could fall into shit and come out smelling of roses."

Aida laughed.

In a fluid pair of movements, Winter curved his body closer to hers while settling his forearm above his head on the top of the glass case. His fingers tapped on the glass. A big body like his possessed an unspoken dominance if the personality commanding it understood its power, and Winter did. He towered over her at an angle that forced her to tilt her face up and back to meet his gaze, and spoke in a lower, more relaxed tone, as if he were sharing a choice bit of gossip, luring her into his web. "Uncle Jakob found the dragon bow a few years ago. Found three, actually—reported one, kept one for himself, and gave my father Drake, here."

"Lawbreaking runs in the family."

He made a grunting noise. "My uncle is fond of shipping black market goods, and my father always had boats. That's why he got into bootlegging in the first place."

"Bo mentioned that your father was a fisherman."

"Crab and salmon, mainly. I've traded most of the fishing fleet for rumrunners and a couple of big, new powerboats that go to Canada. But I haven't gotten rid of the crabbers."

"You still crab?"

"It's good money and a legitimate cover for the booze."

She glanced at a long bay of windows lining the outer wall of the study and left Winter to survey the view. "Oh, look at that. Bet you can see the entire city when it's clear."

Winter's low voice was closer than she expected. He pointed over her shoulder. "You can see Fisherman's Wharf and Alcatraz Island from here. If the bay wasn't foggy, we could also see the northern point of the Presidio where they're going to build a suspension bridge across the Golden Gate strait to Marin County. Have you heard about it?"

"No."

"Will be the longest in the world, if they ever raise the funds to build the damn thing."

"Impressive."

They gazed out over the rooftops for a moment until Winter spoke again. "Velma said you're booked at Gris-Gris through July. What do you do, just go from club to club?"

"Sometimes theaters, but speakeasies pay better. I've worked six of them over the past couple of years up and down the East Coast. This is the first time I've been out West since I was a small child. I'm originally from here—my parents were killed in the Great Fire."

"I'm sorry."

"I was only seven, so my memories are limited. Our apartment building initially survived the quake. It was one of the gas pipe explosions that brought it down. I got separated from my parents when we were trying to escape. One of the neighbors got me out, but my parents never made it. To this day, I'm a little phobic of fire."

"Understandable. I was nine when it happened, but I still dream about the city burning."

God, so did she.

"What happened to you after the fire?" Winter asked.

"I was shuffled off to a temporary camp, then an orphanage. I lived with three families before a couple, the Lanes, took me in later that year. They were moving out east, so I went with them." She glanced out the window. "I have a few memories of living here before the quake, but I definitely don't remember it looking like this. It's going to spoil me. I won't want to leave."

"How do you live like that, moving around all the time? Do you travel with someone?"

"Just me and myself."

Two deep lines etched his brow. "Doesn't seem safe for a single woman to be running around the country."

If she had a penny for every time she'd heard that . . . "I've managed just fine."

"Sounds lonely."

It was lonely at times—terribly lonely. But she did what she had to in order to survive, and she wasn't embarrassed about it. A certain pride came with the kind of independence she had. If you didn't rely on anyone but yourself, you had fewer chances of being disappointed—that's what Sam always told her. Out of habit, her fingers reached for the locket hanging near her heart.

"I live for the moment, not the past or future," she said. Another Sam mantra. "But if you must know, I do prefer private séances to work onstage. They pay better for less work. Building up a client list takes more time than—"

A loud *brring-brring* startled her out of her memories.

"Hold that thought." Winter excused himself and strode across the room to answer the telephone. She was a little relieved to drop the subject of her career choice. It was none of his business, really. And she'd already said more than she probably should. A bad habit of hers, not controlling the things that exited her mouth.

While he spoke in a hushed voice on the phone, she strolled past the windows and looked around, glancing at the book spines on a bay of shelves, mostly commerce and fishing titles. Her gaze fell upon a couple of long books sitting on a nearby lamp table. Scrapbooks? Photos?

Leather cracked when she opened the top book. Not photographs, but postcards attached to black pages with adhesive mounting corners. Postcards from Cairo. Postcards from France. The Eiffel Tower. The Arc de Triomphe. The Louvre. Two French maids wearing nothing but aprons. A girl falling off a bike, her skirt lifted, wearing only rolled-down stockings underneath. A woman sitting on a sofa reading a French copy of *Ulysses* with her legs spread—

Dear Lord.

Erotic postcards. Dozens and dozens. She glanced in Winter's direction. He was quiet, listening to the earpiece receiver while pacing around the fireplace, toting the candlestick base as a black telephone cord snaked around the floor, trailing his footsteps.

She hurriedly leafed through the pages, which seemed to get progressively worse—or better, depending on your view. A fully dressed man kissing a nude woman on his lap. A man fondling a woman beneath her chemise.

Flipping toward the back of the book, Aida stopped on a page with only one postcard affixed to the center—not a photograph, but a colored illustration. It featured a naked woman with bobbed hair. She sat upon the lap of a naked man, who was propped up against a pile of cushions. His cock was drawn to fantastical proportions, and the artist had managed to include an impressive amount of detail in rendering every vein, ridge, and hair as it slid into the woman's exposed sex. She rode him, mouth open, with a look of ecstasy on her face.

And she was freckled.

Aida's pulse pounded. She stared at the shocking postcard, transfixed. It was surely only a coincidence the illustrated woman looked like her—artists often added freckles to make females look younger, after all, and—

"Find something interesting?" Winter's low voice rumbled near her ear.

She jumped in surprise and attempted to shut the book, but his palm slapped down on the pages. When she tried to step away, another hand planted on the other side of the book, pinning her inside his arms. His chest against her back was warm and solid.

Her breathing faltered. Embarrassment created a fog that rolled over her brain. "They were sitting out," she argued dumbly.

"My study. My books. I can leave them where I like."

Her heart pattered like a frightened animal. "You should take more care when you invite guests over."

"I didn't know my guest would be so curious."

"And I didn't know I'd be visiting a deviant!"

"One man's deviance is another man's lunch break."

"Pervert."

His mouth was against her ear, his words spoken through her hair. "Are you referring to me or yourself? You've been staring at that for quite a long time."

Her face flamed. She *never* blushed. Never! "It's . . . depraved."

"How so?" His thumb ran along the edge of the postcard. "Is the artist depraved for rendering a fantasy, or is the woman in the painting depraved for enjoying it?"

"*You're* the one who's depraved for owning it." She shoved her shoulders back against him, grunting. "Let go."

He didn't grip her tighter, nor impede her from ducking out of his hold, but instead distracted her with words. "Look closer," he said, pointing to the woman in the illustration. "There's a trust between them. She enjoys him watching her. Oh, and would you look at that? She's got freckles just like you. How interesting."

Aida's eyes flicked to the bulky arms flanking her shoulders. She twisted inside his trap, defiantly faced him, and shoved at his chest. A useless act against someone built like a mountain; he didn't budge.

She drew back. He leaned forward, erasing the distance. Their combined weight pressing against the lamp table caused it to slide a few centimeters. A frightening, almost unbearable intensity darkened his eyes. She could no longer tell which pupil was bigger, because both were enlarged beneath languid, drooping eyelids.

"Do you like people watching you onstage, Aida?"

The question was, at best, rude, and paired with the postcard, the insinuation behind it was downright vulgar. But it was her name on his lips that unexpectedly triggered lust to uncoil low in her belly. It sounded so startlingly intimate, and he was so close. So close, so big . . . so intimidating. She was overawed and overexcited, all at once.

His gaze dropped. Hers followed, only to find the hands that had shoved at his chest were now grasping his necktie, either in an attempt to choke him or pull him closer.

Maybe both.

"Christ alive," he whispered thickly.

Her thoughts exactly—what on earth did she think she was doing? Rattled by her own lack of restraint, she released the necktie and ducked under his arm, then took several quick steps to put some distance between them.

"Sorry," she mumbled with her back to him. "I'm not sure what came over me."

He didn't answer. God, she'd rattled him. Probably a first. And now that her foggy brain was clearing, she was uncertain about his intentions. *Do you like people watching you onstage, Aida?* Maybe she'd misread this completely. Perhaps he'd only been trying to intimidate her after she'd rudely plowed through his personal things, and she'd only been *hoping* he didn't mind the freckles. Maybe she'd just been fooling herself because she wanted him to want her as much as she wanted him.

But wants and needs aren't interchangeable, and what she *needed* right now was to cool down and gather her wits. She exhaled heavily, and the breath that rushed out of her mouth was a chilly white cloud.

# SIX

IT TOOK SEVERAL MOMENTS FOR WINTER TO COMPOSE HIMSELF enough to turn around. He was uncomfortably hard, aching and straining against the front of his pants. The fact that she provoked such an immediate response in him wasn't a surprise—he had, after all, spent the last few nights conjuring images of her while he stroked himself to sleep. Thank God she hadn't flipped one more page in his postcard collection, or she'd have seen the program he'd taken from Gris-Gris, folded inside out with her photograph bared.

But really, could he be blamed for that? She was beautiful, vivacious, and carefree. Of course he wanted her. It was *her response* that had him thrown for a loop. Because unless the blood now pulsing inside his cock had emptied his brain and made him daft, he suspected she wanted him, too. How was that possible?

The only women who showed him any interest these days were gold diggers who lusted after his money and the perceived excitement it could provide, or fallen socialites who'd become accustomed to a lifestyle that was slipping from their grasp. Women who once knew him before the accident now looked at him with pity. Strangers acted uncomfortable when they saw his scars.

So why was Aida flirting with him?

And the more he thought about it, the more he was certain she really *was* flirting, despite it having been years since anyone had shown interest in him without an agenda. She had no reason to need anything from him. She was independent, earning her own money, and successful enough at it. Hundreds of people lined up every night to see her show. She seemed comfortable with her life. Satisfied. Self-confident. She didn't have the stench of desperation that he could usually spot miles away.

But she did have every reason to hold up two crossed fingers or throw holy water on him. At Velma's he'd collapsed like an injured horse, sick and naked and half mad with the poison polluting his veins. She should've been fainting in horror at the sight of him, running for the hills.

Yet here she was.

And now he'd forever have an image stamped in his depraved mind of the moment her lovely face tilted up to his . . . her eyes big and brown beneath the slender brim of her hat, lips parted, freckles peeking through faded oxblood red lipstick. One particular freckle near the right corner of her mouth was larger than the others, straddling the blush of her lip and the lighter skin of her face. Dear God, how he desperately wanted to swipe his tongue across that freckle.

And maybe suckle one or two of the fingers that had been wrapped around his necktie.

"Mr. Magnusson?"

"Winter," he corrected, turning around. A white cloud billowed from her mouth, and standing between them was the *thing*. "Was this what you wanted me to see?"

It looked the same way it had every day that week: a man with dark hair and a beard, wearing an old-fashioned suit. Usually at this point, Winter would be intently studying the ghost, but right now all he could do was stare at Aida and the breath wreathing her face.

This was the third time he'd seen the ghost, but it was still startling.

"At least you know Velma's antidote worked, because your ghost couldn't be less interested in either one of us." She studied the ghostly man as he went through the same motions he did every day—talking to himself without uttering a sound, putting his hand over his heart. A few moments more and he'd be heading toward the windows.

"I can see through his feet, so he's definitely an old ghost— they usually fade after time. Rare that one sticks around for more than a decade or two. Oh, look, he's got a wooden hand."

Huh. Damned if she wasn't right. Now that she'd pointed it out, Winter could see wood grain beneath paint.

"How long does he stick around?" she asked.

"Another half a minute or so, then he jumps."

"Jumps?" She glanced at the window. "Suicide?"

"Would seem so."

"Did a man kill himself in this house?"

"No idea. A San Francisco judge built the house after the earthquake. My parents bought it a few years ago."

"Interesting. Would you like me to get rid of it?"

"That's why I called you out here."

*Not* because he craved an excuse to see her again.

"Your wish, my command, Mr. Bootlegger." She smiled so beautifully, he nearly forgot all about the ghost standing between them. As whorls of white puffed from her mouth, she reached out with splayed fingers and touched the man. He crackled, then simply . . . disappeared.

Gone.

Along with her snowy breath, which petered out after a couple of exhalations.

Winter stared at her, unable to speak. "Well done," he finally managed to say.

Aida folded her arms under her breasts and looked him straight in the eye, one side of her bewitching mouth cocked in a self-assured smile. "That'll be fifty dollars."

Two nights later, standing behind a folding screen in her dressing room at Gris-Gris, Aida was *still* giddy about that fifty dollars. Well, not so much the money as the wicked postcard collection. And not so much the postcards as the way she'd felt when Winter towered over her like some erotic heathen god. For the umpteenth time, she reminded herself how reserved he'd been after she'd banished the ghost in his study. He barely said another word, just handed her some bills from his pocket—who carries around that much cash?—then clammed up when his housekeeper came in the room.

"You haven't heard from him since," she murmured to herself as she tugged a beaded green gown over her head. It was a straight-cut gown with a dropped waist, a nice fit, but it had a line of buttons in the back that she couldn't reach. Should've thought of that before she put it on. Maybe one of the chorus girls would help her. A knock sounded on the door. She peered around the side of the screen to see Velma's head poking into the room.

"Oh, good. You're dressed," the club owner said.

"Actually, I'm glad you're here, because I need help reaching—"

Velma didn't wait for the end of her sentence, just swung the door open while speaking to someone in the hallway. "She's all yours, but don't hold her up. She's due onstage in fifteen minutes."

Aida slipped back behind the screen and stood on stockinged tiptoes to see over the top.

It was him.

Damn.

"Velma!" she called out.

Her boss just shrugged and shut the door, leaving her alone with Winter Magnusson, who was looking warm and handsome in a smoky brown suit and chocolate coat.

"Hello, Miss Palmer."

She tried to prop her arm on the screen in an attempt to look casual and slipped. As if her heart wasn't already beating fast enough to make its way into a Poe story. "Err, hello."

"You are dressed behind there, aren't you?"

"Just putting on . . . shoes." Shoes? She winced. "What brings you by? Another ghost?"

He squinted at her for a moment, probably wondering why she wasn't coming out from the screen, which would be the normal thing to do if she *were* dressed, then held up a dark bottle. "Krug. Champagne. From France."

What were they celebrating? Her discovery of his erotic postcard collection?

"Just a token of thanks for getting rid of my ghosts, since I didn't pay you for the prostitute."

"The what?"

He stilled. "The first ghost. The night we met."

Oh. "How did you know she was a prostitute?"

He tapped the bottom of the bottle against his gloved hand, then walked to the dressing table and set it down. "Hope you like it."

"I adore champagne, and if it's the same stuff you sell to Velma, it's terrific."

"Better. But don't tell her. It's personal stock."

"Ah, well. I'm . . . honored. Thanks. You didn't have to."

"My pleasure."

"She wasn't yours, was she?"

"What?"

"The Chinese prostitute. Had you seen her before she was a ghost? As a paying client, I mean."

She hadn't realized he'd been tense until his face relaxed into a smile. "No, Miss Palmer." He removed his hat and ran a palm over his hair. "Not that night or any other."

"Good to know." She propped her chin atop the screen and arched her back while attempting to fasten a button. If she held her breath and reached with her fingertips, she might get one or two—

"Speaking of ghosts, I was wondering if you'd be interested in doing a séance for someone. An old family friend who lives in Sea Cliff."

"Oh?" Aida stopped struggling with the button. "Where is Sea Cliff?"

"Small neighborhood on the other side of the Presidio. Very exclusive."

"As exclusive as Pacific Heights?"

Winter strolled to the dressing screen, reaching inside his coat for an envelope. "Sea Cliff is all new money. Big homes, right up near the bay."

She panicked and made herself smaller. "Sounds swank."

"Depends on your style." He hung his hat on a corner of the screen, propped an elbow on the top edge, and handed the envelope over. "The séance would be after a dinner party this weekend. The job pays well. Read it."

Holding her dress closed with one hand behind her back, she reached for the envelope.

He snatched it back an inch. "Sure you're fully dressed?"

"Of course I'm sure," she lied. "Unlike someone in this room, I don't parade around naked in front of strangers."

"I'm not a stranger."

"And you're no gentleman, either, or you wouldn't—stop that!" She leaned back as he stuck his head over the screen and tracked her movement, his face towering inches away and closing the distance ever so slowly, his eyes never leaving hers. If she continued to retreat, she'd be falling backward.

His voice was a warm, velvety lick up her nerves. "Need help buttoning that dress, cheetah?" When she made a panicked noise, he added, "I can see you in the mirror."

She glanced toward the side of the screen without moving her head. The dressing counter was in her sight, just past his hanging fedora, but he still couldn't . . .

"Behind you." He tilted his eyes to a spot on the wall at her back, where a long dressing mirror stood—dammit!—then looked back down at her face and smiled. "A few advantages to this point of view." He raised a level hand above his head.

"A few disadvantages, too—if you lean any harder on the dressing screen, it'll be reduced to matchsticks."

"Not seeing how this is a problem."

A host of rebuttals formed and dissolved inside her head

as she took a step back. "You probably couldn't even manage the buttons with those beefy fingers of yours."

"Oh, I don't know. I think you'd find I'm skilled at managing all kinds of buttons. Big, small, round. Pearl buttons— I like those quite a bit, and I'm *very* good at manipulating them."

What in the world were they talking about? Alarms blared in her head. "It's not like you've caught me in a scandalous position." Why was she talking so loud? "All you can expect to see is a bit of back. You can ogle more skin in the middle of the day on the beach."

" 'A bit of back' is not going to drive me to depravity, Miss Palmer. I'm offering to do you a favor, not asking for one." The calm and sensible way he said this made her feel foolish.

And really, it might be nice to feel his fingers on her skin. Just the thought of it made her nostrils widen.

"The chorus girls will be back any second, so hurry." She turned around and bared her back. "You'll have to come around here."

She waited, heart hammering, and listened to the floorboards creaking under his feet. Heard him stop behind her. Waited . . .

Waited some more.

What was he doing? It took every ounce of willpower she had to stop herself from spinning on her heels to face him. Then she remembered the dressing mirror and darted her eyes to the side. If she leaned forward an inch, she could see him in the mirror—not his eyes, but she could see him below the nose. He was standing behind her, looking down at her back, tugging on the tips of his gloves to remove them.

A thrill shuttled through her bones, sending an anticipatory wave of goose bumps across her bowed back. She'd called him a pervert, but sadly, she was the guilty party, because her breath was coming faster and a familiar pleasurable heat was blooming between her legs.

She watched him surveying her back in the mirror. His

mouth was open, as if he were poised to say something. Maybe he was having trouble breathing, too.

Without warning, he straightened and tugged his glove on again before marching back around the screen.

"What are you doing?" she asked, standing on tiptoes to peer at him.

A big palm snatched the hat off the screen corner. He molded it atop his head at an angle that shaded his wounded eye. "You're right. It's not proper."

Not proper? She never said it wasn't *proper*. And, well, it wasn't, but when did a bootlegger care about conventions? Or maybe that was just a cover-up for something else—did he see something on her back that revolted him? Some ghastly mole? Was she too heavily freckled there for his tastes? Too skinny? Too fat? *Why did he stop?*

"I'll tell Daniels to send in a girl to help you," he said in a rushed voice. "Enjoy the champagne. Thanks again, and please consider Mrs. Beecham's offer. She's interested in spiritualism and will invite all her rich friends. Good potential business for you. Contact her directly if you're interested."

"But—"

He opened the dressing room door and exited without looking back. "Good night, Miss Palmer."

Winter stopped outside Aida's dressing room to compose himself. Christ, that was close. A second more, and he would've had his hands all over her back . . . and her back on the floor. In public, where anyone could walk in on them. It was disgraceful. She wasn't a whore, for God's sake. One look at her bared back and the gentle slope of her bent neck and he was hard.

And a fool.

His record with the medium wasn't good. First he'd collapsed on the woman. Then exposed his naked body to her. Then he'd made rude insinuations while unintentionally exposing her to lewd and indecent material in his study—though, to be fair, if she hadn't been poking around in his things, that wouldn't have happened.

He reminded himself how fast she wriggled away when she came to her senses after the postcard incident. If she knew what was on his mind today, she'd slap him to kingdom come.

Sadly, a slap from her would probably just make him harder.

It had been years since he'd wanted *someone*, not something. Desire itself, well, he felt that every day. It was like breathing. Hunger for food. Thirst. And he sated himself in the easiest way possible—by his own hand, or with someone willing. Since the accident, the only willing women were fast flappers—too drunk to care that he was anything other than a meal ticket until the next party—and the women he paid to pretend that they enjoyed his scarred, lumbering body on top of theirs.

Simple transactions. Interchangeable. They were about the act itself, not the person. Now he was combining the person and the act in one ridiculous fantasy. He'd gone out of his way to see her again, chasing her around like an eager pup, tongue wagging. Couldn't blame the damned poison this time.

He moved out of the way as two feathered chorus girls strolled by, chatting as they headed backstage. Now there, see? That's exactly what he should be chasing: a pretty girl without a name. How long had it been since he'd had a woman? A couple of months . . . three? Too long.

Maybe Aida was just the first person to step into his sights. She was attractive and vivacious. Any man would appreciate that. It was natural to want a girl like her, especially one who was so easy to talk to. Just a sign that he was getting back to normal, nothing more. Sure, he'd been thinking about her a lot—too much—but he thought a lot about bacon, too.

He stuffed his hands in his pockets and started for the alley exit, where Bo was waiting with the car. It wasn't until they were driving away from the club that Winter realized he'd been so wrapped up worrying about his feelings for Aida that he hadn't taken a second look at the half-dressed chorus girls.

# SEVEN

———— ❦ ————

THREE DAYS LATER, ON THE AFTERNOON OF THE SEA CLIFF DINNER party, Winter sat in a barbershop chair and called Florie Beecham from the barber's phone. The operator let the call ring ten times, and then another ten, but no one answered. He slammed the earpiece down on its hook and handed the telephone back to the barber. His overcast mood took a nosedive.

The bell above the door jingled. In the wall of mirrors, Winter watched Bo stride into the shop. He pocketed car keys and plopped down on a nearby swivel chair. "Is the spirit medium coming to Mrs. Beecham's dinner party?"

"Apparently Mrs. Beecham's staff is too busy to answer the damn telephone," Winter replied gruffly as a white barber's cape was snapped open and draped over his torso.

"I'm sure she'll be there," Bo said.

"She's had three days to accept the job." And as of last night, Florie said she hadn't received a definite yes from Aida yet. Did she have another engagement? Because he'd already called Velma and knew Aida wasn't scheduled to work tonight.

"Maybe she accepted late because she's been busy getting rid of other suicidal ghosts."

Or maybe she'd had second thoughts about seeing him again. "Aren't you supposed to be tracking down the person who tried to kill me? Remind me why I pay you?"

"Because you trust me and I'm the only one who'll put up with your bullshit."

Winter shot him a warning look. He wasn't in the mood.

"As soon as I drop you off at that party, I'm following some leads," Bo promised.

"It's taking too long."

"A tong leader in the booze business was found dead this morning. Locked in a room filled with bees. He'd been stung to death. Allergic, I suppose."

Sounded like a horrible way to die. "Interesting, but I'm not sure what that has to do with curses and ghosts."

"Maybe nothing, but I'm checking into it on my way to talk to someone I've had asking around Chinatown about Black Star. I'll let you know what I find." Bo exhaled a cone of smoke as he watched another barber sweep hair around the white tile floor. Traffic rushed by the plate glass window, where a red, white, and blue pole jutted out near the doorway. "Look, I'm sure she'll be there, so stop worrying. Hell, I'd dress up like a gypsy and do the séance myself for that kind of cash."

"Makes no difference to me whether she comes or not." A lie, but he didn't want to sound overeager. It made him feel weak.

"No reason why she wouldn't. She has no idea what a pain in the ass Florie Beecham is, and for some reason, you didn't frighten her away with your big, hairy body last time you saw her."

"God only knows what's on any female's mind," Winter complained.

Even the barber made a noise of agreement.

God help him, but he wanted to see Aida again. He should've just asked her to a proper dinner. That way, if she turned him down, at least he could be out drowning his sorrows at a nightclub tonight instead of putting on a monkey suit and pretending to give a damn about Florie Beecham and her tedious friends.

"She'll be there," Bo assured him again as the barber picked up a pair of scissors.

On her way out to Mrs. Beecham's séance, Aida ate a quick meal of jasmine tea and Chinese doughnuts—long strips of not-too-sweet fried dough—then stopped by the front counter to drop off her weekly rent money. It was a slow night for the restaurant. Mrs. Lin was sitting on a stool behind the register, a pencil balanced behind her ear, reading a Cantonese newspaper printed in Chinatown.

"Evening. Any mail?"

Mrs. Lin glanced up from her reading and looked her over. "No mail."

Aida handed her a stamped envelope, addressed to Mr. Bradley Bix of New Orleans, a confirmation to his request to meet with her about the potential booking at his club. "Would you please put this with the outgoing letters?"

Mrs. Lin set it inside a box behind the counter and nodded to her dress. "Very pretty."

Aida's black gown had a flattering bateau neckline and a hem trimmed in long strands of beaded silver fringe. Looped around her wrist was a small steel mesh handbag. Her best evening coat was several years old, but it would get her from the taxi to the door.

"Thanks. I'm doing a séance for a rich widow in the Sea Cliff neighborhood."

"Whe-ew," Mrs. Lin whistled. "Fancy new houses there. Hope you charge them a pretty penny."

"Oh, don't worry." Though, to be honest, she wasn't even thinking about the séance or the payment. She was only anxious about the possibility of seeing Winter. It was embarrassing just how much she'd agonized over accepting the job after he'd rushed out of her dressing room. She finally decided that if he *didn't* want to see her, she could just say she was there for the money. Maybe he wouldn't even be there at all. Mrs. Beecham hadn't mentioned him when Aida had called to accept the job earlier in the day—she'd only given Aida instructions to arrive an hour after dinner, which was being served at eight.

Twilight fog clung to trolley wires and shrouded the tops of buildings as Aida's taxicab tilted up and down long stretches of the city, heading west to the southwestern edge of the wooded Presidio. The fog was thicker here near the bay, and she lamented not being able to see the view, which the taxi driver assured her was exclusive and divine.

On curvy El Camino del Mar, she was dropped off in front of a terra-cotta Mediterranean mansion. Though it wasn't as large as the Magnusson home, it sat in the middle of a luxurious amount of land. The house on the adjoining lot was in the middle of construction. Everything was new here. Brand-new, in fact; when she ascended winding steps to the front door, she saw that the green lawn had been laid down in squares. Must be nice to afford all this.

A young maid with a dark complexion opened the door when she knocked. Classical piano music, laughter, and gold light spilled onto the stone steps. "Aida Palmer," she told the girl, who stared at her with a puzzled look on her face. "The spirit medium," she clarified.

"Oh! Yes, Mrs. Beecham is expecting you."

Aida pocketed her gloves and removed her coat, handing it off to the maid as her nerves began jumping. It was the sight of the maid that did it: the girl's black dress with its white lace collar and apron reminded her of the French maids in Winter's postcard collection, bending over with no undergarments to dust perfectly clean bookshelves.

Best not to think about that. Best to think of nothing at all. Definitely no need to immediately look for Winter. If he *was* here, what would she even say? Hello, and thanks for getting me this job?

Right. She was hired help, after all, not a rich socialite attending a party. Why had she not thought of this before she spent the afternoon agonizing over what to wear?

"I'll let Mrs. Beecham know you're here in just a moment, miss," the maid said as she dashed off somewhere, leaving Aida alone.

The home's entry smelled of a headache-inducing combination of paint fumes and roasted meat. Additional scents of brandy and cigar smoke fought for dominance as Aida followed sounds of chatter into an expansive room with polished wood floors, long gold drapes, and upholstered ivory furniture. Near the windows, a lively group of guests mingled around a white baby grand piano. A handful of older men in formal tails and younger men in tuxedos were enjoying post-dinner drinks with twice as many women in evening gowns. The room was a blur of feathers and beads and silk.

No Winter. Her heart sank.

As a piano player took a seat behind the baby grand, a gentleman nearby took notice of her. "Why, hello there. I don't believe we've met. I'm Robert Morran, Florie's cousin." He offered her a dazzling smile. By the glazed look in his eye, he was at least one or two sheets to the wind—and by the way he jostled the glass in his hand, clinking the ice against the sides in a futile attempt to get a servant's attention, he was trying for three.

"Aida Palmer."

"An unusual name for an unusually pretty woman." He gave up flagging the servant and fiddled with a light brown pencil-thin mustache. "How do you know Florie, my dear?"

"I don't. I'm the medium."

"Oh! How exciting." He clinked his ice again while perusing her figure. "Tell me, Miss Palmolive—"

"Palmer," she said crisply, adjusting her handbag's position around her wrist.

"Miss Palmer." He chuckled and ran his tongue over his top teeth. "Yes. So very unusual. I'm a great admirer of unusual beauty. Tell me, dear, what am I thinking right now?"

It took everything she had not to roll her eyes. "I'm a spirit medium, not a telepath."

"Oh, that's no fun. Come now. I'm sure you have more than one talent. Maybe some fortune-telling."

Entertain me! Frighten me! Make the table lift from the floor! She could see how this séance would turn out. Why had she agreed to do this again? Oh, that's right: the small fortune being dangled in front of her face . . . and the foolish hope that she'd get a chance to study Winter's backside again. She'd called him depraved, but clearly she was the one who couldn't control her own animal urges.

"Maybe you'd like to read my palm?" her companion suggested.

"Sorry, no."

He took a step closer, undeterred. *Clink-clink.* "Tarot cards, then. What would the cards say about my future chances with you after this party, hmm?"

He reached out and ran a hand down her arm.

As she pulled away from him, a voice rumbled over her shoulder. "I can predict your chances for losing that hand. Or you can touch her again and find out for yourself."

She turned to find Winter Magnusson's tank of a body filling the doorway as he glared at her companion. A fevered skirmish broke out inside her stomach.

He was dressed in a midnight blue tuxedo jacket with peaked black lapels and matching silk bow tie. His white shirt cuffs were perfectly starched and cuff-linked in gold, his shoes shiny enough to reflect heaven.

Dashing. Dark. More than a little devilish. With his smoldering good looks and his high cheekbones, he looked like a brawnier, crueler version of Valentino, rest his soul. To be honest, he looked as if he could squash Valentino like a bug.

Or, perhaps, Mr. Morran.

"See here, now. I was just speaking to the medium. No need to get testy." Mr. Morran turned to Aida for support. "Right, dear?"

The drunken man was a fly buzzing in her ear. She wished she could swat him and his clinking glass of ice away.

The bright light of the room had caused Winter's good pupil to constrict to a tiny black dot, while the injured pupil remained wide, framed by the curving scar. He was only a couple of inches taller than the other man, but he was just *so much bigger.* And with the aggressive energy fuming and sizzling from him, he looked as if he were ready to tear Morran's hand right off his arm.

A thrill bolted through her.

Something else was bolting through Morran, and it caused *his* eyes to widen as he backed up a step. People were beginning to notice something was awry; the outer edges of the crowd around the piano glanced in their direction as the chorus to "Shine On, Harvest Moon" was being sung out of key by several swaying partygoers in the background.

Winter's mouth lifted in something that could've technically been called a smile, but it had the effect of an angry wolf baring his teeth. In a deceptively calm bass-heavy voice, he told the man, "I'll give you ten seconds to make it to the other side of the room."

It only took the man five.

Once Morran had disappeared into the crowd around the piano, Winter looked down at her. His anger drained away. "Hello, cheetah."

It was all she could do not to smile up at him like a child being handed freshly spun cotton candy. Good grief. She had to calm down. "I could've taken care of him myself, you know."

"Any woman who traipses around the country working night shifts at speakeasies surely can, but that idiot is an aggressive skirt chaser. You don't want to let him get you alone."

"Good to know. Thank you for your concern."

Now his mouth wasn't smiling, but his eyes certainly were. He stuffed his hands into his pockets as he lowered his head and spoke to her conspiratorially in a teasing voice. "Let's just pretend that you needed my help. It will make me feel useful."

A thrill flowed through her like an electrical current. "Would you have actually hurt him?"

"In a heartbeat."

"How foolish of me to find that exciting."

His mouth parted and he grinned, big and genuine. She couldn't stop herself from grinning in return.

"I suppose it wouldn't be a party without the threat of violence," an approaching feminine voice called out.

Aida turned to see a beautiful blonde slinking toward them in a long gold gown with a silk cape that draped over her shoulders and flowed behind her like a flag. Several strands of gold beads dripped from her neck, clinking against her stomach as she walked. She was grinning at Winter but turned her attention toward Aida.

"Darling!" Her arms extended to her sides in a dramatic welcoming gesture, a long, silver cigarette holder poised between gloved fingers. "I'm Florie Beecham. Welcome to my home."

Aida smiled tightly as the woman embraced her shoulders and kissed her cheeks, engulfing her in brandy and perfume. "Thank you for having me."

"Nonsense. You're the talk of the party," Mrs. Beecham said with a laugh, waving her cigarette holder, scattering ashes around. Goodness, the woman was drunk. She was also Aida's age, if not younger—certainly not the doddering, lonely widow Aida had expected.

"Your home is lovely, Mrs. Beecham," she said as the piano player finished and the party began shuffling past them into another room.

"Call me Florie. Everyone does. And isn't it marvelous?" Not one single strand of her slicked platinum bob shifted out of place when she tilted her head back to admire her own decor. "I moved in three weeks ago. This is my first party."

"How nice."

"I see you've found Win. Don't mind his brutish manner; that's just a facade. He gave me the idea to hire you. He said, 'Florie, old gal, there's this spiritualist down at one of the black-and-tans who'd make your party more interesting.' And it was a brilliant idea, as usual. All his ideas are brilliant."

Aida flicked a questioning glance at Winter. His look was something between sheepish and apologetic.

Mrs. Beecham teetered past Aida to sling both her arms

around one of Winter's, hanging on to it like the remaining mast on the *Titanic*. He extracted her cigarette holder half a second before it burned a hole in his tuxedo sleeve and set it on a nearby hall table.

"Win and I went to Berkeley together. Before he got the boot." Mrs. Beecham kicked a leg out and nearly tripped over her gown.

Winter pulled the woman to the side and steadied her as guests filed past them into the parlor. "I think you better slow down on those sidecars."

"Says the big rumrunner!"

Aida eyed the woman's perfect pale skin and dimpled smile. An unwelcome tightness squeezed her lungs. She glanced at Winter. "I don't believe I've heard the story of you and Berkeley." Did her voice sound strained? She steeled her posture, hoping that would help.

"Oh, it's a good one," Mrs. Beecham confirmed. "Win can tell you the long version, but the short of it is—"

"Florie," Winter said tiredly.

"Shhh. Lemme tell. See, we had this friend, Nolan, who edited a university literary journal, and he printed a D. H. Lawrence review that was a bit . . . risqué, and even though he left blanks for the offensive words, the university was furious and he got expelled. Then Win here"—Mrs. Beecham poked Winter square in the chest—"wrote a scathing treatise against censorship, only he *didn't* include blanks for the offensive words, and there were a *lot* of them. He had it printed up as a handbill and circulated it around campus. The best part is that he included an unflattering caricature of the dean who fought for Nolan's expulsion—miserable old hag. The drawing was in the buff, if you know what I mean."

Aida cocked a brow at Winter.

"I didn't sketch it myself," he said, almost sheepish.

"Ugh," Mrs. Beecham complained. "One of the art students drew it—a horrible caricature with great sagging breasts. It burned my eyes. Anyway, someone ratted on Winter and he got kicked out. It was terribly boring after he left."

"I'll bet," Aida murmured.

Mrs. Beecham laughed. "The funny part is that he was only one semester away from graduating."

"That's not funny," Aida said, suddenly annoyed. "That's terrible. Why didn't you go somewhere else and finish?"

"Why bother?" the woman answered for him. "Volstead passed and his father traded in the fishing for bootlegging. Pays better than building boat engines and chasing down salmon."

Winter grunted.

"Can you believe that was what—seven, eight years ago? Time flies," she said with a dramatic shrug. "It's been such a blur since college, my whirlwind romance with Mr. Beecham, his unexpected death. It's been trying."

"I can feel your pain inside the walls of this lavish shanty," Winter mumbled.

"It does help to soothe my frail nerves."

"Is gold the new mourning color?" Winter said, looking at her dress.

"I put one of his hideous paintings in the parlor as a tribute. That means more than a boring black dress." She gestured into the dark parlor, where candles were burning and wooden chairs had been set in rows in front of a round table draped in patchwork Romany cloth. Behind it was a garish bohemian painting of what was clearly Mrs. Beecham lying half naked in a field of flowers. Her nipples were painted a shade of blindingly bright pink and her face was blue.

"Maybe you should've married someone who wasn't three times your age," Winter said.

"He was sweet to me, once. But perhaps you're right. Really, Win, just think if you would've stayed at Berkeley— the two of *us* might've been married and I could be decorating your house right now."

"I like my house just fine as is."

"I mean your old house, not your father's. Never mind. Let's not dig up bad memories."

What in the world was she talking about? Aida's head was spinning from all the information this obnoxious woman was unleashing. Every word that came out of her mouth made Aida loathe her more and more.

"Regardless, it all turned out fine anyway. I rather like being a widow. I can do anything I want, with *whomever* I want, and nobody can say a damn thing about it." Mrs. Beecham turned her face up to Winter and grinned like a harpy while her fingers danced up his arm suggestively.

Were they lovers? Was this what he preferred in a woman? Perhaps that protective show with Mr. Morran was just everyday business for someone like him. Maybe he would've done that for any girl standing in her place.

Something snapped inside her. She had her pride, and she'd made a promise to herself that she would take no job she didn't want, and Sam would've encouraged her to stick to that promise. "I'm sorry, but I've changed my mind. I think this party will do just fine without me," Aida said to Mrs. Beecham. "I appreciate your offer, but perhaps your guests would prefer music over mysticism."

"Aida," Winter said, unhooking Mrs. Beecham's arm as he started toward her.

"Come on, darling," Mrs. Beecham said to Aida, as if she were a small child who needed to be coddled. "Don't be that way. Win and I are old friends. Have a drink."

"I don't want a drink."

The widow waved a hand toward the parlor. "Well, let's get started then."

"I said I'm not doing it, and that's final."

"Stop being silly."

"Oh, for God's sake, shut up, Florie," Winter snapped.

Conversation and laugher inside the parlor halted as people turned in their seats to stare.

"Don't you get crude with me in my house," the widow said to Winter, then pointed at Aida. "I'm paying you for a séance, so get inside that room and do your job."

A thousand emotions crackled inside Aida. She had wild thoughts of taking Mrs. Beecham's cigarette holder and shoving it inside the woman's ear. "You want a séance?" she said through gritted teeth. "I'll give you a séance."

Aida stormed to the back of the parlor, ignoring the mumbles and whispers. She stopped at the gypsy table and removed her trusty silver lancet from her handbag, unscrewing a cap on the end to bare a small blade. The garish painting of Mrs. Beecham hung on the wall a couple of feet away. "What was your husband's name?" she shouted back at the widow.

"What?"

"His first name."

"I don't want to participate. This is for my guests. Andy, you go first. Where's the violinist? We can't start un—"

Aida squinted at the corner of the painting. "Harold Beecham."

"Oh, yes, well. I'd rather you didn't—Andy?" Mrs. Beecham called desperately. "Where are you? It's so dark in here. There aren't enough candles."

"Over here, Florie. I'm coming." A brown-haired man sidestepped behind a few chairs to stand next to her.

Aida ignored them. With one hand on the painting, she took a deep breath and pricked her thigh with the lancet blade. Tears stung her eyes as endorphins reared up. Using the pain to enter a winking, oh-so-brief trance state, she reached out into the void, calling for Mrs. Beecham's husband.

Her vision wavered. She inhaled sharply, feeling a silent answer to her call. The spirit came rushing toward her over the veil like a demon released from the pit of hell.

# EIGHT

———— ❧ ————

WINTER HALTED IN THE MIDDLE OF THE PARLOR WHEN AIDA'S
breath turned visible, barely hearing the gasps of surprise
around him. He wasn't unsettled by the puffs of white billowing from her mouth—not anymore. He was more interested in the silver instrument she had in her hand.

Aida's body stiffened, then her face became animated.
Her head swiveled around in all directions until she found
Florie. "Sweetheart," she said. "I never thought I'd lay eyes
on you again."

Florie froze, then backed up as Aida stalked her around
the rows of chairs.

"Aren't you glad to see me?" Aida's voice said. "I remember your last words like it was yesterday . . . when I found
you riding the Halstead boy like a prized pony at the county
fair."

Florie paled, then laughed nervously. Her eyes flicked to
her apparent lover, Andy Halstead, who stood next to her
looking as if he were going to faint and keel over.

Aida walked faster. "When my heart failed, you didn't even
try to save me. You just said, 'Looks like we killed him.'"

Florie's back hit the wall. She yelped. Aida lunged with outstretched arms. Something flew from her fingers and sailed through air, dinging against the wall, but she didn't seem to notice. She was too busy grasping Florie's throat with both hands as she wrestled his college friend to the floor. Winter raced toward them, knocking chairs out of the way while party guests stood by in a drunken daze.

Aida straddled Florie. The mesh handbag dangling around her wrist smacked against the floor as she choked her. A vase shattered. Florie was grasping the leg of a side table, trying to buck her off in a panic. Christ. The medium was going to kill her.

"Aida!" he shouted.

Her head snapped toward his voice. She looked at him with her eyes, but it wasn't her. She was possessed. Feral. Unearthly. A violent chill ran down Winter's arms.

"Aida, let go," he commanded roughly.

She shuddered . . . then fell sideways off Florie and landed in a heap. Her frosty breath swirled away. Florie gulped air and pumped her legs, scurrying backward. People snapped into action.

One of the servants bent to help her up. "Are you all right, ma'am?"

Florie coughed, then pointed at Aida and choked out, "She's crazy! Get her out of here!"

Winter slung an arm around Aida's waist and hefted her to her feet. He brushed dust off her black dress and slid both hands around the back of her neck to hold her steady and get a look at her. He could feel her pulse hammering beneath his hands. "You okay?"

She sniffled. "Fine." Her chest heaved with several labored breaths before she nodded her head. He released her. She looked over her shoulder at Florie and made a low noise of regret, her face contorting with a reluctant embarrassment.

"Come lay down, ma'am," the servant was telling Florie. "I'll bring you water and your pills."

Halstead helped the servant lift Florie onto a settee. Win-

ter watched him with mild interest, unsurprised that the man
had been screwing Florie behind her husband's back. Rather
fascinating what Aida's ability could dredge up.

"I want her out," Florie yelled at no one in particular.

"Don't have to tell me twice." Aida rotated her shoulder
to pull away from him, mumbling, "I just need to get my bag."

As people were filing past, he spotted a flash of silver on
the floor—what Aida had dropped—and picked it up as she
got her bag, nearly cutting himself on a small, sharp blade.
Before he could inspect it properly, he spotted the black lines
of Aida's stockings moving toward the door. He slipped the
silver instrument inside his tuxedo pocket, hearing it ding
against something inside as he ran after her and called for
one of the servants to retrieve his coat.

"Hers, too," he added, guiding Aida toward the entryway
as guests scattered around other rooms—some whispering
in corners, others looking for another drink. He helped Aida
into her coat and instructed the maid to tell Florie that he
was leaving and to call them a taxi.

Outside, he followed Aida down winding steps, then continued up the sidewalk. Packards and Cadillacs lined the
curb, some with drivers asleep at the wheel, napping until
their employers stumbled out after the party. The Magnusson family driver, Jonte, would normally be here as well,
but he had the night off and Bo had dropped Winter off
before heading to Chinatown.

"Where are you going?" he asked Aida.

She stopped in front of a nearby lot with a half-constructed
house. Cement steps built into the hill were still framed in
timber, flanked by two freshly bricked posts on either side.

"Let's wait for the taxi here," he suggested.

She didn't turn around to look at him. Her silence was
confusing. Maybe he was wrong, but the way she'd reacted
to Florie's obnoxious chattering was as if—well, that
couldn't be right. She wasn't jealous, was she? Because that's
damn well what it seemed like in the heat of the moment,
but maybe it was only what he *wanted* to believe.

Frustrated, he stared at the fog clinging to the trees and the roofs of houses across the street. "That was interesting."

"I'm not sure what got into me. I'm sorry if I embarrassed you."

"Florie's smashed. She won't even remember it in the morning. She never does." He reached in his tuxedo pocket and held out the silver knife in his palm. "What is this?"

Her fingers brushed his as she took it. They looked at each other for a moment, then her gaze broke away. She rummaged around in her bag, retrieving a small silver cap. "It's a military snake bite kit. I think it once belonged to a British pilot." She screwed the cap over the blade. "Lancet is here and the other end holds medicated salve."

"A lancet," he repeated, still confused. "Why were you holding it when you called up Florie's husband?"

"Because even though I can send ghosts away without help, I need to enter a trance state in order to call a spirit who's left this plane."

"Wait. If they leave this 'plane' after death, where do they go?"

"Across the veil to the beyond." She made a vague sweeping gesture. "Look, don't ask me to tell you the meaning of life or the one true religion or what happens to souls once they've crossed over, because I don't know. They won't tell you if you ask them, either. All I know is that I can call most of them back from wherever they are to communicate with their loved ones, as long as they haven't been dead too long."

"So you need to be in a trance to do that, but what's the lancet got to do with it?"

"Lots of ways to enter a trance, but since I don't usually have time to meditate, the fastest way for me is pain." She twirled the lancet in her fingers, then palmed it, showing him. "I can hold it onstage without anyone noticing it." Her big eyes blinked up at him. She pointed the capped lancet at her thigh. "I prick myself here."

"Jesus! You injure yourself every time you call up a spirit?"

"It's not bad, and I like helping people. Provides some

resolution to the past." She slipped the lancet into her coat pocket and retrieved her gloves. "Besides, it pays the rent, you know?"

She was tougher than he imagined. He studied the silhouette of her face beneath the brim of her cloche. The upturned tilt of her nose echoed the curved front of her bob, curling ever so slightly against her cheeks. She caught him staring and turned away, testing out the concrete steps. Finding them solid, she ascended one step, then another. She toed the wooden board housing the third step.

"This wasn't exactly what I had in mind when I was telling you about wanting to do séances," she said with her back to him. "I'm sure you feel like you're doing me some big favor by getting me this high-paying gig, but I don't need help arranging work. And it doesn't matter how much money people throw my way—if they don't take me seriously, I might as well be dressing up in a jester suit and tap-dancing."

Why was she so agitated? "Look, I wasn't trying to do you a favor—"

"And I didn't mean to upset your lover, but maybe if you would've just explained the situation to me instead of having her summon me out here—"

"Whoa! Florie and I are not lovers. Haven't been since college. And it wasn't as if we were sweethearts then, it was just . . ."

She turned around and crossed her arms over her middle. "Just what?"

"Convenient," he finally said. "I'm sure that's shocking."

"Shocking?" Her laugh was mean and hard. "Like your silly postcard collection?"

"I believe you called me a deviant and a pervert, not silly."

"You are. That doesn't mean I'm prudish. I may not be as loose and free as Mrs. Beecham, or however many other flappers with whom you've had 'convenient' affairs, but I'm no virgin."

Oh, she was a big talker, wasn't she? Aida might be tough and independent, and she might not be a virgin, but Winter wasn't convinced she was carefree and modern when it came to sex. He could tell by the nervous defensiveness in her speech—the way she blinked rapidly and wouldn't look him in the eyes. The way she'd reacted when she'd discovered the postcards in his study, and how she'd acted in the dressing room. He'd been so worried about his own feelings that afternoon, he'd confused himself in regards to her motives.

She wasn't concerned with propriety—she was skittish.

"How old are you? Sixteen? Seventeen?" he teased.

She narrowed her eyes. "Twenty-eight."

"Practically dead. And how many lovers have you had?"

"That's none of your business."

He rested one foot on the bottom step. "You just accused me of being a promiscuous lout. I think it's a fair question. How many? One?"

"Two," she said, putting distance between them by ascending another step without turning around. "And both of them could barely manage a proper kiss, much less anything else, so I can't say I was impressed. Like I said earlier, I can take care of myself."

Now it was Winter's turn to be astonished. Was she saying what he thought she was saying?

She bit the inside of her cheek and looked away.

Well, *well*. No woman he'd known had ever admitted to pleasuring herself, and being curious, he'd asked plenty of times. Frankly, he'd started to believe females just didn't engage in such depravity, though he couldn't for the life of him figure out why. He was quite fond of the activity himself. He must be; he'd been doing it daily half his life.

His mind conjured an image of her sprawled on a bed with her hand beneath her skirt. Big mistake. He tried to think of what she'd said before the taking-care-of-herself bit, and that didn't help matters. She'd admitted to two lovers, and they weren't any good. The sudden shift of blood from his brain to his cock made that sound like a challenge.

"So you're saying that you can judge a man's worth by his kiss?"

"I . . . no, I don't think that's what I said."

"That's what you implied. Would you like me to kiss you, so you can judge my worth?"

"Just because you look handsome in that tuxedo doesn't mean I want you to kiss me."

Handsome? She thought he was handsome? Perhaps she was blind, because he knew from all the uneasy stares he tolerated every time he stepped out in public that this couldn't possibly be true. But he used to be, once, and oh, how he wanted to believe she meant it, so he allowed himself to do so, just for a moment, and climbed one step.

She made a small anxious noise and tried to do the same, but the top step was barricaded by a piece of timber, while his body blocked the descent. The freckled wildcat was trapped on the step above him.

"Don't come any closer!"

"Are you sure?"

"Of course I'm sure, and that's final."

He chuckled. "You said that to Florie about the séance, then ended up pinning her to floor."

"Yes, well . . . I mean it this time. What are you doing?"

"I'm considering kissing you."

"I really wish you wouldn't."

He lowered his face very close to hers and smelled violets again. That drove him a little mad. His breath was coming faster. So was hers; for a moment, he watched her breasts rise and fall beneath the weight of her coat. "Why not?"

"I'm sure I have a really good reason, but you're making it awfully hard for me to remember it."

He chuckled. She gave him a sheepish smile.

"Maybe you'll even kiss me back," he said, becoming greedy.

"I doubt that. But if you insist on trying, what could I do to stop you?"

The heated look she gave him sent a bolt of heat through his already hard cock.

Jesus. She was teasing him. For a crazed moment, he

wondered if he'd been the one to start this or if she'd manipulated him. Maybe she wasn't skittish after all.

He leaned in closer. She smelled so good, he worried he
might pass out and crack his head open on the sidewalk. He
could see the gossip headline in the newspaper now: *Suspected Bootlegger Succumbs to Spirit Medium's Seductive
Charms, Makes Idiot of Himself.* He put a hand on one of
the brick posts to steady himself. "This is what's going to
happen," he said in a low voice that sounded far surer than
he felt. "I'm going to kiss you—just a kiss. I won't lay a
finger on you. And if you find you don't like it, if you find
my *worth* lacking, you can shove me back down the steps.
Deal?"

She hesitated, just for a moment, before answering him
in a threadbare whisper.

"All right."

Something between victory and vertigo raced through
his veins. He swallowed hard and lowered his mouth—near
hers, but not touching. Not yet. Her breath was warm against
his lips. Their noses grazed. He tried to hold his eyes open,
but his eyelids were heavier than wet sand.

Her mouth was so small. For a moment, he worried over
this, feeling oafish and hulking. But he was too hungry to
withdraw. His pulse swished and pounded inside his ears.
He closed his eyes as his lips brushed hers, testing. So soft.
He felt her mouth open against his as she breathed out the
tiniest moan. The reverberation that went through him was
wildly disproportionate, like a whisper causing a landslide.

Keeping his promise not to touch her with his hands, he
pressed careful kisses on the corner of her lips, on the big
freckle he'd first noticed that afternoon when she was in his
study, then on her bottom lip, tasting salt. Her mouth opened
wider, and that did him in. He was lost. He kissed her fully,
trying not to swallow her whole, but unable to restrain himself when she pressed back.

She was kissing him.

Every cell in his body vibrated. Warm chills ran down

his arms. He lost all good sense. His tongue slid inside her mouth before he could think that this might be crossing a line, but for some miraculous reason, she didn't resist—she moaned into his mouth and joined him.

My God, she was kissing him in the slowest, most erotic fashion that he momentarily forgot where they were. He was hard as iron, barely able to stop himself from grabbing her around the waist and pushing his hips against hers. He'd never wanted to touch anyone so badly.

They broke away from each other, breath ragged. She could've pulled back, could've pushed him away, but she didn't. A single syllable fell from her mouth—"oh"—and her cheek fell against his.

An unexpected tenderness washed over him. He bent his head lower, breathing in the sweet smell of her skin. "Aida . . ." His hand twitched. He wanted to touch her face if nothing else, and he might have broken his promise and done just that, if it weren't for the blinding headlights that shined on them from the street.

Aida turned her head. He lifted a hand to block the light, out of sorts. She said something that he couldn't hear. He made some strange noise in return, and she repeated herself.

"I think that might be the taxi," she said hoarsely.

"Oh."

She wiped her mouth with the back of her glove and cleared her throat as a door slammed in the distance. "The driver's headed up to Mrs. Beecham's."

He pulled away and composed himself. "Seems so." Whistling loudly, he waved a hand in the driver's direction, catching his attention as he was heading up Florie's stairs. The driver lifted a hand in acknowledgment and returned to his taxi to pull forward.

Winter thought of the potentially cramped backseat, which in most taxis was barely big enough for him alone. The thought of Aida crowded into that constrictive space alongside him inspired several ideas all at once.

Oh, the things he could do to her in the back of that dark

cab. Maybe she was right about him being a pervert; he'd certainly never felt more deviant than he did at that moment.

And something more . . . a dizzying lightness. A burden lifted. If a monster's heart beat inside his ribs, her kiss was a sharper lancet than the one she used to pierce the veil: it opened up a small hole that allowed some of the darkness to drain.

She straightened her hat and pulled the brim down tight. Stepping aside, he allowed her to shuffle past him, the fronts of their coats lightly brushing. He followed her to the curb, smiling the entire way.

As the taxi shifted into gear and began rumbling down the hill from Florie's, he noticed movement in his peripheral vision. A figure stepped out of the darkness near his shoulder: a man dressed in a red suit, his hair in disarray. His eyes glowed yellow, reflecting the headlights of the taxi as it rolled toward them.

White smoke rushed from Aida's mouth at the same moment Winter realized that the man's suit wasn't red at all—he was covered in blood.

Ghost.

Aida looked down at her breath. "Oh no . . . not now."

Winter turned to face the ghost, all the hairs on his arms rising as panic tightened his chest. The bloody man looked straight at him—saw him, just like the prostitute. This was no random ghost, no accident victim tied to the street where he'd been hit. This was deliberate. And if the poisonous spell was broken, and he was no longer a walking ghost magnet, then something else was drawing it to him.

This was an attack.

The ghost came for Winter, reaching out with both hands. A strange electrical current crackled through his arm where bloody hands touched him.

Touched. Solid. The ghost was corporeal. Worse—Winter knew his face! From somewhere, someplace. So goddamn familiar, but he couldn't remember.

Recoiling in horror, he jerked back and slammed into Aida. She yelped. He swiveled around in time to witness her, mid-stumble, as she tripped on her heel and fell into the path of the taxi.

Brakes squealed.

Winter lunged.


Aida felt her ankle give way as she staggered into the taxi's path. She heard a terrible squeal and squeezed her eyes shut as headlights flashed across her face.

Her world tilted. She was jerked in the opposite direction, away from the rolling car. A sharp impact shook her bones as her face smashed against linen and wool and male. The taxi skidded by, veering sharply. Then everything was drowned by the sound of the crash. Metal exploded. Burnt rubber and asphalt filled her lungs.

Winter's arm slackened and she tumbled from his grip. Her face scraped against the pavement as the wind was knocked out of her lungs. She wanted to cry out in pain but couldn't. It took her several seconds to get her breath back. When it did come, that breath remained cold and white.

The ghost was still here somewhere, but she couldn't see it.

Arms shaking, she pushed herself up on her elbows and twisted around, terrified until she felt Winter's leg under hers. He was on his side, cradling his arm, grimacing. She shuffled around and quickly surveyed the rest of him. Saw no blood or tears in his clothing. Nothing but a streak of dirt on the bulk of his upper left arm.

He'd been struck on his shoulder while pulling her out of the taxi's path. That was the thud she'd felt in her bones; he'd absorbed the impact.

"Winter?" She didn't want to touch him, fearing that she'd hurt him further. His jaw clenched. "Mr. Magnusson?"

He exhaled on a loud grunt and shifted his leg, pain causing lines to crease around his eyes. He pulled himself up to sit, coddling his arm close to his side. "You okay?" He nodded to a small rent in her coat sleeve.

"Must have scraped the wheel cover or running board. It's fine. Your shoulder hit the car. Is it broken?"

He rolled it and groaned. "Not dislocated. Just hurts like hell. It'll be fine."

Metal squawked behind her as the driver's door of a white and black Checker Cab opened. He'd hit a telephone pole and dented the grille of his car, but nothing was on fire. No broken glass that she could see. "Are you folks okay?" the driver called out from across the street.

They exchanged brief answers, confirming that no one was seriously injured, as a porch light flickered on in a nearby house—neighbors curious about the crash. Aida scanned the street looking for the ghost. She found it a few feet away, bending over in the middle of the road.

"Behind you," Aida warned Winter as she pushed herself up.

The ghost was seemingly unaware of them. It was fixated on something round lying on the pavement. Something gold and shiny and small.

Another glinting object lay just behind Winter, and a third near his hip.

The ghost picked up the first object, admired it, and then focused his attention on the next one, shuffling a couple steps closer.

"What the hell?" Winter murmured, warily watching the ghost bending again.

As he grunted and sat up, Aida squinted at the object closest to them: a gold coin with a square hole in the center that was bordered by familiar characters. "Chinese coins."

"Shit!" He pushed himself to his feet. "I heard something clink in here when I pocketed your lancet." He rummaged inside his tuxedo jacket pocket and pulled out a fourth coin.

"They must've spilled into the street when you pulled me out of the taxi's path."

"They aren't mine. Someone put them there."

The ghost had two coins and was now bending over the third. Bizarre, but the show was over. Aida started toward the ghost with the intent of getting rid of it, but Winter's hand gripped her arm. "He's solid, Aida. Feels like electric flesh."

"Solid?"

"I knew this man when he was alive. Whoever poisoned me sent him."

"The coins are the magnet," she said. "Velma removed the magic in the *Gu* poison. Whoever is after you is trying something new."

The ghost stood, holding the third coin. Its head snapped toward Winter, and then it lumbered toward them.

"It wants the magnet," Aida shouted. "Throw the damn coin!"

Quick as lightning, Winter hurtled the coin into the street. The ghost immediately changed directions and lunged for it. The moment he had the coin in his grip, he . . . disappeared.

Aida's breath returned to normal. It worked. Would she have been able to send the spellbound ghost away on her own? She didn't know. She'd never encountered a solid ghost.

They stared at the street, both of them wary, but when it was clear that the thing was truly gone, she turned to him. "Someone put those coins in your pocket to attract that ghost."

"It must've happened at Florie's."

"Someone at that séance isn't your friend."

The taxi driver was heading toward them, a young boy in a gray uniform, his pants tucked into tall black boots. Up the sidewalk, several guests from Mrs. Beecham's began spilling out of her house. Someone called out to them, inquiring if everyone was okay.

"Winter?" Aida asked in a low voice.

He made a vague noise in acknowledgment.

"You said you knew the ghost when he was alive . . . ?"

He nodded his head once, then looked away. "I couldn't place him at first, but I realized where I'd seen his face when he started picking up those coins."

"Where?"

Winter waited so long to answer, she almost thought he wouldn't. "He was a spy working for a small bootlegger out of Oakland. Pulled a gun on my father when we caught him snooping around one of our warehouses." Winter turned his head and looked Aida in the eyes. "His name was Dick Jepsen. He was the first man I ever killed."

# NINE

---

SOBER AND BROODING, WINTER ACCOMPANIED AIDA BACK TO Golden Lotus after calling for his own car. They did not discuss the ghost's identity any further.

They also did not discuss the kiss.

Granted, it wasn't an appropriate topic for conversation after what transpired in the street. Aida shouldn't have even been thinking about it. And she tried not to; after all, the man was clearly upset. If she were a decent person, she'd be upset, too—she'd kissed a killer. That's what he was, wasn't he? He did say Dick Jepsen was the *first* man he'd killed, implying there was a second. A third? Fourth? How many? It was easy to forget the dark side of what he did for a living. He'd said he was defending his father's life the night he shot Jepsen, but maybe there were other times when he was the aggressor.

Could it be possible Winter was bloodthirsty like the racketeers and gangsters reported in the newspapers? No. She didn't believe that. Not after the gentleness he'd shown when he'd kissed her . . . the restraint he'd used to tease her.

Goodness, how he'd made her body melt.

She tried to tell herself that it wasn't the absolute best kiss she'd ever had, but that was too monumental a lie for her poor heart, which was madly pitter-pattering beneath her dress the entire way home.

Before she made her way up to her apartment, he stepped outside the car and gave her a business card that said MAG-NUSSON FISH COMPANY, with an address off the Embar-cadero, on a pier that housed his legitimate business. He penciled his home telephone numbers on the back: a private line that rang directly to his study, and the main line that his housekeeper Greta answered.

"I'd like to retain your services on an ongoing basis. Whatever you think is fair pay, let me know."

"Uh . . ."

"If you aren't working at Velma's, I want you to be available to me in case I need you."

"For business," she said, thinking of the kiss.

He hesitated. "Yes. As a medium. Or an exorcist." He was being very stern and serious, and she felt quite sure this was how he spoke to his own men—as if he wouldn't take no for answer. And if it were anyone else throwing out this kind of gruff demand, she'd likely tell him to go to hell. But he'd just kissed the bejesus out of her and broke the sensible part of her brain, so she said yes.

In fact, she said, "I'm all yours," but it was lost under the sound of a loud truck rolling by.


At noon the next day, Aida headed down to Golden Lotus to have a quick lunch of tea and dumplings and collect her mail. "Why so anxious?" Mrs. Lin asked behind the counter as she stuck a pencil into the knotted bun of black hair at the nape of her neck.

"Excuse me?"

"Anxious. Jumpy."

"Oh, I don't know, my mind is elsewhere. Listen, you wouldn't happen to have heard of any superstitious practice in the Chinese community having to do with old coins?"

She considered this. "Don't think so. Why?"

"I'm trying to figure out why someone would use four old Chinese coins to attract a ghost."

"A ghost?" She looked around. "Not here, I hope."

"No, no—at that séance last night."

"Oh." Mrs. Lin rubbed the Buddha's belly and mumbled something in Cantonese. "I don't know about ghosts, but four of anything is unlucky for business. Four is a curse. Very bad. Everyone knows that. No specific curse associated with coins, though. Is someone cursing you?"

"No. Cursing . . . a client." She tapped her nails on the counter. "I need to find someone in Chinatown who knows more about ghosts and superstitions and curses. Maybe someone who appreciates my special abilities?"

Mrs. Lin brightened. "I know just the man. My acupuncturist, Doctor Yip."

"A doctor?"

"He owns an herbal apothecary shop off Sacramento. It's located in a small alley. I will draw a map." She lifted spectacles that dangled from the chain around her neck next to the key that unlocked the red lacquered mail cabinet and began drawing a map on the back of a blank ordering slip.

Aida's pulse increased as a cautious hopefulness sprung up. She waited, watching Mrs. Lin silently until she began sketching what looked to be parts of Chinatown that weren't exactly tourist-friendly. "Is it dangerous, that area?"

"You will get some looks, and you should avoid the opium den. If you smell sweet smoke, you've gone too far. It's best to take a man with you. Too dangerous for a young woman alone. But do not be afraid to go to Doctor Yip. He came here from Hong Kong a few years ago. Very educated and kind. You will like him."

"Wonderful. Thanks so much."

"Anytime. Hope he can help."

It might be a long shot, but Aida hoped so, too. Maybe Bo had already talked to this herbalist. Best to just contact Winter and find out. She could send him a note through Mrs. Lin's courier, but that seemed like a silly waste of time when she had Winter's business card propped against a lamp on her nightstand. That was what it was there for. She worked for him now, after all. He'd probably forgotten all about the kiss.

She'd certainly tried.

Retreating to her room, she bolstered herself and tried his private number, feeling butterflies in her stomach when the operator made the connection and his big voice crackled over the wire.

"Magnusson."

"It's me," she said, suddenly forgetting her manners and good sense.

"Hello, you." His voice sounded low and friendly in the telephone's earpiece.

Her stomach fluttered while the line popped and hissed. "I can't talk long and people might pick up—the telephones in our rooms are connected to the restaurant's line. Mrs. Lin doesn't like us to make calls during lunch rush, so if you hear swearing in Cantonese, hang up," she said, trying to sound casual and breezy.

"Duly noted," he replied before adding, "I hear it from Bo all the time."

"How's your shoulder today?"

"Sore. Greta forced some pills down my throat, so it feels better at the moment."

"Good, good. Well . . . ah, the reason I rang is because I have the address of an herbalist in Chinatown who might help with information on the coins. My landlady gave me his name."

"Oh?"

"Don't get too excited. It might not pan out, but it could be worth investigating. I have a map to show us how to get there."

"That's damned resourceful," he said, sounding impressed.

"You hired me to help you."

"Indeed I did. Bo should be back from an errand any

minute. As soon as he arrives, we'll head over there. Shall I meet you in an hour, say?"

Bo was coming, too? A pang of disappointment tightened her chest. "Sure. But I have to be at Gris-Gris around five. I'm doing an early show tonight for happy hour."

"That's fine. I'll get you there in time."

One of the girls who lived in the building clicked on the line and asked to use it.

"In an hour?" Aida said quickly.

"With bells on."

She hung up and changed her clothes, dressing in a camel-colored skirt and a matching jacket. Casual, but smart. Very businesslike. It looked good with her tan stockings, which had pretty little scrolling shapes embroidered on the calves and hid the freckles on her legs. She finished getting ready, then headed downstairs in time to meet him.

Aida's heart pounded wildly as she glanced toward the entrance and found him stepping inside the restaurant wearing a long black coat, black suit, and black necktie with red chevrons running down the middle peeking from his vest. Pausing near the door, he removed his hat and brushed away droplets of rain. Gray light filtered in from the windows behind him, where Chinese characters and the pronouncement "Best Almond Cookies in Chinatown" surrounded a painted lotus blossom.

His eyes found hers. "Miss Palmer," he said politely, as if he were an upstanding gentleman and not a bootlegger. As if they were merely business acquaintances . . . which they were, she reminded herself. "Shall we?"

Dodging customers tottering up to the register, she followed Winter outside into the fresh air, heavy with the scent of wet pavement. She eyed rain dripping from a shallow ledge above the entrance. "Everyone told me it would be dry here in the summer."

"Usually is."

"Where's Bo?" she asked in her best neutral tone as she pulled on a pair of short brown gloves with bell-shaped cuffs.

"He dropped me off."

"Ah." *Flutter-flutter.* She squelched her excitement and glanced around. The newsstand next door had erected a rainy-day tarp that tied to a street sign and a telephone pole. "Maybe we should grab a taxi."

Winter snapped open a large black umbrella. "Nonsense. It's barely raining. Come." He shifted her under the umbrella and out of the entry so an elderly couple could step inside. His hand lingered on her back as they walked to a spot by the newsstand.

Hope and anxiety quickened her hummingbird pulse. Being close to him set her nerves dancing. She was close enough to catch his scent, crisp and clean, a touch of the orange oil that permeated his house. She glanced up and found him studying her. Had he seen her sniffing his coat like a dog? "Sorry. You smell nice."

"Barbasol cream." He was hiding a smile. Amused. Relaxed. Very non-businesslike.

Emboldened by his good mood, she teased him a little. "I thought it was eau de bootlegger."

"No," he answered with a soft chuckle, "*that* smells like money and sweat."

He was joking with her—smiling and laughing and touching her. She was far happier than she probably should be about it. Any second, her feet would be floating over the sidewalk. She forced herself to settle down and dug out Mrs. Lin's map. "Look at this and tell me if you know where it's at."

"All right. No need to be pushy," he said with good humor. As rain dripped from the umbrella onto his coat sleeve, he studied the hand-drawn path through Chinatown's labyrinth streets and noted where he'd make a bit of a detour. "A small tong leader has a warehouse here. We're on decent terms—Bo and I have already ruled him out as a possible ringleader for all the ghost business—but I don't want him to think I'm sniffing around without his permission."

The thought hadn't crossed her mind that it might be dangerous for a notorious bootlegger to be prowling Chinatown, whether or not it meant facing someone he suspected of his recent hauntings. He must've noticed the concern on her face, because he opened up his long overcoat and showed her a handgun strapped beneath his suit jacket. "Just in case. Don't worry."

"Don't worry?" she repeated, looking around quickly to make sure no one else had seen it. "That makes me even *more* nervous. What if you have to use it?"

He curled gloved fingers around her chin and lifted her face. "Then the other guy'll have a bullet in him and you'll be safe. I promise you that."

"I don't like guns."

He released her chin. "Then try to keep your hand out of my jacket and you'll never know it's there." He gave her a quick wink that made her stomach flip, then, with a gentle hand on her shoulder, prodded her down the sidewalk.

Light drizzle darkened the pavement and carried scents of Chinatown: dried fish, exotic spices, old wood, and tobacco leaves from a nearby cigar warehouse. Across the street, tourists huddled under dark red canvas awnings to get out of the rain and browse ceramics and toys on display in wooden crates. Tin Lizzies and delivery trucks rumbled down the street, splashing through puddles collecting near the curbs.

"Bo said he started working for you when he was four-teen," she said as they sauntered down Grant, passing a butcher's window where a row of skinned ducks hung above signs in English and Chinese, promising the freshest meat for the best price.

"He was half your size back then," he said. "Did he tell you how we met?"

"No."

"I box at a club on the edge of Chinatown, a few blocks from my pier—"

"That explains a lot," she mumbled, eyeing a thick arm. Half of him was getting wet, she noticed, as he was tilting the umbrella at an angle to account for their height difference and keep her dry.

He blinked at her with a dazed look on his face and nearly smiled. "Well," he said, clearing his throat. "Bo lived with his uncle. To bolster the family income, he took to pickpocketing. Was good at it, too. Fast as a whip—you never knew he'd been in your coat. He robbed me blind when I was getting dressed for a match."

"Oh dear."

"After the match was over, I caught him in the alley behind the club. He was so small, I could lift him off the ground with one hand. Little degenerate looked me straight in the eye and told me, yes, he'd done it and wasn't sorry one bit." Winter smiled to himself. "I knew he was either brave or stupid, so I asked him to do a little spying here and there, paying him mostly in hot meals at the beginning. He can still eat his weight in lemon pie."

Aida laughed.

"His uncle died a couple years later, on Bo's sixteenth birthday. Bo called me because he couldn't afford to bury the man."

"How awful," Aida said, feeling for her locket.

"Damn disgrace that the old man didn't even leave Bo a penny." His brow lowered, then he shrugged away the memory. "Bo's been living with me ever since."

"I thought he told me he moved in with you after the accident? Wasn't that two years ago?"

"We both moved back to the family home then, yes."

"From where? Mrs. Beecham mentioned an old house of yours . . ."

Winter stiffened. "She had no business bringing that up."

"Oh, I didn't know—"

"I'd rather not talk about it," he said, cutting her off.

His gruff tone stung. She'd unintentionally touched a nerve, and for a moment the air between them was awkward and tense. Bo *had* warned her about prying into his past.

"No one's told you about the accident?" he said after a long moment. "Not Velma?"

"No, but I gather both your parents died."

The subject hung in the air for several steps. "I didn't mean to bark at you. I just don't like talking about it."

"I can understand that. Everyone I've ever loved is dead." His hard look softened.

"Apart from that, people talk to me intimately about death all the time," she said. "Everyone wants to be reassured that there's life after death, but I always beg them not to forget that there's life *before* death—and that's the only thing we really have any sort of control over. Anyway, if you ever feel inclined, I'm a bit of a specialist in these matters, and you *have* hired my services."

He grunted his amusement. "I suppose I have. And I appreciate that, but some things are best left in the past."

"Now *that* I agree with," she said with a soft smile.

It took them a quarter of an hour to make it to the first side street. Avoiding the subject of the accident, they talked the entire way, first about Chinatown, then about what she remembered of the city from her childhood. The smell of fish cooking got them chatting about the Magnusson fishing business and crab season, then he told her a few stories from his childhood—stealing away from school at lunchtime to smoke cigarettes behind the baseball field . . . absconding with one of his father's fish delivery trucks to meet schoolmates at Golden Gate Park.

Once they'd turned down the side street, the scenery began changing. Gold-painted window frames, pagodas, and curling eaves all but disappeared. Forgotten laundry dripped from balconies, and the smell of sewage wafted from dark corners. By the time they'd taken two more turns, they were sloshing through puddles on narrow backstreets where the asphalt gave way to old paving stones.

They found Doctor Yip's storefront halfway down a cul-de-sac, right where Mrs. Lin said it would be. The sign was in Chinese, but they spotted the landmark she'd mentioned, a metal yellow lantern that hung near a door under an arch of honeycomb cutout woodwork. A string of bells tinkled when they walked inside.

Winter shook the umbrella outside the door as Aida looked around. The apothecary shop's walls were wrapped in wooden shelves that stretched to the ceiling, each of them brimming with ceramic jars lined up in neat rows. Tracks of wooden drawers stood behind a long counter to one side. Near the back of the shop, sticks of pungent sandalwood incense smoked from a brass bowl filled with sand.

The shop was empty until a thin, elderly man appeared from a dark doorway. "Good afternoon," he said with a British accent as he shuffled around the counter to greet them. He was shorter than Aida, with salt-and-pepper hair braided into a queue that hung down his back. And though he was dressed in western clothes—black trousers, white shirt, gold vest—he was wearing a pair of Chinese black silk slippers embroidered with honeybees.

"Hello," Aida said. "We are looking for Doctor Yip."

"You have found him."

When Winter turned to face him, Yip froze. Aida tensed herself, hoping the elderly man hadn't recognized Winter as a gangster; Winter had said this street was on the edge of a tong leader's territory. But before she could worry any further, Yip exhaled. "Forgive me, but I do believe you are a very large man." He grinned, laughing at himself, then nodded at Aida. "Quite wise to have a protector like this when walking some of these streets, young lady."

She introduced the two of them and the herbalist heartily shook their hands before ushering them farther into the shop. "How can I help you?"

"My landlady sent me here."

"Oh? Who might that be?"

"Mrs. Lin. She owns the Golden Lotus restaurant on the northern end of Grant."

"Ah yes. Mrs. Lin—always brings me cookies, trying to fatten me up."

Aida smiled. "Yes, that's her. She said you might be able to help us."

He stepped behind the counter and faced them. "I can try. What do you need? A remedy?"

"Information," Winter said as he propped up the closed umbrella and removed his gloves.

"About . . . ?"

"Black magic."

"Black magic," Doctor Yip repeated, drawing out the words dramatically. "Sorcery? Spells and things? Can't say I know much, I'm afraid. I'm a healer, not a sorcerer."

"We don't need a spell," Aida clarified. "Something's been done already. We're wanting to know how to stop it."

Curious eyes blinked at Aida. "What kind of something?"

Aida said what she'd rehearsed with Winter on the walk. "We have a friend who's been cursed. A sorcerer used a spell to open his eyes to the spiritual world—ghosts and things of that nature. And now he's being haunted by ghosts that have been manipulated by magic."

"Oh my," the herbalist said. "Very interesting."

"Do you believe me, or do you think I'm crazy?" Aida asked with a half smile.

"Strange things happen every day. If you say it's true, I believe as much as I can without having witnessed it myself. I've felt things that I couldn't explain. I am a Shenist. Do you know what that means?"

Aida nodded. "Mrs. Lin says it's the old Chinese religion."

"Most religions are old," he said with kind smile. "I believe in *shens*—celestial deities made of spirit. I also believe in lower spirits, other than the ones I worship—what you would call ghosts. It is not a stretch to think that someone could manipulate a spirit of the dead. Though I wouldn't know how, exactly."

"Four Chinese coins were found on the person being haunted," Winter said. "We've been told that's considered unlucky?"

Doctor Yin crossed his arms over his black and gold vest. "Four is very unlucky. In Cantonese, the word for 'four' sounds like the word for 'death.' In Hong Kong, many buildings do not have fourth floors—or fourteenth, or twenty-fourth. People are careful to avoid the number four on holidays and celebrations, like weddings, or when family members are sick. Westerners call this tetraphobia. But four Chinese *coins*, you say?"

"Yes. Old gold ones." Winter described them briefly.

"There is an old folk magic belief that if you leave four coins on someone's doorstep with ill intent, you curse the home's owner. I've heard stories of businessmen in Hong Kong leaving four coins under the mat of a rival's shop to give them bad luck and steal their customers."

"What about in regards to a spirit or a haunting?"

He shook his head. "Sorry, that I don't know."

Winter groaned softly.

"But . . ." Yip added. "Someone else might. One of my customers has told me about a man who reads fortunes at a local temple—what used to be called a joss house."

"Yes, I'm familiar with those," Winter said.

"My customer, she says rumors are that this man knows more than fortune-telling. That he's also a skilled sorcerer."

Aida glanced at Winter, then asked Yip, "Can you tell us where the temple is and what the fortune-teller's name is?"

"I don't know which temple, sorry."

"How many temples are there in San Francisco?" she asked.

Winter grunted. "Dozens."

"He's right, unfortunately," the herbalist said. "If my customer returns, I can ask for the exact temple. I doubt the name of the man is known to her, but the moniker he uses for fortune-telling is Black Star."

# TEN

———— ❦ ————

AIDA FELT WHAT SHE IMAGINED HER SHOW PATRONS DID WHEN
their lottery ticket number was called: excitement, disbelief,
and the thrill of a small victory won. As Doctor Yip waxed
poetic about Shenist and Taoist temples in Hong Kong, she
half listened while exchanging looks with Winter. Doubt
began creeping in. It seemed too simple. Too easy. But how
many Chinese sorcerers called themselves Black Star?

Maybe it *was* that easy. They thanked the herbalist pro-
fusely and Winter offered to pay him for the information.

"No, no," Yip said, waving his hands in dissent at the
generous bill that Winter held out in offering. "It is nothing.
Not a well-kept secret or trained knowledge. Just gossip."

"I insist," Winter said.

"How about an exchange for services? If you'd like to get
rid of that pain you're carrying, I'd be happy to provide some
relief."

Winter stared blankly at him.

"The arm," Yip said, pointing. "I can see how you're
holding it that it's causing you discomfort. If it's an injury,

I can make the pain go away and speed the healing. Bring healthy blood flow to the right spots."

"I don't think so. No offense, but I've had some bad experiences with folk remedies recently."

"Not a remedy. Acupuncture."

"Needles?" Aida said.

Winter frowned. "Oh, no-no-no."

"Doesn't hurt. Doesn't bleed. My needles are a fine quality, brought with me from Hong Kong. Very clean. Will only take seconds to place them, then you relax for a few minutes, and the pain will be gone. I have patients who come every week. Not just Chinese, but Westerners, too."

"Oh, go ahead," Aida encouraged Winter. "Why don't you do it?"

Winter shook his head. "It's kind of you to offer, Mr. Yip, but—"

"He's afraid of needles," Aida finished.

Winter narrowed his eyes down at her. "That's not going to work."

"Isn't it?"

"Probably not."

She laughed, and he grinned back at her. *Flutter-flutter.*

"I do it right back there," Yip said, pointing to a long wooden bench and chair at the back of the shop.

"A needle seems much smaller than, I don't know, let's say, my lancet," she said, grinning.

Winter sighed dramatically and slid his money across the counter. "Outmatched by a tiny woman."

"Excellent!" Yip said. "Right this way."

The herbalist questioned Winter about the state of his injury as they followed him to the bench at the back of the shop, where he shifted a carved wooden privacy screen and instructed Winter to remove his shirt while he disappeared in the back.

Aida glanced at Winter, and memories of Velma's bathroom sprung into her mind. Well, what did she expect? The herbalist wasn't going to poke needles through his shirtsleeves. Looked liked it was turning into her lucky day. She plunked down on a nearby chair and tried to act casual.

Winter set his fedora on the bench, then turned to her, shrugging out of his overcoat. "Hold this for me." She took the heavy coat from him and folded it neatly on top of her lap.

"And this." He stood inches away, towering over her with his suit jacket dangling in front of her face. She took it and folded it on his coat while eyeing the gun holstered at his ribs. After unbuckling the strap across his chest, he slid it off his good shoulder. "It can't fire itself," he assured her as he handed her the heavy leather holster. She made a face at him as she accepted it.

He proceeded to remove clothing until he was standing in nothing but his too-tight pants, suspenders dangling at his hips, and a sleeveless undershirt—which molded over every muscle in his broad chest and bared his tree-trunk arms. Her gaze flew to his injury.

"Good lord, Winter!"

Most of his left shoulder was mottled black and purple. She'd never seen an uglier bruise.

He tucked his chin to peer at his shoulder. "It's not as bad as it looks."

Yip came out of the back room rolling a metal cart. He stopped to inspect Winter. "Oh! Very nasty. It's okay, though. I'll help you. Sit."

An array of slender silver needles lay fanned upon a white cloth on the herbalist's cart. "The newest type of needle, stainless steel," Yip said. "Sharp and clean."

Winter eyed them warily. "It's the sharp part I don't like."

"You will. Dull needles are painful. Sit still." Very delicately, Yip inspected the injury, prodding the skin around it and asking Winter questions about his range of movement. He rotated Winter's arm until he grunted in pain. Yip seemed to be happy about this. "Ligaments injured. The bruise is bad, but superficial. I will help you. Relax."

Winter looked ill. Legs spread, he hunched over, bracing his good arm on his knee while the herbalist used a small metal tube to hold a needle at the top of his shoulder. He tapped it with one finger. Winter closed his eyes. Aida cringed. The needle wobbled, standing proud on Winter's shoulder like an errant dart.

"That's it?"

"That's it," Yip confirmed.

Winter grinned at Aida. "It doesn't hurt."

Half a minute later, five more needles porcupined his arm. Winter moaned.

"Feeling drowsy?"

"You didn't tip these needles in poison, did you?"

Yip laughed. "What you're feeling is your *qi* flowing. Natural energy. When it is blocked, you have pain. I've opened up a channel for your energy to flow. Just relax and enjoy it for a few minutes."

A telephone rang. The doctor excused himself and went behind the counter up front to answer it, speaking in quick Cantonese.

Sandalwood smoke wafted from a dozen joss sticks standing in the brass bowl near Aida. "That looks like your arm right now," she said, pointing to the incense stand.

"I feel . . . drunk," he said, closing his eyes.

"In a good way?"

"In a very good way."

Bells jingled again near the entrance. "Don't pass out. I don't think I could carry you to a taxi."

"Mmm." He took several breaths through his nose, and then murmured, "Do you think it's really our guy? Black Star?"

"I hope so. Though, I was thinking, if he's such a popular fortune-teller, I wonder why Bo hasn't been able to turn up his name? Seems to me—"

"Aida."

"—that if he's working at one of the temples—"

"Aida," he said sharply.

"Yes?"

"Come stand behind me." Winter's voice was strained, his gaze fixed behind her. "Now."

She started to ask why, started to turn around to see what he was looking at, but an arm wrapped around her shoulders and yanked her backward. Winter's clothes spilled out of her lap as her body lifted into the air. Her ankles knocked against the rungs of the chair. A man's foot kicked it out from under her, and her back slammed against someone's chest.

It happened so fast.

Winter charged, a snarl on his face, but another approaching voice gave him a rough command as a gun and a second man appeared at her side. "Sit back down."

Winter held up his hands in surrender and sat. Doctor Yip stumbled past her with his hands up, as well.

She struggled to get away, clawing at the arm around her shoulders. His grip tightened painfully. She gasped for air and dug her nails into her assailant's arm. He shoved her head to the side. Low Cantonese grated against her ear. His arm was beefy. Not as tall as Winter, judging from the way he felt against her, but solid enough. Her initial shock and confusion trickled into a deeper panic.

Winter addressed the man standing next to her in a barely restrained rumble. "You just made the biggest mistake of your life."

"No, *you* did, Magnusson. This is Ju's territory."

"Did Ju send you here?"

"Ju hears Bo Yeung poking around, asking questions. Now you show up? He won't be happy to hear we found you here. Not at all. Maybe you think now that your daddy is gone, you'll get your hands on tong business." The man took a step toward Winter. His black suit was creased. A bowler was perched crookedly atop his head. His ear was cauliflowered—bulbous and protruding around the upper shell. An old injury. "Why are you in Ju's territory?"

"None of your goddamn business."

"Why is Bo sniffing around?"

"Call off your dog and let her go. Then we can talk."

The man said something in Cantonese that made her captor laugh. Fat fingers clamped over a breast and squeezed. Aida struggled to pull away. "Get your hands off of me."

Winter lurched to his feet. "You dirty fucking pig—"

The cauliflower-eared man shoved the muzzle of the gun against Winter's forehead as he grabbed one of his acupuncture needles and jammed it farther into Winter's shoulder. He shouted incoherent blasphemies as his eyes watered.

"Do not spill blood!" Doctor Yip cried out. "This is a holy place."

The man ignored the doctor. "Sit down," he repeated to Winter.

Winter complied.

Aida's panic shifted into anger. She could continue to stand by and do nothing while Winter got hurt—or killed! Or she could do something and help him.

Her mind raced. Her lower arms were free. The man holding her was becoming lazy as he watched his friend torment Winter. Doctor Yip was huddled against the far wall, talking silently to himself. Praying to his spirits, maybe. She hoped like hell they were listening.

The overpowering scent of sandalwood was making her ill. She glanced down at it in irritation. The brass incense bowl was within her reach, the tips of the sticks glowing orange.

*Ah . . .*

Fast as she could, she whipped her arm out and grabbed several sticks in one swoop. She felt the gripping arm tighten around her shoulders, but he wasn't fast enough. She stabbed backward over her shoulder using all her strength, aiming the joss sticks for what she hoped was his face.

# ELEVEN

———❧———

THE STICKS JAMMED INTO FLESH. HER CAPTOR'S SCREAM PIERCED her ear.

She fell forward, stumbling away from him.

Distracted by his friend's screaming, the cauliflower-eared man let his guard down for one heartbeat too long. Winter flew off the bench. In two beautiful movements, he snatched the gun from the man's hand as he jabbed an angry fist square in the middle of his face. It was brute strength, skillfully wielded—she'd never seen such a violent motion delivered so precisely. The punch made a sickening *crack!* like a bat hitting a ball. The man's body flew backward and collapsed on the floor.

His muffled cries were pained and feral as the copper-bright scent of blood wafted in the air. He was not going to get up again. Aida's attention flew to her captor. Both hands covered his cheek. She'd missed his eye by centimeters. A shame.

"Get down!" Winter bellowed at the man, loud enough to rattle Aida's nerves. He was savage—the devil himself. And Aida was, all at once, frightened and strangely thrilled.

Winter stepped between her and her captor and motioned with the gun. The man dropped to his knees.

Lying on his side, the cauliflower-eared man loosely held his hands over his nose and took desperate gasps of air through his open mouth. Blood seeped between his fingers.

"No shame in crying." Winter told him in a calmer voice. "That nose is broken and probably hurts like hell. You might want to have someone set it, or it's going to look ugly when it heals."

The man twisted in place to shoot Winter a hateful look.

Winter clucked his tongue. "You've got nerve, coming in here today to question me without Ju's permission. I can only imagine what you were thinking. But let's get some things straight. I'm not interested in Ju's territory, or any of the other tongs'. We do not have overlapping interests. Never will. Secondly, this cul-de-sac is not technically Ju's. It's free territory."

The man shuddered, rolled onto his shoulder, and spat blood out of his mouth.

"And if Ju has a problem with Bo 'sniffing around,' as you put it, then he will come talk to me directly. I don't do business with peons."

Her captor was saying something in Cantonese. His partner didn't answer.

"But let me make one thing clear. If either of you lay a finger on Bo, I will hunt you down and break every bone in your body. And if you or any other man so much as even stands too close to *her* ever again, I will blame *you* personally"—he tapped the man's elbow with his shoe—"and I will put a bullet in both your brains. Do you understand?"

The cauliflower-eared man made a short grunting noise in confirmation.

"I'm going to send word to Ju that the two of you assaulted us without provocation. I'll let him dole out your punishment. Now get the hell out of here before I change my mind and take you out into the alley."

Fifteen minutes later—after Winter had made promises to Doctor Yip about ensuring his protection—Aida scooted across the backseat of a taxi to make room for his big body. She decided it was better to drop her off at Gris-Gris, as there wasn't time for her to return to her apartment. He instructed the driver, and soon they were pulling out onto a rain-slicked street, away from tong territory.

"That was a stupid thing to do, burning that man in the face," Winter said staring out the window. "He could've hurt you."

"But he didn't."

He turned and looked at her. "Did you think I wouldn't protect you?" His tone was intimidating, his mouth stern. Was he angry, or was his male pride wounded?

"I wasn't thinking about anything at all," she protested. "I just acted on instinct." When she got no response to that, she asked, "Would you have done worse to them if I wasn't there?"

"I don't go around killing everyone who threatens me. I'm not a thug."

"That's not what I asked."

He didn't answer, which hurt her feelings.

Fine. He could be mad at her and brood in the corner all he wanted. Only, there wasn't a corner in the taxi, and he filled up every inch of the space with his enormous body, the scent of his clothes, and the dark cloud of emotions radiating from him. She squirmed, trying to cram herself against the door.

He noticed her moving away. "You afraid of me now?"

"No, I just . . ." What? What did she want from him? One moment she was bragging that she could handle herself, then the next, she was upset that he was short with her. If she was being honest with herself, she wanted him closer, not farther away. She wasn't frail and timid; she didn't need to be comforted. And she knew exactly what he was, what he did. Saw proof of it last night in the ghost of the man he'd killed.

The violence didn't surprise or offend her. It was unsettling how little it offended her, to be honest. She just didn't like the cold-shoulder treatment. Maybe after spending so much time in nightclubs, she'd come to admire the bruisers who guarded the doors and kept the drunks out of her dressing room. They were tough on the outside, but polite as could be backstage. The big guys were always the kindest to her.

And Winter was the biggest man she'd ever known.

A strong wind blew rain against the window as the taxi's engine noisily rumbled around a curve and up a steep incline. She allowed gravity to pull her back against the seat and glanced down at Winter's hand. Knuckles were reddened from the punch, the skin bleeding around one.

Gingerly, she reached out across his lap and touched her bare fingers to his, inspecting the wound. Her own hand was half the size of his. "Does it hurt?"

He shifted the arm between them and laid it across the back of the seat, behind her shoulders. This both relaxed and electrified her. She could smell the rain on his coat, the pomade in his hair. "Yes. But it will hurt more tomorrow. Always does."

"You need to get some ice on it."

"Probably."

"That punch was impressive."

"Mmm."

"But I'm not afraid of you."

"You sure about that?" he said softly near her ear.

His bass-heavy voice resounded through her body, unexpectedly kindling warmth between her legs. She shifted in her seat, but the warmth changed to heat. So she tried clamping her thighs together, which only made things worse.

Maybe she shouldn't be leaning into him, tracing the red pattern around the edge of his injured knuckles. But her poor reasoning skills were at war with her body, which liked his body quite a bit.

"I'm sure," she told him.

The arm resting behind her shoulders shifted until she felt its weight against her neck.

This was not business anymore.

Her hand stilled on his. She turned her head, slowly, and

glanced up at his face. Lazily blinking eyes looked down at hers. His nostrils were flared. She wanted to say something, but she wasn't sure what, exactly.

Maybe that's why when she opened her mouth to speak, she ended up pressing it against his. He stilled. His lips didn't move. Had she shocked him? She'd shocked herself. She didn't go around kissing men, especially not men who punched people in the face. Certainly not men she worked for. She should definitely stop this foolishness right this second and beg his forgiveness.

And she would have, maybe, had he not kissed her back.

His mouth opened to hers. The little noise of triumph she made in response was embarrassing, but not enough to stop. The arm circling her shoulders pulled her closer. His lips were soft and wet and sent legions of tingles down her arms and back. And that was before his clever tongue slipped between her lips and danced with hers.

She lost all thought and kissed him back savagely. She was desperate and wanting, and his big arms were wrapped around her and it was . . . bliss. Their first kiss was unforgettable, but this was a new level of thrill, to be touched, to touch him back. Her hand slid up either side of his chevroned necktie and strayed around his neck, seeking contact with his skin. She pushed her fingers into the back of his dark hair, fingernails lightly grazing his scalp, and he made a pleasurable sound of approval.

Good lord, he was an expert with his mouth. She didn't know or care where he learned to kiss like this, tongue rolling as he possessively molded his lips to hers. But whatever skills he'd mastered seemed to magically transfer to her, because she was oddly confident he was enjoying what she was doing. She was certainly enjoying doing it. And that confidence changed to certainty when her left leg, which was draped over his lap—and she didn't know how in God's name this happened without her realizing it before now— strayed a little higher up his thigh. And a little higher. And just when she was nearly straddling him, like some wanton whore, her leg brushed against something hard.

Winter moaned.

She nearly fainted with excitement.

And yet, some part of her that had been taught to repress urges and feelings warned her that she was doing a Very Bad Thing, and going way too far. That part of her piped up and mumbled, "Sorry," against Winter's lips.

Catching her breath, she rested her cheek against his and agonized over either starting up again like she wanted to or pushing away from him like she *should* do. But he solved the problem without her when his head dipped to her neck. He began trailing wet kisses across the side of her throat, soft ones . . . rougher, pulling ones. She may have possibly made a series of desperate noises. She definitely arched against him, bumping into his erection again. Well, rubbing herself against it, to be truthful.

She didn't apologize this time.

But Winter did. "I'm sorry, as well," he said against an intensely sensitive spot on her neck, just beneath her earlobe.

She shivered in response to his voice. Then hazily said, "For what?"

"For this."

His hand ghosted up the back of her leg, under her skirt, over her garter . . . and beneath the loose silk of her step-in chemise. He cupped one bare buttock with his palm and gently squeezed.

Desire shot through her. She cried out against his neck, something between a moan and a half-formed encouragement.

He opened his mouth against her neck and ran his teeth across her skin as his palm massaged her backside, rougher now—demanding. She went limp in his arms. She was afraid if his long fingers explored an inch farther, he'd discover how wet she was. Unbelievably wet. Her thighs were slippery with arousal from all the wanton rolling around she'd been doing on his lap.

She was half ashamed over it. Half not.

And she was half a second from telling him—no, *de-*

*manding* he take her, right there, right now. She didn't care anymore, she just wanted—

A loud, judgmental throat-clearing sounded from the front of the taxi.

The taxicab driver. The car was stopped outside Gris-Gris.

Good grief. They were inside a public taxi, with nothing but a seat between their lewd activities and a stranger's body. She'd completely forgotten—*How* could she have forgotten? *What is wrong with me? I am an immoral human being.* This seemed far more wicked, *far* more risqué than her previous two brief sexual experiences had ever been.

And she liked it.

It was at that moment she realized that she was, sadly, just as perverted as she'd accused Winter of being that afternoon she'd found the postcards in his study.

"Fifteen cents," the taxi driver said as she shifted off Winter's lap. He resisted, holding her in place for a moment before reluctantly sliding his hand out of her underclothes.

"Hey!" Winter snapped at the driver. "I'm paying you to drive, not to ogle. Eyes off her."

Winter instructed the man to wait. She couldn't get the door open fast enough, nearly tripping over the curb as her Mary Janes scrambled to find purchase on the wet sidewalk. Her legs were wobbly. She had trouble standing and experienced a flash of panic as she wondered if the pedestrians walking by knew exactly what she'd been up to.

"You okay?" Winter asked behind her as drizzle beaded on her coat.

She let out a breath and turned to face him. He seemed so much bigger out in the open air. And terribly good-looking. She found herself smiling dumbly at him. "Yes."

He pulled his overcoat closed and smiled back, just as dumbly. "Good."

"Do you do this kind of thing with all your employees, Mr. Magnusson?"

"Hardly. Then again, Bo isn't half as tempting as you."

A prideful pleasure leapt up inside her chest. "No need to butter me up. Your hand's already been up my skirt."

"My hand is very happy about that." He grinned at her, big and wide, tapping the brim of his fedora against his leg.

They stood in the gray drizzle in silence for several moments, just looking at each other, as people passed by on the sidewalk. Raindrops began snaking down the collar of her coat. Her hair was sticking to her cheeks. She'd have to wash it before her show. "I'd better . . ." She pointed behind her, toward the barred entrance to the speakeasy.

"Of course."

"You'd better . . ."

"Yes."

"Okay, then. Good afternoon."

"Good afternoon."

She forced herself to turn and walk toward the club, her body still tingling from the heavy petting. As she was reaching for the door buzzer, a hand clamped around her shoulder and spun her around. Winter kissed her firmly on the mouth, just for a moment. He released her and fitted his fedora tightly on his head without saying another word. Just walked backward a couple of steps, then turned on his heel and marched back to the waiting taxi, leaving Aida breathless and swooning with joy.

# TWELVE

———— ❧ ————

LATE AFTERNOON SUNSHINE BROKE THROUGH THE DRIZZLE A COU-
ple of hours after Winter left Aida at Gris-Gris, happy as a
clam. The taxi dropped him off at his house. He returned a
couple phone calls, made a couple more, then stepped out
onto the side porch and waited for Bo to return. They needed
to recalibrate the search for this Black Star sorcerer and
focus on fortune-tellers at the Chinatown temples.

The Queen Anne didn't have much of a yard, but what
little grass they had stretched out from the driveway to the
tall wooden fence that separated his property from the Victorian on one side and the Italianate on the other. A fragrant
bay laurel tree stood in the corner near a wooden swing.
Winter used to sit there and watch the boats glide across the
bay until the neighbor across the street added a wing to his
house last year and blocked the view, the bastard.

He leaned against the spindled porch railing, thinking
of Aida. It was hard to keep his mind on anything else,
truthfully. The way she looked up at him in the taxi with
those big, haunting eyes of hers, the surprise he'd felt when

she kissed him. How warm and plump her backside felt in his palm. How she'd lustily rocked against his lap.

Thank you, God.

But what he was thinking about now was the feel of her slender fingers tracing his tender knuckles. They were sore as hell, and though she'd been careful to use a light touch, her explorations had caused jolts of pain to shoot up his arm. He'd refrained from telling her this, because . . . well, because she was touching him, unafraid, and nothing else mattered.

And when she'd turned her face up to him and he saw the longing blossoming there, he was gone. Despite promising himself that he would try to be a gentleman around her, if she hadn't kissed him then, he probably would've instigated it himself.

She was just too irresistible. So beautiful. So full of life.

Christ. He was crazy about her.

The Pierce-Arrow's maroon and black body pulled through the open iron gate near the sidewalk and squeezed into the driveway next to his mother's old Packard. Jonte, a middle-aged first-generation Swedish immigrant who did most of the driving for the household, called out to Winter as he climbed out of the car. "You want the gate closed?"

"Leave it," Winter answered. "Bo and I are going out to the pier when he comes back with the truck." He leaned over the railing while the back door of the car opened. His sister's lemon blond hair bounced into sight.

At seventeen, Astrid Magnusson was thirteen years younger—a surprise, his mother had said when she was conceived. And she was the spitting image of their mother, which was painful for Winter at times. But where their mother had been soft-spoken, Astrid was loud and opinionated. She acted like the world was hers, carrying herself with a defiant tilt to her chin and a fearlessness behind her eyes. And for that, he was eternally grateful. He already had enough to worry about, raising her. Knowing she could stand her ground was a small comfort.

God bless the modern female.

Astrid strode toward him in a striped blue dress that cost him more than the monthly grocery bill for the entire household. But it made her happy, and he was a pushover when it came to anything that did. "How was school?"

"A waste of my good looks and devastating charm. Why are you in such a good mood?"

Aida's freckled face popped into his mind. Was it that obvious? It couldn't be. He narrowed his eyes at Astrid in challenge. She lifted one blond brow. Too observant for her own damn good.

"The sun's shining," he answered.

"Fine. Don't tell me. I'll assume you just made some unseemly amount of cash, and I'll be dreaming of ways I can spend it. Speaking of, I need new art supplies. Can Bo take me to Hale Brothers on Market tomorrow after school?"

"Why didn't you ask Jonte to take you on the way home?"

She hefted her book satchel and smacked a mouthful of gum. "I forgot."

"Then he can take you tomorrow."

"I don't like the way he sits in the car at the curb waiting. Bo goes inside with me."

"Bo's not being paid to be your nanny."

Astrid gave him a cross look. "I just feel safer when he's around."

"That better be all you're feeling."

She tucked a blond strand of her bobbed hair behind one ear and leveled him with a look so tragically bored, he almost believed it. "I have no idea what you're talking about."

The screen door creaked open. Greta poked her white head outside. "Telephone, Vinter. It's some man named Ju with heavy Chinese accent. Very polite."

"Coming." Winter urged Astrid ahead of him. She flashed him her middle finger. When he pretended to chase after her into the house, she ran, laughing. The screen door banged against the wood frame behind him as her blond bob disappeared into the hallway.

"Is this man Ju responsible for the ghost trickery?" Greta

whispered as she held the mouthpiece of the downstairs telephone against her stomach.

Winter's good mood darkened. "I sure hope not."


Aida finished her happy hour show and took a streetcar back to Golden Lotus, returning home before nine. The early slot hadn't drawn the same crowd that her usual ten o'clock show did, but it was successful enough to make Velma happy. In turn, Aida was happy to be home at a decent hour.

When she passed by the counter, Mrs. Lin leaned around a paying customer to flag her down. "A note for you was dropped off."

Aida warily accepted the envelope from her landlady's hand and studied the front. Nothing but her name scrawled in long, bold script on the front and a gold leaf monogram inside a diamond on the back flap, with a prominent M in the center.

Her heartbeat quickened. M for Magnusson? Why did he write? Did this have something to do with what happened in the taxi?

She mouthed a thank-you to Mrs. Lin and hurried to her room. Once the door was locked, she kicked off her shoes and set the envelope on her nightstand like it might explode, nervous and curious at the same time. Pondering its purpose, she stripped down to her step-in chemise and rolled down her stockings. Her leg was aching. She decided to take care of that first, just in case the letter was bad news.

In her small bathroom, she wet a washrag with cool water and gathered up her supplies, plunking them upon the nightstand next to the envelope. She laid the cool washrag over her hip, where the lancet pricks from the show were pink, swollen bumps, and used rubbing alcohol to wipe down her lancet blade.

Once she'd smeared medical salve over her wounds and put everything away, she had no choice but to read the letter. Wedging her pillow against the wall, she lay back and opened the envelope. Two things spilled out: a letter, and something slightly smaller wrapped inside opaque tissue paper that had been taped shut. She opened the letter first.

*Dear Cheetah,*

*I have received word from the boss of the two gentlemen who accosted us today in the apothecary shop. He would like to apologize to us in person, and has requested we join him for luncheon tomorrow. In spite of his employees' bad behavior, I feel confident that we will be treated with respect, and would not put you in further danger if I believed there was a chance that this wasn't safe. Please trust me. Bo will drive us. I'll pick you up at noon.*

*Yours,*
*Mr. Bootlegger*

*P.S. I hope your show went well this afternoon.*
*P.S. #2 I'm not sorry about what we did in the taxi, in case that wasn't clear.*

A bubbling giddiness replaced Aida's previous anxiety. She read it twice more and admired the severe slant of his masculine cursive, written in heavy hand. Then she thought of that hand on her skin, and how his big arms circled her as he smothered her throat in kisses. *Goodness.* She fanned herself with the letter and used a fingernail to pick open the tape on the smaller flat package. It weighed nothing, and she couldn't for the life of her guess what it was. But when the tissue fell away, she dropped the letter beside her onto the bed.

It was the pornographic postcard of the freckled woman.

Dreary skies greeted Aida the following morning when she headed downstairs to wait for Winter and Bo. It wasn't quite noon, so the restaurant wasn't full. Mr. Lin was manning the counter instead of his wife. He looked at her strangely when she stood by the door, squinting against the plate glass window. It hadn't gotten warm enough to burn off the fog that lingered around the building tops.

Unlike the overcast weather outside, Aida was burning up. Being anxious made her overly warm. Every minute that she waited for Winter's car increased her nervousness by another degree. By the time his devil-colored limousine rolled up, she was almost sweating in her thin coat.

The shades were pulled down in the back windows, so she couldn't see inside. Bo hopped out of the car before she made it to the curb. "Hello, Miss Palmer," he called out. "This promises to be interesting."

For a moment she was mortified, thinking of the last time she'd crawled into a backseat with Winter . . . wondering if Winter had told Bo anything.

"This meeting," he clarified.

*Oh!* "Yes, I'm not sure what to make of it."

"Ju is a small tong leader, but it's still an honor that he's inviting you. I doubt many white women have seen the inside of his home."

"I'm always up for a new experience."

He laughed and opened the back door, offering her a hand as she entered the car.

It was dark inside.

Scents of shaving cream and starch wafted as her knee bumped against muscled shadow. The door shut behind her. A tiny light clicked above the shaded rear window, and she found herself looking at Winter's bear of a body lounging catercornered on the seat. She sucked in a quick breath as her eyes darted over his expensive suit and the fantastical breadth of his shoulders . . . the endless length of legs stretching across her section of floorboard. Her gaze climbed those long legs, skimming over his torso, to settle on his face.

He stared back at her, one eye shining like polished pewter, the other blue as the Pacific. High cheeks were ruddy from the heat that radiated throughout the car. His mouth opened slightly, as if he intended to speak but suddenly forgot what he wanted to say. *Yes, me, too*, she thought. They remained mute. All of her practiced casual questions fell out of her mind. She couldn't have formed a word if her life depended on it.

The moment stretched out, suspended like a fly in honey, while an unexpected tumble of feelings rose inside her like the first slow notes of a violin concerto: a foreign, desperate hope, quivering with possibility and a longing so painful, it stuck in her throat like regret. He was right there, his face only a few feet away, his knee touching hers—but it was like sitting in front of a cake so luscious, you cannot bear to take a bite for fear that you will never want anything else.

Only, she'd already stuck her finger in the frosting, hadn't she?

"Hello, cheetah."

"Hello, Mr. Bootlegger."

"You got my note."

"I'm here, aren't I?"

Something playful and mischievous sparked behind his eyes.

*Do not think about the postcard*, she told herself, but it was already too late. "I could get arrested for owning something like that, you know."

"Good thing you immediately tore it up and threw it in the trash."

"Well—I was busy, but I'm definitely *going* to do that."

"Might should burn it, just for good measure."

"Excellent idea."

"Ready?" Bo said as he climbed into the front seat. The privacy window was lowered. Probably for the best, all things considered. She had no desire to repeat yesterday's behavior in front of Bo, and if Winter continued to tease her about the postcard, she wasn't certain she'd be able to concentrate on being proper.

"Ready?" Winter repeated, tossing the question to her.

"Yes, I think I might be."

The corners of his mouth curled like paper on fire.

Bo turned the Pierce-Arrow onto Grant, and the three of them chatted casually as they retraced the same path Winter and she had walked. Only, instead of navigating through the narrow streets and cul-de-sacs toward Doctor Yip's, Bo slowed in front of an unmarked garage and waved a hand out the window. A man smoking a cigarette waved back, and Bo waited while the man hauled open a massive door on wheels, allowing them access to a dimly lit garage.

Once they'd parked, the man pointed at Winter while asking Bo something in Cantonese. Winter must've recognized a word, because he opened his jacket and flashed a holstered gun. "That stays with me, buddy. You can forget it."

Bo translated and shooed the man, urging him to back off. He yielded.

They were led through a series of dingy corridors, out a door, across an alley, and into another building, passing several men she could only assume were guards along the way. A dull anxiety settled over her as they headed into a massive warehouse space. Just what did Ju do, exactly? She assumed it was bootlegging, but all she could hear was loud machinery.

Sewing machines.

Several rows of them, all operated by Chinese women, who looked up with blatant curiosity at Aida and Winter.

"One of Ju's enterprises," Winter explained near her ear as they passed bolts of brightly printed silk stacked on shelves. The warm air smelled of fabric dye and machine oil.

Aida removed her gloves and pocketed them. "This is his fishing company?"

"Exactly. He makes costumes for theater productions. Quality stuff."

"Ah." The sounds of sewing machines faded as they headed down a dark corridor to an open area with several carved doors, the middle of which was flanked by two armed men. Their guide spoke some aggressive words in Cantonese to the men and knocked on the door.

A tiny woman in a bright yellow traditional Chinese dress answered. Her black bob was shinier and straighter than

Aida's. She smiled at Winter; her front teeth had an attractive gap.

"*Nei hou*, Mr. Magnusson."

Winter groaned under his breath. "Hello, Sook-Yin."

Their guide snapped at Sook-Yin and a short argument ensued in Cantonese. The spat ended with her looking angry and saying, "Follow me."

Her quick strides led them through a gilded foyer, past a set of heavy wooden doors, and into a large six-sided room—an indoor courtyard with double-high ceilings and a second story ringed with balconies. Like Golden Lotus, the room was decorated with traditional ornamental flair: gilded screens, silk curtains, and ornate trusses lining the ceiling.

In the center of the great hall was a large, round dining table. A lone person sat at the table, two bodyguards at his back. The chair he sat in was so wildly thronelike, Aida could only assume that the person lounging in it was Ju.

# THIRTEEN

———◆———

"WINTER MAGNUSSON, THE VIKING BOOTLEGGER. IT IS GOOD TO see you, my friend. It has been several months. We've missed you."

With polished black hair and a big smile, Ju was rather dashing and well attired. He looked like someone who should be in Hollywood pictures, not running an underground gang in Chinatown. Aida guessed him to be in his forties.

"You've got more goons around than usual," Winter said. "You worried I might steal something?"

Ju's smile grew. "You are big and slow—easy to catch. This must be the woman we spoke about on the telephone."

"Aida Palmer, this is Ju-Ray Wong."

"Everyone calls me Ju, my dear." He held out his hand, inviting her to step forward. When she took it, he kissed her knuckles. "It is an honor to meet such an extraordinarily lovely woman."

"Thank you for inviting me into your home."

"Please, have a seat. My grandmother is making us a very nice meal."

It did smell rather nice, whatever it was. Winter held out

a chair for her, then sat down next to Ju. Bo hung back until Ju prompted him forward. "Go on, Mr. Yeung. You're Magnusson's trusted man. You can sit with us."

Bo didn't act like he was comfortable doing so, but he sat to her left. Several of Ju's men joined them. And if Aida felt uneasy being the only female seated at a massive table full of gangsters, it only got worse when an army of women began bringing dishes out to the table, under the instruction of Sook-Yin. Their faces were painted, their dresses traditional. Several of them placed platters of steaming vegetables and scafood on a rotating wooden tray in the center of the table, while others brought green bottles of Chinese beer.

Aida had grown accustomed to tasting unusual dishes since living over Golden Lotus, but the style of food presented here was much more rustic—no pretty dumplings and hand-pulled noodles. She didn't recognize the vegetables, and Ju laughed as she stared at the intimidating spread. "You need a knife and fork?"

"I can use chopsticks," she said proudly, having been taught by Mrs. Lin.

"Everything is very fresh. Have some chicken."

She peeked at bubbling liquid inside a clay pot, from which a serving girl speared small, unfamiliar pieces of chicken, each glistening with rubbery dimpled skin and strange bone fragments. One piece was definitely the chicken's clawed foot.

"The Chinese butcher chicken differently," Bo explained in a soft voice.

"Killed fresh this morning," Ju said, while making an enthusiastic hacking motion with his hand.

"I can practically see the cleaver marks," Aida agreed.

Ju chuckled and translated to the table. A round of male laugher erupted. Winter draped his arm across the back of her chair and gave her quick wink.

The women filled her plate with this and that, while Bo steered her away from some dishes and encouraged others, his advice mostly on the mark. Winter ate heartily, his steely leg pressed against hers, while conversing with Ju.

"So tell me your story, Magnusson. Why were you really

in this neighborhood yesterday? I know it's not for acupuncture. Bo has been poking around asking questions about other tongs. You finally deciding to do what your father would not and take over the alcohol business in Chinatown?"

"Not in a million years. I'm making plenty of money, Ju. If I made more, I'd have to find something else to spend it on."

"You've certainly gotten your daddy's business all shipshape. Cleaned up all his messes. Everyone knows you are a much better boss than he was. A born leader. Maybe because you have all your marbles?"

Winter narrowed his eyes at Ju. "Watch it."

"I'm not telling you anything that you and I don't both know. All I am saying is that people around Chinatown are talking. They see you're more successful than your father—so successful that they covet what you have."

"Someone's coveting, all right. And when I find out *who*, they'll wish they'd minded their own business." Sook-Yin bent low to pour beer into Winter's glass. Aida didn't like how close the woman got, or how she put her hand on Winter's shoulder. "You haven't heard about anyone in particular, have you, Ju?"

"I've heard rumors about a handful of different tongs. If any of those rumors had substance, I'd share them. We've always had an understanding, you and I. I've treated you well. You've treated me well."

"That understanding hasn't changed on my part. Has it changed on yours?"

"You are speaking of yesterday's insult. Let us take care of it." He whistled and said something in quick Cantonese to one of the men behind him, who turned and headed through a doorway. A few moments later, the cauliflower-eared man and his companion were hauled out and pushed in front of the table.

"These are the men who accosted you yesterday?" Ju asked. It took Aida a moment to realize he was speaking to her, not Winter.

She glanced at the first man's bandaged nose and the

discolored burn on his companion's cheek. "Yes, that's them."

Ju motioned to the guard holding them, who immediately pulled out a revolver and stuck the muzzle against the head of the man she'd burned. "Do you want his death as payment, Miss Palmer? I will gladly do this."

*Good grief!* "That's not necessary," she said.

"Are you sure? It is within your right. They acted out of turn and insulted you."

"I was just hoping I'd never see them again."

Winter put down his chopsticks. "If Miss Palmer doesn't mind, I'd like to propose a trade." Aida nodded her consent. Winter continued. "Instead of their lives as payment, maybe you can give me some information."

"What kind of information?"

"The private kind."

Ju dismissed everyone from the table but one guard, and Aida let out a long breath as their attackers were marched out of the room.

When they'd gone, Winter asked, "Have you heard of a fortune-teller named Black Star working at a local joss house?"

Ju's brows shot up. "A fortune-teller? Why do you need to know this?"

"Because another tong is using him to try to scare me. Do you believe in superstitious things, Ju? In spirits and ghosts?"

Ju chuckled nervously, looking between the three of them. "Are you teasing me, or is this an honest question?"

"It's honest. Someone's playing around with witchcraft, and I need to hunt them down."

"The alleys of Chinatown are crawling with dark magic. There are some things I don't want to stick my nose in, and that is one of them."

"So you won't help me find this man?"

The tong leader considered it and let out a heavy sigh. "I should refuse, but you've been good to me. If I do this for you, and another tong catches me, I will ask for your protection."

"You'll have it."

"Then I'll see what I can learn. Might take me a few days. I'll need all the details you already have."

"Thank you."

Ju sighed and said something to his guard while pulling a silver cigarette case out of his pocket. "That is all you want? Just the location of this man? Usually I'd offer you something else, but in light of your company—"

Winter made a loud growling noise.

Ju held up his hands. "I was only going to suggest something for Miss Palmer. My dear, would you like a new gown? My ladies can make beautiful things."

"That's not necessary," Aida said.

"Go on," Winter encouraged. "They do nice work."

"It's the least I can do," Ju said. He fired off another string of Cantonese commands to someone. Several minutes later, two women carried bolts of silk into the room. "Sook-Yin will take you to be measured and show you gown styles."

Winter's face was blank. Should she be worried?

"It's a high honor," Bo whispered as he gave her an encouraging prod. So she followed Sook-Yin and her two girls into another part of the home. Someone's bedroom. It looked too feminine to be Ju's. The girls unwound measuring tapes and deftly coiled them around her—bust, waist, hips, wrists. You name it, they measured it. Sook-Yin spoke to her while they worked.

"I have seen freckles on the Irish women's faces and arms, but never so many."

"Yes, I hear that a lot." She suffered through Sook-Yin's brash inspection as the girls worked, jotting down figures after each measure. "I'm not Irish."

"I wondered why Winter had not visited me in so long, but now that I see you, I guess I understand."

"Pardon me?"

"You are to be the new wife, yes?"

"New wife?"

"Second wife."

Aida stared at her. "You were married to Winter?"

Sook-Yin's eyes widened, then she laughed. Loudly. "Me? I am Ju's woman. You do not know Ju's business?"

"Sewing?" Aida guessed, unhopeful.

"The other business."

Aida stared at her.

"I am a paid woman," Sook-Yin said. "All of Ju's women are paid."

"Prostitutes?" Aida squeaked.

Sook-Yin held her chin high. "I am one of Ju's honored women. These girls"—she gestured to the girls taking her measurements—"are whores. They are lower than me. They have no choices. Ju tells them to work in the factory, they work. Ju tells them to work in the bed, they work. But I have choices— I can say no, and I earn more money. Do you understand?"

"You're a concubine."

"Yes, you could call me that. I only choose the best men. Winter was one of my favorites."

Aida studied Sook-Yin, seeing her in a different light. She was pretty, her figure slim. It was hard to tell her age, but she was fairly certain the woman was many years older than her. Maybe older than Winter. Aida's stomach knotted painfully. She worried she might be sick. "Were you in love with him?"

Sook-Yin laughed. "No, but he was very kind. I always liked to make him smile. I could see he was ugly after accident, and Ju warned me that he was angry and sad, but he smiled for me. I made him forget about his wife."

"Which wife?" Aida said carefully.

"First wife. She died. You know." Sook-Yin used her finger to make a slash over her eye. "Accident."

Aida tried to swallow and failed. Her mouth was dry as dust. "His parents . . ."

"Yes," Sook-Yin said. "Mother, father, first wife. All together in automobile with Winter. All dead but him. Very sad. Last year, Winter began coming to see me. I made him forget about dead wife."

Understanding hit Aida like a punch to the stomach. The "other" house that Bo had moved into with Winter—the house that Mrs. Beecham had brought up at the séance. The one Winter had clammed up about. It belonged to him and his dead wife.

She felt sick and confused.

"Did they have children?" Aida dared to ask.

"No children. First time I saw wife was three years ago, before accident. She was very sad. Sick and frail. Unhappy. Too serious. Not a good match for a big man like Winter. But I watched you at the dining table." She nodded toward the front of the house. "You are much better match."

"We aren't a match," Aida said weakly. "It is only a business arrangement."

"Like me?"

"No," Aida said angrily. "Not like you at all."

Sook-Yin didn't ask any more questions, and Aida was ashamed to have snapped at her. Didn't she herself hate when people turned their nose up at her profession? What made her think that she was any better than someone like Sook-Yin?

When they finished, Sook-Yin led her back into the courtyard, where the boys were joking and talking boisterously. She glanced at Winter and felt a tumble of conflicting emotions. Anger. Pity. Hurt. Disappointment. When he lifted his face to smile at her, she turned away.

"Which silk?" Sook-Yin asked, poking her shoulder. She pointed to the bolts of fabric.

Aida couldn't have possibly cared less. She didn't want the gown. She just wanted to get out of that house and go back to her room at Golden Lotus, as far away from here as she could get.

"Red is pretty but would not look good with your freckles."

"It doesn't matter," Aida answered. *Why didn't he tell me any of this? Why?* A fresh wave of anger and hurt renewed itself inside her constricted chest.

"What about yellow, like mine?" Sook-Yin gestured to her own gown.

"No," Winter said unexpectedly behind Aida's head, making her jump. "Use that." He pointed to an oyster color, softer than gold, darker than cream, with a hint of gray.

"The very best silk from China," Ju said, joining the discussion. "Magnusson has excellent taste. A peacock feather design embroidered on silk means royalty and beauty. A very good choice for you."

Aida stared at the fabric until her sight blurred. *Standing in a room with Winter's whore,* she thought. *How utterly delightful.* She had to get out of there, or she'd cause a scene and embarrass herself.

She glared at Winter, defiant and bitter. "I'll take the yellow."

# FOURTEEN

———◆———

AS SOON AS AIDA SLID INTO THE BACKSEAT OF WINTER'S CAR, HE
rolled up the privacy window and lowered the shade.

"What's wrong?"

"Oh, gee, nothing at all. What would be wrong?"

Winter shifted, stretching his legs. He removed his hat,
scratched his head. Put his hat back on. Took it off again.

Oh, he knew. Of *course* he knew.

"I mean, what could Sook-Yin and I have possibly talked
about?" Aida said, crossing her legs. "The weather? Poetry?
Politics? Oh, wait. I know. How about the fact that she's a
prostitute, and you're her favorite customer?"

"Shit."

"Yes, shit. That's what I thought, too, especially when
she was going on about how she could make you smile—"

"Aida—"

"So there are others? This is routine for you?"

He groaned in angry frustration. "This is *not* routine.
Sook-Yin was the only one."

Was that worse or better? Aida honestly didn't know.
"She did brag about how special she was and seemed to

know you quite well. She even asked me if I was the 'new wife,' because apparently there's an old wife that *nobody told me about*."

Winter said nothing. Just stared ahead at the canvas shade as the car began rolling out of Ju's garage.

"Were you ever going to tell me?"

"She's dead," he said without looking at her. "There's nothing to tell."

Aida rocked her foot and opened the side shade to stare outside. "I asked you about the house and you growled at me," she said in a much calmer voice than she thought she was capable of at that moment. "You could've told me. I told you things about me. I've told you secrets about my job—about the lancet. About my plans for the future. How many lovers I've had. I told you all these things, and you couldn't be bothered—"

"This is a business relationship. I am paying you to do a job."

Her mouth fell open. "Then why was your hand up my skirt yesterday?"

"You attacked *me*!"

"I did not!"

He narrowed his eyes.

"Okay, maybe I did attack you a little bit," she said in frustration. "But I'll tell you what. It's one or the other. Either you pay me and I advise you about spiritual matters, or you don't. Because if you think I'm going to take money from you when you're kissing me and holding me, you can think again. I'm not a whore."

"I've *never* thought of you that way," he said in a low, angry voice. "Never."

"You don't have to think of me in any way at all. Why would you? I'm just a low-class spirit medium you picked up in a speakeasy."

"My father was an immigrant fisherman. I make my living by breaking the law. If you're low-class, so am I, and—Jesus, Aida."

She swiped below her eyes. "These are angry tears, not

sad tears. I'm not crying over you. How could I cry over someone I don't even know?"

The question hung in the air for a moment before he spoke again. "Just because I haven't told you my life's story doesn't mean you don't know me."

"I don't know you as well as Sook-Yin, apparently. You could have at least warned me before you took me there."

"I haven't seen her for months. I told Ju I didn't want her there today—I told him."

She stared out the window. "It was humiliating."

"I don't know what to say."

"Me, either." She tugged the tassel of the privacy shade and lifted it. Wide-eyed, Bo stared back at her in the rear-view mirror. She looked away.

Winter pulled the shade down. "I was lonely. Is that what you want to hear? I'm not proud of it. But in case you haven't noticed, I'm not exactly prime husband material."

"Boo-hoo, you have a scar. You're easily the most hand-some man I've ever met in my life, *and* you're rich and influential. If you'd stop scowling and quit being so damn defensive—"

He stuck a finger in front of her face. "You can't begin to imagine what I've been through. I lost everything in one day. Everything."

A wave of pity crashed over her, subduing her indignant anger. She couldn't bear to look at him. "I'm not judging you about Sook-Yin. I'm just hurt that you didn't tell me about any of it. About your wife."

"I don't like to talk about her."

"It's fine. You don't owe me anything. I made assump-tions I shouldn't have."

She raised the shade.

They sat in silence for several seconds. He lowered the shade again.

"All right. I'll tell you everything. What do you want to know?"

"I . . . I want to know about your wife."

He hesitated. "Her name was Paulina. Her family was

from Nob Hill. Lost their fortune after the earthquake. My mother encouraged the marriage to distract me from getting caught up in the bootlegging with my father. She thought it would bring us a certain status that the money alone didn't. We were married for a year."

Aida waited for more. It was slow to come.

"The summer of 1925, when one of Paulina's relatives invited us to a charity dinner at the Elks Club, my parents accompanied us. My father's mental health was not stable. He was having manic episodes when he wasn't himself."

*Oh . . . Io's comment about Winter having all his mar-* bles. Aida didn't know what to say.

"He'd been seeing a doctor for several months. During the charity dinner, he went through one of his fits and caused a scene. Embarrassed Paulina. We left the dinner in a rush, to get him home and call the doctor. He was screaming in the backseat. Paulina was arguing with my mother, telling her that my father's fits were caused by the devil, or some such nonsense. And I was trying to calm everyone down. I accidently jerked the wheel as a streetcar was turning a corner."

Aida made a small noise.

"One second of distraction. That's all it took. One second, and I killed three people. It was my fault."

"You can't believe that," she whispered.

"People have told me that again and again, so why do I still feel guilty?"

"Oh, Winter."

"I'm not looking for pity. Just don't tell me that my life is all champagne and caviar, because it damn well isn't."

He tugged on the shade to lift it once more, and they spent the remainder of the ride in silence. As they pulled up to her building, she said, "Maybe it's not a good idea that I work for you anymore." When he didn't answer, she exited the car.

"Aida!" he called after her. As he stepped onto the sidewalk, a woman with an unruly toddler passed. The child, attempting to escape her mother's grip, twirled around and looked up at Winter. The tiny girl wasn't even the height of his knees, and Aida could only imagine what he looked like in her eyes: an angry giant towering above her. But it wasn't just his size. The girl saw something Aida didn't notice anymore: his mismatched eyes and scar. She screamed bloody murder and ran to the shelter of her mother's legs, sobbing in terror.

Winter's face fell.

Ever loyal, Bo lurched from the car, shouting in Cantonese at the woman, motioning for her to take her crying daughter away. Protecting the monster from the child.

Aida's throat tightened as her own eyes welled with tears. She took one last look at Winter and walked away in the opposite direction from the crying girl, more depressed than she'd been in years.


With one hand on the open car door, Winter stared out over the black roof of the Pierce-Arrow, watching Aida retreat inside Golden Lotus. He slammed his fist against the car frame. Pain shot up his wrist. He angrily threw his hat into the street.

"I take it she found out about Sook-Yin," Bo said as his gaze tracked the hat.

"And Sook-Yin told her about Paulina."

Bo whistled. "You probably should've told her that yourself."

"Not another word."

Bo managed to stay quiet for all of five seconds. "Is she never-want-to-see-you-again angry, or just temporarily angry?"

"How the hell should I know?" Winter felt as if Aida had just pulled on a loose thread of a sweater, and he was left watching it unravel before his eyes, powerless to do anything to stop it. When he picked her up that morning, he'd felt happier than he had in years.

And now he wanted to pummel every stranger on the sidewalk.

The crying girl didn't help, though he couldn't say he blamed her—or that it was the first time, either. A face that makes children cry. What a perfect ending to a perfectly pissy afternoon. "She doesn't want to work for me anymore," he said miserably.

"Maybe that's for the best," Bo said. "Now you can ask her out to dinner and not feel conflicted."

"Doubt she'd agree to that at this point."

"She did say you were the most handsome man she'd ever met."

Winter looked askance at his assistant.

"Hey, I tried not to listen," Bo argued, "but you were both shouting and . . ."

Winter stomped off into the street to retrieve his hat, then rammed himself into the backseat of the car and slammed the door.

Bo climbed into the driver's seat. "Home? Pier?" he asked. "Or do you need to hit something?"

Hitting something sounded beautiful. And after Bo dropped him off at the boxing club, he spent the rest of the afternoon doing just that.

And the next afternoon.

And the next.

But it didn't help. His hellfire mood only worsened.

He busied himself with work, visiting his warehouses and overseeing deliveries. He spent an entire morning taking apart a small boat engine and putting it back together. His employees began looking at him as if they wanted to toss him in the bay. He didn't give a damn.

He'd nearly convinced himself that he never wanted to see Aida Palmer again—that he'd be just fine if he didn't, because a woman like her would only drive him to violence, what with her insisting that he tell her every godforsaken thing about his life, screwing up his orderly routine, making him feel guilty.

Making him hope.

On the fifth afternoon, Bo breezed into his study carrying a box under his arm. "I just had an interesting conversation with a butcher in Chinatown."

Winter lay on his leather sofa, one arm and leg dangling off the side, staring at the ticking grandfather clock his father had shipped over from Sweden. "If it's not about Black Star or those symbols, I don't want to hear about it."

"It's not directly about Black Star, but it might be."

The pendulum on the clock swung several times while Winter waited for Bo to elaborate. "You going to tell me, or make me guess?"

"This butcher says that his cousin joined a secret tong two years ago. He said that no one knew the name of the leader, where it was based, what it controlled. But his cousin underwent a strange initiation that involved enduring insect bites."

Now Winter was interested. "Insects? Like the *Gu* poison?"

"Maybe, and remember the tong leader killed by bees? I've heard of blood initiations, but this . . ."

"It does sound strange," Winter admitted.

"There's more. The cousin said that the leader of the tong claimed to be a descendant of a mystical group of Chinese rebels from the Han Dynasty. A military group. Their leader was a necromancer."

"What is that? Black magic?"

"Calls up the dead. Could be nothing but legend, but it's the first connection I've heard between sorcery and a tong, and it's awfully strange."

"Damn right it is. We need to talk to the butcher's cousin who joined this tong."

Bo shook his head. "The night after he spoke to the butcher, he turned up dead in a gutter. The butcher thinks the tong killed him for blabbing about the initiation ceremony. The butcher also said after his cousin's death, he was so worried the secret tong would come after him and his wife that he moved his business to the opposite end of Chinatown."

"Christ. A secret tong with mystical roots . . . This has to be it, Bo."

"I'll keep my ear to the ground and let you know what else I can dig up."

Unease wormed its way into Winter's gut. Bo was savvy and sharp; he knew what he was doing. But Winter had already lost too many people in his life. If anything happened to Bo while he was slinking around Chinatown's alleys, Winter would never forgive himself. "Tread carefully," he told him. "If any of that is remotely true, and if they're connected to this Black Star, God only knows what they'd do if they thought someone was poking into their business."

Bo flicked the cap on his hat and winked. "I'm always careful."

"I mean it, Bo."

"Your concern for my well-being is touching. I will agree to be careful if you agree not to bite my head off for giving you this." He handed over the box. "A courier dropped it off."

Winter walked to his desk and dug around in a drawer for a letter opener to cut the strings. When he lifted the top of the box, he found himself staring at the gown Ju had made for Aida. The pain he'd been nursing for the last few days reared up, making his chest tight and hot.

*"Helvete,"* he swore under his breath.

Not the gaudy yellow fabric, but the color he'd wanted, so delicate, like silver and sand. At least Ju had some sense. It was finely made. Looked like something a goddess would wear. He imagined Aida wearing it, and the unending hollowness he'd felt since their fight grew wider.

He crammed the box top back on, crushing one side of it in frustration. He should just throw it in the trash. She wouldn't take it anyway.

"It's a beautiful gown," Bo noted.

Yes. Ju's girls had gone to a lot of trouble making it, and it was exceptional work.

A shame to let it go to waste.

Maybe Astrid would want it. Then again, if she ever wore it, it would likely just remind him of the spirit medium.

Only sensible option was to just give the damned thing to Aida. She might not accept it. He wasn't going to get his hopes up—he knew better now. This was just the logical thing to do, that's all.

Someone pounded on Aida's apartment door when she was getting ready to leave for her late show at Gris-Gris. Who would be calling on her at seven on a Friday night? And why did it make her so angry? Everything made her angry lately, and it was all Winter Magnusson's fault.

She was ill—physically sick to her stomach. She'd lost her appetite and had spent the last four nights rolling around on her narrow bed, feeling every spring, kicking the covers, cursing Winter's name.

Even one-way conversations with Sam about the matter, usually a comfort, gave her no support or relief. She tried to recall a Sam-ism that would apply to the situation and only remembered warnings about the uselessness of love, which she didn't care to consider—maybe because she was weaker than he'd been when it came to these matters.

It was ridiculous, all this anger and disappointment Winter stirred up inside her. She wasn't mad at him anymore about Sook-Yin, now that the shock had worn off. She wasn't even secretly mad about his dead wife, because that would be petty and selfish of her to be mad about something like that. It was none of her business, and he was obviously struggling with grief she couldn't fathom, and it would be silly to be jealous of a dead woman.

She was, however, still angry.

Because he'd given up on the two of them.

And if he could just give up without a fight, then he wasn't losing sleep like she was. And that meant she was lovesick over someone who didn't give a fig, and that made her *furious*. It was a self-loathing kind of fury, yes, but it was easier just to blame him. Much easier.

Feminine laughter seeped into her apartment from the hallway. Maybe one of the other tenants needed something. Aida opened the door to find a striking girl, not quite college-aged, with ringlets of blond hair peeking beneath a soft pink hat. She stood next to a young black girl about the same age. Both girls were giggling, both carrying shirt boxes.

"Hiya," the blonde said brightly, a little breathless. She looked familiar, but Aida couldn't place where she'd seen her. Nor could she figure out why she was standing outside her door. Maybe they were here to call on someone else and got the apartment numbers confused.

"I'm Astrid Magnusson," the girl said. "Winter's sister."

Aida's chest tightened. "Oh. Uh . . . oh." *What in the world is she doing here?*

"The woman at the restaurant counter let us come up. Your apartment is a hellish hike."

"No elevator."

"Someone needs to get one installed, and pronto. Can we come in? This is Benita, by the way."

Benita smiled over the big shirt box. Her hair was bobbed a little shorter than Astrid's, and she wore a pretty blue plaid dress with a bow at the neck under her coat. Aida greeted her and ushered them both inside.

"Benita's my seamstress," Astrid explained. "She can alter anything that doesn't fit. She's a genius. Gosh, this is a tiny apartment." She deposited her box on Aida's bed and looked around, wandering to the window. "Oh, but you can see the entire street. I love Chinatown. It must be so exciting to live here. Bo tells me stories all the time about growing up here."

While Astrid chatted, Benita hefted the largest box onto the bed. It was stamped with a gold I. Magnin logo, a high-end department store downtown at Geary; Aida had gazed at their window displays, but she'd never been inside.

"Astrid?" she said.

"Yes?"

"What are you doing here?"

Winter's sister smacked gum while giving her a crooked grin. "Winter sent me. He said you'd ripped your coat when he hurt his shoulder last week, something about a taxi hitting a telephone pole. He's terrible at explaining things. He always leaves out the interesting parts."

"That's an understatement," Aida murmured.

"Anyway," Astrid continued, "he told me he'd promised to buy you a new coat, so he sent me out to find one. Bo helped me. He's got an eye for fashion. Whenever I go shopping, he waits outside the dressing room and gives me his opinion when I model things for him." She hesitated, grimacing. "Umm, don't tell Winter about that. Not that there's anything wrong with it—it's not as if Bo sees me undressed or anything."

Benita made a small noise.

"Hush," Astrid told the girl, looking mildly embarrassed, but probably not as much as she should be. "That was an accident."

Aida raised a brow.

"Anyway, all I'm saying is . . . well, I've forgotten now. Come on, take a look at what I picked out."

"Astrid, this is really kind of you, but things may have changed since your brother asked you to do this."

"He just asked me a few hours ago."

"Oh." Aida's heart pattered inside her chest.

"Believe me, even if you've already found a new coat, this one is better. I'm so excited I can barely stand it. Don't worry, I've got excellent taste." The girls bent over Aida's bed together. "Oh, I almost forgot. Let's show her the gown, first."

"Gown?" She was incapable of doing anything more than repeating Astrid's words.

"I didn't pick it out, but Winter showed me. He called it a 'goddess dress,' and he's sort of right. It's gorgeous. Hold on." Benita untied the string on the smaller box and wiggled the top off. After pulling back layers of crinkly tissue paper, the girl lifted out a delicate oyster-colored sleeveless gown. It gathered over the shoulders with gold-threaded cords tied into long bows, and draped around the hips like a Greek chiton. Tiny freshwater pearls and golden beads danced across the sheer bodice.

Astrid and Benita both looked up at her with happy, expectant faces.

"It's stunning," Aida admitted.

"Look, the bodice is silk crepe-georgette. Two layers,"

she said, slipping her slender fingers behind the fine, diaphanous material. "And when you look at it in the right light, you can see tiny peacock feathers embroidered on the skirt."

Aida's heart skipped a beat. She leaned in to inspect the fabric. Yes, it was Ju's. The fabric Winter had liked. She never expected . . . well, she didn't know what she expected.

"It's beautiful, but I can't accept this."

"Winter told me you'd say that. He also said you might be offended, angry, or stubborn."

"Oh, did he now?"

She held up her hand. "Before you say anything else, let me show you the coat I found. If you say no to cashmere and fox, you're either a fool or an idiot."

Good grief, the girl had a mouth on her, didn't she?

"Look, my brother thinks you hung the moon, so I hope you're not planning on breaking his heart," Astrid added, giving her a cool look. "He's been through enough already."

Aida had never broken anyone's heart. She never stayed in one place long enough for that to happen, and if she did, she certainly wasn't heartbreaking material.

"He's not a monster," Astrid added. "He likes to think he is, but he wasn't like this before. I mean, he's always been arrogant, but he used to be happy and fun to be around."

"Before the accident."

Astrid shook her head. "Before Paulina. The accident just made it worse."

If the girl was trying to make Aida curious, she'd done a fine job. "Why didn't Winter come here himself?"

"He did. He's waiting in the car downstairs."

# FIFTEEN

———— ✦ ————

AIDA STARED AT ASTRID FOR A MOMENT, HEART POUNDING, THEN walked to the bed. "Where's the fur? Here?"

Benita quickly unpacked the coat. It was cashmere, all right, a soft camel color. And the collar was made of the longest, thickest, *softest* deep brown fur she'd ever seen. Aida could barely look at it, the thing was so ridiculously lovely. She averted her eyes and looped the coat over her forearm. Her apartment keys sat on the bedside table. She grabbed them and headed toward the door. "You coming?" she asked the girls, who scrambled to follow her out, Astrid begging to know if she liked the coat. Of course she liked the coat. That wasn't the point.

Mrs. Lin waved at them as they marched through the front door of the restaurant, Astrid complaining and fussing the whole way. Aida saw Bo on the sidewalk first, then Winter. He was lounging back against the Pierce-Arrow, ankles crossed. She thought she saw a flash of surprise in his eyes when he noticed her stalking toward him, but it quickly cooled.

"Mr. Magnusson," she said, stopping in front of him.

"Miss Palmer."

Damn him, he looked unfairly handsome. And he was giving her the frostiest look, slanting it down at her while his head remained still. He was intimidating, and she knew she should still be angry with him, but his clean scent wafted toward her with the breeze, and that lulled her into a softer mood.

All she could manage to feel at that moment was a tremendous amount of comfort and relief. Like when she'd tried to stop drinking coffee and went without for several days, until she walked into a diner and smelled it being brewed—then she forgot why she'd been trying so hard to avoid it, so she gave in and had a cup. That first sip was pure joy and warm pleasure.

That's how she felt, standing there in front of him, only a few inches away.

And it was a feeling that didn't pair well with the words she'd been repeating inside her head the entire trek down from her apartment, but she said them anyway: "I cannot accept this coat."

"Why not?" he said in his seductive, low baritone. "Do you hate the design?"

"It's gorgeous."

"The color?"

"I love the color."

"It doesn't fit?" He turned his head to the side and called out to Astrid. "Can it be altered?"

"Sure, but she hasn't tried it on," Astrid called back. She was standing on the sidewalk with Benita and Bo, several yards away, as if Winter were contagious and they didn't want to get too close. She probably should've kept her distance as well; one minute in his company and she already wanted to sway closer. It was pathetic, truly.

Winter glanced down at her. "How can you say it doesn't fit if you don't try it on?"

"I never said that. I—"

"Here, let me help." He pulled the coat out of her arms and shook it. "Looks real enough. It's not shedding, so hopefully it's not made of rat hair."

"I heard that," Astrid shouted.

"Can we speak alone, please?" Aida said to him under her breath.

"Are you going to tell me why you can't take this coat?"

"Maybe."

"Then no, we can't be alone. Hold out your arm."

She scowled at him, or tried to, at least, and held out an arm. He slipped the coat onto one arm, over her shoulders, then the other arm. He was very close, and he was touching her again, and that was only making her Comfort and Relief feelings grow stronger. He tugged the coat closed. "There. Looks as if it fits just fine to me."

She glanced at the length of the arms, the hem, hoping to find something to latch onto for argument fodder, but no. It fit. It fit well.

"Told you," Astrid called out.

"She's very irritating," Aida complained in a low voice.

"You have no idea," Winter answered with a merry twinkle in his eye, keeping his voice quiet to match hers. "You look lovely. That coat couldn't possibly be any better. It suits you perfectly." He ran his fingers along the side of her bobbed hair and smoothed down flyaway strands, causing a flurry of goose bumps to spread across her scalp. "Tell me why you can't accept it."

"I have a very good reason."

"You always do. I'm listening."

"Give me a second. You're distracting me with your handsome looks and sensible arguments."

She shouldn't have said that. He puffed up like a balloon, seemingly growing several inches in height. He almost started smiling. Almost. He leaned closer. "You may not want to keep it, but I have a good reason why you *should*. You'll need it tomorrow night."

"Why?"

"I'd like you to come to dinner with me."

She gave him a suspicious look. "Is this like the last meal you invited me to? Or have you seen another ghost? Wait, don't answer that. I'm not working for you anymore, and that's final."

"No ghost, and I'm not asking for business reasons. I'm asking if you—the person, not the spirit medium—would join me, the person, for dinner tomorrow. Just the two of us. No prostitutes or armed guards."

"Oh. Well. I, uh . . . I don't know if that's such a good idea."

"Why? You just said I was handsome."

"Too handsome."

"Let's not get carried away. A few days ago you were yelling at me like you wanted me dead."

"A few days ago, I did."

"And you've forgiven me?"

" 'Forgiven' seems too strong a word, especially when I've been so unhappy since you dumped me here five days ago and seemed to forget I existed."

"You stormed off—I didn't dump anything. And I tried to forget your existence, believe me. I tried very hard. I made it my top priority. All I could think about was how I was trying not to think about you."

"That sounds taxing."

"It was. And we can argue about who stormed off and who dumped whom over dinner. I know you're off tomorrow night, because I called Velma and she told me your schedule. So you can't use that excuse."

"That's—"

"And you have a new coat. And a new gown, though you don't have to wear it if it reminds you of that afternoon. It was a lousy afternoon."

"Yes, it was."

"And I've missed you ever since."

She stilled; her heart was beating far too fast. "You have?"

"I'm not sure why. Last time I saw you, you made it clear that you hated my guts."

"I don't hate you."

"You certain about that?"

"Fairly certain."

He nearly smiled again. "I'll take what I can get. Eight tomorrow night, right here. I'll pick you up. I'll even promise to keep my hands aboveboard if you do the same."

A short laugh escaped her lips. She glanced to the side and spied Bo, Astrid, and Benita watching them with undisguised interest. "They are awfully nosy," she murmured to Winter.

"Worse than the gossip rags," he agreed. "Aida?"

"Yes?"

"Please go to dinner with me."

She touched the locket beneath her dress; Sam would be furious with her for caving in too easily, but for once in her life, her whispering heart drowned out his persistent voice.

"Okay," she told Winter. "But no Chinese food."

He closed his eyes for a moment and blew out a long breath.

The following night, she stood in the same exact spot, while the Magnusson family's driver, Jonte, greeted her as he opened the limousine door. Winter waited in the backseat, dressed in a tuxedo. Her gaze flitted over the white of his shirt and the luxurious heft of a long blue black coat; his gaze flitted over the fur-collared coat and headed down her pale silk stockings.

"You look . . ." he started. "Oh, hell. You look breathtaking, Aida."

"I don't believe anyone's ever called me that." She couldn't hold his gaze. "Please stop looking at me. It's making me anxious."

"Is it? I can't tell."

"I'm good at hiding it. A stage trick."

"Maybe you should sit closer. I think that might help."

"Last time I did, I ended up attacking you."

"Yes, well, hope springs eternal, but I'm sure that would never happen again. And I have promised to keep my hands aboveboard. Come here." He shifted to make room for her, and she scooted into the crook of his arm, tightly clutching her handbag against her lap with both hands. The side of his body warmed hers within seconds, and she found herself relaxing, just a little. She didn't dare look up at his face. Lord knew that was her downfall the last time she did this.

"See, it's fine," he said in his deep-velvet voice. "Anyone who saw us would think we're old friends. No one would imagine that we were crazy about each other before I went and screwed everything up."

"Who knows. Maybe we still *are* crazy about each other, despite your best efforts."

"That would be something, wouldn't it?"

She leaned her head against his fine coat and breathed him in, grateful and content.

He made a strange noise, then she felt the hesitant weight of his arm wrapping around her shoulders. "Let's look out the window. I'll give you a quick tour of the city along our route. Point out things that have changed since you were a child."

Ten minutes later, she was soft as butter, lounging against him, listening to his voice as it vibrated inside his big chest, pointing out which blocks were destroyed in the Great Fire, telling her about Lotta's Fountain, where a crowd of people were gathered to listen to someone playing a violin as the sun set behind the downtown buildings.

"And here we are."

She perked up. "Where? Which building?"

"The big one there. The Palace Hotel," he said as the car inched its way in the direction Winter pointed, an eight-story concrete building with curved corners that sat squat on New Montgomery Street, the top floors obscured by evening fog. Dozens of cabs and limousines lined the curb in front of the hotel, competing with three rows of streetcars and cable cars as they whipped in and out of traffic.

"John D. Rockefeller and Oscar Wilde have stayed here," Winter said. "Hollywood actors and famous opera singers, too. And it just so happens that I supply their booze."

Even a deaf person could hear the note of pride in his voice. She grinned up at him. "You're their hero, I suppose."

"It's a tough job, being a hero to rich drunkards and party girls."

"Yes, I can imagine. Is that why we're here? So you can show off?"

"Only a little. We're mainly here because they have a chef who cooks a beautiful chop," he said, offering his arm.

Beaded gowns and tuxedos draped the haut monde that paraded through the illuminated entrance alongside them. Once inside, Aida's gaze tried to take everything in: polished floors, staggering floral displays, beveled glass, and gleaming brass. She wondered what it would be like to stay in a room here. Like royalty, she supposed.

In the main lobby, they stopped at a concierge coat check to exchange their outer garments for a numbered ticket. She hated to give up the new coat but reluctantly opened the large square button over her hip and shimmied out of it. Winter turned to take it from her. Reaching hands stopped midair as his eyes wandered over the peacock-embroidered chiton gown, over her elbow-length white gloves, over bare shoulders . . . until his gaze finally lit on her breasts.

"Christ alive," he mumbled. "That dress is sheer."

Warmth rose to her cheeks. "No sheerer than half the gowns here."

He made a garbled, low sound of doubt. "I can see *everything.*"

She looked down. "You cannot!" She'd checked in the mirror before coming—twice. The golden beads on the torso covered most of her breasts. It wasn't obscene, for Pete's sake. A little daring, maybe, and she couldn't wear a chemise or brassiere beneath, or it would show through. But it was still sophisticated. She wore dresses onstage that were comparable in style, if not in quality.

"I can count the freckles over your nipples."

Her face twisted as she darted a wary glance at the coat check girl. "Keep your voice down," she complained. "And you can't see my nipples."

"*We-e-ell*, maybe my recent supernatural woes have fortified me with more than just ghost-sight, because I can make out the exact size of—"

She smacked his arm. "The girl is waiting for my ridiculously expensive fur coat."

His eyes danced merrily as he draped the fox over his own coat and handed both to the girl, then pocketed the coat check ticket inside his tuxedo jacket. "I really do owe Ju a big thank-you."

"I hope it wasn't Sook Yin who made it."

"She can't sew, so I think you're safe."

"It was made by one of the younger prostitutes, then? Hopefully one you haven't slept with."

"Careful, cheetah. And I haven't slept with any of the younger ones."

"Hallelujah."

A slow grin spread over his face, plumping up high Scandinavian cheekbones. He held out his arm. "Shall we dine, Miss Palmer?"

They headed out of the lobby and walked into the Palm Court, a large, bustling room that was partitioned into a lounge with a piano at the front, and a restaurant at the back. The host at the podium took one look at Winter and snapped his finger at a waiter several steps before they arrived. "Mr. Magnusson, always a pleasure. We have your table ready."

Well-dressed patrons lounged and dined around clusters of lazy palms under a domed iridescent glass ceiling. Aida watched diners' reactions as she and Winter wended their way through the tables: first Winter's size caught their eyes, then they recognized him, and finally they looked at her in curiosity. Table by table, this was how it went, until they were seated off to one side beneath a balcony, where potted palms and a marble column gave them some privacy from the rest of the floor.

"Is this always how it is for you?" she asked after the waiter brought menus, stripping off her long gloves and tucking them in the handle of her handbag. He watched her actions over the top of his menu, staring at her hands with great interest.

What on earth was so interesting? She looked down, wondering if her fingers were covered in ink from a leaky pen. They weren't. His mind seemed to be elsewhere. She dipped her head to catch his eye. "Does everyone recognize you, I meant."

He blinked and shook away his daze. "Depending on where I go, yes. It will stop in a minute, once they realize I'm not doing anything interesting. Surely you must be used to some of this yourself."

"I never stay anywhere long enough to garner a following. People recognize me now and then at the Automat across the street from Gris-Gris. I can barely read this menu, it's so dark back here. Tell me what's good."

With a hand under her seat, he scooted her closer, chair and all, oblivious to the whispering at neighboring tables. Now that their arms were practically touching, he browsed the entrées with her, talking up the merits of his beloved chop, which sounded as if he liked it so much, they should probably consider adding his name next to it on the menu. She ended up ordering what the waiter recommended, including a French wine that Winter cockily assured her was some of the best in the city; the very best, he hoarded in his own cellar.

Winter was served the thickest chop she'd ever seen in her life—certainly not the size that was listed on the menu—while she had prime rib and salad with dressing the Palace had made famous, or so they claimed: something called green goddess. They talked as they ate. Conversation was so effortless and easy, it was almost as if the visit to Ju's had never happened. She watched him in surreptitious snatches while he chatted: his animated mouth with its deep indentations at the corners, made deeper by the flickering candle at their table; the sleek wave of his brilliantined hair, so dark it was almost black; and those bewitching mismatched eyes, which now looked so merry.

*He used to be happy and fun to be around*, Aida thought, remembering Astrid's words. This was what she meant. This was the real Winter. She understood Astrid mourning him, if this was something she didn't see much anymore, because

Aida could think of no recent company she'd enjoyed half as much.

The only pause in their conversation came after the waiter cleared their plates away and promised to return with something for dessert. After a few moments of silence, Winter surprised her by saying, "I didn't love her."

She glanced up at his face. "Sook-Yin?"

"No, my wife."

"Oh."

"You told me I shouldn't feel guilty about the accident, and I try not to. But that's what still bothers me. I didn't love Paulina when I married her, and she definitely didn't love me."

Was he really talking about this? She couldn't believe it. She was scared to say anything for fear he'd stop, but he seemed to need some encouragement, so she gave in. "Why did you marry her, then?"

"I married her to please my mother, and I suppose I thought my feelings would deepen after the wedding. But we couldn't even manage small talk, much less love. The more we grew apart, the more I helped my father out with the bootlegging, which only made things worse. She detested the bootlegging. Her family is Pentecostal—are you familiar?"

"The religious people who speak in tongues."

"Holy Rollers," he confirmed. "Paulina wasn't active in the church when we met, but I suppose that I was so inherently evil, I made her long for fellowship. She tolerated my father's bootlegging, but knowing I was out making deals after dark became a sin too big for her to ignore. She once told me she didn't know which was worse—staying awake at night worrying I'd be killed, or finding out that I hadn't been."

"What an awful thing to say."

"It made me never want to come home. I stayed out just to avoid her. She accused me of being unfaithful, which I never was, Aida—not once."

"You don't have to convince me."

He scratched his neck and remained silent for a time, staring at the flickering candlelight on the table. "It's not just that we made each other miserable, because we did. The worst part was that we wasted each other's time. Several months of courting and a wedding that cost my family enough to shame William Randolph Hearst, only to find that we were complete opposites. She didn't like rich food, sex, foul language, drinking . . . or jokes. I swear to God, I never once heard her laugh. Not once. I don't think she even knew how."

"She sounds delightful, Winter."

"I—" He looked down at her in wonder, then laughed. "Yes, I suppose so. Those were all my favorite things, so she pretty much ripped the joy out of my life. Especially when she made the decision to go back to her church and started attending services every weekend. I thought it would make her happier, but the congregation just encouraged her to divorce me, because I was a known criminal."

She waved around the luxurious dining room. "All of us are criminals. There's not a dry table here. You're Robin Hood, taking back what the government took away—not Jack the Ripper."

He crossed his arms and rested them on the edge of the table. "Regardless, I should've just let her go. I'm not sure why I didn't. I think maybe I saw it as a failure, and that was unacceptable. So we had a bad fight, and I told her divorce was impossible, that I'd never let it happen."

"What did she do?"

"Nothing. That was two weeks before the accident."

"Oh."

"If I would've just let her leave, she wouldn't have been invited to her aunt's dinner, and her family wouldn't have tried to tell us that we were going to hell, which was the thing that spurred my father's last fit. So that's why I feel guilty—because even though I didn't love her, I refused to let her go. If I had, everyone would still be alive."

The waiter returned with some sort of sponge cake and more wine. She waited until the man left, then said, "I can understand why you'd feel that way. I probably would, too, if I were in your shoes. But you can't continue to pummel yourself. You can't let one moment in time define you for the rest of your life."

"Easy to say, harder to do."

"Paulina made the decision to marry you. You didn't hold a gun to her head."

Winter toyed with the stem of his wineglass. "No, but I might as well have done that when I didn't let her leave."

"She had two feet and a mind of her own. If she wanted to leave, she could've walked out the door."

"Not every woman thinks like you."

"Which is a damn shame, to be sure, but you can't be held responsible for her character defects. Nor can you spend the rest of your life allowing human mistakes to mold your future."

"Yes, well—"

"Nothing is more important than right now. This moment." She tapped the table with her fingernail. "Not what happened yesterday. Not what will happen tomorrow. You once asked me how I could be happy moving from place to place, and that is the answer. I live for the moment. I enjoy what I have, not what I've lost. Not what I don't have yet."

Upon finishing her passionate speech, she found him staring at her intently with the strangest look on his face. Something about that look made her chest warm.

"Let's have an affair."

"What?"

"An affair," he repeated. "A temporary relationship. Companionship. Sex."

The heat in Aida's chest climbed to her cheeks. "Ah . . ."

"We like each other," he said in a very businesslike manner. "Might even be crazy about each other, like you said. We're both single. I passed your kissing test."

She snorted. "Confident about that, are you?"

One brow lifted.

"*You* invented the kissing test," Aida argued. "All I said was that my previous lovers were terrible kissers."

"Which brings me to my next point. Wouldn't you like to be with someone who knows what he's doing in bed? I'm *very* good."

"Gee, don't sell yourself short or anything," she said, looking around to make sure no one nearby was listening as her cheeks flamed higher.

"Just being honest."

"I don't think this sort of thing is something people plan and negotiate."

He ran his hand over the back of his neck. "Maybe they should. You're only in town for how much longer? A month?"

"About that, yes."

"Not much time, but you've made it clear you're not interested in long-term relationships because of your traveling, and God knows I'll never be interested in anything permanent again after my failed experiment with marriage."

A cynical voice whispered inside her head. "You want me to be your new Sook-Yin."

"That's the last thing I want. That was a pretend relationship." He sipped wine. "Though, I'm not really sure what I had with Paulina was much different. She wanted my money, too."

"Money is nice. I'm not above its allure. I love that you brought me here," she said, looking up at the dazzling chandeliers. "I love that damn coat."

He chuckled, then gestured with his glass. "But pride is more important to you, and that's the difference."

"Perhaps."

"I don't want to talk about the past anymore. You just told me to live in the present."

"You're right. I did."

"And what I want right now, in the present, is you in my bed. Do you want me?"

She licked dry lips. No one had ever spoken to her like this. She wasn't sure if it was crude or refreshingly honest.

Winter looked down at the table and brushed his thumb along the curve of her wrist. "I lay awake at night thinking of you. I have since we met. Do you ever think of me?"

Her heart flamed up like a pyre. And he was looking at

her with such intensity, it made lights twinkle in her brain. If he didn't stop telling her all these things, it would get so bright up there, she'd go blind and start shouting *Yes!* at the top of her lungs.

As it was, she managed to say it in a normal voice, after downing the remainder of her wine in two gulps. "Yes."

"You don't have to answer now. You can—" His hand stilled on hers. "Did you mean 'yes' you think of me, or 'yes,' you want to have an affair?"

"Yes to all your questions."

He smiled oh-so-slowly, like a dockyard cat eyeing a fish flailing on dry ground, and she knew right then she was a goner.

# SIXTEEN

———◆———

THEY LEFT THE PALM COURT WITHOUT EATING DESSERT. WINTER'S body was flying, but his brain was stuttering along, half a step behind, still in disbelief. They stopped in the main hall that led to the lobby, allowing a bellboy to pass with two luggage carts.

"How do we do this?" Aida said, almost whispering. "We can't go to my place. Mrs. Lin doesn't allow men in the apartments."

Winter pulled her off to the side. "We could go to mine, but it's still early. Might have to sneak you past Greta and Astrid, otherwise I'll never hear the end of it. Everyone's still ribbing me about you calling on me in my study that afternoon."

"Your car?"

He stared down at her. No way in hell was he taking her in the car. "Jonte would certainly get a thrill straining his gnarled old ears trying to hear us, but no."

Aida glanced around. "Well, we *are* in a hotel."

No need to tell him twice. "Stay here. Do not move. Do not talk to anyone. I'll be right back."

He rushed off to the registration desk, rushed back with a golden key to a suite and their coats. Part of him expected her to be gone when he got back, but she was still there, looking like an exotic goddess, freckled and golden and sparkling. Not a dream. Not a figment of his overactive imagination. Not a ghost. He touched her bare shoulder, just to make sure, and the heat from her soft skin nearly made him drop to his knees in prayer.

"Elevators are this way," he said, gripping her hand as if she might blow away.

As they ascended to the top floor, he watched her laugh at the elevator operator's jokes. On the surface, she was open and carefree, as she often was. But the way she clutched her handbag made him realize how anxious she was. He was anxious, too.

The room was on the top floor, at the end of the hall. No one occupied the neighboring suite. His hand shook as he unlocked the door.

"Oh, good," she said, noticing. "It's not just me."

Once he got his hands on her, he'd calm down. He was too keyed up. He felt like a boy, overexcited and bouncing with energy. Practically ramming the door open, he hurried her inside, hung the DO NOT DISTURB sign, and locked the door behind him.

She switched on a lamp and set her handbag and coat down. He watched her inspect their surroundings. The suite was big. Clean, but not properly prepared for guests: no fresh flowers, no turned-down linens. He was in too much of a hurry to wait for niceties.

Strolling to the window, she looked out over downtown. Hazy fog clung to the rooftop. "I'll never get over the views here," she said. "Everywhere you go, there's something to see. I think some of these views must be stuck inside my head from childhood, because nothing out East compares. Everything seems so flat and claustrophobic out there."

She turned to face him. He saw her throat working as she swallowed hard. Noticed the way she tightly held one arm beneath her breasts, gripping her opposite elbow, as if she was trying to shield herself. He hated that. She glanced at the bed. "Oh, Winter, I'm so nervous."

Her voice was small. *She* was small. How had he not noticed how small and fragile she was? That blustery attitude of hers was deceptive. And now that it was gone, and she was unable to meet his eyes, he was reminded of Paulina, timid and guarded—worse, he was reminded of how he used to feel around her. Like a monster and a bully. Like the bad guy.

Her fingers touched her breastbone as if she were searching for something, and then glanced down in panic when she didn't find it. She snatched her hand away and exhaled heavily.

A pang of worry went through him. This was not at all how he'd imagined this going, and he'd imagined it plenty of times, plenty of ways. It definitely wasn't what he had in mind when he proposed this harebrained idea in the restaurant. Maybe she'd been right. This wasn't how it was supposed to be done. He should've been patient and let things happen naturally.

But *God*, how he wanted her.

It's just that he wanted free-spirited Aida, not this tense, nervous rabbit version.

He approached her and held out a hand. "Let's just sit here on the sofa." It faced the window. Maybe the view would be soothing. He removed his tuxedo jacket and laid it on the back of the sofa, unstrapped his leather shoulder holster and gun, then sat down next to her. "Deep breath, cheetah. It's just me."

She exhaled and anxiously laughed at herself, smoothing her dress down her legs.

He made a quick decision.

"I changed my mind. We're not going to have sex tonight."

She looked up, eyes big and brown. "Why?"

*Because you are scared of me.* "Because we need to get used to each other."

"Maybe that's wise," she said. "I mean, if you think so."

Enough of this awkwardness. "Come here. I want to hold you." He pulled her sideways onto his lap and wrapped his arms around her, then spoke to her in a hushed voice. "Hello."

"Hello."

So warm. He stroked a palm across her back and felt tense muscles relax against his thighs. "This is better."

"Yes. Much better." Her fingers fluttered over his bow tie. She fiddled with the knot, then glanced up at his face and smiled. All her lipstick was gone, wiped away on her napkin at dinner. Now he could see every freckle on her lips, including the one near the right corner of her mouth that he liked so well.

He spoke without thinking, his voice sounding rough to his own ears. "I swear on my life, you are the loveliest thing I've ever seen."

She softened in his arms. He held her closer, running a hand down her bare arm, feeling chills race down his own arm in response. His mouth brushed her face. He kept himself in check, slowly relaxing, enjoying the weight of her body. Grateful for it.

"Please kiss me, Winter," she said against his cheek. "Or I'll be forced to attack you again."

There she was. His Aida.

He complied, trying to go gentle, but her mouth was so hot and eager, and her hands were slipping over his shoulders. His cock stirred, pulsing to life against her leg. She twisted in his arms and pressed closer.

He forgot all about the tense start. "C'mere," he murmured against her lips. "Like this." He prodded one of her legs across his until she was straddling his lap. "Oh yes. That's better." He slouched lower and gathered her closer, until her gown hiked up. Soft breasts pressed against his chest as her mouth returned to his. His hands slid up the back of her thighs. He stuck his index fingers beneath the tops of her stockings, under her garters. Two fingers. Three. He wanted to rip them off. And he almost did when her hips shifted and her soft heat covered his cock.

"Oh," she said in a high voice. He extracted his roaming fingers from her stockings and pulled her down more firmly, fitting himself along her sex, nothing but a few thin layers of fabric between them. *"O-oh,"* she said louder.

His thoughts exactly.

He gathered her closer, thrusting up against her heat. She rocked in reply, rubbing herself against him. Christ, he was hard as iron. He thrust harder against her, drunk with pleasure, craving more . . . wanting to be inside her. She flinched. "Oww."

He pulled away.

"I'm sensitive, sorry." She let out a little breathy laugh, then settled back down and rubbed against him again, softer, studying his face.

He pushed her bangs away from her forehead and kissed the exposed skin there. "Never apologize." He was the one who couldn't control himself. If he didn't get her off his lap, he'd be inside her in another minute. "Hold on to me." He secured her against him with an arm around the small of her back, then pushed off the sofa, taking her with him. Her weight felt good in his arms. He walked her across the suite and climbed onto the bed with her clinging to him. She made a noise when he set her down on the mattress.

Anxiety reappeared in her eyes.

"I'm just going to touch you a little," he reassured her, kissing her softly. "Yes?"

She nodded and kissed him again. Her hands slid up his chest. "Can we take this off?" she said, tugging a button on his vest.

He blinked at her in surprise. "Yes."

"It will make me feel more comfortable," she said defensively, as if he was going to protest, then, in a softer voice, "I want to see you. Again," she added with a coy smile.

God only knew why, but whatever she wanted, she could have. If she asked him to sign over the Pierce-Arrow to her, he'd do it in a heartbeat. He fumbled with the top button on his vest while she started on the bottom button; they met in the middle. She pushed the vest over his shoulders, then his suspenders.

"No need to rush," he said, untying his bow tie under the wingtip collar points of his formal shirt, which tiny fingers were already busy unbuttoning. He yanked shirttails out of his pants with one hand while she struggled with his cuff link on the other.

"How?" she asked.

He showed her the mechanism, and together they unfastened them. She kissed him as he pocketed his cuff links and shrugged out of his shirt. He tossed it behind his back. Warm hands slithered up the front of his undershirt. Shivery pleasure blanketed his skin. She lifted the cotton and peered at him. He watched her gaze follow her stroking hand down the line of dark hair bisecting his stomach, down to the intrusive bulge of his cock straining the fly of his pants.

Her mouth opened with a garbled noise.

He could only imagine what she was thinking. Jesus—it looked lewd and mammoth, even to his eyes.

"Oh my." Her eyes tilted up to his. One corner of her mouth curled.

Well.

"Ignore that," he said. Then added, "For now."

"I don't think I can."

"Sure you can—I do, every day. Especially around you." He halted her reaching hand. "But I can't if you touch me." Christ! Was he really stopping her? He had to, or he'd be finished before they even started, and both of them would be embarrassed. "Hold that thought, and just let me . . ." What? Possibilities crowded his mind, but he pushed them away for one specific starting place, first conjured during dinner, when it was all he could do not to take a bite out of her shoulders. Her dress was held up by golden cords tied into draping bows at the tops of her shoulders. He tugged one to loosen it. A second tug, and the entire right side of her bodice dropped to reveal one pert breast.

His mouth went dry.

Her freckles were lighter here, but they dusted every inch of her skin. They even covered her nipple, which was high and small and peach, jauntily standing at attention. He cupped the lush weight of her breast in one hand. A scant palmful—not too big, not too small. Just right. Encouraged by a moan, he stroked her nipple with his thumb and felt her shudder. It did him in. He hastily untied the cord on her other shoulder and bared her to the waist.

His brain emptied as he gazed at her, tracing the curve of her shoulder, the elegant ridge of clavicle. "Goddamn," he murmured. "You're beautiful." He kissed her mouth and trailed his lips across her jaw, urging her back onto the mattress. "Beautiful," he repeated, drawn to the rise and fall of her breasts. Stretching out next to her, he captured one dusky peak with his mouth, worrying it with his lips, his tongue, his teeth.

"Oh . . . yes," she mumbled, as the warm pressure of her hand clasping the back of his neck held him in place. She liked it. He felt like a jockey jumping a hurdle, breathless and triumphant. His cock kicked inside his pants, as if to cheer him on.

He released her flesh with a soft *pop* and licked his way to her other breast, giving it the same treatment as he rolled the now-wet abandoned nipple between his thumb and finger. She bowed her back and moaned so loudly, goose bumps rose over his arms. He plucked harder, sucked harder, savoring the taste of her skin as he pressed himself against her soft thigh like a schoolboy, desperate for any sort of relief.

His mouth returned to hers as his hand wandered lower, over her soft belly, half covered with her fallen gown. He went lower, running the heel of his palm over the hilly apex between her legs. "I just want to touch you," he assured her in a gravelly voice.

"I . . ." she began, mumbling something incoherent.

He slipped his hand down her stocking, to the inside of her knee, then back up her inner thigh. He stilled halfway to his goal.

Just above her garter, her thigh was shockingly slick. He

took a ragged breath and went higher. Slippery, everywhere. "Christ alive," he whispered in amazement. He hadn't even touched her!

"Oh, *God*," she said, as if she were ashamed. Her cheeks reddened beneath the freckles.

"Aida, you are . . . Jesus—you are a miracle." He kissed her mouth to quell her unspoken protests and slid his hand to the silk between her legs. "Soaked," he reported in amazement, as if she didn't know. He plundered beneath the thin fabric. Greedy fingers glided along one slick fold bordered in damp curls, then the other. And without any trouble at all, his thumb found her taut bud between them, sweet and ripe and stiffening beneath his touch.

She cried out and bucked against his hand.

A mad sort of joy rose up inside him.

"Yes, you were right," he murmured against her ear. "You *are* sensitive. What if I rub you like this?"

Her breath hitched, then a garbled string of words came out of her mouth in a rush as she grabbed his arm. She squirmed. Cursed. Her hips jerked this way and that as he rubbed and circled and flicked, experimenting . . . listening to her response in the pace of her breathing, the sounds she was making in the back of her throat, the intensity of her grip.

But he wanted more.

He withdrew his hand for a moment to give himself better access. Shifted his weight and hushed her complaining moan as he eased her silky tap pants down. They matched the color of her nipples, peachy and golden, trimmed in lace. He leaned up on one elbow and slipped them over her knees. They tangled around the heels of her shoes. She laughed, a little breathless, until he finally got the wretched things off.

But when he went to push her gown up her legs she sat up and slapped her hands over his. "No," she said, panicked. "I don't want you looking at my hips."

"What?" He could barely get the word out. She might as well have said "I hate bacon," because who in their right mind hates bacon? No one, that's who. Why wouldn't she want to let him see her hips?

"My scars," she clarified.

"What?" he said again.

"My lancet scars. I don't want you to see them. Please, Winter."

Dear God. She'd scarred herself? He shouldn't be surprised. God only knew how many times she'd cut herself. Several times a night for the last couple of years? Of course she had scars. But—

"Do you not see the gash around my bad eye?" he asked.

"That's different. I'm not ready for anyone to see mine."

Why this smarted, he didn't know, but he wasn't going to let it spoil things. He pulled his hands out from under hers and shifted them to her inner thighs. "I'll keep my eyes closed," he lied as he urged her legs apart.

With her hands holding her gown over her curving hips, propped up on her elbows, she watched him as he kissed the inside of one knee, then the other. The edge of one garter, then the other. The slippery inside of one slender freckled thigh, then the other.

"What are you doing?" she said with a look of astonishment in her eyes.

"I just want to taste you a little." His gaze roamed over more of her beautifully freckled skin, a nest of golden red brown curls, and the glistening pink flesh below. Luxuriously, gloriously wet, and all for him.

He pushed her dress up above her sex while she stubbornly clutched the loose fabric of her gown over her hips. "You . . . I . . . no one's ever . . ." she tried to say.

No one had? Not those two idiot lovers of hers? This thrilled him to no end. Spurred on, he stuck his nose into her curls and breathed in deeply, groaning with pleasure at her heady female scent. He gave her a long, lazy lick and she gasped. Then he set his lips to her and drew her delicate, swollen flesh into his mouth.

She flopped back against the bed and said, "God, yes," to the ceiling.

He kissed. He suckled. He licked.

She moaned. She panted. She swore.

But nothing happened. He tried slow and fast, soft and hard, side-to-side flicks—he tried every trick he knew. She wasn't nervous anymore. Seemed to be enjoying it. Was certainly moaning loud enough and twisting beneath his mouth. Still extraordinarily wet. Most women he'd tried this on had no trouble coming. Most women he'd bedded came—period. Except Paulina, but he refused to conjure her face at this moment.

He thought of Aida's confession about her past lovers, implying she didn't enjoy the encounters. It wasn't a leap to assume she didn't climax with them. But she certainly wasn't frigid. Anything but. A wildcat on the outside and inside—he'd bet his life on it.

All women were different. He just needed to recalibrate his efforts.

Keeping his mouth where it was, he slid one finger inside her. *Christ.* So tight and slick and petal-soft. She inhaled sharply, then cried out, "Yes, *God* . . . please."

Much better.

He stroked her on the inside until she widened her legs welcomingly. When he added a second finger, she began shivering and shaking so hard, he nearly lost his mind. Forgetting herself, she released her dress and grabbed his head, fingers diving into his hair. She tried to pull him closer, rubbing herself against his mouth, as if this would alleviate the tension building in her trembling thighs.

She was wild. Beyond shame. Beyond anxiety.

All his.

When her hips swayed off the mattress, he laid his arm across her lower belly to give her something to rock against. Then he crooked his fingers and rubbed the small, spongy patch of skin he found inside her as she tightened fiercely around his fingers. Aha!

"Oh, Winter. Oh, God. Oh, Winter."

*That's right*, he thought, drunk on power. *One and the same.*

Her arms fell to her sides, gripping the bedcovers. She was very close. He slowed his pace to tease her, draw it out.

For the briefest moment, big eyes looked down at him in bewilderment.

She turned one cheek to the mattress and broke apart, crying out in long, wavering sobs.

# SEVENTEEN

———❦———

AIDA LAY IN A DAZE, UNABLE TO MOVE, EVEN AS WINTER TRAILED
three slow kisses between her breasts and shifted to her side.
He nestled a leg between hers, and she felt his arousal, firm
and hot against her thigh. Something was going to have to
be done about that . . . in a second, when she could actually
lift her head. When her limbs didn't feel like they weighed
a thousand pounds and the center of her wasn't melting into
the mattress.

How in God's name had he learned to do that? Intellec-
tually, she knew people *did* do that, of course—the ancient
Romans, probably. The French, definitely. The women who
posed for pornographic photographs that graced the postcards in Winter's study certainly seemed fond of providing
the service to men. No woman she'd ever known had mentioned anyone doing it.

Perhaps she was just lucky. Very, *very* lucky. She certainly
felt that way, with Winter's face hovering over hers. A mussed
lock of hair rakishly fell in a dark slash over one eye. "Still
with me?" he asked.

She squeezed his leg between her knees.

"Is that a yes?"

"Yes," she croaked. "I'm just . . ."

"Yes?"

"My *God*."

He smiled down at her, clearly pleased with himself. "You," he said between kisses, "are a joy"—she tasted sex on his lips—"to satisfy."

"And I *am* satisfied. Was. Am. Utterly. I . . . loved it."

"I could tell. You are vocal."

"I couldn't help it."

"I know."

"Oh, God," she murmured. "You think anyone heard?"

"I certainly hope so. Makes me look good."

She wrapped her arms around his neck and pulled him closer. "You, sir, are no gentleman."

"Aren't you glad?"

"Delighted," she admitted.

He started to kiss her again but held still, listening to something. She heard it, too, out in the hallway. Loud knocks on nearby doors. People shouting. Next to the bed, the telephone rang, startling both of them.

"What the hell?" Winter mumbled, pushing himself up to reach the nightstand. He growled an agitated, "What?" into the mouthpiece. Every muscle in his face tightened as he listened for several moments. He hung up without responding. A stream of curses spilled from his mouth—half of them in what she could only assume was Swedish—while he gripped the massive bulge in his pants as if he were trying to will it away.

"What is it?" she asked.

Aida got her answer from a shouted word that shot through the hallway outside their door.

Raid.

Winter pulled her up and said, "Get dressed. Feds have already secured the restaurant and the ballroom."

"Can't we just wait it out up here?"

"They're sending agents up to search the rooms." He snatched his shirt off the floor. She watched him slip it on over his undershirt as she pushed her dress down and struggled to tie her gown's golden cords over a shoulder. "The hotel sends booze up to rooms when guests call the front desk and ask for a 'birthday treat,' or some other such nonsense code."

"But we didn't."

He stopped dressing for a moment and gave her a hard stare. "No, but I'm the one who supplied it to the hotel."

"Right." She tied one shoulder of her dress into place and twisted to find the second set of cords.

"And I'd prefer that our photograph doesn't end up on the front page of tomorrow's newspaper, no matter if all they did was question me—which they will, if they catch me."

"I wouldn't think anyone would bat an eyelash over a bootlegger caught in a hotel room with a speakeasy performer."

He lifted her chin with one knuckle. "I couldn't give a damn about myself. It's your reputation I'm worried about."

Perhaps he was a gentleman after all. She ran her hand down his stomach, pausing over loose shirttails. "I'm sorry. We weren't finished."

"I'm not happy, either, believe me. Rain check?" She nodded, and he kissed her briefly before returning to dressing and strapping on his gun. He didn't bother tying his bow tie. "Don't leave my side," he said calmly as he herded her out the door. "And don't panic." She barely had time to snatch up her coat and handbag as they left the room.

Out in the hallway, guests talked excitedly as they breezed past, headed for the stairs behind another couple. Near the elevator, Aida nearly bumped into a half-dressed man who was hunched over a potted palm, turning up a gurgling bottle of gin into the potting soil. Toilets flushed behind doors on either side of them as other guests got rid of their own incriminating evidence. Winter and Aida might've been the only people on the whole floor who hadn't ordered a birthday treat from the front desk.

They clattered down several flights of stairs, others joining their exodus along the way. Winter guided her away from the small crowd and took her on a circuitous route around the Palm Court. When two men with shotguns appeared around a corner, he ducked into a pair of doors, pulling her along, before they could be seen. They found themselves inside a ballroom where a private party was in the middle of hysterics. Tuxedoed guests were emptying champagne glasses when cries broke out near the front of the dining area. Several men in suits charged into the room, brandishing guns.

"Federal agents," the leader shouted. "Everyone stay where you are. This is a raid."

Chaotic shouting broke out. Tables toward the back of the room emptied as diners joined several waiters who were fleeing out a back door. A Fed stepped into the doorway, blocking their retreat. He raised his gun in warning and the line reversed direction.

Winter yanked them against the wall and surveyed the mounting chaos, looking for an alternate escape route. "There," he said, nodding toward a shadowed door hidden behind a standing screen, where pitchers of water sat on a console table. They slipped around the edge of the anxious crowd and made their way there.

It may have taken a minute, but it felt like an hour to sneak toward the unwatched door. She kept her eye on the Feds as they went. When they were a few feet away, one of the younger agents looked their way.

"Winter," Aida whispered as the man raised a rifle.

"Go." He shoved her behind the screen as the Fed shouted in their direction. Her hand shot out for the door handle. Unlocked! They burst through the door and found themselves in a small back hallway.

"Kitchen?" she said, hearing clamor behind a set of swinging doors.

"Obvious place to find liquor—might be blocked with Prohis on the other side," he said, pulling her down the hallway. "We need to get to the front desk without being seen."

That sounded like the *last* place they needed to be.

"Trust me." They sprinted together, Winter leading her through back corridors of the hotel, inside a supply room, up stairs, down stairs, squeezing past rolling luggage carts until they finally made it to the front desk. Two Feds guarded the front entrance as another argued with the concierge and someone who appeared to be hotel management.

They hid behind an elaborate floral arrangement and waited. Aida's heart knocked inside her chest. Winter gripped her hand so hard it began to throb. She peeked around the flowers to see the hotel manager's face reddening as his voice rose—the raid was an outrage, he was saying. They were ruining his guests' evening and besmirching the hotel's sterling reputation. When the Fed turned his back to answer the manager, Winter jerked her toward the registration desk. "Up and over," he whispered, lifting her by the hips onto the curved counter. She scooted across as he leapt the desk neatly and helped her down on the other side.

At the end of the counter, a door led to a small room with several large safes. Dead end. "Can we wait it out here?" she whispered. "We can't walk out the front door. Will they recognize you? Do the Feds know you?"

"Oh, they know me, all right. And we're not going through the front door. He stood on tiptoes and touched something on the wood paneling. Part of the wall opened to reveal a small door; he opened it.

Aida peered into darkness until he flipped a switch. A string of temporary warehouse lights illuminated a steep set of stairs, from which cool, dank air wafted. "What is this?" she whispered. "A basement?"

"This," he said as he urged her down the stairs, "is a tunnel that runs beneath the road. They dug it when prohibition passed. Used to be a glass bridge between the Palace and the building across the street—before the earthquake leveled the hotel, which gave someone the idea for the tunnel. We drop off shipments at a gentleman's club called House of Shields, and the hotel stashes it there and only takes what it needs a little at a time through the tunnel. That's why the Feds aren't going to get the big bust they want tonight. They'll haul a few people away—high-profile guests, if they can nab 'em—but the hotel's fairly clean."

The tunnel was narrow and poorly lit, the walls lined with brick and patchy concrete. Winter's head nearly bumped the arched ceiling . . . the head that had been between her legs a half hour ago. Had she really just let him do that to her?

His shadowed face peered down at her. "Hello."

"Hello."

"Still okay?" he asked in a teasing voice.

*God, yes.* "As long as we don't go to jail." She felt a low, erratic rumbling in the soles of her broken shoes and looked up.

"Cars and trolleys," he said.

"We're under the street right now?"

"We are."

Rather exciting. The passageway was barely wide enough for the two of them to walk abreast. Their feet kicked up dust from the concrete. "Does this happen a lot?" Aida asked.

"Raids? Not really. It did in the early days, or so my father said."

"Do you worry about your customers giving you up if they're caught? Your employees?"

"I don't have a paperwork trail leading away from my customers, and my people know that they'll make more money keeping their mouth shut than ratting me out. Feds questioned my father once in '23. They couldn't make the charge stick."

"Are they watching you?"

"Off and on. I employ a lot of people—dispatchers, truck drivers, ship crews, warehouse workers. So on one hand, I generate a lot of money, and that always gets the Feds' attention. But I don't make as much as a couple other bootleggers in town, and I don't pursue other illegal enterprises— gambling houses, narcotics, that sort of thing."

"Do you worry?"

"All the time," he said, steering them around a murky puddle. "But I've made some changes to the way my father set things up. I've ditched most of the high-risk customers, I pay taxes on the fishing business, and I bribe the police, which keeps things quiet."

He sounded nonchalant, but she knew better. Though half the city might see bootleggers as Robin Hood figures, if his illegal import operation was ever uncovered, he could go to jail. For years and years. Lose his house. Be unable to take care of his family. Maybe his dead wife had legitimate reasons to worry. This kind of business certainly wasn't for the faint of heart.

Then again, neither was what she did for a living.

He changed the subject. "You know President Harding died here four years ago."

"Sure. Everyone knows that. Apoplexy in a penthouse suite at the hotel."

"Nope. He died across the street in an apartment above the House of Shields, drunker than the devil with a bed full of women. His aides dragged his body through the tunnel so that he'd be found in his hotel room and his family spared the disgrace."

"No!"

"Oh yes. He—"

The sight blocking their path halted them in their tracks.

A short man stood in the middle of the tunnel, his face lit by the string of crude lights scalloping the wall. His suit was so wet, Aida could hear water dripping from his sleeves onto the concrete floor. His face was striated and bloated; his eyes were solid white—no pupils or irises.

It didn't take Aida's cold breath to prove to either of them that the bloated man was a ghost.

# EIGHTEEN

---

**NOT AGAIN.**

Winter stared at the bloated corpse of Arnie Brown standing several yards down the tunnel while his mind flashed back to the day he died. It was almost three years ago, right after he'd married Paulina and moved them into their Beaux Arts home on Russian Hill. He'd been fighting with her about Bo. Winter thought she was worried about Bo's character, as she complained that things were missing around the house, and the obvious culprit in her mind was a boy who'd been raised as a thief. But there was more to it. She didn't trust Bo because his mind and mouth were both sharp. She also didn't trust him because he was Chinese.

Winter and Bo had stayed out late one night making a deal at the pier—rather, trying to save a deal that Winter's father had nearly lost after berating a client during one of his manic fits. After the deal was salvaged, Bo was telling Winter he'd rather move out of the Russian Hill house than have Paulina insult him with accusations of stealing. Winter knew he hadn't stolen anything. Hell, he knew Bo's character better than he knew his own wife's. Spent more time with him, too. But Bo had his pride, and Winter was caught between it and the burden of having to placate his parochial wife.

That long-ago night, as Bo locked up the back door on the pier, Winter had walked the dock and came face-to-face with the man he'd just renegotiated the deal with—Arnie Brown. Arnie had a gun and was prepared to kill Winter so he could rob the booze being held at the pier. But the bullet grazed Winter's arm when Bo sneaked around and grabbed Arnie from behind. The three of them grappled, but it was actually Bo who shoved the man off the pier. He couldn't swim.

And now he was slowly shuffling down the tunnel toward Winter and Aida, bloated as he was the day the police found him floating a mile down the bay.

"Coins," Aida said, already rummaging through his coat pockets.

As they backed away from Arnie's ghost, he checked all his inner pockets . . . pants pockets. Nothing.

"Nothing tasted funny at dinner, did it?" she asked. "You aren't poisoned again?"

"No, no—I felt strange almost immediately last time."

Aida pulled off his hat and felt around under the band. "Shoes?"

"I've had those on the entire time we were in the room together."

Arnie's ghost picked up speed, shuffling with greater intent.

They backed up several feet, but Winter realized now that they were trapped. Couldn't go back the way they came dragging a ghost with them into the middle of the raid. Couldn't go forward. He hand went to his gun holster. The last ghost was solid—if Arnie was, too, could he be shot?

"No," Aida said when he withdrew his handgun. "You might slow him down at best, might not. Let me see if I can send him away."

"Absolutely not."

"Absolutely yes. It's a ghost, for God's sake. This is my territory, not yours. Let me try."

He hesitated. Released the gun's safety. "I'll stay right behind you."

"Don't shoot me."

"I'll do my best."

Aida stalked down the tunnel toward the ghost a little too fast for Winter's preference. The inexperienced woman in the hotel room was all confidence now. No fear. Winter supposed it was good that he had enough for both of them.

The ghost was grotesque, his face an unearthly color. No life behind his eyes, yet he walked. And unlike the brutal shock Winter had felt when he recognized the ghost of Dick Jepsen, he felt something different now: a slow-building anger.

A few feet from Arnie, Aida blew out a hard blast of cold air and charged forward with one hand extended. The slap of her mortal flesh against his ghostly chest echoed off the tunnel walls. White sparks shot through his form. The tunnel lights dimmed and popped on and off.

"Arghh!" Aida jerked her hand back like it was on fire and shook it out. "That hurt!"

Enough of this bullshit. Winter grabbed her around the waist and pulled her backward, away from the ghost.

"He won't budge," she said, breathing hard as she twisted out of his grip and stood her ground. "Feels strange—solid, but unreal."

"Move behind me or so help me God, I'll put you over my shoulder. And do not touch that thing again. It's dangerous, Aida. Jesus! Here he comes again. Move!"

"All right, I'm moving." She ducked under his gun arm and started to shuffle past him, then grabbed his coat. "Buttons . . . Winter! Four of your buttons don't match. They're—"

He glanced down quickly, shifting his gaze back and forth from the coat to the approaching ghost. She was right—they didn't match. They weren't cabochon. In fact, they were embossed with dragon heads and looked as if they'd been hurriedly sewn, with loose threads sticking out like spider legs.

Four coins. Four buttons . . .

Some rat bastard had switched them out during dinner when he'd checked his coat. He'd been so desperate to get Aida's clothes off—and back *on*, when the raid started—that he hadn't noticed. That was careless and stupid.

Aida didn't wait for permission. Just ripped them off and spun around to face Arnie. "After these, are you?" She held the fisted buttons above her head.

The ghost's head tilted as dead eyes tracked the magic inside them.

"Ha!" she said triumphantly. "You want these, huh?" She shook the buttons in her hand like she was baiting a disobedient puppy.

Arnie's bloated body lunged for her. So fast! Winter's heart nearly exploded in shock.

She jerked away from the ghost but dropped one of the buttons. It bounced off a wall and skipped across the tunnel's uneven floor.

Winter froze.

The ghost stumbled against the wall, lumbering, then bent to pick up the fallen button.

"Goddammit, throw the rest of them, Aida!" Winter shouted.

As the ghost stood up and refocused his attention on her, she shifted her gaze to some sort of sawed-off drainage pipe jutting from the wall where it was embedded. Dirty water dripped from the pipe's hollow mouth. "If you want them, old man, you'll have to find them," she said to the ghost, then clamped her hand over the pipe and forced the buttons inside. They made a horrible racket as they clanged through the pipe—first sideways, straight into the wall, then down. Yes, definitely down below the tunnel.

Pulse pounding, Winter snatched Aida backward, ignoring her protests. He brandished his gun at the ghost and they both watched him, waiting for a reaction.

Arnie Brown walked to the pipe. Turned to face the wall. And walked right through it.

"Mother of God," Winter whispered.

"Unbelievable. Did you see that?" Aida said, unmistakable awe in her voice.

Yes, he damn well did, and he wasn't sticking around to find out if the ghost was going to reappear. All he knew was that he didn't have the damn buttons to attract it back and that was enough for him. He whisked Aida through the tunnel's length, looking back over his shoulder a couple of times. It wasn't until they climbed the steps to the House of Shields' storage room and shut the tunnel door that he holstered his gun and allowed himself to relax.

He'd been stupid to let his guard down. Whoever wanted to scare him wasn't finished. Was he going to have to endure the sight of every person he'd killed? The list wasn't long, but he sure as hell didn't want to relive it.

It came back to him again, the memory of Arnie Brown's death. Winter hadn't killed him—Bo had. Was the ghost gone now that the buttons were sitting under the street? What if the sorcerer sent another set of four Bo's way?

"Did you know him?" Aida asked from his side. "Was he like the other ghost?"

Winter nodded as another dusty memory popped into his head. After Bo and Winter had watched Arnie Brown drown in the bay, they'd gone back home to his house on Russian Hill. The police were in his parlor, talking to Paulina as she stood in her robe and slippers while they hauled Mr. Johnson away in handcuffs. It was the cook. She'd blamed Bo, but it was the cook the whole time—one she'd brought with her from her mother's house.

"What?"

He glanced down at Aida's confused face. Had he said that out loud? Maybe seeing Arnie Brown had unnerved him more than he wanted to admit.

"Nothing," he said. "I have to . . . I need to check on Bo."

# NINETEEN

———⁂———

IT WAS ALMOST MIDNIGHT WHEN THE TAXI DROPPED HER OFF AT Golden Lotus and immediately sped Winter away to God knew where. To find Bo, he'd said after he'd briefly explained how Arnie Brown had come to his grisly end. And to warn his men about the raid.

She wanted to go with him, but he was a bull about refusing her. Said he wasn't dragging her into danger. When she protested, he kissed her soundly—an unfair trick. "I'm not going to sit around worrying about you," she'd said grumpily when he left.

And she *didn't* worry about him . . . not much, anyway. She actually meant to, no matter what she'd said, and she stayed up for an hour or so, in case he called needing her for another ghost. But as soon as her back hit the creaking Murphy bed, she was out. Probably Winter's erotic exertions in the hotel room that did it. That was certainly what she was dreaming about when the telephone rang the following morning.

She almost never got calls. Especially not before noon, and the little pink Westclox by her bed said it wasn't quite ten, so the call couldn't be for her. But as she laid her head back down, it rang again. She snatched the earpiece off the hook.

"Hello?"

"Were you sleeping?" Winter. His low voice hummed through the line.

"No, no . . . not sleeping."

"You were."

"Yes," she admitted with a laugh. "Wait—is everything okay? You're not calling from a shady doctor after some gangster pumped a few bullets into your legs, are you?"

"Nothing that dramatic."

"Bo is okay?"

"Yes, fine. I'll tell you everything that happened over breakfast, if you'll join me."

"For breakfast?"

"You *have* heard of this meal, yes? The one served before lunch?"

"I'm usually too busy sleeping to bother."

"Well, you've done yourself a great disservice, because breakfast is the best meal of the day. My absolute favorite meal. There are few things I like more than breakfast. Very few."

Aida twirled the telephone cord around her finger and smiled to herself. "You don't say?"

"Pancakes. Bacon. Eggs."

"All right. I might be able to crawl out of bed for bacon."

"That's my girl. You work tonight?"

"Eight o'clock show."

"Did you have plans this afternoon?"

"Not a single one."

"How about breakfast first, then we spend the afternoon having spectacular sex."

She dropped the earpiece and fumbled around in the sheets to retrieve it.

"Aida?"

"I'm here," she said as her racing pulse tripped.

"I'm going crazy for you. Please don't say no."

"Okay. Yes."

He made a small, satisfied noise. "I'm at the Fairmont in Nob Hill. California and Mason. I had a long night, so I just got a room here rather than go home. I'll call Jonte to come pick you up—"

And have the driver gossip to the rest of the Magnusson staff that he took Aida to Winter's hotel room? "I can take a streetcar," she said quickly.

"Are you sure?"

"I take them every day."

"Be careful and keep an eye open for—"

"Ghosts?"

He grunted. "That's a smart mouth you have, young lady."

"You liked kissing it well enough last night."

"Mmm, I liked kissing all of you last night."

Aida flopped back on her pillow and grinned wildly at the ceiling.

He gave her the suite number. "Just come straight up. No need to stop at the desk."

An hour later, stomach somersaulting with nervous energy, Aida was stepping off a streetcar into a terrible storm that came out of nowhere. The skies were perfect and blue when she left her apartment—a genuine summer day, for a change—and now she was dashing through puddles as a black sky opened up and hurtled torrents of rain. By the time she'd skidded onto the marble floor of the Fairmont's column-lined lobby, she was drenched from head to toe and completely miserable. Her reflection in the glass door was not kind. What in the world was she doing here, anyway? Racing across town to meet a man in a hotel . . . it was disgraceful.

She considered going back home, but the lure of promised spectacular sex overrode both her pride and shame. She shook rain off her thin coat and cloche hat, ran fingers through her dripping hair, and marched past staring eyes to the elevator. *Everyone knows what I'm doing here.* A few minutes later, she was standing in front of his room, teetering somewhere between a mild nervousness and a raging panic. She knocked on the door, prepared to flee if he didn't answer in five seconds, four seconds, three—

The door swung open.

Winter's big body filled the doorway. His hair was wet and neatly combed back, dark as rich soil, and he was wearing nothing but a white damask hotel towel wrapped around his hips.

Smelling of soap and shampoo, he propped his forearm on the doorframe. Everything below was all long, ropy arm muscles, bunching shoulders, and that massive chest of his, covered in damp hair. Her gaze dropped to admire impossibly thick thighs. The towel was *just* big enough to tuck around all . . . that.

This certainly didn't look like breakfast.

She shivered, whether from cold or anticipation or fear, she didn't know.

"Christ alive, Aida. You're shivering."

"I don't own an umbrella."

He pulled her inside the room with a firm hand on her shoulder. "Get in here before you catch pneumonia."

This room was just as exquisite and decadent as the Palace's, filled with heavy brocade draperies and beautiful furniture, and what might have been one of the finest views of the city if not for the storm. "You have a balcony?"

"Unless you want to get electrocuted, I'd advise that you wait until the storm's over before venturing out there." After helping her out of her coat and cloche, he pulled her through the sitting room and into a small bedroom. A second set of glass doors on the far wall opened up to the same balcony, only the doors were wide open there, letting in a cool, damp breeze that sent another shiver through her. She caught another glimpse of the storm-wracked cityscape before Winter made a sharp right and urged her into a brightly lit bathroom. "Get your shoes off," he said, reaching for a stack of thin towels that matched the one around his waist.

She obeyed without thinking, toeing off her Mary Janes at the heels, leaning on a gold-fauceted vanity for balance.

Her hand touched metal. A small round tin stamped with the words MERRY WIDOWS and a quantity: 3. It took her a moment to realize what was inside.

She wrinkled her nose, half embarrassed, half offended. "I'm not disease ridden."

"Neither am I. What's the matter?"

"It makes me feel cheap."

"I don't know why. They aren't just for disease. I'm not exactly the best candidate for fatherhood at the moment. What precautions have you previously taken?"

"I guess I got lucky," she admitted. "It was only the two times."

"I suppose if your lovers were incompetent enough to fail you in other ways, it should come as no surprise that they didn't care enough to see to this, either."

She'd never thought of it that way, but it made her feel both grateful and ashamed at the same time. Her brain searched for a witty retort, but she was too frazzled to fight.

"One thing at a time, okay?" He slid the tin out of her reach, kicked her shoes aside, and began toweling off her hair. "You look like a homeless beggar," he said with amusement in his voice.

"I feel like one." She was relieved to change subjects.

He tossed the damp towel on the tiled floor and picked up another, then stopped to look at her. "I know you're not going to be happy about this, but there's really no way around it, so this is what's going to happen. I'm going to take off your wet clothes, and I'm going to look at the scars on your hips."

She squeezed her eyes shut, groaning under her breath.

Winter pushed back her damp bangs with one swooping, warm palm and dropped a gentle kiss on her forehead. "I scare children on the street." His fingers reached for the hem of her striped top. "If you are black and blue and grossly disfigured, I will not even blink."

She raised her arms as he pulled her top over her head. "It's not that bad," she mumbled.

"Has your skin turned green and putrid?" he said in a

teasing voice as he slipped his hands around her back to unfasten her bandeau brassiere.

"No."

"Does it look like you've been run over by a lawn mower?"

"No."

Winter paused to look at her as cool air breezed across her bare breasts. The front of his towel expanded, temporarily distracting her from his fingers, which were unbuttoning and sliding off her skirt. When she stood in nothing but stockings and lacy-edged silk tap pants, her anxiety ramped back up. She stared at the wall as he tugged her stockings down.

"Aida," he commanded as he stood. "Look at my face."

The bright light from the bathroom vanity made his good pupil constrict to a fine black point—a drastic contrast to his dilated eye. He pressed a kiss between her brows and slowly rubbed his hands up and down her arms. "It's only me."

"I know," she replied as her muscles began relaxing under his petting hands. "That's what makes it worse."

"Why?"

"Because—" She lost her train of thought when his hands moved from her arms to her waist. Before she could protest, warm palms slipped beneath the waist of her tap pants and ran down her hips.

"I can barely feel them." A moment later, silk slid down her legs, and there was nothing she could do but endure his inspection. Dense patches of toughened, bumpy skin started at the outer curve of her lower hips and spread down, mid-thigh, each patch about the size of her hand. The freckles both hid the scars and made them more noticeable in places.

"This is what you're worried about?" he said, running the pads of his fingers over her scars. "How long have you had them?"

She let out a long breath. "Since I began working nightclubs. They've gotten thicker over the last year. And I know you can see them, so don't tell me you can't."

"Yes, I can see them," he said softly.

"I've tried to use the lancet on other places, but this is the easiest to hide onstage."

He studied the other hip and brushed his knuckles over a tender spot. "It's red here."

"That was from two nights ago, my last show. I try to switch sides every show."

"Probably wise." His hand ran up the scars, over the upper curve of her hip, up her ribs. Then he cupped her breasts, catching her off guard. "Now, are we done with this ridiculousness?"

"Yes," she said, feeling as if she'd cleared some small hurdle or received a passing grade on a test. And when he traced circles around her nipples with his thumbs, she gasped for breath and forgot about the scars altogether.

"Good." The erection tenting his towel brushed against her stomach. "See what you do to me?" he whispered roughly against her hair. "Even the sound of your voice makes me hard. Your smile . . . your laugh. You smell so damn good. Christ, Aida—you turn me into a babbling fool."

*"Winter."* Her forehead fell against the damp hair on his chest. He was always so warm.

"I want you, cheetah. Every inch, scars and all. I want all of you."

His words emboldened her. The corner of towel tucked into his waist looked as though it wouldn't take much effort to come loose. She took hold of that corner and tugged.

# TWENTY

———◆———

AIDA STARED AT WINTER'S HARD COCK. SHE COULDN'T HELP IT. IT was long and shockingly thick, jutting proudly from a forest of dark curls. And it curved upward at the end like the stalk of a shaded plant desperately seeking sunlight.

His knuckles brushed her belly as he casually took himself in hand. One stroke pulled the foreskin back to expose a fat, glistening tip. "What do you think?" he asked, half mischievous, half serious, as if he already knew the answer but wanted to hear her say it.

What did she *think*?

She thought he was bigger and more exciting than anything she'd seen before. She thought maybe the crazy pornographic drawing on that wicked postcard of his wasn't as exaggerated as she'd believed.

After another stroke, he aimed toward her hip and rubbed himself across the scars there. It could've been crude; it wasn't. He was speaking to her in a primal language she was disarmed to realize she not only understood, but craved.

She wanted to speak that language, too.

When she reached between them, he guided her hand to

replace his. He was shockingly hot and smooth, velvet over a core of steel. The fingers circling his girth did not meet her thumb.

She ran her palm down his length and felt him shudder. His hands cupped the back of her head as he kissed her hotly, his tongue filling her mouth above as he filled her hand below. She was inexplicably happy, feeling an urge to plea-sure him, to make him feel as good as she'd felt last night. He made low, hungered noises as she stroked him with more confidence, then pulled back on a groan. "You have to stop," he said in a gravelly voice. "I've wanted you too badly for too long."

A thrill raced through her.

He urged her toward the bathroom door, grabbing the round tin off the vanity along the way, then herded her to the bed.

Rain pounded on the balcony a few feet away. Cool wind carried scents of the city into the room—concrete and rust and brick—as they crawled onto the bed together. He dropped the tin on the embroidered matelassé coverlet and wrapped her in his arms, kissing her mouth, her neck.

Pleasure rippled over her, flooding her body from the out-side in as they rolled together. They were skin to skin: her breasts pressed against the whorls of hair covering his chest, his erection trapped against her belly, her legs tangling with his, intertwined. Just this indulgence alone was an extrava-gance, and she explored the planes and contours of his body, touching him freely without shame.

Such a joy.

She marveled at how solid he was. Not just his chest and arms, but his back. Muscles she'd never felt before on another man. Her hands found the twin dimples above his buttocks that she'd often fantasized about touching since spotting them at Velma's. And when she pressed her fingers into those dimples and traced their shape, his mouth opened wide against her cheek—

And he *bit* her.

Not hard. Not gentle, either.

It was startling. Strange. And it sent desire racing over her skin in waves. When he licked the place he'd bitten, her hips pushed against him, a response she couldn't have controlled if she tried. He pushed back, rubbing his length against the triangle of hair between her legs. "Are you wet for me?" he whispered against her cheek.

"Yes."

He frisked her curls with questing fingers, cupping her as she spread her legs. When he touched her aching center, she cried out and moved against his hand. "All of this for me?" he murmured, kissing her ear as he began stroking her. "You're amazing."

Her eyes fluttered shut as she gave in and relished the intense sensations he stoked up as he rubbed a thumb down and around her clitoris, making her whimper. It was too much, too intense. "Please—"

"Please, what?" He slid a thick finger inside her. "This?"

"Yes." Her voice sounded far away as he stroked her, putting pressure against the same aching place he had the night before. A second finger stretched her. Then he pushed deeper, twisting those fingers inside her, as if he were testing. *Making a way for himself*, she thought, and contracted around him, testing back. He groaned.

Extracting his fingers, he rubbed his thumb along her swollen entrance and pushed himself up to kneel on one knee. She lay on her back and blinked up at him, squirming under his touch, her gaze moving over his chiseled, aroused body. He took her hand and guided it between her legs, pressing her own fingers on top of his, slick and warm. So foreign and intimate to feel him there. Until he moved his hands away. She started to retreat as well, but he stopped her. "No, keep them right there."

"Winter—"

He reached for the metal tin. "I want to watch you keeping yourself ready for me."

She hesitated, but savage instincts took over.

"Yes, just like that. Most beautiful thing I've ever seen."

He watched her dazedly for a moment, eyes hooded, then pried the lid off the tin and retrieved a small piece of rolled rubber cinched in the middle by a sleeve of paper. She'd never seen one before, and watched in fascination as Winter removed the paper band and fit the rubber sheath over his tip. "Don't stop," he instructed, eyes between her legs. Only when she continued did he unroll the sheath over the length of his cock, practically strangling it.

"Looks uncomfortable," she said, more compliment than criticism.

"It's a tight fit. But you'll be even tighter, and I can't wait. Come here." He slung an arm under one of her thighs and tugged her closer, parting her legs wider, until he was kneeling between them. Prodding her fingers away, he took himself in hand and rubbed the head back and forth through her slickness. It felt extraordinary. Better than his fingers. And when he settled himself against her entrance, her heart hammered furiously.

Everything seemed to pause as her awareness sharpened in that hanging moment. She smelled the city rain, felt it mist across her arm as the wind blew. She felt the mattress springs beneath her back. Saw the diffused light from the bedside lamp and heard the alarm clock softly ticking.

And then he pushed inside her, and it all disappeared.

She cried out in surprise, her shoulders coming off the bed as her muscles tensed. It was too much, all at once. He was too big; she was too small. An unyielding fullness that stretched her uncomfortably. And he was barely inside her. Without thinking, she tried to scoot away.

"It's okay," he assured her in a strained voice, flattening his palm on her stomach while the other hand reached for her hip. "Just relax. I'm not going to move."

She remained propped up on her elbows, breasts heaving, willing herself to calm. But she didn't have to try. He was right. It was okay. It was *so* okay, after a few moments she found herself tilting her hips upward to urge him deeper inside. He groaned and pushed with her, then retreated, pulling all the way out. Her body instantly changed its mind and decided she was now empty and aching, which was far worse than before. "Winter," she pleaded sharply, unable to communicate anything more. By some miracle, he understood, and was pushing back into her again, this time fully, all in one long stroke.

Nothing had ever felt so good.

Nothing.

The moan that came out of her mouth twined with his, carried through the open balcony doors, and got lost in the storm as he began moving inside her. She tried to remain still, vaguely remembering Freddy's complaints that she moved too much, but when she lost herself and rotated her hips, Winter said in a tortured voice, "That's right—grind on me. Christ, you feel good."

She fell back and adjusted her legs, trying to find a place to put them. Everything about him was big—even his hips— and she was unsure of herself. He seemed to understand her floundering and lowered himself over her body, resting his weight on forearms that pressed into the mattress on either side of her head. Then he hooked one of her legs around his waist and sunk deeper into her.

"O-o-oh."

"Too much?"

She wrapped her other leg around him in answer.

"Dig your heels into my ass," he commanded roughly. She did. It opened her legs wider and changed the angle again.

"Yes!" she cried out with more enthusiasm than intended. "Oh yes!"

He chuckled in response, and she felt so happy, she laughed, too, breathless. Then his mouth found hers and she accepted it, greedily kissing him back as he rocked into her steadily. A lock of dark, damp hair brushed across her face as he dipped his head to her neck, sucking and kissing. His shoulders bunched. She ran her hands through the hair on his chest, then skimmed around his sides, feeling every taut muscle in his broad torso tight and hard and shifting beneath her exploring fingers as he moved.

She made strange, savage noises, but he felt so good, she couldn't make herself care.

"Aida, my God," he whispered against her ear. "You feel like heaven. So perfect. Even better than I imagined."

Her pleasure was honed by his words, abruptly quickening. The slick muscles at her center wanted to clench and bear down on him, but he was too big. She cried out in frustration, feeling the urgency of what was coming, almost frightened by it.

And it was gathering within her with alarming speed.

If he'd brought her to orgasm the night before with his fingers and mouth, that was one thing. This was wholly different. He was *inside* her. Sharing the same pleasure. Filling her. Surrounding her. She was humbled by the intensity of emotions that bloomed at the horizon and raced her thundering heart.

"Goddamn," Winter cursed appreciatively as her center constricted around him again, this time with greater success.

"Oh, *God*, Winter! Please don't stop."

"I won't, I won't," he said, pumping his hips with urgency. "Come for me, *älskling*."

She grasped his solid shoulders, slick with sweat. Her breath caught as she tightened around him a final time. Deliverance rocketed her to great heights and the world fell away. Euphoric spasms pulsed through her center, bringing wave after wave of astonishing pleasure. She shook. She whimpered. And just when she began to fall back down to earth, Winter pounded into her a handful of times with such intense strength, she opened her eyes to watch him.

Mouth slack and wide, he bucked, squinted his eyes closed, and bellowed out an extended cry that reverberated through her as he shuddered in her arms like a great, divine beast taken down by a single bullet.

She didn't know if she was the gun that fired the bullet or the hunter who'd pulled the trigger, but when he rolled to his side, taking her with him, and she heard his heartbeat pound in time with hers, slowing and heavy, she felt an unyielding sense of brutal possession and knew she had made a terrible miscalculation.

She was the one who'd been shot.

# TWENTY-ONE

***

WINTER TOOK ONE LAST SWIG OF COFFEE, THEN PUSHED THE ROLLing cart away from the bed with his bare foot. Two in the afternoon might be a brow-raising time for breakfast service, but the hotel staff didn't argue when he phoned down the request.

"That was the best meal I've had in years," Aida said from his side, propped up on feather pillows. One bent freckled leg peeked out from beneath the white sheets. "Maybe there's something about your pro-breakfast stance."

He rolled onto his left hip to face her. "Stick with me and you'll eat breakfast every day."

She gave him a slow smile and closed her eyes, the picture of satisfaction. This is how he wanted to see her, stretching like a cat, cheeks flushed, eyes lazy. Unable to do anything more than lift a spoon. "Are they your customers?" she asked.

"Who?"

"This hotel."

"No," he said, eyeing the open condom tin on the bedside table. Only one of three left, dammit. He should've bought another tin. He'd never gone through an entire one in an afternoon; then again, he'd never bedded a woman who was so eager to help him empty it. "They aren't one of my customers. They just lost their supplier."

She cracked open one eye. "Does this have to do with the raid last night?"

"Raids, and yes."

"Tell me everything. Where did you go after you left?"

Winter heard his father's voice somewhere in the back of his mind, reciting a list of rules for bootlegging. *Never tell a woman details* was one of them. He'd warned him that pillow talk was the downfall of many a great man, and forbid him to tell even Paulina where their warehouses were, who their customers were, when the mother ships from Canada came into port. And he never did, mainly because Paulina never wanted to know.

While he was trying to decide how much to tell her, his eyes fell on the golden locket around her neck. "What's inside?" he asked, fingering the engraved floral pattern on the front.

"Just a photograph." She sounded defensive, which set off warning bells inside his head. He clicked the small mechanism on the side before she could stop him. A tiny oval photograph was set inside. A young man.

"Who is this?"

"No one." She tried to shut it, but he wouldn't let her. "Stop. It's just Sam."

"One of your lovers?"

"No," she said. "Sam Palmer. My brother."

Winter was confused. "You told me you lived with a foster family."

"I did. The Lanes. Sam and I were rescued from the earthquake together. He was a year older than me."

He studied the photograph with greater interest. Perhaps there was some resemblance, hard to tell. Then he remembered what she told him when they were walking in Chinatown. *Everyone I've loved is dead.* "You said Sam *was* a year older than you. Is he . . ."

"Sam and I lived with the Lanes together in Baltimore until he turned eighteen. He joined the army in 1916 after President Wilson called for volunteers."

"Did he end up in the war?"

"He got assigned to a cantonment in Virginia. He was there for six months, and was due to be deployed overseas when America entered the war. He was shot during a training exercise. Just a fluke accident." In a blink, her eyes became bleary. "I didn't take it well. We were inseparable. He was my only real family—you know, flesh and blood."

"I'm sorry."

She gave him a tight smile. "The Lanes were killed in a train derailment a month later. I was seventeen. They had some money— not a lot, but they weren't poor. Only, they never officially adopted us. They thought they had, but Sam and I kept our surname. We called them Aunt and Uncle since we were little. And I think the surname confusion was mishandled in the paperwork. I don't think they ever knew. Mr. Lane's brother showed up for the funeral, and within two weeks, he'd fired the staff, sold the house, and dumped me off at an orphanage. This photograph is the only thing I was allowed to take with me. That and the clothes on my back."

"Christ alive, Aida."

"Good old Emmett Lane. Lovely man," she said sourly. "I'd only met him once before. He never gave a damn about his own family, much less Sam and me, so it wasn't a big surprise in hindsight." She snapped the locket shut. "Anyway, I lived in the orphanage until I finished school. It wasn't pleasant. When I turned eighteen, I got out of there as fast as I could and struck out on my own. Sam always told me to be independent, count on myself, no one else. And he never was afraid of my talents— he encouraged them."

"Could he . . . do what you can do?"

She shook her head. "I started seeing ghosts when we moved to Baltimore. The Lanes just thought I was having nightmares about the earthquake, but Sam believed me. I didn't know I had channeling skills until he introduced me to another medium before he joined the army. Mrs. Stone. She took me under her wing after I left the orphanage. Gave me a room for a few months, showed me how to make money with my talents. Got me on my feet."

"And you've been on your own for ten years?"

"Never look back, always move forward—that's what Sam always said. He wouldn't want me feeling sorry for myself, so I don't. I just keep getting up every day and moving along." She smiled again, this time more genuinely.

"Live in the moment," he said, repeating her sentiment from the night before.

"Exactly. Sam believed in the value of independence, and I honor his memory by appreciating today."

So confident. But anyone could see the sadness beneath her bravado.

They were alike in a way. Both had lost their parents, and though he'd lost Paulina, Aida had not only lost a second set of parents, but her brother.

And then she was forced to support herself with no family help?

He tried to imagine Astrid in the same predicament and wondered how she'd fare. It made him feel ill to think about her utterly on her own. And even without the bootlegging fortune, even when they were just a fishing family, no man in his household would abandon a female. Not Astrid, not his mother, not Greta . . . not even Paulina. What kind of man does that? Not a real one.

Winter suddenly felt both more pity *and* respect for Aida.

"There. Now you know the story of my life," she said.

He pushed her bangs back from her forehead and kissed her there, softly, lingering. When he pulled back, she met his gaze and something passed between them. Something that made his chest tighten. He just wasn't sure what it was.

She quickly redirected the subject. "So, you were about to tell me what happened last night with the raids."

Oh . . . that again. He'd only known Aida for a couple of weeks, and already he'd violated all sorts of rules with her— his father was probably rolling over in his grave. But when she looked up at him with those big brown eyes, all he could hear was her angry accusation during their fight on the ride back from Ju's: *I told you things about me.*

And now she'd told him even more.

His father had been right, no doubt. It was a sensible warning. But Winter was tired of being sensible. He'd tell her everything, give her the combination to his basement vault and all his bank account numbers if she'd meet him in this hotel room every day. As long as she'd look up at him like this, trustful and expectant, genuinely curious about his work—not plugging her ears and pretending he was somebody other than he really was, like Paulina had.

"You haven't seen the headlines?" he asked.

"You might recall waking me up," she said, lifting the sheet to cover her breast. "I came straight here, because I apparently have no self-control around you."

His heart leapfrogged joyfully. He dropped a kiss on her nose and sat up to fetch the newspaper from the cart. "There were five raids at five hotels last night," he said, pointing out the *Chronicle*'s headline. "All of them were executed within minutes of one another. The Feds were tipped off that this man would be personally delivering a big shipment to one of the hotels."

Aida skimmed the article, reading aloud under her breath. Her fingernail traced the caption below the old man's photo. "Adrian St. Laurent. He looks like a nice old grandfather."

Winter snorted. "I've known him for years. His operation is smaller than mine, though he used to be part of the Big Three in the Bay Area—and before you ask, yes, I'm one of them."

"Oh, I seriously doubt any of them are as big as you," she teased, circling a finger around his thumb as she continued to read the article.

"Keep talking like that and I'm going to be forced to call up the desk and beg them for a bellboy to go out to the druggist for another tin."

"And I won't be able to walk out of here. Tell me more about the bust."

He slipped an arm beneath her head and settled his leg across hers. "St. Laurent does a lot of cheap deals, but he also has half the hotel business in the city. Had, rather. The Feds' tip was on the nose. They found him in the Whitcomb, eating dinner in the kitchen while his crew unloaded a quarter million in rum for a big fund-raiser party. Had enough evidence to haul him in. Just like that, he's gone."

Winter was shocked when he got wind of the bust last night. If he had any lingering worries about St. Laurent being responsible for his hauntings, those doubts were now gone.

"But why did the Feds show up at the Palace if they're your client?"

Winter folded the newspaper and tossed it on the floor. "They weren't three years ago. Used to be St. Laurent's, but he made a deal with my father when he thought the Feds were after him back then."

"So last night the Feds thought the Palace was one of his."

"Yep."

"They weren't after you."

"Nope." He ran his fingers over the curve of her shoulder. Her skin was so soft, he almost worried his calloused fingers would scrape it, but he couldn't stop himself from tracing random lines of freckles that led to the ridge of her clavicle.

"Do you think that this has any connection with what's going on with you?"

"Raids happen all the time, and there's no indication of anything supernatural going on with this one. But there are two things that worry me. On that first night when I was poisoned, St. Laurent told me something was changing in Chinatown. The tongs who control the booze there are getting pushed out of business."

"And the second thing?"

"Rumor is that the Feds were tipped off by someone in Chinatown."

"O-oh."

"Odd that there's unrest in Chinatown's booze distribution, and someone's attacking me from Chinatown, and now St. Laurent gets hauled away on a tip from Chinatown."

"More than odd." She stared out the balcony doors. "I was thinking about the ghost last night, and those dragon buttons. You think it's a coincidence that they were sewed on, and you know someone in Chinatown with a sewing factory . . ."

"Ju? No. Couldn't be him. That truly has to be coincidence."

"Are you sure? What if Sook-Yin is upset that you haven't been seeing her? What if Ju takes your rejection of her as a rejection of him? And at that lunch, he did make a point about how successful you've become—warned you people would be jealous of that success."

As much as he hated to admit it, things *had* been more relaxed between him and Ju back when he was still visiting Sook-Yin. "I don't know. Ju isn't a big tong leader, but he's not stupid, either. Besides, if he wanted me dead, he's had plenty of opportunities to kill me. Why all the hocus-pocus with the magical poison and the hauntings? Doesn't add up."

"Maybe you're right." She gave him a thoughtful look. "The hotel we're in now wasn't raided. Were they one of St. Laurent's customers?"

"They *were* raided."

"Why aren't they shut down like the Palace?"

"Prohis didn't find any booze. I talked to the manager this morning. Apparently St. Laurent was behind on shipments. Regardless, they are now without a supplier, and in light of everything I just told you, I think it's possible whoever ratted out St. Laurent did so because they either wanted him *out* of business, or they *want* his business."

Intelligent eyes squinted up at him; he liked the way her nostrils flared when she did that. "Is that why you got this room? You waiting to see if anyone shows up to offer the hotel booze?"

"Believe me, I was thinking about you when I checked in."

She hooked her leg around his while her fingers toyed with the line of hair that bisected his stomach. Christ, she was just as bad as he was—they couldn't stop touching each other. "But . . ." she prompted.

"But I might've taken last night's events into consideration when I choose the Fairmont specifically. So I'm going to be nice to the hotel manager, and wait and see what transpires."

Her fingers walked up his breastbone. "And if you can discover who ratted out St. Laurent while helping out the Fairmont with deliveries in their time of need, all the better, yes?"

"Just being a good neighbor."

She laughed, and the sound made his balls tighten. "Winter Magnusson: friendliest man in the city."

"You should've seen the concierge. Nearly pissed his pants when I walked up. I'm nothing if not recognizable," he said, winking his bad eye.

She craned her neck and kissed him there—right on his eyelid—and trailed two more kisses over his scar, then fell back against the pillow, grinning at him prettily. Jesus. Did she know what that did to him? It felt as if she'd poked a hole inside his chest. If she didn't stop, he'd be telling her how he rode around last night in a daze, thinking of the way she trembled beneath his tongue. How much he'd hated leaving her, and how he had to stop himself from calling her at three in the morning when he'd finished his work.

How he couldn't get enough of her, even now. Even after he'd just had her twice, he was getting hard. And not because she was trying to seduce him. Not because she'd been trained for pleasure, like Sook-Yin, and knew exactly what to do to turn him on. But because she was so easy to talk to. Because she laughed and smiled at him without wanting anything in return. Because she made the past disappear.

And because she accepted him freely, scars and all.

"Only one left, huh?" she said, running tiny fingers up the ridge of his cock. "And, let's see . . . four hours before I have to leave. This is very unfair. If you're going to insist on using those things, you better bring more next time."

He laughed and pulled her close, until he felt the peaks

of her nipples against his chest. "Let's be creative and see what we can do without using the last one just yet."

"Creative." She stroked him leisurely, up and down. "Like this?"

He groaned in pleasure. "Exactly like that."

"What about this?" Her fingers strayed lower to his balls, sending soothing shivers through his groin.

"Christ alive, cheetah. That feels nice."

"It does?" She cupped him. "Like this?"

"God, yes. Be gentle, though. Whatever you do, for the love of God, don't squeeze."

"How do you walk around with all this?"

"The same way you walk around with these," he said, massaging one breast.

She made a little moan, then whispered dreamily, "I'm so glad we're having an affair."

"Best idea I ever had," he agreed, and inhaled the scent of violets in her hair.


Aida's performance at Gris-Gris later that night was one of her finest—dramatic, emotional, and enthusiastically applauded. When she left the stage, she wondered if her confidence had been increased since her afternoon with Winter. The sinful hum of well-used flesh lingered as she strolled to her dressing room, and this gave her a puzzling sort of satisfaction.

What was even more puzzling was how happy it made her. Not just the sex, but the experience of being so close to him when his guard was down. What would it be like to have a man like that all the time? Someone to confide in? It seemed like an impossible luxury, to know someone for more than a handful of months. Best to be sensible about things and just enjoy what she had in the moment, not worry about things she couldn't control.

But her future caught up to her as she approached her dressing room door. The club manager, Daniels, was waiting there for her with a tall, slender man dressed in a cream-colored suit. His skin was darkly tanned, as if he spent every daylight hour in the sun, and the sides of his dark blond hair were streaked with silver.

"Miss Palmer, I have someone here to see you," Daniels said formally. "Mr. Bradley Bix from New Orleans. Mr. Bix, this is Miss Palmer."

The speakeasy owner. Of course. He said he'd be here visiting his cousin, but she'd put him out of her mind. Still, it was surprising to see him standing before her now. She shook away a sense of foreboding and picked her manners off the floor. "Mr. Bix, how do you do," she said, extending her arm. "I thought you were coming in another week. I hope your travel was pleasant."

"Three days of jostled sleep, but I made it in one piece," he said with a kind smile, his hand warm and leathery on hers. "I've had some changes to my summer bookings so I thought I'd come see you earlier. I hope you don't mind." He smiled, flashing her a smile. "Your show was spectacular. Just astounding. I'd heard things from people who'd seen you perform on the East Coast, but to watch it in person was a treat."

"Thank you," she said.

"I'd like to offer you an official invitation to perform at the Limbo Room," Mr. Bix said. "We'll buy your train ticket, of course, and my business partner owns a hotel next to the club, so we can also provide a temporary apartment for the duration of your stay in our city."

No one had ever offered her as much. She was immediately wary that the hotel he spoke of was a brothel of some sort. Velma had friends in New Orleans; perhaps she could check on it.

"Is there somewhere we could speak about salary and other details?" Mr. Bix asked.

"Daniels, if you wouldn't mind, please show the gentleman to the bar." He nodded a curt response. "Mr. Bix, it will only take me a few minutes to get ready. I'll meet you out there when I'm done."

Mr. Bix canted his head politely before setting a pale straw Panama hat on his head. "I should mention that I'd like to have your decision rather quickly. I'd need your debut performance to coincide with a spiritualism convention in the French Quarter."

"And when would that be?"

"July 15."

She'd have to be on a train the day after her last night at Gris-Gris if Mr. Bix wanted her onstage that soon.

She should be elated. None of her previous bookings had dovetailed so nicely to provide her with a steady income, so hard to come by in this business. But as Daniels escorted the man back out to the club floor, it was all Aida could do to fight images of Winter's big hand curving around her naked breast, and the lazy satisfaction she'd felt dozing in his arms.

She'd known it wasn't permanent, but now they had less time than she thought.

# TWENTY-TWO

WINTER TOOK A TAXI TO THE FAIRMONT THE NEXT DAY. WHEN HE left Aida the night before, he'd asked her to meet him there at the same time today, but he half expected her to change her mind—maybe she'd have regrets about the things they did with each other. It seemed too good to be true.

A rap on the hotel door made his pulse jump. He rushed to answer it too quickly, but when he threw open the door, it was only an attendant from the kitchen with a cart. The boy cowered under Winter's glare and waved a gloved hand at the pitcher of orange juice and coffee service. "Your order, sir?"

Winter exhaled heavily and signaled the attendant inside the room. After he wheeled the cart into the sitting area, he asked if Winter required anything else, then acted like he was going to bolt for the door; Winter stopped him.

"You know who I am?"

"Yes, sir."

"Anyone asks, you don't." Winter pulled out a stack of bills and removed a gold money clip, then peeled off what was likely a month's worth of the attendant's wages. "Make sure my men outside get coffee and food at lunch. If I'm back tomorrow, I'll give you the same."

The attendant brightened considerably. "Yes, sir. You can count on me."

As Winter handed over the tip, a figure appeared in the doorway. Winter's chest squeezed.

"This is a private room, miss," the attendant said quickly, pocketing the money as he strode to block her entrance.

"Yes," Aida said, tapping her handbag against her leg. "I'm Mrs. Magnusson." She arched one brow Winter's way: teasing, playful, attractively arrogant. Only a day ago—no virgin—she'd been nervous about her sexuality, and now she was brimming with confidence. It gave him a deep-seated satisfaction to know he was responsible for that change.

"*Mrs.* Magnusson?" The attendant gave her a pointed look of disbelief.

"Ah yes," Winter said. "Please don't disturb my . . . wife and I again until I call, unless it's an urgent matter with my men."

The attendant cleared his throat and nodded before exiting.

Aida locked the door, then dropped her handbag and dashed to Winter in a delirious rush. With her arms around his neck, he lifted her off the floor and kissed her like she really *was* his wife and he hadn't seen her in months. She smelled so good, felt so warm and soft, that if relief and gratitude hadn't weighted him down, he might've floated away in happiness.

"What have you done to me?" she said breathlessly when they broke for air. "You've turned me into a fiend, Winter Magnusson."

"There *is* a God," he mumbled against her neck as he pressed kisses on her rapid pulse.

"I went to sleep thinking of you," she whispered, "and woke up wanting you."

A big, bright happiness flooded his senses. *Thank you, thank you, thank you.*

She gave a little squeal of delight as he pushed her back

against the wall. "Please tell me you brought more Merry Widows this time."

"I cleaned out the druggist," he said, grinning down at her. "At the rate we're going, I should own stock in the damn company."

Her happy laugher followed them to the bed.

The Fairmont became their daily routine. Nothing in the outside world interrupted them—not ghosts nor raids nor threats of any supernatural nature. The primary anxiety that plagued Winter came in the form of regular updates from Ju about the liquor trade in Chinatown spiraling out of control. Warehouses had been burned, robbed, smashed up. Infighting broke out among friendly tongs. Everyone suspected their neighbor, but no one knew who was actually leading the shake-up.

It even made the newspapers. Headlines questioned how safe the "new tourist-friendly" Chinatown truly was. Rumors spread of the old pre-earthquake tong wars being revived. It was all anyone talked about at Golden Lotus, Aida reported, and her landlady was worried because the restaurant's business was starting to suffer.

Businesses outside Chinatown were feeling the effects of St. Laurent's raid. The Fairmont was hurting. Winter managed to sneak in a few cases of champagne and whiskey for their important guests, but the manager refused to risk anything more. Winter put more men watching the hotel, but no one had seen or heard anything.

Not until the sixth afternoon, when Winter got the call about Black Star.

Bo's voice was barely audible over the hotel's telephone wire. He had to plug his free ear with his thumb to even hear him.

"Say again, Bo."

"Ju found the man. He's a fortune-teller at Lion Rise Temple, but only on Saturdays, when the tourists come.

We've got three hours before his shift finishes, so we need to leave now."

"I'll be ready in fifteen minutes."

"A couple more things. Ju says the guy isn't affiliated with any tongs. He's probably just a hired gun."

"Then we'll just convince him to tell us who's paying him. What's the other thing?"

"Anthony Parducci turned himself in early this morning."

Winter froze. "What?"

"Showed up at Central Station, spooked as hell, saying the voice of God had spoken to him and told him to turn himself in. They thought he was doped at first, but now they're saying he just went crazy. Police chief tried to talk some sense in him and get him to calm down, but two Feds had stopped by the station and heard what was going on, so they arrested him. Parducci gave up the locations of all his warehouses, suppliers—everything."

"Holy shit."

"Whoever's conducting all this is starting to land some blows."

"I don't want to be the next one. Pick me up out back," Winter said before hanging up.

Aida started dressing before he could even finish telling her. "I'm going with you. If there's any ghost business, you're safer with me along. Especially after the business with this other bootlegger turning himself in. Let's hope this Black Star is your guy."

He watched her rolling the welt of her stocking over a pink garter that sat snugly on her lower thigh, just above her knee. "I might have to threaten him. I don't want you to see that."

"You mean that you don't want me to be repulsed by it," she clarified.

"Yes."

"Well, I won't be. And I trust you will protect me if something goes wrong."

He watched her pull on the second stocking, amazed by her nonchalance. By now he shouldn't be surprised. "All right."

Both stockings were in place now. She stood up, wearing nothing else. Absolutely gorgeous. But something was changed about her today, even before Bo called, and Winter could see it in the line etched between her brows. He captured her wrist.

"What?" she asked.

"You seem different."

"Do I?"

"Something wrong?"

"Not at all."

"Are you sure?"

Her chin dropped. "No."

"Tell me."

"It's silly. I just got something delivered to me at Golden Lotus this morning that made me sad." She gently tugged her arm away and picked up a shell pink chemise. "I met with my future employer a week ago. He came to the club and offered me a gig in New Orleans. A new jazz hall called the Limbo Room."

The unexpected news unstrung his nerves. "You've already got another job?"

She stepped inside her chemise and shimmied it over her hips. "They're offering me room and board at a hotel next door to the club. Will pay me double what Velma's paying. The most money I've ever been offered in my life." She slipped silky straps over freckled shoulders. "It'll keep me employed through October. The owner bought my train ticket. That's what was dropped off at Golden Lotus this morning."

"Do you know anything about this man?"

"He's middle-aged. Owns another speakeasy in Baton Rouge. Seems nice enough."

"And you're just going to run off to a strange city halfway across the country to work for a complete stranger?"

"It's what I did when I came here."

A rising panic tightened his chest. "You won't have anyone there to look after you."

Slender fingers tucked the front locks of her bob behind

her ears as she bent to pick up her skirt. "I've made it this far on my own."

God only knew how—a miracle she hadn't been raped or robbed or killed in some dark alley after leaving one of her shows in the middle of the damn night. The only unescorted women roaming the street that late were . . . Christ, he didn't know if there *were* any. Even prostitutes had sense enough to stay behind closed doors. It panicked him to think about her off somewhere, out of his reach, where he couldn't be there in minutes. "New Orleans is a vice-ridden port city, cheetah."

"San Francisco is a vice-ridden port city, Mr. Bootlegger."

Swearing in Swedish under his breath, he hunted down his clothes, trying to hide the unsettling mix of anger and hurt churning inside. This was preposterous, her traipsing off. He knew she had to leave—of course he knew. But in the back of his mind, he'd pictured her in Seattle or Portland, maybe Los Angeles. Somewhere on the West Coast, where he could take an afternoon train and be there in time to catch her show. And where the hell were his socks? He didn't for the life of him remember taking them off.

"Here." She handed him two limp black dress socks.

"When do you leave?"

She stilled and bit the center of her upper lip.

"When?" he insisted.

"About a week."

His throat felt as if he'd swallowed wet cement. "One week?"

She nodded. "Now you know why I'm sad."

That was nothing—no time at all. "What if Gris-Gris offered you a longer contract?"

"Velma already has a telepath booked, and don't you dare storm into her office and force her to keep me. I can already see the wheels turning. I won't take something I haven't earned honestly, and I can't stand being in debt to someone else. I'm not sure if you understand that, but it's important to me."

Unfortunately he did understand. Even if his work was

illegal, it was hard work, and he didn't cut corners to get it done. His father had always told him there were few greater shames than debt. It was a matter of pride.

But what they had together was bigger than pride—his or hers.

"A week, a month—it makes no difference," she said. "We both knew I'd be leaving eventually. You didn't want anything permanent when you suggested we share a bed, remember?"

Yes, he remembered. He buttoned the fly of his pants and plunked back down on the bed. "I can't believe you're really going."

Her stockinged legs stepped between his. She cupped his cheeks with small, warm hands. "Only live for today—that's what Sam taught me. But if I'm being honest, I've never wanted to leave a place less . . . or a person."

If that was really true, then why was she going?

The temple was located in a narrow, nondescript three-story brick building crowded between a dozen others just like it. A steady stream of locals and western tourists paraded under strings of triangular orange flags that hung above the entrance. The main sign, from which swaying lanterns hung, was painted in Chinese characters. A secondary cloth banner below read LION RISE TEMPLE.

Winter tried to summon up the will to care that the man who poisoned him was inside, and that he might soon be where Parducci was if he didn't watch himself, but his mind was fixated on Aida's news. Every time he looked at her, she was staring out the window, lost in her own thoughts, unreadable. Meanwhile, he was slowly sinking.

*Only live for today.* Complete and utter bullshit.

In a week, she'd be gone, on to some new adventure. Maybe even another lover. The thought of someone else touching her made his stomach harden into a black lump. His hands curled into fists.

She acted as though she had no qualms about walking

away and never looking back. As though he was merely a choice for dinner—beef or chicken, and tomorrow she'd be dining somewhere else. Goddamn casual affair. Possibly the stupidest idea he'd had in years. Casual was Sook-Yin, or Florie Beecham.

Casual was *not* Aida.

Had all of this meant nothing to her? The time she spent in his arms? He stole a look at her as Bo parked the car across the street from the temple. That same deep line divided her brows. She chewed on her bottom lip. Either he was a fool, falling for someone who didn't feel the same way, or she was lying through her teeth with this breezy, live-for-today act. God give him the strength to figure out which it was before it was too late.

Spice-tinged floral smoke drifted from the temple. Winter surveyed the area and found nothing out of the ordinary, so he, Aida, and Bo approached by foot. A few cars behind, four of his men shadowed them to the entrance.

An attractive pair of girls wearing embroidered red silk cheongsams collected donations from entering patrons. Winter stuffed a bill into their tin as they stepped into a wide chamber—something between a lobby and a museum. Gilded columns, elaborately carved wooden screens, and ornate statues of Chinese deities filled the low-ceilinged space. Two red doors at the far end of the room opened into a courtyard, open to the sky, where a red and gold pagoda housed the temple's shrine bookended by a pair of iron Chinese lions.

The smoke was thicker here, nearly choking. Coils of burning incense hung from the pagoda's ceiling. Temple employees sold incense sticks and bundles of joss paper. Beneath the pagoda, visitors carried their offerings while chanting prayers.

Winter's gaze lit on a table where two women were distributing cylindrical bamboo cups. THE KAU CIM ORACLE: CHINESE FORTUNE STICKS, as the sign proclaimed. Querents knelt on their knees in front of the shrine and held the cups sideways, shaking them until a single stick fell onto well-worn cobblestones. The sticks were numbered, each one corresponding to a fortune. People carried their fallen stick to a small canvas tent in the corner of the courtyard, where a fortune-teller provided interpretation.

*His* fortune-teller. The goddamn pissant who poisoned him.

"That should be our man," Bo confirmed.

Winter nodded. "Let's have our oracle read."

After a customer exited, Winter ducked into the tent's opening under a line of gold fringe and found himself inside a dim space not more than six or seven feet wide. An oil-burning lantern sat on a small portable table, behind which sat a wizened man dressed in a black ceremonial robe with gaping sleeves. A long gray queue lay braided across one shoulder.

"Please, sit," the man said without looking up from writing something. He waved his hand toward two folding chairs in front of his table. A flat box containing slips of paper, numbered fortunes, sat near his elbow. A placard off to the side identified the man as Mr. Wu.

Aida took a seat while Winter unbuttoned his suit jacket and sat beside her, stretching out his legs in the small space as best he could. Bo untied the tent flap and closed it behind them.

"Your fortune stick, please," the man said, then glanced up at Winter and flinched.

"I'm here to get some information about my past, not my future, Mr. Wu. Or should I call you Black Star?"

A muscle in the man's eye jumped. "What do you want?"

"I want to know why you tried to poison me with *Gu*."

Knobby fingers tightened around the pencil he was holding.

"Know who I am, now?" Winter asked. "Or do you poison so many people that you can't remember?"

"Magnusson," the man whispered.

They held each other's gaze as discordant sounds from the temple seeped under the heavy canvas of the tent. "You drank the *Gu* but are unaffected?" The old man was genuinely surprised.

"Another magic worker removed the curse."

Shadows clung to bags of loose skin beneath his eyes. "I should've never taken that job."

"You really shouldn't have." Winter moved his jacket aside and watched Wu's gaze settle on the gun strapped next to his ribs.

The old man gave him a dismissive wave. "I lost my wife ten years ago, and with her passing, the will to live, so threatening me is futile. I am looking forward to the afterlife far too much to worry about dying. Save the violence for someone younger who is still under the illusion that there is happiness on this plane."

If anyone understood apathy born of grief, Winter did. And when he pictured harboring that kind of hopelessness for an entire decade, he almost pitied the old man. But not enough to excuse him. "Your problems are your own. I just want information."

"All you had to do was ask—I have no loyalties. What would you like to know?"

"Everything."

Wu leaned back in his seat. "I was hired to do a job, and was told that an anonymous party was interested in ensuring that you do not work anymore. That you have a family history of mental instability—that you had inherited your father's fragile mind. I was asked to make a potion that would draw ghosts to you and make you crazy."

He hadn't inherited his father's mental illness. The doctors said it could be genetic, but no one else in his family had showed any signs of it. His father had been ill since he was young man—Winter's mother knew about it when she married him. It just didn't get out of hand until a few years ago, when the frenzied episodes worsened.

"So you are telling me that someone paid you to mix up a poison that would draw ghosts to me because they believed this would drive me insane," Winter said. "And when the poison didn't work, you were hired to conduct additional spells to draw ghosts to me with coins and buttons."

"I just found out from you that my *Gu* was unsuccessful. I was hired to make the poison, nothing more. That is my speciality."

"What about Parducci? You make any poison for him?"

He looked at Bo and began speaking rapid Cantonese.

"He doesn't know Parducci. Says he was hired by an old Chinese man in May," Bo interpreted. "He came to his tent, gave no name. Asked for the poison and paid him half up front, half when he came back to pick it up two weeks later."

"Talk to me, not him," Winter said to the old man, patience wearing thin.

"He mentioned your name specifically—no one else's," he replied in English. "The poison is custom-brewed for one individual. Can't be used on everyone."

If that was true, and Wu was a hired gun, then it stood to reason other magic workers were being hired for their specialties. Maybe whatever had been done to Parducci was a different kind of magic.

"In early June the man who hired me collected the *Gu* I made for you," Mr. Wu added. "Haven't seen him since."

"The man gave no name at all? Surely you must have some idea who he was. What did he look like?"

"Western clothes. Maybe fifty, sixty years old, maybe younger. Average height and weight. Nothing special about him. He had a forgettable face and he never gave a name. Apart from what you already know about the poison, he was insistent that the *Gu* not kill you directly. Some recipes for *Gu* are used for other purposes—sometimes to kill. He said I must be absolutely sure it wasn't deadly. It was only meant to cause a nervous breakdown."

This just didn't make sense. It was cowardly. Passive.

"He claimed he was working for someone with a higher cause," Wu said.

"What kind of cause?" Aida asked, speaking for the first time since they'd arrived.

"One that would liberate Chinatown from the *Gwai-lo*."

Aida's brows knitted. "Who are the *Gwai-lo*?"

"White men," Bo said quietly.

Winter shook his head. "Nonsense. I have no business in Chinatown."

Wu spoke in a hushed voice. "I don't know for certain, but I think they mean to liberate Chinatown from the entire city. A quiet rebellion, the man told me. Take power not by force, but by controlling the money."

A quiet rebellion. And one of the easiest ways to control money these days was to control booze. Winter thought of all the booze problems in Chinatown . . . St. Laurent getting nabbed by the Feds in the raid. And now Parducci. Sweat bloomed over Winter's forehead. "Have you heard of a secret mystical tong?"

The man shook his head.

Winter pressed further. "One that's headed up by a purported necromancer?"

Wu's eyes narrowed. Bo rattled off a longer explanation in Cantonese.

"I've never heard of such a thing," Wu said. A lie. Winter had seen something in the old man's eyes when Bo was talking. "I'm sorry. I've already told you more than I should have." Before Winter could protest, the man was scribbling something on the back of one his fortune cards. He slid it across the table. It read, the Hive.

Winter's mind was jolted back to something Bo had told him back when all of this started. He'd said that a tong leader who dealt in booze had died locked in a room filled with bees. A chill raced down Winter's spine. "Where can I find them?"

Wu shook his head, a look of defeat, maybe even commiseration behind his eyes. "I truly do not know. This temple isn't under tong protection, and my work is the only thing that holds my interest. I am uninterested in politics and would prefer to be left alone. I only helped the man who requested the *Gu* because I needed the money."

Winter stared at him for a long moment. The man finally held out his hands and made an appeal to Bo in Cantonese.

"He says that's everything he knows," Bo translated.

Maybe it was, maybe it wasn't, but Winter suspected he wouldn't get anything more out of the man by threatening him. He'd have the old man monitored night and day, find out who he visited, who visited him. And in the meantime, they now had the name of the secret tong. Something small, to be sure, but hope is often kindled by small things.

Winter leaned closer. "If anyone else comes to you asking for any more of these kinds of favors, I'd appreciate if you'd get word to me at Pier 26 before accepting the work. Whatever they pay, I'll pay more. I can be a good friend for a temple like this. I can even ensure that you are left alone to live out the rest of your hopeless, depressing life in peace and quiet."

The man laughed. "Now *that's* something. Much more motivating than a bullet."

"Then we have an understanding?"

"Yes, Mr. Magnusson. I believe we do."

"One more thing," Aida said, surprising Winter. "Can you really see the future?"

Mr. Wu gave her a tight smile. "If I could, I very much doubt I'd be wasting my talents in a place like this."

# TWENTY-THREE

———— ✦ ————

WINTER CLAIMED HE WAS TOO BUSY TO SEE HER THE FOLLOWING day, chasing down this Hive tong, and talking to the last remaining bootlegger in the Big Three. Even so, she suspected part of the reason for his busy schedule had to do with punishing her for the news about New Orleans. Maybe some time apart would help him come to his senses, so she didn't protest. Just went to work the next night, a little sad, a little anxious, and took the midnight streetcar home to an empty apartment.

After getting ready for bed, she opened her locket and thought of her brother. Before he'd left for training camp, Sam told her about something he'd once read: that people could fall in love with anyone, given the right circumstances. This meant that there was no such thing as soul mates or a One True Love for anyone, he said. Love was something people used to prop themselves up. It created dependency and distracted from learning and personal growth. It also inevitably led to loss. Therefore, one's goal in life should be to remain single, he theorized; avoid love, avoid a lifetime of pain and suffering. The world was falling apart anyway—

why would anyone want to get married and, heaven forbid, bring another child into such a mess?

For once in her adult life, Aida heard Sam's words in her head and had doubt. This upset her on a couple of levels. It upended her world to even consider for a moment Sam might've been wrong. And yet, at the same time, it felt as though she was defacing his memory, wronging him from the beyond. Not for the first time, she wished she could discuss it with him. Ironic that she was a medium but couldn't channel him. Couldn't even find another medium to help her, because she had nothing of his to use for memento mori; the photograph she owned wasn't in his possession long enough to act as a magnet. He would probably say this proved something about the absurdity of life.

Setting the locket on her nightstand, she slipped beneath the bedcovers and tried to block out Sam's words. It took a long while to fall asleep, and when she did, she dreamed of Winter standing outside the incense-filled temple from the day before. Then the scene changed, and she was watching his hand slipping away from hers as she reached out the window of a departing train. When he was just a speck on the receding landscape, she sat down in an empty train car and unwrapped candy with a beehive printed on the wrapper. It tasted of honey, only far too sweet and bitter. She tried to spit it out when she saw a shadow moving across the window. Just as she turned to study it, the train burst into flames.

Even inside her sleeping mind, she distantly recognized the recurring dream. It was like an old enemy that she'd held at an arm's length for so long, they were almost friends by default. The earthquake. The Great Fire. Holding on to Sam while the city burned to smoldering ash. Her parents out of reach.

She tried to wake herself up, but the dream was so vivid. So *real*.

She came awake with a start to find that it *was* real! She was not dreaming.

Yellow and orange flames leapt from her apartment door,

quickly spreading across the floor and over the inner wall. Aida lurched from her bed and spied movement outside her window.

Someone was racing down the fire escape.

Billows of black smoke rose from the flames. She coughed and stumbled. Her vision wavered. She tried to walk, but her knees buckled.

What was wrong with her?

"Help!" she shouted, again and again.

It was her absolute worst nightmare. The fire was consuming the small apartment. Already, the door to her bathroom was blocked by flames. The only way out was the window.

Dizzy and confused, she glanced around and despaired. She was going to lose everything.

This couldn't be happening.

She crawled to the open closet and pulled herself up by the door handle. Her handbag was here on the back of the door, thank God, along with the the fox coat. Tearing it from its hanger, she coughed against her forearm and waved away smoke, desperately looking for Ju's dress, but it was impossible. She couldn't see her bed anymore, the smoke was so thick.

She shoved her arms into the coat's sleeves and sloppily ducked onto the fire escape. The iron creaked and groaned as she zigzagged down the steps, back and forth, one story at a time, until she reached the bottom, one story above the sidewalk.

She pushed a bare heel against the drop-down ladder. It was rusted. Not budging.

A blaring bell nearly startled her off the fire escape. Someone had pulled the alarm. The girls on her floor would hear it. Mr. and Mrs. Lin—dear God! The whole building might be lost if the fire department didn't get here quickly.

She kicked at the ladder again, surveying the streets for people. It had been after midnight when she'd fallen asleep, and she had no idea what time it was now. Two A.M.? Three? Not late enough for the milkman.

In the distance, a group of late-night revelers sauntered down Grant. She screamed for them at the top of her lungs. Had they heard her? It was too dark to tell. Yellow light pooled at the bases of the dragon lampposts dotting the sidewalk. The lights swayed as a wave of dizziness rolled over her.

"Hey!"

The people *had* seen her—they were rushing up the incline. More onlookers emerged from the apartment building next door. She called out to them, trying to get someone to knock on Golden Lotus's door to wake up the Lins. The other girls living in the apartments were in danger; just because she'd gotten out didn't mean they'd be so lucky.

The stairs creaked. She glanced up and saw flames pouring from her window. Then the iron railing made a horrible sound. Rusted bolts ripped away from the brick building.

The world fell away beneath her feet.

She blindly gripped the railing as the bottom flight of the metal stairs collapsed and crashed to the sidewalk with an explosive *Boom!* that rattled her bones.

Flung from the fire escape, she sailed sideways. Her back smashed against the building, knocking the wind from her lungs. Pain ripped through her body. Her vision went blinding white for several moments, then slowly pulsed back to reality.

Not dead.

A rusted iron dragon skeleton groaned in front of her as a cloud of dust swirled from its fallen carcass.

She inspected herself. The pain receded, which was odd. She should be really hurting, but all she felt was numb, physically and emotionally. Her tongue darted out and swept the side of her mouth, tasting blood and sweetness and that awful honeyed bitterness from her dream.

Strange hands lifted Aida to her feet, then steadied her wobbling. Her foot was bleeding.

Cantonese and English erupted around her as a crowd gathered. She assured people that she was okay, which might not have been entirely true. She was so dreadfully sleepy and dizzy. It was all she could do to stand without aid.

"Miss Palmer, Miss Palmer!"

Aida turned to see Mrs. Lin's tiny figure racing toward her in a housecoat and slippers, her tightly wound hair now tumbling loose to her waist.

"Are you badly hurt?"

"I'm fine." Aida's handbag still dangled around her wrist. A small miracle.

"What happened?"

"Someone came up the fire escape and set fire to my room."

"Oh, no, no, no—this is terrible."

"I broke the fire escape on the way down. I'm sorry for that and the fire."

Mrs. Lin shook her head dismissively. "All the girls are out. We have insurance. I'm the one who should be apologizing to you— I should have done something about the fire escape."

"You couldn't have known."

"Oh, but I did," she said, distressed. "My mother warned me to repair the fire escape last time you channeled her for me. I should've listened."

Wailing sirens announced two fire trucks. Everyone craned their necks to watch the men setting up wooden ladders to reach what was left of the fire escape so they could drag a hose up to the window. Across the street, Aida leaned against a brick wall, half dazed, watching the fog-capped neighborhood fill with cars and gawkers.

Police arrived. Mrs. Lin dragged an officer to Aida, who took down her story with the nub of a worn pencil: no, she didn't see a face, nor did she know how the fire was started or why. Someone else chimed in, saying he'd spied two men jumping from the fire escape into the bed of a truck that idled at the curb, but it took off before he could make out the model.

Early morning wind rustled her hair and sent shivers through her, even inside the fox coat. Nothing made sense. Why would someone set fire to her apartment? Thinking about it hurt her head. She started to close her eyes, just for a moment, when she heard her name again.

"Aida!"

Strong hands gripped her shoulders. Shook her. She opened her eyes to Bo.

Why was he here? How did she get on the sidewalk? She must've slipped down the wall.

"Are you okay?" he asked. "Do you need me to take you to the hospital?"

She repeated what she'd told Mrs. Lin and the police officer, but the words weren't coming out right. Light from a dragon lamppost cast triangles across Bo's face, highlighting his sharply chiseled cheekbones. His normally perfectly combed-back hair fell into his eyes, reminding her of Winter in bed after sex. "You're very handsome, Bo," she heard herself saying.

"What's wrong with you? Your face is flushed." He leaned in close. Was he going to kiss her? No, that was all wrong. She tried to back away, but he held her firm. Sniffing, not kissing. That still didn't make sense. He opened up the front of her jacket and looked at her nightgown. She tucked in her chin and did the same. A reddish brown stain coated the front of her gown.

"Where did that come from?" she said. "Is that the sweet taste in my mouth? I woke up tasting honey. Bitter honey. And brandy. I think I might be drunk, but I don't remember drinking."

He said something in Cantonese.

"What?"

"Laudanum," Bo translated. "Opium."

Her eyes widened. "*N-o-o.*"

"Someone didn't want you leaving that room."

"That's . . . wait—why are you here?"

"I keep an apartment a block away. Can you walk? Let me take you there. You're freezing to death out here."

"Mrs. Lin—"

"She's the one who told me what happened and pointed you out. Let me tell her where we're going. Come."

Bo's place was in a tiny apartment building squeezed between a furniture maker and a tea shop. He didn't lead them through the front, however. Instead, he hustled her down a side street, through a door that led into the furniture maker's storage room, and finally into the apartment's empty lobby. Very sneaky, that Bo. The stairwell was musty, but his room on the second floor was clean and sparse: only a small unmade bed, a tiny table with two chairs, and a love seat, on which she collapsed.

"I don't stay here often," he said, before making a hushed phone call. When he was done, he left the room for a few minutes and came back with a mug of something warm. "Drink. All at once."

Her throat was dry. She took a gulp from the mug and made a face. Warm salt water.

"All of it. Hurry."

She drank half, then felt her stomach constrict violently. He placed a ceramic bowl in front of her face, and she promptly began vomiting. When she was done, he gave her a wet towel to wipe her face and a drink of cool water to rinse her mouth out.

If she was weary before, she was doubly so now. He left the room again, taking away the bowl and the salt water, then returned empty-handed.

"You can see Golden Lotus from your window," she noted as she watched the firemen in a sleepy haze. The fire was extinguished. She wondered what was left of her room.

"I eat there sometimes. The Lins are good people."

That surprised her, but she was too drugged to make sense of it at that moment. "Best landlords I've ever had. I can't believe this happened."

"I should've been watching. Winter's going to be furious."

She looked up at him, puzzled. "He has you watching me?"

"Sometimes. Just to make sure you get home okay from Gris-Gris. It's dangerous being out so late."

"I've managed just fine the past few years, and I'll manage when I'm in New Orleans."

He sat down next to her on the love seat. "You're breaking his heart, you know."

"Who?"

His dark eyes narrowed in irritation as he cast an incredulous look her way. "He'll never admit it, and when you leave, he'll go back to being mad at the world. So I don't like you very much right now."

Aida was mildly embarrassed that he was speaking to her about this. "Well, that's too bad, because I like *you*. Thank you for helping me. I'll just need to find a cheap hotel somewhere close by." She thought of her financial situation and reconsidered. "If you'd let me sleep here on the couch, I'll be out of your hair by morning."

He didn't answer.

She was having a hard time keeping her eyes open. "I lost everything I own. My clothes. My savings . . . I can't believe it's gone. Every penny I scraped together for the last three years. All I have is a few dollars in my handbag." Tears slid down her cheeks, but that seemed strange, because she wasn't crying. "Every time I try to plan for the future, the world conspires against me and rips it away." She tried to gesture, but it took too much effort to raise her arm. "Look at me. I don't even have shoes. I'm right back where I was when I was a child."

"I'm sorry."

She shrugged. "What can I do but start again in New Orleans? I'm not happy about leaving, in case you think I am."

"Then don't."

"I have to earn a living."

"Get a job running a switchboard. A secretary, maybe."

"I have no experience. Can't even type. And could you do a job like that after working for Winter? After the freedom he gives you?"

He stared at her for a moment before shaking his head.

When Bo left the room for a third time, she lost track of time and fell asleep. The next thing she knew, she was being jostled down a flight of stairs, carried in someone's steely arms, crammed against a warm, hard chest.

"Mind your feet." The familiar cadence rumbled through her shoulder.

"Winter?"

"I've got you."

Her voice was weak and far away. "Guess what? I've been drugged."

"And injured. We'll get your foot patched up when we get back to the house, okay?"

"I rescued the coat."

"I see that."

"I just don't understand why this happened."

"Someone wanted you dead, and they went to great lengths to ensure that they didn't kill you directly. And I'll wager it's no coincidence this happened after our visit to the temple. We were seen together."

"Do you think it's that tong Mr. Wu told us about? The Hive?" she asked, closing her eyes. His arms were strong and safe, and she was so . . . very . . . drowsy.

He dropped a kiss on the crown of her head, then his deep voice whispered near her face. "Whoever it was, they won't be alive when I get my hands on them, I promise you that."

# TWENTY-FOUR

───◆───

THE LAUDANUM BECKONED HER TO SLEEP AGAIN, AND SHE GAVE in, waking up briefly during the car ride, the side of her head sweating against Winter's shoulder as he held her in his lap.

When she woke again, it was inside the Magnusson elevator, and she was being carried again. "A girl could get used to this," she said, her voice rough, "but I need to find a cheap hotel. And I might need to borrow a couple of dollars."

"You're not going anywhere," Winter replied. "If I have to lock you up in the turret attic, I will. Consider yourself my prisoner."

She was too weak to argue. "Do prisoners get baths? Because I can't stand the stink of smoke all over me. It's burning my eyes."

"Yes, prisoners get baths."

"Will you bathe me?"

A throat cleared. Aida tilted her head to see cold-as-ice Greta operating the elevator in a housecoat, a scarf tied around her head. Wonderful. God only knew what she thought of all this.

The elevator groaned to a stop.

"Thank you, Greta. I'll ring if I need you," Winter said. "Get some sleep."

Aida smelled orange oil. Wood paneled walls blurred by. Then she found herself being carried into a sumptuous, warm bedroom with rosewood flooring, window seats, and a lavish Nile green rug. "Where is this?"

"My room."

"O-oh, it's even nicer than the Fairmont. We should've been coming here."

He set her on the biggest bed she'd ever seen, covers pulled back, sheets wrinkled. A dragonfly-patterned Tiffany lamp cast muted light from a bedside table. He struggled to get her out of her coat. "We'll have this sent to the cleaners. Get the smoke out."

"I need to find out if anything survived the fire," she said.

"Don't worry about that now," Winter said. He knelt down and inspected her foot. "A little swollen. Could be sprained. Can you move it?"

She could. It was tight, but any pain she felt was far, far away in the distance.

A new voice startled her. "You want me to call a doctor?" It was Bo. He set some first aid supplies on a mahogany chest of drawers with modern, sleek lines. Her handbag hung from one of the drawer pulls.

Winter shook his head. "He'd just elevate it and give her more drugs, which she doesn't need. We'll call someone in the morning. Go ahead and alert the warehouses about the fire, in case someone tries that trick again."

"Already called Frank. And there's something you should know."

Winter sighed heavily. "What is it?"

"The fortune-teller from the temple. Same time Aida's apartment was being set on fire, Mr. Wu jumped from his apartment window and killed himself."

The news sobered Aida for a moment. "Oh no."

"Christ," Winter said.

"Charlie was on shift watching him. Said he saw the man

racing into his apartment like he was trying to outrun something. Charlie checked the stairwell, windows—nothing was there. Then he heard screams outside, and that's when he went out and saw him on the sidewalk. Neighbors had already found him. Stuck around until the police came, just in case someone else showed up. Never saw anything else."

"Ghosts," Winter mumbled. "Or some other kind of black magic."

"That's what I'm thinking," Bo said. "Charlie sounded unnerved. He also mentioned that he heard Wu repeating something when he was running into his apartment—'beekeeper.'"

Winter's jaw shifted to one side. "The Hive."

"Maybe that's what the leader calls himself?"

"Maybe."

"Regardless, it rules Wu out for the fire," Bo said. "Not that I really suspected him."

"Poor bastard."

A wave of sadness washed over Aida. She had rather liked the depressed old fortune-teller, even if he had poisoned Winter. Maybe he'd found his dead wife beyond the veil. She hoped so.

Winter talked with Bo in soft murmurs outside his room for several moments before he dismissed him and shut the door, turning his attention back to her. "Still with me?"

She nodded. He stripped off her laudanum-stained nightgown and left her naked on the bed, while he stepped into the adjoining room and started running a bath.

Several framed photographs crowded the back of his bedside table. The most prominent was a family photo in front of a fishing pier: a couple who could only be his parents, Astrid as a younger girl, a blond man about Bo's age—his brother, the archaeologist—and Winter, looking several years younger, smiling, squinting into the sun with no scar.

Happier times.

Behind that photograph was a smaller one, a posed portrait of a strikingly beautiful blond woman, her long hair pinned up, porcelain skin, and a stoic look on her face.

Winter strolled back into the bedroom, barefoot and shirt stripped off, wearing nothing but pants and suspenders over a sleeveless white undershirt. The unyielding breadth of his mighty bare shoulders and well-muscled boxer's arms made her heart skip a beat.

"Who is this?" Aida asked, reaching for the silver-framed blonde.

"No one."

Hmph. It had to be Paulina. A dull feeling of jealousy taunted Aida from a distance. "Why would you have a photograph of *no one* next to your bed?"

"Why would you care? You're leaving in a week." He took the photograph from her hand and put it back on the table, then reached to lift her off the bed.

"I can walk," she said irritably, pushing his hands away. As she struggled to her feet, she flipped the photograph facedown when his back was turned.

His bathroom was spacious with gleaming white tile and polished wood cabinets. A beveled glass window was cranked open to the opposite view seen from his study: instead of the Bay, it was the south side of Pacific Heights rising up steep hills, its prestigious homes wearing a crown of fog beneath the night sky.

An enormous, grand slipper claw-foot tub sat to her left. Winter twisted the silver handles to shut off steaming water. Before she could protest, he lifted her off the floor and set her down into the hot water. It stung her ankle for a moment, but the rest of her felt so good, it didn't matter.

"Too warm?"

Her muscles turned to mush as her shoulders slid down the high-backed tub. "Perfect. You could fit a car inside here." Or a giant-sized bootlegger. The heated water sent ripples of pleasure through her limbs.

He folded his big body up to perch on a wooden stool next to her. "Put that foot up here," he said, patting the side of the tub.

She propped her leg where he instructed and sank farther into the water. A firm hand held her leg while he soaped up her foot, carefully cleaning her cuts with a soft washrag, sloughing all the grime away.

"Winter?"

"Yes."

"I have three dollars to my name. All my savings was in my room. I have no clothes. No cosmetics, no jewelry—"

"I will replace everything. You wouldn't have lost it if you weren't affiliated with me."

"You don't know that."

"You normally have people trying to kill you?" he asked.

"Well, no."

"And I *do.* This is the same passive bullshit that's being used on me with the hauntings. My fault, therefore my responsibility. End of story."

"I don't want charity. I'll repay you once I've earned the money back. Velma still owes me one more payday, and the salary I'll earn in New Orleans—"

He slapped the washcloth onto the floor. His face was taut with outrage. "You're still thinking about New Orleans? You almost *died* tonight. Do you know how terrified I was? How close you were to being burned alive? I could've received a call from Mrs. Lin instead of Bo, telling me to come arrange a casket for your charred body."

She inhaled sharply on an unexpected sob. "What else can I do? It is the only work I know." Sniffling, she wrestled with her emotions, and lost. Her fears jumped off her loosened tongue before she could censor them. "I will not stay here and play mistress to you until you grow tired of me and find someone blonder or prettier or more glamorous."

"Why the hell is our imaginary breakup *my* fault?"

Because she couldn't fathom herself finding anyone else she could want more than him. But she didn't say that. "I've built a reputation—club owners are seeking me out, not the other way around. I don't have to beg for work or try to prove myself. If I don't take advantage of it, my time may pass. Can't you understand that? This is all I have. I'm not fit for anything else but this life."

He surged up from the stool, biting back a reply as flames

danced behind mismatched eyes. The surface of the water shook under his angry footfalls as he left the bathroom.

Winter fought the urge to throw something against the wall. Goddamn New Orleans. If he never heard the city's name on her tongue again, it would be fine with him.

*Find someone blonder . . .*

What the hell was wrong with her? Had the fire melted her brain? Why the devil would he want someone—

His gaze fell on the silver picture frame lying facedown. Paulina. He picked it up and looked at her photograph. Aida was jealous of a dead woman? Did she think he kept this here out of grief or love? Far from it. He kept it out of respect. Maybe it would be more accurate to say that he kept it to feed his guilt. Because if he didn't see it every now and again, he found himself forgetting what she looked like.

Even worse, he found himself not thinking about her at all, which wasn't much different than when she was alive. Sometimes he wouldn't see her for days at a time when they were married, even living in the same house. And that had never bothered him.

He should've let her go when she wanted the divorce.

Was he now so quick to repeat the same mistake with Aida? Her association with him made her a target. His fault. Again.

He thought of the numbing panic that unfurled inside him when he'd gotten the call from Bo: *Someone tried to burn down Aida's apartment with her inside it.* Death by fire. Few things were worse.

But she didn't die. She was safe, here with him. That was all that mattered for the moment.

Exhaling heavily, Winter picked up Paulina's photograph and headed to his study. He sat in front of the windows, looking out over the city as dawn broke. After a few minutes, Astrid peeked inside the door, her arms filled with clothes.

"I heard all the commotion," she said. Her slippers slapped against the floor as she walked, nightgown billowing behind her. "Bo told me what happened. I thought Aida might need some clothes."

"*Tack, mitt hjärta.*"

"You're welcome." She laid the clothes on the windowsill. "Bo said it was faulty wiring that caused the fire, and that she lost everything."

"Mmm."

"But I have a feeling it had something to do with the bootlegging." When he didn't answer, she perched on his lap. "I can tell you're upset. I'm sorry."

He ran his fingers along one strand of her lemony blond hair. "Someone is trying to scare me into giving up the business. I don't want you to be frightened. I'll take care of things."

"I know you will."

"But until I put a stop to it, I'd like you to be mindful when you're out. Not frightened, but mindful."

"I always am."

"Use good sense and have someone with you at all times, but if we allow ourselves to be intimidated, then—"

"They win. Got it. I'll be sensible."

"Good girl. How do you feel about another shopping trip?"

"For Aida?"

"I'll call the department store and coax them into letting you in before they open to the public. Bo can ride with you. And Jonte." And a couple of extra guards to man the doors, and take a circuitous route in one of the old cars. Better safe than sorry.

"Count on me. I can be ready in an hour." She gave him a sleepy smile and clasped his hand. "Will Aida be moving in here permanently?"

"She leaves for New Orleans in a week."

"For good?"

He shrugged.

The tips of her slim fingers folded over his. "Are you in love with her?"

His stomach tightened. Was he? He remembered how

miserable he'd felt those few days when they'd been apart after the fight about Sook-Yin. And he knew how relieved he felt now, knowing she was only a few yards away, safe inside his home. He wanted her to sleep in his bed . . . wanted to see her when he woke up.

He wanted all of her, not just an affair.

And he definitely didn't want her to leave. The thought of it filled him with a black despair that rivaled the pain of losing his family.

"I might be," he finally answered honestly.

"I think she might be in love with you, just from the way she was looking at you that day when she tried to give the coat back. I don't think I've ever seen anyone look at you that way. Definitely not—"

"Don't say her name."

"Sorry."

He lightly squeezed her hand. "It doesn't matter. I can't force Aida to stay."

Maybe not exactly *force* her, but he could tip the scales. Talk to Velma behind her back and get her to extend her contract. Only, he'd already promised he wouldn't.

He could take a train to the speakeasy in New Orleans and threaten this new club owner to drop her. Tempting, but he nixed the idea almost immediately. She would see through that deception in a heartbeat.

No, he couldn't force her.

Why couldn't Aida just see what was right in front of her face? They were so good together. Great in bed. More than great: exceptional. Marvelous. And they got along famously. Honestly, she was one of the few women he'd enjoyed as much out of a bed as in one. Christ, he even enjoyed arguing with her.

And she loved it out West—she said as much all the time. So why shouldn't she put down roots and start her séance business here? Not only could he help her buy a place she could work out of, like she wanted, but he could help steer rich patrons her way. She could have what she'd dreamed about. And if anything ever did tear them apart, God forbid, she'd be set up to do what she wanted, instead of injuring herself every night for a roomful of drunken idiots.

And he'd be right here to take care of her if she needed anything.

It was a simple solution. Why was he the only one seeing it? Worse, if he tried to convince her, she'd probably just stubbornly argue her way around it.

"So you're just going to let her go?" Astrid said. "That doesn't seem like you at all."

He let his head drop back against the chair. "What can I do? Lock her up? Threaten her?"

"Sure, that's what every girl dreams of, Winter."

He gave her a cross look, then glanced out the window, watching golden light piercing through a blanket of fog. "What do you suggest, then? Since you're such an expert in these matters, what with your many years of experience."

"At least I've got sense enough not to marry someone I didn't love."

He couldn't disagree with that.

She stretched her legs out, releasing his hand, and stood to leave. "Pappa once told me that everything he did in life was something to please Mamma, and that he was only happy when she was happy."

"Yes, so?"

"So if you want her to stay, maybe you should make her happy. What does she want?"

It sounded so simple, but what if the thing Aida wanted most was to leave?

"Figure that out," Astrid said as she padded out of the room.

He shoved the photo of Paulina inside the bottom drawer of his desk. Maybe he'd eventually put it in storage or send it to her parents. If he forgot Paulina's face . . . well, then he just did. He'd flagellated himself for too long. It was time to let it go.

He exhaled wearily and headed back to his bedroom. Aida was lying facedown on his bed, a towel draped around her, hair wet. The contents of her handbag were strewn across the bedspread—some crumpled bills and change, a metal lipstick tin, a cheap pocket mirror, her lancet, a few opened letters.

He strode to the bed and lifted her up. "What's wrong, cheetah?"

"My locket," she said, voice worn. "I thought I had it, but I took it off before bed."

"I'm sorry." He tried to pull her into his arms, to comfort her somehow, but he struggled with something to say. "It's just an object, not your brother himself."

Tear-stung eyes narrowed in anger. "*Just* an object?"

Wrong choice of words.

"Nothing is 'just an object,'" she said. "Possessions aren't meaningless—everything is connected. If it weren't for these things, I couldn't call spirits."

"I spoke carelessly," he said.

But she wasn't listening. "And now all my possessions are gone. I had so little, and now I have nothing." She shoved at the contents of her purse. "My only photograph of Sam—the last remaining piece of my family, and I lost him."

# TWENTY-FIVE

---

MIDDAY SUN WARMED THE TILE BENEATH AIDA'S FEET AS SHE looked around Winter's big bathroom, mildly anxious. Her head throbbed and the injuries to her foot ached with each step. Someone had left her a robe. Kind, but it was a little on the small side, and she needed real clothes. She also needed to find out if anything in her apartment survived the fire.

And to find out where Winter was.

She remembered nodding off in his arms. He pulled the covers over her and left, and now his bedroom was empty. No indication of where he slept—*if* he slept.

Bending to drink from the tap, she rinsed last night's lingering tastes from her mouth and hunted for a comb, feeling out of sorts in the strange home. When she finally discovered Winter's toiletries inside a frosted glass cabinet, she stood in front of the sink and realized what was odd about the bathroom: no mirror—not a proper one, anyway. Just a small shaving mirror that extended from a scissored arm attached to the wall. No dressing mirror in the bedroom, either.

No mirrors, so he didn't have to see his scarred face every day?

"Oh, Winter," she murmured on a sigh.

Low voices in the distance derailed her attention.

On the wall opposite the bathroom stood another door that accessed an adjoining room. Aida followed the voices here and peeked inside. A guest room, perhaps. A four-poster bed at the far end of the room was stripped of linens and pillows, in disuse, and covered with mounds of clothes.

Her eyes darted around the room.

A dressing table was laden with new boxes of expensive cosmetics and shampoos, an electric curling iron and hair dryer—luxuries she couldn't afford. Nearby, a large wooden steamer trunk stood open on its side, hangers slotted into place on one half, and six drawers lining the other. It looked like something a Hollywood star would own for traveling around the globe. Boxes of shoes were lined up next to it, brown and black leather peeking out from fluffs of tissue paper. Several evening gowns, glittering with beads and sequins, hung from the top of an open armoire door. Day coats, hats, handbags were spread across the bed, and sitting on a bureau, open boxes of jewelry sparkled under a slant of sunlight.

A pretty young servant stood with Astrid and her seamstress Benita, all three of them organizing the chaotic spread. It looked as if they might be planning to open a department store. Blond hair swung as Astrid turned and spotted her, eyes lighting up. "Oh, you're up—excellent! How do you feel?"

"I've been better," Aida admitted.

"Gee, I'm sorry about what happened. Bo said the wiring in those old apartments is always catching on fire."

"Uh . . ."

"You're lucky you got out. But on the bright side, you get all new things!" She spread her arms, showcasing her handiwork with a look of ecstasy on her face.

Aida choked. Astrid patted her on the back. "You okay,

there? Need some water?" She rattled off several commands in Swedish to the maid, who scurried out of the room. "She'll bring up some juice and breakfast. I bet you're starving."

"I—"

"Anyway, isn't this all great? I'm so jealous. I told Bo I was going to set fire to my room so I could experience the thrill of a new wardrobe. But Winter said if I did, I'd be wearing a potato sack until I graduated. Anyway, come look at what we picked out. Some of it might not fit, but Benita will take care of that for you."

"Astrid," Aida complained, feeling mildly sick to her stomach. "I can't possibly afford all this."

"Don't worry, Benita and I kept a tally," Astrid said, scooping up a small ledger. "Winter said you insisted on paying everything back when you could. It's all logged right here."

Aida scanned the entries, pangs of worry accumulating with every subtotaled figure written in flowery feminine print at the bottom of each page, until she got to the latest running total: four hundred and fifty-eight dollars.

Her mouth fell open. "I could buy a car for this—my life savings was . . ." Half that. And it took her years of scrimping. "This is crazy. This is—"

Dimples appeared as Astrid grinned. "Guess that'll teach you to take up with a Magnusson."

*"God middag."* Winter's housekeeper breezed into the room wearing a dour day suit. "Here you go."

Aida accepted a thick envelope. "What is this?"

"First-class tickets," Greta said in her singsong voice. "Train leaves same day as your original ticket, late morning. Train company was sympathetic about your ticket being lost in fire. You only owe Winter the difference between ticket prices, and sleeping arrangements will be much more comfortable. Winter insisted."

Good grief. She'd never traveled first-class. And Greta handled this? The woman probably cursed her name the entire way to the train station.

Aida was so confused—last night Winter had been shouting at her like an angry bull about going to New Orleans; now he was practically shoving her out the door. "I'm overwhelmed," Aida admitted, gripping the train ticket.

"*Ja*, I can imagine," Greta said. "But consider that all you lost were material things, easily replaced, and you now have comfortable, safe place to stay for the remainder of your time in city."

"I suppose you're right. Where is Winter?"

"Hunting down people who did this to you."

Aida's stomach twisted.

"Enough of all that, let's get on with the fun stuff," Astrid said brightly. "Changing screen's in the corner."

"Yes, by all means," Greta said, crossing her arms beneath her breasts. "Astrid will now demonstrate what a girl with no sense and an open charge account can do."


Winter stood in the hallway looking through the burned-out hole where Aida's apartment door once stood. Nothing was salvageable: clothes and luggage, charred; hiding place for her savings, nothing but ashes; and the locket, now melted into her bedside table.

"That was kind of you to arrange repairs," Velma said at his side as she looked on.

How they'd ever get rid of the acrid burnt stench was beyond him. "Both Aida and Bo are fond of the owners. Can you do anything?"

Velma surveyed the damage for a long moment, the picture of poise in an elegant chartreuse coat. The brim of her matching hat hid her eyes from him. "What did you have in mind?"

"Some sort of tracking spell?"

"To lead you to the men who did this?" She shook her head. "I'm not sure I'm that good. You'd have a better chance finding them by chasing leads."

"The witnesses saw a truck and two men. One of them said the men were Chinese, the other said they were white. Neither could identify the truck model."

"So no leads, is what you're saying."

"No leads, and I already talked to the police. They've got nothing, either. There's nothing you can try?"

Velma tugged the cuffs of her cream-colored gloves, tightening the fit. "I don't know a spell that can track them and return logical information concerning their where-abouts. I can, however, light a fuse from this point that will burn until it finds them."

"What does that mean?"

"It means I can work a curse on them. Punish them. But before you agree, hear me out. This is nothing to play around with. A curse deals out the same amount of punishment as the wrong they did. Eye for an eye. And once I set it in motion, there's no stopping it. I might end up killing these two men, and frankly, that's not something I want on my conscience."

"Well, *my* conscience is happy to take responsibility."

"Not that simple," the conjurer said, squinting up at him with sharp eyes. "Curses have a way of causing new rifts. If this is connected to the secret tong you're talking about, and they have a powerful sorcerer on their side, it might make some waves. You might be setting something in motion that won't stop until someone else gets hurt—or killed. So if I do this, either you or Aida have to bear the blood-debt. Anything I send out will come back to one of you, not me. Do you understand?"

He didn't, exactly. But if cursing them sparked a war, then at least all this bullshit would be out in the open. He was tired of shadowboxing. "I take full responsibility—not Aida. She's a bystander. All the blame should fall on my shoulders."

Velma nodded. "So be it. I'll need to collect some ashes."

Between shuffling in and out of clothes for the better part of the day, Aida unabashedly gobbled down a mid-afternoon breakfast of toast triangles piled with soft, buttery scrambled eggs, dill, and smoked salmon—Magnusson fish, Astrid proudly clarified. Fresh orange juice and strong coffee washed it all down.

And when all her new belongings had been sorted into piles—keep, return, alter—she settled on a raisin-colored casual dress to wear. Astrid took her on a tour of the house, traipsing through dozens of rooms brimming with objets d'art collected from exotic places—including a sitting area dubbed the Sheik Room, outfitted to look like something out of *Arabian Nights*.

She met Winter's mostly Swedish staff: a cook; three maids; a woman whose entire job was handling the laundry, who she later found out was Benita's mother; a handyman; the driver she'd seen before, Jonte; and keeping watch over all of them was Greta. They eyed Aida with great curiosity. Some spoke little English, and Aida listened in amazement as Astrid vacillated between English and Swedish with ease.

Under Greta's supervision, Astrid also showed Aida how to operate the elevator and the intercom system installed on each floor. Led her through the kitchen, formal dining room, and downstairs library. Walked her out to see Winter's cars, where Greta asked her to write down her work schedule for Jonte, who assured her he'd be ready to chauffeur her back and forth from Gris-Gris.

Astrid talked a mile a minute to Greta as the three of them stood in the driveway next to a cream two-seater Packard coupe with its convertible canvas top down. A beautiful car. Far more feminine than Winter's hell-colored Pierce-Arrow. Aida gazed at her reflection in one of the car's side mirrors and tuned out Astrid's chattering.

Aida was bone-weary. Her foot ached. She wanted comfort. Wanted Winter. It was strange to be peeking behind the scenes of his home without him there. Over the past couple of weeks she'd gotten too used to him . . . the way he smelled, the way he laughed. How the mattress sank when he crawled into bed. How he sounded when he came inside her.

Their routine at the Fairmont had been nothing short of

bliss, and now it was over. Now she was back to her normal life, where every day was different and nothing could be counted on. Because now that she'd had the entire day to mourn the loss of her possessions—and the locket, in particular—she reasoned that maybe she'd been so devastated to lose them because before Winter came along, *they* had been her routine. Things. They'd been the only constant in her life. City to city, job to job, stranger to stranger, she could always count on the comfort that her dependable pink Westclox and Sam's old photograph provided.

The locket had grounded her. But now it was gone, and there was nothing she could do to bring it back. She had to hold her shoulders high and keep going. Besides, Sam would've hated that he'd become her crutch, after he'd spent years encouraging her to live fearlessly.

She was good at being fearless. Damn good. That was something. And she wasn't destitute like she'd been when Emmett Lane had shoved her into the orphanage. Her possessions had been replaced. She was surrounded by nice things and nice people. Lots to be thankful about.

If she only had Winter by her side, she might even be *more* than thankful—she might be happy. After all she'd been through over the last twenty-four hours, imagine that. If Winter could make her happy on a dismal day like this, how could he make her feel on a good day?

"Do you require anything else?" Greta asked, breaking into Aida's thoughts.

"What's that?"

"Anything else?"

After everything they'd already done for her? Aida couldn't possibly have any other needs. If anything, she should be asking what *she* could do for *them*. Then inspiration came to her. A whim. "I would like someone to hang a mirror over Winter's bathroom sink."

Greta and Astrid stared at her. "Oh, he won't like that," Astrid finally said.

"I know. But I'd like to have a mirror in there for grooming, and Winter needs to stop feeling sorry for himself. Sometimes people require a little push."

"I do not—" Greta started.

"Blame it on me," Aida said firmly. "And while you're at it, have someone bring the full-length dressing mirror into his bedroom. How he dresses without help is beyond me."

"He had the dressing mirror in his closet lowered so that he only sees himself from the neck down," Astrid volunteered.

"Astrid Margaret Magnusson!" Greta chastised.

"Well, he did. And Aida's right. It's time for some changes."

Aida smiled. "Good, it's settled then."

"Anything else?" Greta said, her voice thick with annoyance.

Aida looked at Astrid. "You said you've never driven a car, not even once?"

She shook her head. "Winter won't allow it."

"And this coupe just sits here collecting dust? Shame, don't you think?"

"It was my mother's."

"It's lovely. Does it run?"

"All the cars run. Jonte takes them out around the block every Wednesday."

Aida caressed the curve of the spare whitewalled wheel attached to the side of the car above the running board. "Someone taught me how to drive in Baltimore a few years ago. I think I still remember. Want to learn? My treat for everything you've done for me today."

"*Nej, nej!*" Greta protested. "He will be very angry."

"Just around the block," Aida assured her. "You can stand here and watch us."

"Really?" Astrid said, suddenly swept up in the idea of it. "Bo showed me how to shift gears once. I think I could do it."

"Of course you can. Duck soup. Easy as pie."

Greta mumbled a string of Swedish words under her breath.

"Greta!" Astrid said with a grin.

The housekeeper's pink cheeks darkened. "I will not fetch the automobile key. If you are planning mutiny against your brother's rules, you can ask Jonte to help you."


After dropping Velma off at Gris-Gris, Winter spent the day in his Embarcadero office making calls. When dinnertime rolled around, he asked Bo to take him to Russian Hill. He hated driving by the house he'd shared with Paulina; though it had been sold more than a year ago, the sight of it still filled him with guilt and gloom. But what brought him here this time didn't have anything to do with his past. It concerned *Aida's* past, and it had taken him all day and a shameful amount of money in long-distance calls and lawyer fees to find it.

Worth every goddamn penny.

The address he was hunting ended up being down the street from his old house, two blocks from Lombard. Small world. Winter asked Bo to park the Pierce-Arrow right in front of a three-story Spanish Colonial attached home. Well kept. Cypress trees flanking the crooked steps. Shiny white Duesenberg behind an elaborate metal gate in the driveway.

"I'll be right back. Shouldn't take long." Winter buttoned his coat and marched up the steps to the entrance. A bored maid answered his knock and blanched at the sight of him.

He removed his hat. "Winter Magnusson to see Mr. Emmett Lane."

"Oh . . . yes, well, Mr. and Mrs. Lane are entertaining clients for dinner right now."

"This will only take a second."

"Can I tell him what this is in regards to?"

"Yes, you may. You tell your boss that we can discuss the inheritance of his deceased brother's child alone or in front of his guests—his choice."

The maid hesitated for a beat before opening the door wider. "Please come in, Mr. Magnusson. Drawing room is to your left. I'll bring him straight in."

And to her credit, she did just that, for Winter only waited a handful of seconds before a tall man with gray hair and shrewd eyes sauntered into a slice of lamplight illuminating the front room. "Mr. Magnusson, is it?"

"It is."

"State your business. I'm engaged with a dinner party."

Winter removed a folded telegram from his suit pocket. "Have a look at this."

Mr. Lane's scowl deflated as his eyes scanned the brief message.

"You'll note that was wired to my attorney two hours ago from Baltimore. See, when Miss Palmer told me the story about her foster parents dying, something stuck with me that I didn't quite understand. Why, I asked myself, would a well-to-do couple raise two children for ten years without ensuring the adoption paperwork was in order? After all, their will was thorough. Seems to me their lawyer would've made sure everything was up to snuff."

"What business—"

"So I did some poking around. And as you see on that telegram there, the adoption was legal, and the state of Maryland is happy to provide a notarized letter stating that the documents are on file. The lawyer we're working with in Baltimore is taking care of that tomorrow."

Mr. Lane's hand dropped. "It's been ten years."

"Eleven."

"There's no money left from that estate. It's long been sold, the gains lost in the stock market."

"Not my concern that you can't manage money."

"Whatever scam that girl's running on you, I can assure you that *my* lawyer will investigate every possible legal angle to prevent—"

Winter stepped closer and spoke in a lower voice. "Do you know who I am, Mr. Lane?"

The question hung between them for a moment. "Yes, I believe I do."

"Then you know I don't really have a great deal of love for the law. I'm also an extremely impatient man. So we can either handle things with grace and dignity, and you can prove to me that you aren't the conniving prick I suspect you are, or I can come back later with my men and convince you in other ways."

The man stared at him, nostrils flaring. "What do you want?"

"I want Sam Palmer's army footlocker. I know it was sent to you, so don't tell me it wasn't. The army still has a record of the shipment—military efficiency is a thing of beauty."

Mr. Lane stared at him, mouth agape, then brushed away invisible crumbs from his suit lapels. "It's in storage. I'll have to dig it out."

"I want it delivered to my place of business by Friday." He handed Mr. Lane a business card and took back the telegram, folding it as he talked. "If it isn't delivered by five o'clock sharp in the afternoon, I will break a finger for every minute it's late. If I run out of fingers . . . I'll just have to get creative. Do we have an understanding?"

The man's face was puce with rage. "I don't know what you think you're going to find inside."

"Not everything is profit fodder, Mr. Lane. It is simply of sentimental value to the boy's sister, and I want it."

"Fine. Are we done?"

Winter's gaze fell upon a photograph on the mantel. The man's wife, he presumed. "One more thing. Your brother's estate in Baltimore was appraised at twenty thousand dollars."

"Now, you look here—I have no way of getting my hands on that kind of money. The estate was sold off for far less than it was worth, and that was a decade ago."

"I know exactly how much you're worth, Mr. Lane. I also know you have $5,607.02 in your account at Hibernia Savings and Loan. I want a check made out to Aida Palmer for that exact amount to be sent along with the footlocker."

Sweat glistened across Mr. Lane's forehead.

Winter picked up the picture frame on the mantel, removed the photograph, and handed the frame to Mr. Lane.

An idle threat, but the man was a piece of shit who deserved to squirm. "Five o'clock on Friday. Enjoy your dinner."

Winter knew something was wrong when Bo pulled into the driveway. The gate was standing open, the day's last rays casting long shadows over the empty space where his mother's Packard should've been sitting. But it was his staff lined up on the side porch that made his heart rate shift from flustered to panicked.

"What's happened?" he said, slamming the car door behind him.

The maids fled, retreating through the screened door. Only Greta and Benita remained, and their dueling looks of worry versus titillation did nothing to calm his nerves.

"I warned her not to," Greta said, shaking her head. "I told her you'd skin her alive."

"What are—"

Excited shouting exploded from the street in front of the house. Bo was already jogging out front. By the time Winter raced to catch up with him, the source of the shouting revealed itself as Jonte. The reserved old bastard was running down the sidewalk, long arms akimbo as he signaled wildly to a car puttering down the street. Winter had never seen him so animated. What the devil was going on?

"Oh my God," Bo muttered as he tore off his cap and stared at the spectacle.

Winter's mind finally grasped what was happening. Jonte was running alongside Winter's mother's car, which lurched fast, then slow, then fast again. "Brakes!" the old Swede shouted. "Use the brakes before you turn, not after!"

The blood all but drained from Winter's body when he spotted the Packard's driver. Astrid? Mother of God, it was. His sister was squealing with either terror or delight—he couldn't tell which—as she shifted gears and the car's transmission made a sound that no one should ever, *ever* hear their car make. And Aida was perched in the passenger seat, cheering her on.

"Shit," he murmured. *"Shit, shit, shit."*

He scanned the street and saw a couple of other cars pulled over to the side, their drivers probably in fear for their lives—and he didn't blame them. His sister was on a mad path of destruction that flattened a flower bed when she made a jerky, sharp turn into the driveway, veered erratically to the right, nearly smashing the car's mirrors against the open gate, then came to a screeching halt a mere inch away from plowing into the back of the Pierce-Arrow.

Jonte stopped in the middle of the driveway and bent over, clutching his heaving chest. Bo ran to check on him, but the man was only winded. Probably the most exercise he'd had in years. Winter breezed past them and made a beeline for the Packard.

Astrid saw him coming and flattened herself against Aida on the car's seat. "I only took it around the block a couple of times."

His gaze skidded over the length of the Packard, looking for damage as he approached. He could hear the staff tittering on the porch behind him, all of them now back outside to witness Astrid's exhibition.

"I didn't hit anything!" she said, then something caught fire behind her eyes. "And guess what—I loved every second of it."

A goddamn challenge. Wicked little girl . . . he wanted to . . . Christ alive, he didn't know what he wanted. He looked at Aida.

"Go on and be mad at me," she said, just as defiant. "It was my idea, and I don't regret it. She did just fine. Might've scared a few of your neighbors, but some of them looked like they needed a little excitement."

He counted breaths, staring down at them while the staff grew quiet.

For a moment, he didn't know what he was thinking or how he felt. A strange numbness took root inside his chest. Looking on the scene in front of him, he expected to be reminded of the accident . . . to feel the same fear he'd felt during the weeks after, every time Bo drove him somewhere, every time

Astrid got in a car. Sometimes he'd wait outside for Jonte to return with her, making himself sick with worry while he remembered the sounds of the accident . . . remembered how he'd been pinned by the steering wheel, unable to move as he called out to Paulina and his parents and no one answered.

But forcing himself to think about those things was different than the memories coming without warning. And he *was* forcing it, wasn't he? As if he were testing himself.

He stared at his baby sister, trying to will his mother's face in place of hers, but all he saw was Astrid's rebellion. Behind her, Aida offered him a patient smile that made his insides quiver. He wanted to pull her into his arms and hold her; he wanted to scream at her. For God's sake, didn't she understand what he'd been through today? He'd been fighting for her—threatening people, pushing his lawyer, ordering up black magic from Velma to get revenge on the people who nearly killed her . . . ringing the house every few hours to check on her like a nervous mother bird.

He felt raw on the inside. Overwhelmed. Defeated.

"Did you see me?" Astrid asked Bo, a little breathless and puffed up with pride.

Winter cut a sharp look Bo's way. If he said *one* single word of encouragement to her, he'd pummel the boy's head into the pavement for pulling a Judas and siding with the girls. But his assistant just stuffed his hands into his pockets and rocked on his heels as he locked gazes with Astrid. He didn't give her a verbal approval, but he might as well have applauded—anyone could tell he was fighting back that damned smart grin of his.

"I wasn't great, but I think I'll manage it better next time," Astrid said proudly.

"Not bad," Aida agreed, poking his sister affectionately on her arm. "Not bad at all."

Christ. They were all teamed up against him, and witnessing Astrid's burst of self-confidence, Winter had the sinking feeling he was on the wrong side of this argument. His own guilt and fear had prevented his sister from experiencing this moment of happiness.

And in one day, after losing everything she owned—after nearly being burned alive in her own bed—Aida had done what he was never able to do: she'd stepped into his home and swept away two years of melancholia hanging over the household.

Winter tried to say something, failed, and headed into his home.

# TWENTY-SIX

———— ❦ ————

AIDA GAVE WINTER SOME TIME TO CALM DOWN. QUIET FURY HAD transformed his face into something she barely recognized. She'd overstepped and pushed him too far. God only knew what was going on in that mind of his right now. He might be thinking of the accident. She probably made the memory fresh for him again and could only imagine how painful it could be.

Maybe she was wrong to think his life could be changed with a simple push, and maybe this wasn't the right way to go about it. Too much at once. She should've thought it through instead of acting on impulse.

Night fell, and the temperature on the porch dropped as the fog began rolling off the bay. Leaving Astrid chatting with Bo, Aida struck out into the house to find Winter. He wasn't in the kitchen. Wasn't downstairs. Wasn't inside his study.

The mirrors.

God, she hoped the staff hadn't already seen to her request. Hopefully Greta had sense enough not to listen to her. She approached his bedroom door, heart hammering with dread. It was closed. She rapped lightly, and hearing no reply, almost walked away. But considering that she hadn't heard one word from him all day, if she didn't at least try to talk to him, she might be sleeping on the sofa in his study.

She opened the door. Winter was standing in his shirt-sleeves on the opposite side of his bed, staring into the corner. The dressing mirror had been moved there. He wasn't looking in it, but rather looking *at* it. As if it were an alien enemy breeching the safety of his room.

Aida closed the door behind her. "That was my doing, too, I'm afraid. I didn't do it to hurt you. I just . . ."

He didn't turn around to look at her. "You just what?"

"I just wanted you to see yourself as I did."

"And how is that, Aida?" He sounded weary or sad. Maybe angry. She wasn't sure which.

She stood behind him, catching both their reflections in the long mirror. The planes and contours of his long face were changed by shadows, his eyes downcast, feelings shrouded. "I see someone strong and resilient. Someone who pushes himself hard and expects others to do the same. Someone smart and fair. Decisive. Protective. I see a good man."

"You see a mirage."

"Better to use my sight for hope than remain blinded by guilt." She put a hand on his arm. "And if you're a mirage, how is it that you feel solid to me?"

His head turned. He looked down at her hand as if he could will it away. She gripped him harder. When his eyes met hers, she saw nothing but cold outrage and a barely checked rancor that made goose bumps swell across her arms. It was as though he was daring her—just *daring* her to look away.

She dared him right back.

An explosion of fire leapt behind all that coldness. His big arm shot out, snagged her around the waist, and lifted her right off the floor.

He meant to punish her, but she met him halfway, wrapping her legs around his waist and digging her nails into the back of his neck.

How do you punish someone who wants to be punished?

The kiss was angry. Aggressive. Searing. His cock hardened immediately. Christ, she felt good, and he was starved for her. Had it been two days since he'd had her? It seemed like years. He pulled her hips against him and slid his tongue into her mouth, teasing a tortured moan out of her. Yes, that's the sound he'd been missing. Her capitulation. Her pleasure.

She wrenched herself away from the kiss, gasping for breath, breasts heaving. "We were supposed to be lovers, nothing more." She was practically shouting in his face. "That was the agreement. You didn't want anything permanent—that's what you said."

"Nothing's changed." A lie. The biggest lie in the world.

She slid down his body until she was on her feet again. Fingers fumbled at his fly, freeing his cock, heavy and aching for her. His balls tightened while she gazed at it, watching it bob between them.

And she dropped to her knees.

One warm hand wrapped around his cock—the sensation of her soft skin on him nearly enough to rocket him through the roof—as she gave the head a few tentative kisses that sent a dark shudder through him. Big, brown eyes looked to him for approval. He urged her on with a hand on the back of her fine, straight hair. Soft kisses gave way to a teasing lick, then another—*oh please, oh please, oh please*—then she took him inside her mouth.

He nearly died with pleasure.

Were they fighting? He forgot instantly. Forgot everything but her mouth, wet and warm and doing her best to take as much of him as she could. He made desperate, uncontrollable noises, completely at her mercy. Unable to reason out the *why* behind what she was doing, only astonished and grateful that she was. Gaining confidence, she took him in deeper, another inch, cheeks becoming concave as she suckled.

He glanced to the side and saw her from a different angle . . . their reflection in the dressing mirror. *Mother of*

*God.* Aida on her knees servicing him. He'd never seen a more beautiful sight.

Was this on purpose? Damn her, and damn her again.

His hips bucked. Her fingernails dug into his legs. She pulled back to get a breath, continuing to pump at him with one hand, then gave him a smile, an exhaled single delirious laugh of joy, before going at him again. *She's enjoying it,* he thought madly as he looked in the mirror. But why wouldn't she? He enjoyed burying his tongue between her thighs.

This was something more, though. She was angry . . . wanting control—of him, or of her dismantled life? Of the unseen bond that pulled them together? If she wanted him to admit defeat, he would shout it across the city. She defeated him with far less than this.

After a few more pulls from her warm mouth, he felt an unmistakable pressure at the base of his cock, the urge to thrust. He wouldn't last much longer if she kept this pace.

"Enough, enough." He hooked his hands around her shoulders and pulled her up. "Christ, Aida, I want to be inside you. Help me."

He made quick work of her clothes: dress lifted over head, chemise yanked down over hips. The stockings could stay. Why was she insistent on unbuttoning his shirt? Keyed up and anxious, he slung his arms around her waist and lifted her off the floor, excited by her protest, and threw her on the bed.

His brain was barely working. He was in a singular savage mode, racing against his own drive to have her, and couldn't process anything besides the basic mechanics it would take for his monstrous body to align with her petite one in the simplest way possible. He dropped his suspenders over both shoulders so he could shove his pants lower, struggled with the tin of Merry Widows in the bedside table drawer—nearly dropping it in his haste—and prepared to flip her onto her hands and knees, so he could take her while standing at the edge of the mattress.

"No." She pressed the heel of one palm between her legs,

as if to quench an ache—possibly the single most arousing
sight he'd ever seen. "Like the postcard," she demanded.

He tore his gaze from her hand. It took a moment for his
dull brain to catch up. *The postcard*. She wanted to be on
top—there was that damned control of hers. Hell, did she
think he'd stop her?

"Yes, yes," he murmured. "Fine idea. Let's do that. Come
here."

He sat up on the bed, his back against the headboard,
and helped her as she crawled to straddle his lap. Damp curls
brushed across his balls, making his cock jump. He slipped
fingers between her legs. Unbelievably wet. Warm. Swollen
with need. Ready for him. He guided her down, and when
she impaled herself on him, taking as much of his length as
she could in one fierce movement, gasping loudly, he nearly
lost his mind.

"Aida, Aida," he said, a fervent prayer. A devotion.

She chased a frenetic rhythm, hands gripping his shoulders hard enough to leave bruises. It only made him harder.
He helped himself to her body, rolling her nipples between
his finger and thumb, tasting the sensitive skin beneath her
jaw, memorizing the curve where her hips flared from her
waist . . . brailling over her raised scars with his palms.

His eyes lingered over rose-adorned garters biting into
her thighs, then followed the lines at the back of her stockings to the lightly scuffed soles of new shoes. Every so often,
he slipped a thumb down where their bodies were joined
and rubbed her stiff bud until she moaned and clenched
around him so tightly he had to stop for fear he'd come
before she did.

"That's it, take me," he praised. "Punish me."

She gritted her teeth and cried out in frustration and he
loved it. She was a goddess above him, hell-bent on conquering, making him pay with each rocking stroke of her
beautiful body. He adored every bit of her: the gleam of
sweat on her brow, the sounds of pleasure she was making,
the scent of her sex.

It was far better than anything his debauched brain had ever imagined.

Her breath became ragged. Flesh smacked. Freckled breasts quivered and bounced hypnotically. The moment she faltered, thighs shaking with effort, he angled himself farther down on the cushion beneath her and took over, vigorously pounding up into her as she arched over him.

His mind emptied. He was nothing but a body serving to meet her pleasure. And when that pleasure finally gathered strength and crested, her eyes locked with his. The look on her face was so vulnerable and open, and God help him, somewhere in the back of his barbaric, dull mind, he thought: *This one. Her. Only her. No one else.*

Her eyes closed. A long, soulful wail broke from her mouth. She came so intensely, so ferociously, he was almost jealous. The absurdity of this thought was washed away by his own brutal need. His turn, now—thank God.

She was boneless, weightless, ready to collapse. "Not yet," he said. "Hold on." He lifted her up and down on his cock in time with the pumping of his hips, reviving her. She shuddered and squeezed around him again, another orgasm taking them both by surprise. And as she bucked in his arms, sobbing, every muscle in his body tensed in anticipation.

His pleasure crashed through him, surging forward. He held her hips down and came into her endlessly, a glorious, blinding moment of complete surrender that he felt in the base of his spine, the pads of his toes, the tips of his fingers.

When it faded, he was gasping for breath below her, muttering broken Swedish that he knew she couldn't understand, but damned if he could reach for the words in English. Funny that his mind had trouble making the switch, when it was usually second nature.

Her head lolled against his neck. He stroked her hair as their hearts slowed, finally finding the right words in the right language, which he whispered against her cheek. "Everything I have is yours. My home, my body, my protection . . . my heart. All of me."

One salty tear slid down her cheek. He captured it with

a swipe of his tongue, and this started an avalanche of great, convulsive sobs. He didn't ask why. Just folded his arms around her, pulling her into the rocky cave of his body, and waited for the crying to stop. And when it did, he held her until she fell asleep in his arms. Somewhere inside his blackened heart, he knew it would be the last time.

# TWENTY-SEVEN

———◆———

AIDA BARELY SAW WINTER THE REST OF THE WEEK. A FEAT, really—and an ironic one, at that. She was staying under his roof, sleeping in his bed, and yet she was never alone with him. He was gone when she woke every day. Sometimes he'd eat dinner at home, but by the time she'd rush off to do her show at Gris-Gris, then rush back afterward, he'd already be on his way out again. She waited up for him until the wee hours of the morning, but he never came to bed. On the third night, she found him sleeping in his mother's old bedroom; he claimed he didn't want to wake her when he got home.

Aida spent more time with Astrid, and with Bo. Good grief—even Mrs. Lin spent more time with her when she stopped by to check in and bring almond cookies.

Aida knew Winter was avoiding her. He was mad because she was leaving—maybe mad that he'd said those things to her that night they were together. *Everything I have is yours.* At the time she'd thought he meant it. Now she worried it was merely a lover's oath, said in a moment of passion, forgotten the morning after. And yet the words hounded her thoughts days later. She felt silly for letting them affect her, sillier still for *wanting* to believe them. But she couldn't help but wonder if she'd been able to say something back, would he be avoiding her now? Would she still be going to New Orleans?

She wanted to talk to him, but she didn't know how.

On her next-to-last night in the city, she followed him into the kitchen after dinner, where he was talking to Bo at a large prep table that sat in the center of the room.

Aida felt the temperature change as she stepped across the doorway; the room was humid and warm with earlier dinner preparations. "I am leaving in a day," she announced to Winter's back. "Are you going to refuse to look at me until I walk out the door?"

His body stilled, but he didn't turn around to face her. The cook did, however—and after shelving the plate she'd been washing on a rack above the sink, she mumbled something in Swedish, then scurried out the door, wiping her hands on her apron.

Bo coughed into his fist before scratching the back of his neck. "I'll . . . just be in my room." He gave her a sympathetic look as he passed.

The heels of her leather pumps clicked on black-and-white checkerboard tiles as she walked around the table. Steam puffed from a simmering pot on the stove behind her, where bones from their meal were being used to prepare stock for tomorrow.

"If you're angry at me, I wish you'd just come out and say it."

He still wouldn't look at her. Just gathered the paperwork that was spread out on the table. "I've been busy."

"Liar."

His hand flinched. "What do you want me to say, Aida— have a great trip? It's been nice knowing you?"

"It's not easy for me, either. I'm not jumping with excitement to leave. I'm dreading it, if you want to know the truth. I don't want to go."

Mismatched eyes slanted toward hers. "Then don't."

"I have to."

"Why?"

"Because it's my job. I've made a name for myself. Try to understand. I used to beg for work, now clubs are seeking *me* out. I've been given this window of success—if I squander it, I might never have it again."

"You said yourself that you don't want to do this forever."

"I don't. But what am I supposed to do? I just lost everything I've saved for the last few years—"

He tossed the paperwork on the table. "Oh, for the love of God, you know I'll replace that. I've probably got it in petty cash in my study."

"Of course you do," she said bitterly. "Because it's nothing to you. Do you have any idea how hard I struggled to save that? Years of scrimping, choosing second-best, doing without, only to have all of that brushed aside as your petty cash?"

"So I'm to be penalized because I have money?"

She waved a hand in frustration. "This isn't about money. It's about my independence—my life. Who I am. I won't sacrifice everything I've worked for on a whim."

"I thought you lived in the moment."

"I do—but I'm not careless. I plan for my future."

"Then plan for it here," he said, planting both palms on the wood as he leaned over the table and spoke intently. "The Bay is where you were born. This is your home."

"I don't have a home."

"Then make one."

"I will. That's what I'm trying to do—I'm trying to save, but it's hard."

"You know what I think?" he said, biceps straining his suit as he crossed his arms over his chest. "I think this isn't really about money at all."

"It's about *my* money. My pride."

"And what if you were to find out that you *do* have money. Yours."

"I'm not looking for a handout—how many times do I have to say that?"

He started to reply, then thought better of it and shook his head. "It doesn't matter. I don't want you to make a decision to stay because of money. I want you to *want* to stay. I told you how I felt. You obviously don't share those feelings."

"What do you know of my feelings?"

"I only know what I see when I look in your eyes. What I hear when I listen to the emotion behind your words." He paused, then spoke in a lower tone. "What I feel when I touch you."

Her throat tightened. "And what do all those things tell you?" She meant to sound tough, but the words came out reeking of desperation.

"They tell me that no matter what you might feel, you are too stubborn to take a risk when it comes to your heart. Because even though you accuse me of being weighted down by my past, you're the one living in yours."

"Me?"

"I might be depressed and angry at times, but I didn't stop living after the accident. I picked myself up and kept working. I didn't let my family down. I didn't abandon my clients or my workers or my staff."

"And that's exactly what I'm trying to do!" she argued.

"Here's the difference: I don't work because it would make my father happy. I work because *I* enjoy it— me —and because people are counting on me."

Was he insulting her? She wasn't sure. "I enjoy what I do."

"Do you really? You enjoy hurting yourself? You enjoy giving yourself scars?"

She struggled for a breath. Her voice cracked. "You said you don't mind them."

"I don't and you damn well know it. But you told me you use the lancet because it's fast. You wouldn't have to use it if you were spending an hour with one client, calling up one spirit, for the same amount of money you make calling up a dozen in front of an audience."

"I can't do that until I've saved enough money."

"How many years will that take? Five? Ten?"

"I d-don't know."

"But you won't accept a loan? What if it came from an outside source? People get loans from a bank every day. That would hurt your pride so much?"

Good grief, he was exasperating, trying to talk her into a trap. "This isn't about my career," she complained. "You want me to stay for us."

"Hell yes, I do! Guilty."

"But if I stay, then I lose my career momentum. And how long will we last, Winter? Ask yourself that. You've already tried marriage once, and you said yourself it wasn't working, even if the accident never happened. You told me you weren't interested in anything more than a fling because of your marriage."

"Feelings change."

"Yes, and quickly. Because we've only known each other a month. And what if your feelings change again in another month? Sam always told me that nothing lasts, and that relationships destroy the individual. And clearly that's what you've experienced yourself with Paulina. Why would it be any different for the two of us?"

"Did you ever stop to think that Saint Sam might not know everything?"

Anger heated her cheeks as she pointed a shaking finger. "Don't you *dare* talk about him."

"Why not? You brought him up. I'm sure he was a fine fellow, but he's dead, Aida. He's been dead for more than ten years. When are you going to stop living your life to please him?"

"He's none of your damn business!"

"Unfortunately he is my damn business, because he's come between me and the woman I love."

Love? She didn't mean to gasp—if that's what the noise coming out of her mouth could be called. It was so loud, it sounded as though she were choking. She felt like she was. A brutal weight struck her chest and strangled her heart. She stood in place, unnaturally glued to the tile floor as if under a spell.

"That's what I thought," Winter said. "No response. I suspect you'd let your martyrlike mission to preserve Sam's idiotic ideas overshadow anything at all you might feel, so God only knows whether you care for me in return."

*I do.* She wanted to say it out loud, but her throat wouldn't work. Her fingers were going numb. She felt . . . she felt as though she were going into shock.

If she could articulate what she felt, she'd have told him she was overwhelmed with feelings for him. But it was something she'd never experienced before, and she was terrified. She'd have told him that she wanted more than anything to stay here and be with him.

But Winter didn't give her time to manage it. "Sam was an eighteen-year-old boy who was trying to rationalize the meaning of life," he said. "Did you ever stop to think that he may have changed his tune after a few years?"

"I'll never know, because he didn't get a few more years."

"But you'll spend the rest of yours molding your life around a memory?"

Tears came, fast and strong. She felt like a quaking rabbit cornered by a wolf, unable to think properly. Unable to do anything but position herself to cut and run. "W-why am I the only one forced to take a risk? You want me to stay, but only as your mistress. Did you ever stop to think how I will be perceived if I stay here permanently? Everyone knows you. Everyone will know me, too, and they will talk."

"Who cares if they do?"

"I do! It will affect me and any kind of business endeavors I'd attempt to make."

"Bullshit. No one cares about that anymore."

"Your parents did, or your mother wouldn't have pushed you into a marriage with someone you didn't even like." She swiped tears from her eyes. "If Sam's memory taints my choices, then your horrible relationship with Paulina taints yours."

Cold eyes stared at her from across the table. A muscle in his jaw jumped. He took a deep breath and looked at his hands. "Maybe Paulina just opened my eyes to what marriage really is."

"And pray tell, what exactly did dearest Paulina teach you about marriage?"

"That it's a piece of paper—a legal document that has nothing to do with feelings or trust or affection or friendship. It's a goddamn business transaction, and I will not reduce what's between us to a court filing whose only purpose is to bind people together for the sake of money!"

"And I will not keep repeating what you already know—if you think I want money from you, then you can damn well keep believing that while I'm on the train to New Orleans!"

Rage transformed Winter's face into something demonic, the kitchen's pendant lights casting harsh, craggy shadows down the planes of his face. He slammed his fist on the table, making both it and Aida jump. As his paperwork scattered, some of it fluttering to the floor, he stormed around and stalked her. She backed up, but he kept coming until he was towering over her like a fiend rising from the abyss. Steam from the simmering stockpot whirled around his dark head.

"Go on, then." His breath was hot on her face, his anger hot as flames licking her skin. "Get out of my house and don't fucking come back. I don't ever want to see your face again."

His words boiled her heart right inside her chest. And the tears that spilled down her cheeks weren't enough to extinguish the damage he'd done.

"GET OUT!"

She stumbled backward, turned, and without another word, fled the room.


Winter slammed the heel of his palm against the porcelain icebox. Did that really happen? He could hardly believe it. He listened to Bo's voice, hearing snatches of his conversation with Aida outside in the hallway. A minute later, he heard an engine, and assumed Jonte was driving her to Gris-Gris for her last show.

The telephone rang. He let someone else answer. After a few moments, Bo slipped inside the kitchen. Winter prepared himself for the speech, but to Bo's credit, it didn't come.

"I know you might not want to hear this right now, but that was Velma on the line."

Winter grunted. It was all he could manage.

"She was calling to say that they're reporting on the radio that two unidentified men in Chinatown were burned alive inside a black truck that misfired outside a grocer's shop. Witnesses said a couple of folks tried to help the men when the truck started burning, but the locks were stuck on both doors, and they were afraid it would explode—which it did."

*Christ alive.* The curse worked.

"No identification on the bodies. No registration plates on the truck," Bo added. "Cops think it might've been stolen. I'll check in with one of our guys on the inside and see if I can get any other information."

After Winter muttered his thanks, Bo retreated, leaving him alone in the kitchen with nothing but his incoherent thoughts. His world was breaking apart. He was numb on the inside, worn down on the outside. He couldn't move or think properly. Could barely focus his eyes on Greta when her silver head appeared in the doorway.

"Are you all right, *gulleplutten*?" she asked.

He stood up and pulled the front of his suit into place, trying to wrestle some control over his feelings, and heard the crinkle of paper from his inner suit pocket. Emmett Lane's check to Aida. He could've handed it over, given her the chance to make an informed choice, but he wanted her to choose to stay for him, not money.

He'd put his heart on a plate for her, and she wouldn't say the words back. Maybe he'd been fooling himself to believe she felt the same way.

He glanced up at Greta. "Have her things packed and brought down to the foyer."

Aida's last performance at Gris-Gris was her all-time worst. Unable to call spirits for not one, not two, but three audience members—and unwilling to fake it—she was booed off the stage.

A career first.

Maybe a career last, if word got back to her future employer down South.

"It happens to the best of us," Velma said generously, patting her on the back as she handed over the last of her wages. "Maybe you're distracted by something you want to talk about?"

Aida shook her head. She would only start crying again.

After Hezekiah and Daniels both hugged her, after she'd said all her good-byes, she left in disgrace, heading through the back delivery door.

Pausing under the doorway light, she pulled her gloves from her handbag and stared up at the fog tenting the narrow alleyway. Well. What now? All her new things were at Winter's house.

And so was Winter.

She closed her eyes and exhaled heavily, then slipped her hand into a glove. "Okay, Palmer," she muttered to herself. "Let's think about this rationally."

Maybe he'd been right that no one would care about their affair. She wasn't leading a Girl Scout troop, after all. And how could she argue that they didn't know their own feelings well enough after a month, but insist that he make a public demonstration to last a lifetime?

Right or wrong, it didn't mean she had to leave the state to prove her argument, stomping off like a petulant child. Yes, she loved this city, and some insistent part of her *did* feel like it was home. So he was right about two things.

And really, when she considered, she *could* get a bank loan—he was right about that, too, damn him! Just a small one, enough to pay for a few months' rent at a cheap place, perhaps one with an apartment attached, so she could live and work out of the same place to save money.

*He's come between me and the woman I love.*

Did Winter mean that? Did he really love her?

On a sigh, she let her arms flop to her sides. Her handbag

slipped off her wrist, dropping to the pavement. The contents of her handbag scattered. She bent to collect them all.

"You all right, Miss Palmer?"

She looked up. One of the club's guards, Manny, was leaning out of the back door.

"I'm fine," she lied as she scooped everything back into her handbag. "Thank you."

"Miss Palmer!" A new voice called to her several yards away, at the mouth of the alley. A man stood next to a car with the door open, waving to her. Clouds of exhaust pumped from the tailpipe as the engine rumbled. It took her a second to recognize the man's face.

"Doctor Yip," she said with a smile, standing to greet him. "What brings you out to North Beach?"

"A long story," he said as she approached. "Would you have time to listen to it, over tea perhaps?"

She hesitated, wanting to get back to Winter and talk. But the herbalist's face was friendly, and perhaps he had some information they needed. "Is this about Mr. Magnusson?"

"Yes, in fact it is." He gestured toward the backseat of the waiting car. "Please."

"You all right, Miss Palmer?" Manny repeated from behind her.

She lifted a hand in answer. "It's okay."

"Please," Doctor Yip said again, encouraging her into the car. "Won't take long. I think you will be quite interested in what I have to tell you. We can drive across the street to the Automat."

It was silly to be hesitant about getting in a car with the old man. He'd helped them, after all, and they'd attracted Ju's thugs into his quiet shop. She glanced down and saw he was still wearing his quaint Chinese embroidered slippers. The least she could do was listen to whatever news he had. He gave her a kind smile.

She slid in the backseat, bumping into a man who was already sitting inside. "Excuse me," she said. "I didn't know anyone was in here."

She looked up. The man held a rag in his hand that smelled of noxious herbs. A dark scab marred his cheek, just below his eye.

All at once, she noticed the driver's nose was taped up; his hat nearly covered up his cauliflower ear.

The door shut behind her as Doctor Yip spoke from her side. "Now, my little spirit medium—are you going to play nice, or shall I have one of my new worker bees make you go to sleep?"

# TWENTY-EIGHT

———— ❧ ————

AN HOUR AFTER AIDA LEFT, WINTER FELT THE AFTERSHOCKS OF
their fight lessening. Two hours, and his heart was heavy
with regret. By the time eleven o'clock rolled around, he
was pacing the floors, working himself into a state that see-
sawed between impatience and desperation.

"Should I fetch her from the club?" Jonte asked.

Her show would be ending now. It usually took her a half
hour to sign a couple of autographs, get out of her stage
clothes. "I'll go with you," Winter decided, grabbing his hat
and coat. A couple of minutes later, they were pulling out
of the driveway.

In the dark of the car, Winter watched his sleeping neighborhood sail by the window. It was selfish to have withheld
the news of Emmett Lane's check from her—he understood
that now. Stupid, stubborn pride. She was obviously worried
about a safety net if she was talking about marriage.

Marriage.

He still couldn't believe she brought that up. She knew
how he felt about the subject. Never again, not after what he
went through with Paulina. Maybe she was trying to wrestle

some kind of sacrifice out of him, because she saw leaving her club career as a compromise. Because what else could it be if she wasn't after his money—and of course she wasn't, so ridiculous of him to even entertain that idea for a second—and she wasn't in love with him.

Was she?

She wouldn't say the words. And that upset him more than he cared to admit.

Maybe she would come to love him. If it took her more time to get to that place, better it be here than somewhere across the country, days away by train. Christ, when it came down to it, he'd rather she hate his guts and open her business here, where he could protect her and watch her and keep her safe.

"You should let her drive the Packard."

Startled, Winter glanced at Jonte in the rearview mirror. "What's that?"

"If you marry her, you should let her drive the Packard. She's been taking it out with Astrid all week. Whether or not Astrid learns to drive is one thing, but a girl that young in a family this notorious should not be driving alone. One of your rivals could harm her. Miss Palmer is older—she's not naive like Astrid. Miss Palmer should drive the Packard."

Winter sat in silence, unable to believe what Jonte was saying. The old man never butted into his business. Granted, everyone *else* in the household did—God knew Greta couldn't go two hours without giving her opinion—but Jonte was an island, silent and stoic.

And second, his driver had just made the assumption that Winter might marry Aida. Where did that come from? Surely half the staff heard them arguing, and five minutes couldn't have passed before they told the other half what they'd heard. Was Jonte so far removed from the gossip that he didn't know what had happened?

"Not my business," the old man said. "But she would make a fine wife. Help you forget about the first one, which, by the way, I told your pappa many times was a bad match.

Your mother was only trying to look out for you, but she made a mistake."

"Maybe some people aren't meant to marry. I might be one of them. My job is dangerous and disreputable."

"It's the same job your pappa had, and he was married and raising a family."

"Mamma hated it."

"She was afraid one of you would get killed or end up in jail. She was not ashamed of the work. She was proud of your pappa. Proud of you, too."

Winter glanced out the window in silence.

"And if you don't mind me being frank, Miss Palmer is made of sterner stuff than your mamma ever was."

"I had no idea you had an opinion about such matters," Winter admitted.

"You don't pay me for advice. That doesn't mean I don't have opinions."

"I'll be damned. Maybe all that running you did when you were chasing down Astrid and Aida knocked some of those opinions loose, eh?"

"Maybe so," Jonte said with a quirk of his lips, then returned to his usual silent self.

Winter lifted his hat and swiped his hand over his hair.

How had life gotten so complicated?

All he could wrap his head around was that he'd made a terrible mistake in sending Aida out of the house like he did. She probably thought he was a monster, the way he yelled at her. He didn't want to be that person anymore. Especially when it came to her. All of this bullshit with hauntings and the fire and the goddamn Hive or Beekeeper—whatever the hell the enemy was calling himself—all of it was making him agitated, bringing out the worst in him.

Because that wasn't really him . . . was it? It couldn't be. He didn't want to live the rest of his life being that person.

He would not.

An accident at Broadway and Columbus held them up. When they finally made it to the club, it was almost midnight. They idled by the curb for several minutes, then Winter sent Jonte to see if she was still inside while he scanned the taxi line out front. He didn't want to miss her.

He waited five minutes for Jonte to return. Ten more. When the old man finally strode back, he knew something was wrong.

"Daniels claims she left half an hour ago."

"Where did she go?"

"Men working the entrance said she didn't leave that way."

Winter directed Jonte into the alley. He'd go up and find Velma. Maybe Aida told her where she was going. He could call home and see if they'd crossed paths.

Stepping out of the car, he spotted one of the club's bouncers guarding the door. One of the men who'd carried him up to Velma's apartment the night he was poisoned.

"Evening, Mr. Magnusson."

"Manny, is it?"

"That's right."

"I'm looking for Miss Palmer. Did you happen to see her leave?"

The man nodded. "Half an hour ago, thereabouts."

"Did she happen to say where she was going?"

"No, but she seemed to know the man she left with."

Every muscle in Winter's body tightened. "Which man?"

"Old Chinese man pulled up and waved her into a black Tin Lizzie. I asked her if she was okay. She seemed surprised to see him, but she said it was fine."

Winter's heart began pounding. "Did he give a name? What did he look like?"

"She called him 'doctor.' Funny old man with a long gray braid. British accent."

Doctor Yip. Confusion clouded Winter's thoughts.

"The man said he had some information about you, in fact," Manny said. "Said he wanted to talk about it over tea. I asked her if she was okay, and she said yes," he insisted again. "Did I make a mistake?"

Out of the corner of his eye, he saw silver shining on the

asphalt. He picked up Aida's lancet. His mind raced to fit puzzle pieces together, and he suddenly remembered the way the herbalist had flinched when he set eyes on Winter—not in fear, but in *recognition!*—and he remembered the man's Chinese slippers, embroidered with honeybees.

Shock struck his solar plexus like a physical blow.

"No," he told Manny. "I think I did."

Doctor Yip's car sped out of North Beach. But instead of heading to Chinatown, as Aida expected, they took side streets through Telegraph Hill and turned south on the Embarcadero.

She was trying to stay levelheaded about the fact that she was being kidnapped, and that the man who'd held her hostage and put his hand on her breast was now pressed against her side and sporting a hard-on. He was also still in possession of the noxious cloth. Though it had been put away inside an old shaving tin, he held it like a threat, and if it weren't for the window being cracked, she might pass out from the fumes.

And on her other side was the man who was haunting Winter, who'd killed the fortune-teller, set her apartment on fire . . .

"Where are you taking me?" she asked for the third time as they motored up the coast. They'd passed Winter's pier and the China Basin almost half an hour back, and had since crossed three sets of railroad tracks. All she could see now were warehouses on one side of the road and freight slips on the other, and the signs she glimpsed hinted they might be driving through a meatpacking district. Best she could tell, they were heading out of the city, somewhere along the coast. Definitely unfamiliar territory.

Doctor Yip finally answered her, speaking for the first time since she'd gotten inside the car. "We are going somewhere Mr. Magnusson will never find you. You might call it my little nest." He smiled.

"You are the Beekeeper?"

"Some call me that."

"That afternoon we came to your shop—"

"Oh yes. That was quite a surprise. For a moment, I thought you'd uncovered my identity. Very surreal to see Mr. Magnusson standing in front of me. Providence, as you say here in the States, was smiling down on me that day."

"These two were working for you?"

"Not when they came into my shop that afternoon." The herbalist crossed his legs, pushing himself closer as he settled an arm on the back of the seat like they were old friends. "But Ju-Ray Wong is a weak boss who is uninterested in expanding his territory. After he banished the boys from his tong, I convinced him to work for me."

"Because you are going to take over Chinatown by controlling the liquor supply?"

"I was chosen by celestial deities to lead a quiet rebellion. My *shen* spirits brought me across the ocean from Hong Kong to save my people from the *Gwai-lo*. The Chinese have been treated like slaves in this country, captured like pigs, forced to build your railroads. After the Great Fire, the city tried to move Chinatown and seize our land, and when we resisted, you kept us in cages on Angel Island, separating our families for years."

"*I* didn't. And *you* were in Hong Kong."

"But my brother was not. He was detained on Angel Island for almost a decade before he died. He was jailed for no crime, but they treated him like a criminal."

Aida certainly could empathize with grief for a lost sibling, but she didn't lash out and kill people for revenge when Sam died.

Yip rocked his foot. "I am here now, ready to avenge my brother's life and lead my people to reclaim what is theirs. But I will do it my way, by my own creed. My mission is a peaceful one, because the *shen* spirits have given me a prophecy: I will help my people gain control of the city without spilling one single drop of blood."

It took several moments for this to sink in. Winter's hauntings, the "voice of God" telling the bootlegger to turn himself in, the tipoff for the raid, all the unrest in China-town . . . her fire. And the way Yip had gotten upset when these two thugs had broken into his shop—he'd shouted at them not to spill blood, claiming his shop was holy.

"I'm a peaceful man, a healer—not a killer," the herbal-ist said. "I have no blood debt on my hands. I am clean."

"Just because you didn't pull the trigger doesn't mean you're not guilty."

He gave her a patient smile. "Death is part of war, Miss Palmer. That is hard to hear when you are on the losing side."

"And on whose side are the tong leaders in Chinatown? Haven't you halted their business?"

He rocked one bee slipper near her shins. "They were given a chance to be on the winning side, but they all chose money over honor. And regarding guilt, every soldier knows that there are both good and bad ways to kill. I am taking the higher path by avoiding death if possible. And if death *is* necessary, I arrange for the killing to be done by the victim's own hands."

"Like the fortune-teller?"

"Suicide was the only honorable option. Mr. Wu violated an oath of silence and betrayed his own people to the enemy."

"And what about me, huh? That fire nearly killed me. How is that not on your hands?"

He sighed. "The fire was to scare you away from Mr. Magnusson. I only found out about the laudanum after the fact. They took it upon themselves to stray outside the guide-lines of my orders and took things too far. Ah, look—we are almost home."

The car slowed as they headed past a sign for Hunter's Point, then another for a dry dock, where several massive ships sat inside channels, moored on land by networks of planks and stilts. "What is this?"

"Where unseaworthy ships are repaired. The rusting hulk in front of us is the ship that brought me over from Hong Kong. Unfortunately for the Royal TransPacific Steamship

Company, the *Jade Princess* would not be able to make the return trip to China, because a strange and terrible fever struck her crew several days before entering port, and during that time her boiler went defective. The repair expenses were too high for the owners to manage, and permit problems seemed to plague them. Luckily I was there to pay the dry-docking costs, so she was signed over to me."

In the moonlight reflecting from the dark bay water in the distance, the beached passenger ship looked like a great derelict beast. Faint lights flickered inside a couple of the port windows; someone was inside.

Ju's former employees hauled her out of the car and shoved her toward a locked wooden fence that guarded entry to the dry dock. A foghorn wailed in the distance.

"We are quite invisible out here," Doctor Yip said as he unlocked the gate, the planks of which were covered in Chinese characters and strange symbols. "You and I have similar talents, Miss Palmer. Rather infuriating for me, as you ruined my hard work. But now that I have you contained, my efforts with Mr. Magnusson will be more successful. And I have something very special in store for him. Would you like to see what a necromancer can do?"

# TWENTY-NINE

———⟡———

WINTER STOOD IN THE MIDDLE OF DOCTOR YIP'S SHOP, GLASS crunching below his shoes from where he'd busted the door open. His stomach was knotted, his chest tight with a dull, pulsing terror.

The shop was deserted.

Not a damn piece of paper with another address or phone number. No paperwork whatsoever: the desk in the back office was completely empty. The shop itself looked as it did when Aida and he first came—minus the broken door.

And the row of glass jars behind the counter, which Winter had smashed with the register.

He now stared at the dark spot on the counter where the register had been. A twenty-dollar bill sat there, both sides painted with red symbols.

"See if Bo's done checking the alley, would you?" Winter said to Jonte. The driver stepped outside the shop and came back with his assistant, who'd met them there with a crew of men after Winter had called him from Gris-Gris.

"You know what any of this Chinese means?" Winter asked.

Bo strode to the counter and laid his gun down to examine it. "Black magic."

"I know that much." He couldn't help but wonder if this was the same bill he'd given Yip that afternoon. How many twenties would an herbalist get? Not many.

Then again, Yip was no herbalist.

Winter flipped open a matchbook, struck a match, and lit the bill on fire.

The rest of his men met them out front after canvassing the neighbors, which included an opium den, a locked warehouse, and one small well of apartments. No one knew where the herbalist lived. One lady said a black car dropped him off and picked him up every day.

He forced himself to stay calm. He would not think of the fire in her apartment, or how she'd been drugged. He would not think of what atrocities a kidnapped woman could be forced to suffer in the hands of a man who was trying to liberate Chinatown.

He only thought of what he'd do to that man when he got his hands on him.

Focusing on that, he had Jonte drive back home to keep an eye on Astrid while Bo drove him to Golden Lotus with his crew of men following. But after waking the Lins at an ungodly hour and scaring them half to death, all he discovered was that Mrs. Lin had never asked the herbalist where he lived.

"Is Miss Palmer in trouble?" she asked, gripping her robe closed as she stood in the apartment stairwell next to the restaurant, Mr. Lin standing over her shoulder.

"I think Yip is the one who had the fire set in her room and now he's taken her."

"Oh no. This is my fault," she said in a pained voice. "He seemed like such a nice man, but I should have never sent her to see him."

"Don't blame yourself. He's after me, not her."

His fault, but he would fix it. He would not lose her. Not if he had to destroy half the city finding her.

He could spare a man to watch Golden Lotus, make sure they wouldn't be left vulnerable. Mrs. Lin said she'd start calling her friends and find out if anyone knew anything about Doctor Yip. Doubtful, but Winter wasn't going to discount anything at this point.

He asked the Lins to call his house and leave a message for him there if they heard anything, then walked out into the chilly night air with Bo to rejoin the rest of his men.

"We should go to Ju," Bo said. "If the men who attacked you at Yip's shop were patrolling Ju's territory, then their replacements might be working the same area. They might've seen something."

"If so, that's great, but I'm not going to sit around waiting for information while Yip does God only knows what to Aida. We'll drive to Ju's, but he's not going to be happy, because I'm going to ask him to call all the tong leaders together for a meeting. If they want to take back control of their booze, they're going to have to help me find Aida." He stopped in front of the car. "Doctor Yip seems to want a war. He's got one."

Aida entered the ship on a wide gangplank. The deck was unassuming and quiet, the picture of disuse. The inside was another story. The first-class entrance, a large two-story open room with a staircase, was filled with wooden crates of alcohol—row after row of teetering stacks, some stamped with recognizable brands, others simply marked GIN. Half of them were painted with Chinese characters.

A small fortune in seized booze.

Aida couldn't quite determine the breadth of the haul, because the ship had no electricity. She could, however, spot the occasional guard meandering in the distance. Maybe ten or twenty men. Probably more she couldn't see. A path of portable lanterns led them through the maze of crates to the staircase at the far end of the room. Tables had been pulled together here to create a small work area, where more armed men sorted through stacks of paperwork and labels. Nearby, several crates stood open, brimming with bottles nestled inside piles of wood shavings.

When they passed, all workers looked up at Yip, hailing him by some Cantonese name Aida didn't catch, and bowing their heads.

"You've managed quite a collection here," Aida noted. "Is this where all the booze in Chinatown went?"

"Quite a bit outside of Chinatown, too," Doctor Yip said with a smile as he stopped to talk with someone at the tables. They spoke in hushed voices for several moments while Aida's gaze jumped around the room, looking for anything that might be helpful: an unguarded door, a weapon . . . an escape route. The man with the cauliflower ear tightened his grip around the back of her neck.

"Just try it," he whispered in her ear as pain shot down her shoulder. "I might not be able to hurt you in front of him, but wait until later."

His grip softened when Yip ended his conversation and rejoined the group. "All right, Miss Palmer, onward."

A few steps away, lanterns, fuel, and matches were lined up on a desk. Ju's former thugs both took lanterns. Yip took out a flashlight. They were going deeper into the beached whale.

They headed down a flight of steps to the first level below, passing by more guards. The scents of gin and wood changed to something danker when they stepped into a long corridor. Yip turned on his flashlight and shone the beam in front of them.

"I hope you find your accommodations to your liking," Yip said as he led them past doors lining either side of the hallway. Passenger cabins. First-class, from their location.

*Only the best*, Aida thought blackly. But this was no luxury liner built for rich European families to cruise the Mediterranean. This was an old steamer built for transporting large numbers of third-class expatriates from Hong Kong.

Yip opened a locked door at the end of the corridor.

"Here we are, my dear. Please enter." He held the narrow door open.

The cauliflower-eared man shoved her inside the tight quarters. Her knee banged against something hard. She yelped and tried to get her bearings in the dark. Yip carried one of the lanterns inside and hung it on one corner of the double-bunk berths lining one wall. One chair sat beneath the port window behind her, and a small sink sat at her left hip, on the wall opposite the berths. The room smelled of mold and must.

"It's a tight squeeze, but you'll make the most of it," Yip said. "No plumbing, so the sink's useless for anything other than a urinal. If you get desperate enough, you'll appreciate it more."

"How long are you keeping me here?"

"Not long, don't worry. I have something to show you tomorrow."

"Tomorrow?" She suddenly felt claustrophobic, trapped in the narrow space, and tried to grab Yip's collar.

He lunged out of her range. "Now, now, Miss Palmer. Please show me the same courtesy I've shown you."

The man she'd stabbed in the face with burning incense shoved her backward into the chair as they exited.

"Make yourself at home," Yip called out from the dark hallway. She couldn't see his face anymore. "The fuel in the lantern should last you another hour or so. It will keep the rats and cockroaches away."

The door shut. Aida rushed forward, throwing herself at it as the key turned in the lock. Twisting the doorknob was a waste of energy, but she did it nonetheless. "What do you want from me?" she shouted. No answer came. She pressed her ear to the door and listened to the sounds of retreating footfalls on the squeaking hallway boards.

When they were gone, she began thinking of anything she could use as a weapon. Her handbag was still tangled around her wrist, but her lancet was missing. She groaned, remembering how she spilled everything in the alley before Yip drove up. Had she lost it? Now of all times?

Disheartened, she explored the rest of the cabin. The door was solid and locked. The porthole didn't open, nor could she fit through it if she were to break the glass.

After she'd exhausted every corner, she plunked down in the chair in defeat and thought about Winter.

"Do you even know I'm gone?" she said, despondent. If tonight was like the last few, he'd be out working until morning. The thought of him just heading out to work after their fight hurt her feelings, but that he might be doing that right now, when she'd been kidnapped? Oh, that made her furious.

Angry was good. If she was mad, then she wouldn't worry about what Yip had planned. She wouldn't notice that the light from the lantern was beginning to dim as it ran low on fuel.

And she wouldn't have to regret that the last words she'd ever hear out of Winter's mouth might be when he told her to leave his house.

Indignant and annoyed, Winter strode out of the Tea Rose brothel with Bo at his side. Several of his men detached themselves from shadows and flanked them as they headed toward the car. It would be daybreak soon. Six hours since that bastard Yip had taken her.

And he still had nothing.

Four tong leaders sat inside the parlor of the whorehouse—five, including Ju. A small miracle that he'd been able to gather them together so quickly. Not every tong in Chinatown, but some of the big players. And all of them had sat in silence while Bo translated Winter's words. Not a single one of them knew about Doctor Yip or the Beekeeper or the Hive—rather, not one of them *admitted* to knowing.

They just stared at him with untrusting eyes. One of them looked at him as if he were crazy, organizing a hunt for one woman. A couple others looked at him in pity, maybe for the same reason. They knew his weakness now. A dangerous thing for someone in his position.

"All of that for nothing," Winter grumbled, anger trumping the dread and fear pulsing beneath his skin.

"Give the bosses time to talk," Bo encouraged. "Right now, they are intimidated that you summoned them. Once they loosen up, maybe someone will remember something."

"And by the time they do, Aida could be raped or dead."

"You can't think like that."

"The man who tried to burn her alive in her bed—"

"I know," Bo said firmly. "But he also wouldn't do the deed with his own hands. He's a coward. We will find him."

No other choice existed.

Winter eyed the lights inside a large Chinese bakery and pointed it out to Bo. "Ask to use their telephone. Check in with the house and the pier. Then call up the police station and tell them we're coming in to talk to Inspector Manion."

As much money as Winter pumped into the police force, the inspector better damn well be there to receive them. Manion headed up the vice squad in Chinatown. Winter normally would've hated like hell to ask for a favor, but at that moment, he just didn't care. If Manion could help him find Aida, nothing else mattered.

Waving away an open car door offered by one of his men, Winter pulled his collar up and huddled against a wall outside the bakery while he waited for Bo. The adrenaline that had been pushing him forward was fizzling away, leaving him with nothing but imagined glimpses of Aida in increasingly horrifying situations. She wasn't dead. Couldn't be. He would know—completely illogical, but he repeated it in his head until he believed it. She was alive, and he would find her.

And when he did, he would rip out every vertebra in Doctor Yip's spine.

Winter paced the sidewalk, watching Bo inside the bakery as he made the telephone calls; a few curious workers peered back out at him. Winter exhaled heavily and pulled down the brim of his hat. How the hell was he going to find the herbalist? Bo had been scouting Chinatown for weeks and had barely found crumbs. Winter tried to reassure himself that Aida could hold her own, but it didn't help his mood. Even the strongest man could be pinned down when it was many against one.

Winter had never felt so impotent and useless. Scared out of his mind. Plagued with what-ifs. What if they were hurting her? Maybe using fire again, or something else just as sick. After all, this was the man who killed one of the biggest tong leaders in Chinatown with bees.

Maybe the worst of his fears was something he hadn't yet considered. What if he never found out what they were doing to her—*what if he never found her?* The crushing darkness that had descended on him after the accident threatened to fall again. He pushed it away.

He watched Bo count off several bills to the bakery owner before marching out into the cold early-morning air. "The house?"

Bo buttoned up his coat. "Greta says Jonte's sitting in the foyer with a shotgun. The men outside haven't seen anything."

"Pier?"

"Same there. Called Gris-Gris again—Velma said no one's seen anything there, either, but she'll keep the telephone next to her bed, so we can call her on her home line."

Winter grunted in acknowledgment. He'd already begged Velma to help with magic, but she said there was nothing she could do.

"Talked to Dina down at the station," Bo said as he tugged his gloves on. "She said she'd call the inspector to meet us at the station, and she's putting the word out."

"Fine. It'll take us twenty minutes to get there."

Bo put a hand on his arm. "There's one more thing. Dina said you were already on the inspector's call list. Apparently they already called the Seymours."

Winter stilled. "Paulina's parents . . . why?"

"The good news is I think I know how Yip has been manipulating the ghosts haunting you. Remember I told you the original rumor about the secret tong—that the leader was a necromancer? Dina said there's been a lot of grave robberies over the last few months."

"Digging up graves?" Winter mumbled.

"Dina said most of the graves weren't notable. But early last night one particular grave was reported from Oakland, and I don't think it's a coincidence."

"Oh, Christ."

"Paulina's grave was disturbed. Her coffin's been stolen."

The lantern's fuel had long extinguished, but dusky tendrils of daylight from the port window outlined shapes within the cabin. For hours Aida had been listening to every thump, creak, and groan within the beached ship. She heard, at one point, the distinct sounds of a couple having sex—maybe a few rooms away—and occasionally heard doors opening and shutting, but the door she heard now was louder, and it was accompanied by deep voices: one speaking, one answering.

And both voices coming closer.

Heart thumping, Aida silently hefted the lantern then herself into the top bunk and waited. The voices were speaking Cantonese. They stopped at her door.

As the key rasped in the lock, Aida crouched in the cramped space with the lantern in hand. The door creaked open. She didn't wait to see who was on the other side.

Using all her strength, she swung the lantern from her perch and smashed it into someone's face. A man's voice cried out in pain.

She leapt off the bunk and rushed the doorway, shouldering aside the body that was hunched there. She didn't have a plan—didn't have time to make one. All she could hope was that the surprise of the lantern would put them off guard long enough for her to race down the hall.

She shoved at the second man, trying to get past him as light from his lantern scattered dancing shadows across the walls.

He grabbed her arm and spun her around.

Cauliflower-eared man.

The air whooshed out of her lungs when her back hit the wall.

He struggled with something in his pocket.

She pounded his arm with a fist. Kicked him in the shin. He growled and slapped a wet rag against her mouth.

The noxious cloth from the car.

She tried not to breathe, but her aching lungs betrayed her. And as she inhaled the wretched herbal fumes, she heard shouting down the hall—someone had heard them. She also caught sight of a young Chinese girl carrying a tray of food, and standing nearby, the person she'd thunked with the lantern, who was, serendipitously, the man she'd stabbed in the face with incense sticks.

*Should've aimed for your balls*, she thought as darkness took her.

It was almost two in the afternoon when Winter stepped out of the runabout and onto his pier, having returned from Oakland. Another fruitless exercise. No one had witnessed the robbery of Paulina's grave; the night watchman had been drugged. He paid a couple of men to watch his parents' graves, which were untouched—small favors.

Leaving Bo to moor the runabout, he marched up the dock and headed into the bulkhead building that housed his shipping warehouse and offices. Several of his men greeted him. No, they hadn't heard anything. He nodded and made his way from the reception area, bright and warmed by the midday sun glinting through its Embarcadero-facing window, back to the dark cave of his private office.

He hung his hat on the coatrack and settled behind his father's big old desk, wanting badly to lay his head down. Lack of sleep was starting to wear on him. He'd send someone out for coffee; he'd rest when he found her.

Even though he'd just been informed no one had called, he was compelled to pick up the telephone and ask the operator for the same numbers he'd been calling every hour all night—home, Velma, Dina at the police station . . . As if all it took was persistence, and one of these times he'd get the news he wanted.

He picked up the telephone receiver but pressed the hook switch down when he heard commotion up front in reception.

"Magnusson!"

His pulse sped. He knew that voice. "Let him through," he shouted to his men as he hung up the receiver and rose from his chair.

Ju strode through the doorway. "I thought they were going to shoot me where I stood. You need to train your people better, my friend."

"Did the tong leaders talk?" Winter asked in a rush. "Do they know something?"

"Don't know about the tong leaders, but someone else has been talking." Ju smiled and signaled to the person behind him.

Sook-Yin stepped into view. He'd never seen her outside Ju's place. She was dressed like a respectable lady, wearing a dark coat over a black dress. She looked a little older in the dreary light of his office. "*Nei hou*, Winter."

"Sook-Yin." He canted his head and looked between them. "What's this about?"

Ju leaned against the doorway. "After the tong meeting at the Tea Rose, the girls started chatting. Sook-Yin knows another girl who works for the tong leader Joe Cheung. She's heard a rumor. Go on, Sook-Yin. Tell him what she told you."

"One of Joe's girls, my friend, has a sister. Sister is another *gei* who is not under tong protection."

"She's a prostitute?" Winter asked.

Sook-Yin nodded. "She took a new job two days back. They pay big money and blindfold girls on drive from brothel to ship."

"Ship?"

Sook-Yin nodded. "She says every day they pick up girls late afternoon, take them to ship. Early morning, take them back."

"Tell Mr. Magnusson what's on the ship," Ju said.

*"Zau."*

Winter stilled. "Booze."

"Crates piled up like skyscrapers, apparently," Ju said. "Tell him what else."

With a smile revealing the small gap between her front teeth, Sook-Yin gave him a very particular look he'd seen before. It was a sly sort of look that communicated she had something he wanted. And though he'd seen it under different circumstances, damned if she didn't have something he wanted more than anything she'd offered in the past. "My friend's sister say last night they brought a white woman." Sook-Yin repeatedly tapped a finger across her cheek. *Freckles!* "She's locked up in a room on ship."

Relief and agony flooded him in equal amounts. His knees nearly buckled. It took several moments for his brain to spin into action. "A ship. What ship?" There were dozens lining the coast. Big ships, small ships—miles and miles of them. Knowing that she was on a ship was only slightly better than knowing she was in a building. Maybe worse, if that ship was sailing before he could find it. "Does the girl know anything else that would hint where it was docked?"

Ju gave him a slow grin. "She knew one important thing. The ship isn't on water."

The dry docks. His mind spun in several directions at once. Part of him wanted to race over there now, gun blazing. But he might be putting her in even more danger if they saw him coming. An agonizing choice.

"It will take me a few hours to get all my men together." He glanced at Ju. "Will the other tong leaders help if it gets them their booze back?"

"I'm sure of it," Ju answered.

Winter turned to Sook-Yin. "One last thing. Do you think your girl can ask her sister to sneak something on the ship when she's picked up this afternoon?"

Aida sweated through a never-ending series of bizarre fever dreams in which she was on a boat at sea, pitching and rocking during an angry storm. She woke occasionally, unable to move her limbs. And during those brief waking periods, she was sometimes able to recognize she was still on the beached ship. Other times, she imagined she was in Winter's bed, and wondered why it was so cold.

But it was the jangle of keys on the other side of the door that woke her fully. She lay on the bottom bunk of the cabin. Her head ached, and her body was weak. She glanced down at herself. Clothes were in place, and aside from the head-ache and lethargy, she didn't appear to be harmed—miracle of miracles. But if Ju's thugs wanted to come back for her, she might not have any fight left.

It wasn't them, however.

The door swung open to lantern light. A new man stood in the corridor—a much bigger man who looked as if he could give Winter a fair fight in a boxing match. He held keys and a lantern, and ushered a young girl inside. Aida pushed herself up on one forearm. The girl walked through a crimson col-umn of twilight beaming from the porthole. Good grief, had she been trapped in this hellhole for an entire day?

The girl bent low, wielding a small wooden tray in front of her. It was the same girl from the hallway. She had food—a bottle of beer and something that smelled of dried fish. She murmured something in Cantonese.

"O-oh, no—I'm not touching that," Aida said in a rough voice, waving the tray away. "It's probably got poison in it. You tell Doctor Yip if he's going to kill me, he's going to have to do it properly. I'm not jumping out a window or being burned alive in my own room. And I'm ab-so-*lute*-ly not poisoning myself."

The girl shook her head. She quickly tapped a napkin on the tray as she whispered something in Cantonese while giving her a strange, intent look.

The man outside the door bellowed a gruff command at the girl. She set the tray down on the chair and backed out of the room, bowing. The man snatched her by the neck and roughly shoved her down the hall, then shut the door and locked it.

Aida waited until their footsteps faded, then rolled off the bunk and crawled to the tray of food. She lifted the napkin and found the most beautiful sight she'd ever seen.

Her silver lancet.

# THIRTY

—◆—

WHO SENT THE LANCET? VELMA? WINTER? WHOEVER IT WAS, someone knew where she was—or at the very least, knew how to send something to her.

Reeling with hope, she spent several minutes considering how to hide the lancet, and decided to wedge it under her garter, as it was less likely to be found and taken than it would be if it were palmed in her hand.

No one returned for her, so she began inspecting the food. The beer was capped. She smelled it, poured some out to inspect the color, then tasted it in incrementally larger amounts, until she was as certain as she could be under the circumstances that it was untainted. Once it was finished, out of sheer desperation, she relieved her aching bladder in the rusting sink. Not her finest moment, and she cursed Yip's name for treating her like an animal.

An hour after the food was delivered, the big man returned with a partner. He held up the tin with the noxious cloth as a warning before herding her out of the room. A terrible rush of anxiety rattled her nerves as she was led down the corridor. But instead of heading back to the booze storage, they took her to a room with double doors. The metal plate on the wall, stamped with both Chinese characters and English, read FIRST-CLASS DINING ROOM. They entered.

"Ah, Tai," called a cheery voice in the distance. Yip. "Bring in Miss Palmer."

Her eyes darted around the expansive room. Like the rest of the ship, it lacked electricity, but lit lanterns had been set upon round tables. She could imagine those tables, when the ship had seen better days, covered in white linen and silver tableware; now, they were pushed to either side of the room to make an aisle, broken chairs piled near the walls. Two other sets of doors had been nailed shut with boards.

A large chandelier hung in the center of the room. Some of the bulbs were broken, and a few dripping candles had been stuck in their place. The candles cast a meager golden light on two tables below that had been shoved together. A long, dark box sat atop them, and behind stood Doctor Yip.

"Come, come," the herbalist said, waving her closer. "I hope you're well rested now, and you've eaten."

Aida didn't answer.

He gave a command in Cantonese to the big man, who dismissed his partner, and closed the doors. Yip spoke to her again. "Tai will mind the door while we talk, yes? Step closer, please. I have something marvelous to show you."

No need to panic, she told herself. She was armed, and by calling her forward, he was putting several yards between him and Tai. She'd be alone with him, and the lancet sat snug against her leg.

He should be the one frightened.

Steeling herself, she slowly approached the doctor, but didn't make it halfway before she halted.

"What's on the table?" she said.

"It's a coffin, my dear."

"An empty one?" The second the words were out of her mouth, something putrid and foul wafted. She recoiled and clapped her hand over her mouth. Something crunched under her shoes: dirt and gravel. A line of it led to the coffin.

Yip chuckled. "You would think someone with your skills would be less wary of the dead. Though, I do forget that your talents are different than mine. Not accustomed to graveyard work, I take it?"

"No," she managed.

"It's not pleasant, I'll admit. But you must remind yourself that it is just a body."

"Whose body?"

"Come closer, and I'll show you."

Another smell hung over the stench of death. "Are those herbs? More of your spellwork?"

He laughed. "No, that's to help with the odor of the body. If I wanted you drugged, I would've already done so. I'm trying to show you something, please."

She stepped closer, giving the coffin a wide berth as she tried not to breathe through her nose.

"Let us be frank," Yip said, wiping his hands on a soiled handkerchief. "I know you have been seeing Mr. Magnusson. I also know you are booked in New Orleans, so I am assuming your time spent with the bootlegger is merely a dalliance."

"It's none of your business, is what it is."

He waved a hand, dismissive. "I don't care about that. What I'd like to talk to you about is a partnership." He tipped his head her way. "All hives have a queen, yes?"

She nearly choked. "What?"

"I don't suggest anything physical. I am referring to a working partnership. An indoctrination into my organization." He held up a hand when she balked. "Now, hear me out. We are cut from a similar cloth, you and I. We both can call spirits from the beyond. My powers are stronger, but you are able to do something I can't, which is to speak to them. I cannot do this, I confess. I can bring them back and command them—and truly, this gives me more power than you."

"Truly," Aida muttered.

"You've seen my results, yes? Mr. Magnusson's murder victims? I think he's been using you to get rid of them."

"It's a fine trick, luring them with the coins and buttons," she said.

"I knew it! You can send them back. Is this a skill you've been taught?"

She didn't understand why he was so excited, and she wasn't going to admit that she hadn't been able to send them back—at least not when she tried it on the bloated ghost in the tunnel under the street. "So you basically channel spirits into dead things instead of yourself."

"Yes," Doctor Yip said, throwing his handkerchief aside. "It is one difference between us. I can call them and give them life again. Command them. You can call them into you temporarily. You cannot command them."

"I can send them back."

He smiled at her, as if this was the best news he'd ever received, then cleared his throat. "Yes, yes. And you can speak with them. I cannot. They will follow my commands, but they will not talk to me. And someone with your particular talent might be helpful in obtaining information from the dead. Not this plebeian work you've been doing, but real information from important spirits."

"Why in God's name would I want to help you with that?"

"I know you are sympathetic to the Chinese people—"

"I'm sympathetic to most people, as long as they aren't trying to kill me."

He made an impatient noise. "What I'm offering is a chance to use your abilities for a greater cause. You will be given a place of honor in this organization."

"And live on a rotting boat like a rat?"

"Live wherever you'd like. I will pay you a salary that will allow you a luxurious lifestyle, if that is important to you."

"Forgive me if I don't believe that. You *did* try to burn me alive in my old apartment."

He idly brushed the front of his vest. "I was only thinking of you as a problem then. I've been doing a lot of consideration and prayer, and I see now that I was wrong. You're much more useful to me alive."

"That's a comfort."

"You are suspicious. Very smart. And we can talk about this for hours, but you will not be convinced until you can see what I'm capable of. Action will convince you where words fail. And I truly believe that something in you will understand better."

He cracked open the lid of the coffin.

Aida recognized the moment for what it was: an opportunity. She should stab him now, while he was weak, while his goon stood across the room. She could kill him, or injure him badly enough to escape. But how loyal was the big man, Tai? Would he stop her at the door?

Her mind whirled.

"Like speaks to like," Doctor Yip said as he stood the lid open on its hinges. "We are the same, you and I. No one can truly understand who you are like I can."

The stench worsened considerably.

Yip leaned over the open coffin and chanted something she didn't understand several times. *"Hay-sun-la, hay-sun-la . . ."*

Aida's breath turned white.

She scanned the coffin for a ghost and saw nothing.

Yip's shoulders drooped. His breath wasn't like Aida's— no ghostly fog billowed from his mouth. His breathing was, however, strained. He gulped air like he was drowning and made a crude hacking noise.

Aida's focus splintered when something thudded from inside the coffin.

He'd called something over the veil, her breath told her that. And she expected it to look much like the ghosts he'd sent after Winter.

It didn't.

A decomposing corpse came into view as it sat upright in the coffin. Half bone, half decayed, rotting flesh, it turned its head toward Yip. It was hard to tell if it was male or female, as most of the hair and flesh was missing from the back of its skull. It was wearing clothing, but it was soiled beyond recognition with decomposition, its chest sunken. Shriveled lips remained, sutured closed. The eye sockets were filled with dark sludge.

"You channeled the spirit into the corpse," Aida whispered.

He coughed and placed a hand on his vest, as if to steady his laboring lungs. "Yes. I don't use memento mori, as you say in your show. I use their bones as a beacon." He mumbled incoherent words to the corpse, which promptly lay back down in the coffin. But he didn't send her back over the veil, because Aida's breath was still cold.

"What is this?" she asked.

"Westerners would call her a revenant."

"Animated corpse."

"If I command her to seek a person, she will walk for miles until her legs fall apart—and when that happens, she'll crawl. Her hands will scrabble across dry desert, long after her head has fallen in a ditch. I bound her spirit to her bones, and she can do nothing but obey my commands."

She. That thing was a *she*.

"Behold," he said with breathless excitement. "This is the kind of power I wield."

Aida stared at the corpse in horror. "Put her to rest, for the love of God. You've proven your point, and I can't stand the sight of her."

"She is alive now. I can't kill her."

"You've created an immortal creature?"

"I didn't say immortal. She can die again, in a manner of speaking."

"How?"

He inhaled deeply, ignoring her question. "Besides, this girl is special. Today I will pack her up and let her loose on her husband."

Aida held one exhalation of cold breath for several beats.

"Who is her husband?" she finally asked in a small voice.

Yip smiled very slowly.

It can't be—no, no, no . . .

"Take heart," Yip said. "I am not arranging for Mr. Magnusson's death because of his respect for my people. I'm just pushing forward what would naturally occur in the future—Mr. Magnusson has the burden of too much death by his own hand, and his mind is weak like his father's."

Dear lord. Winter wasn't crazy, but Yip was. A very rationalized, polite insanity, but crazy nonetheless. Aida stared at him, both horrified and feeling pity for the man.

Yip gestured toward the coffin. "Now that you've seen my power, what is your decision?"

"If I declined your offer?"

"Do you know how to swim?"

Aida started to shake her head in answer until realization sunk in.

"That is the best way. Your spirit will travel fast—very little chance of it staying here as a ghost if you've drowned in the Bay. And no one will grieve you, which is a small blessing. I will simply send word to your future employer in New Orleans that you've changed your mind, and no one will even know you're gone." He smiled at her as if he were a kindly old lawyer, breaking tough news about a judge's decision.

A loud noise coming from somewhere on the ship made her jump.

Then again. A sharp *bang!*

The report of a gun

Doctor Yip blanched. His men carried no guns.

Aida knew someone who did.

More shots were fired in quick succession, and suddenly gunfire reverberated inside the belly of the ship. It sounded like a battlefield lay beyond the walls of the dining room. Not single shots anymore, but the distinct *rat-a-tat-tat* of machine guns. Muffled shouting followed. The teardrop crystals in the chandelier clinked; the boards beneath her feet vibrated.

"Tai! Get out there and see what's going on!" Yip yelled at the big man as he rushed to close the casket top.

While he pulled it down, Tai swung both doors open. A shot exploded. The big man stumbled backward. Movement in the dim doorway took the shape of an even bigger man whose arm lashed out to shove Tai. His teetering form crashed to the floor. He did not get up.

The gunman who'd shot Tai stormed into the ship's dining room holding someone else in front of him like a shield, a handgun pressed to the side of his head. When he walked the hostage into the light of the first lantern, Aida, with a start, recognized the man being held at gunpoint.

Ju's thug. The man she'd burned with incense.

The gun fired. Flesh and bone exploded. Ju's thug dropped to the floor.

The gunman kicked him away and stepped into the light.

Splattered in blood, Winter strode into the room like a furious titan.

Aida cried out in relief, but a strong arm wrapped around her shoulders and yanked her sideways. Yip crushed her back to his chest and pinned her there. "Mr. Magnusson," his voice called near her ear as he shoved her forward. "I had plans to visit you at your house later tonight. I have men there watching your sister."

"I know. They're all dead."

"Ah." Yip's grip tightened. "And I see I miscalculated the depth of your allegiance to the spirit medium. Is it really worth damning your soul further to take more innocent lives on this ship?"

"Winter—" Aida started.

Yip slapped his bare hand on her mouth. Ghostly breath, now stoppered there, shifted paths and streamed from her nostrils in quick pants.

"I couldn't care less about her," Winter said.

Aida's chest tightened. Surely he was bluffing.

"Your actions betray you," Yip said.

"She's leaving the city tomorrow. It was a fling. She was giving it up for free—just a skirt, nothing more."

Aida's throat constricted. Anger and hurt welled up in equal parts.

"Then why have you come for her?" the herbalist asked.

"I didn't even know she was here."

It couldn't be true—no! Why did he send the lancet? She struggled to throw Yip off, but he only held her tighter. After huffing several strained breaths near her ear, he snapped at Winter. "You mean to tell me that you brought death into my house—that you're killing my workers—because of a few ghosts I sent your way? I don't believe that."

Winter's face was stone. Lantern light cast shadows over his eyes, making his scar stand out in sharp relief. His mouth was the same immovable grim line he'd worn when she first met him, as if he'd never learned how to smile. "I'm here to look out for my business and take back what you've stolen from my associates."

Aida's pulse pounded in her temples as panic shot through her limbs. Did he mean it? Her heart didn't believe it, but her mind pulled at the loose thread of their fight. The way he'd shouted at her. The way he'd ignored her for days before the fight. Maybe he'd only sent the lancet as a token— maybe it was his way of telling her she was on her own.

She searched his face for some sign of hope but found none. Her confidence unraveled.

"I wasn't aware you had any associates," Yip said.

"You'd be surprised how quickly the dollar will make friends of rivals."

"If you are that intent on saving your business, then go ahead and shoot the girl."

"I'd rather shoot you. Let her go and face me like a man." Winter took another step. His nostrils flared. A brief flash of repulsion crossed his face. He smelled the corpse. His eyes finally flicked to the coffin. Hesitation chinked his steely exterior—Aida could see it. Yip saw it, too.

"Before you shoot anyone, why don't we see if another woman might change your mind?"

All of Yip's muscles seized. He barked out a rough command. Aida struggled against him, trying to get away. His grip changed from firm to bruising. Pain sliced down her arm as his fingernails jabbed hard enough to break skin.

The coffin lid creaked open, blocking her view of Winter.
A gunshot cracked. Shellacked wood splintered.

Yip reacted immediately, dragging her backward as he circled around the coffin like a clock—a ticking second hand trying to outpace Winter's steady minute hand. She attempted to slow Yip by biting the meat of the palm gagging her mouth. Yip stomped on her toes. Pain radiated through her foot as tears streamed down her face. He dragged her farther and shouted another command.

They stopped at the head of the coffin.

Winter aimed a gun at her from the coffin's foot.

Their gazes locked. She saw nothing in his eyes—nothing at all!

The corpse's head lifted. Winter's focus shifted. She watched horror dawn over his face as he looked upon the rotting body of his dead wife.

"No introductions are necessary," Yip shouted to Winter. "True love never dies, yes?"

The body crawled out of the coffin, sloshing viscous dark fluid as it stood with creaking bones. Her dress was plastered to her limbs, indistinguishable from the pieces of embalmed skin clinging to her arms. Most of her flesh was gone around her upper legs.

A grotesque nightmare.

Yip gave her another command. Her head twisted toward her former husband.

Aida heard Winter make a pained noise. He aimed his gun at the walking corpse.

"You killed her once," Yip shouted near her ear. "Will you again? I called her spirit from the beyond. The body is crude, but it holds her, truly. She is alive, for all intents and purposes. And she still loves you, even from the grave. Would you really kill her with your own hands?"

Aida stared at Winter, hoping he wasn't falling for this insane man's words. He'd contradicted himself so many times, even she didn't know what was true. He'd said the revenant wasn't immortal. It was just a spirit occupying a dead body . . . nothing more than what she did when she channeled, only the spirit didn't have a live shell to occupy.

Winter hesitated, unsure, whispering, "Paulina?"

The broken sound of his voice was like a shock of cold water over Aida's nerves. Twisting in Yip's arms, she sloppily hiked her dress up and snatched the lancet from her garter. Yip shouted some threat in her ear, but she wasn't listening. Four quick twists and the lancet cap bounced on the floor.

Reaching behind her, she stabbed the blade into the only place on Yip she could properly reach: his right hip.

"A-a-ah!" he yelped as his hand released her mouth.

Not a serious wound, but enough to free her.

His grip around her shoulders sagged. She spun around and hit him again, slashing his bicep. He screamed in Cantonese and lunged for her, grasping at air when she jumped.

"Move out of the way!" Winter roared from the other side of the coffin.

Aida glanced over her shoulder. Was he talking to her, or to his dead wife?

Yip shouted a command at the revenant. The rotting corpse turned and lumbered toward Aida.

"If you kill me now," Yip yelled at Winter, "you will doom both of them. Your wife will not stop until Miss Palmer is dead—only I can command her. And if she kills the medium, her spirit will be tainted with blood debt. She will no longer be innocent, and she'll be stuck in limbo on this plane."

Stuck on this plane.

The words jarred something loose in Aida as she backtracked, eyeing the revenant as it shambled toward her, moving faster with each step. Doctor Yip had been too happy about the knowledge that she could potentially send his ghosts back across the veil.

Because he couldn't.

Could she?

The ghost in the tunnel hadn't budged, and this one carried the weight of a dead body. She honestly didn't know if that was better or worse, but Yip had used the bones to call the spirit, and maybe she could use them to send the spirit back. All she could do was try.

White breath clouded her eyes. She concentrated. The revenant lifted rot-bedraggled arms and reached for her as Winter shouted something jumbled and elusive in the distance. Aida made a whip-fast decision to boost her chances by doing something she usually only did to *call* a spirit: she raised the lancet and jammed it into her own thigh with all of her force.

One second of brightness. One second of a clear mind, free of chatter and thought.

One second of trance.

She grabbed cold, slimy bone and pushed her willpower into a single command.

*Leave.*

Current crackled inside the revenant, sending a shock through Aida's fingers. She jerked her hand back as the corpse quivered for a moment . . . then collapsed.

Aida's next breath was clear.

With a grunt, she pulled the lancet out of her leg and glanced up. Winter stood a couple of feet away. His gun was pointed at the fallen corpse. Their gazes locked briefly. His nod was barely discernible, but she caught it right before his eyes flicked to Yip. His gun followed.

"Are you hurt?" Winter asked, voice even and low. He was looking at Yip, but talking to her.

"I'm okay."

"Did they touch you?"

She knew what he meant. "No."

The herbalist spoke up. "Do what you will, Magnusson. I will not run from you or beg for my life." Blood stained the slice in his shirt where Aida had slashed. He held his hand over the wound on his leg.

Winter stepped over the corpse. "And I won't enjoy taking it. But you put my family in danger. You kidnapped and nearly burned Miss Palmer alive, and she is under my protection. You cursed and poisoned me, and you defiled my wife's corpse."

"I don't deny it. They are war crimes, and I don't regret them."

"Turn around, Aida," Winter said in a quiet voice.

She could have protested. She didn't. More for Winter than her own qualms. A little for Yip's dignity. Some part of her still pitied him, even then. She turned around and closed her eyes. Her shoulders jumped when the gunshot cracked.

# THIRTY-ONE

———◆———

DOZENS OF MEN FILLED THE SHIP. SOME WERE WINTER'S MEN, some were tong members. Aida felt like a sideshow curiosity as Winter marched her past them while they took stock of the liquor. She kept her eyes forward and tried not to look too closely at the aftermath of the siege.

Both Bo and Ju were welcome sights outside. Bo squeezed her hand, and she gave them all a brief summary of what happened, but was interrupted when two police cars pulled into the dry docks' gates in the distance. No sirens, no lights. But she doubted they were on a regular patrol route.

"I'll deal with them and buy us some time," Winter told Ju. "Tell everyone inside to stay calm and be prepared to truck the booze out before daybreak. Whatever can't be hauled out tonight will have to be forfeited. And if any of Yip's survivors want to defect, the tong leaders are going to have to decide if they want to give them safe harbor."

"Both my men are dead?" Ju asked.

"By my hand," Winter confirmed.

"Thank you." Ju turned to Aida and bowed his head briefly, then strode to the ship.

Winter tilted Aida's face up. Exhaustion weighted his eyes; his face was grim. She couldn't imagine what was going on in his mind after seeing his wife's body, but he didn't speak of it. "I have to take charge of this, and it may take me hours. I want you to go back to the house. When I'm finished, we need to talk."

She wanted to talk *now*. Wanted to tell him how sorry she was that he had to face Yip's cruel creation . . . how sorry she was that he had to crusade onto the ship and do what he did. She knew he didn't relish it.

She wanted to tell him how grateful she was that he did it.

But most of all, she wanted to throw her arms around him and tell him she was sorry about their fight and how stubborn she'd been and how stupid she'd been not to answer him when he confessed his feelings to her. "Winter—"

The police cars rounded a building and headed toward them, halting any chance of her saying anything she needed to say at that moment.

"Bo," Winter said. "Get Will to drive her."

He gave her once last glance, exhaled heavily, then walked away.

Cold and empty, she complied and left in a daze, riding in silence with one of Winter's men back to Winter's house in Pacific Heights. Four armed guards emerged from the home's gates. Her driver gave three of them a mumbled update while another let her inside.

Lamplight kept vigil in an otherwise quiet house. The clock in the side corridor said it wasn't quite midnight. Breathing in the consoling scent of orange oil, she plodded to the foyer with no thought other than a hot bath, but halted on her way to the elevator.

Lined up against one wall were her things—the elegant steamer trunk and several other pieces of luggage Astrid had bought her after the fire. She stood in front of them as her last remaining column of strength collapsed.

"He wants me gone," she murmured to herself.

This was what he wanted to talk to her about when he got back. Not reconciliation, but a good-bye. Her weary mind dredged up the sting of his words on the ship. *It was a fling. She was giving it up for free—just a skirt, nothing more.*

"Miss Palmer."

Aida wiped away tears and turned to face Greta. "He's delayed . . . I'm . . ." She inhaled deeply and righted herself. "I need a bath and a change of clothes, something to eat. Then I'll need a ride to the train station, please."

The frosty housekeeper didn't reply as Aida walked past her and headed upstairs.

She bathed quickly, sloughing off sweat and blood and the scent of death. One of the maids brought her fresh stockings and underclothes, a dress from her luggage. It wasn't until she was fixing her hair that she noticed all the mirrors had been removed again.

After eating, she trudged to the foyer and found Jonte waiting for her.

"Miss Palmer," he said. "I'm relieved to know you are all right."

"Thank you."

"But I must implore you to stay. Wait for Winter. Talk to him."

"I think we've done all the talking we need to do."

"Are you certain?"

She nodded and spoke rapidly to keep herself from falling apart. "Can you take me to the train station? I didn't realize there was so much luggage. I'm not sure how I'm going to manage it all. The steamer trunk is bigger than I am."

Jonte started to say something, but Greta strode in.

"You'll hurt your back, Jonte," she reprimanded in her singsong voice. "Get Christopher to help."

They began speaking in Swedish—an argument, from the tone of it—so Aida turned away to give them privacy and surveyed the luggage. Something unfamiliar sat next to the steamer trunk. A battered wooden footlocker. She stepped closer to inspect it.

Over dull green paint, black words were stamped across the top. Her gaze rapidly jumped from one to the next: U.S.A. 36TH DIVISION. PVT—a rank, private. A brigade. Distantly familiar numbers. And two words that stilled her breath: SAM PALMER.

She dropped to her knees in front of the locker.

Her pulse drummed in her fingertips as she flipped the unlocked latch and cracked open the lid. The musty scent of old canvas and boot polish wafted up . . . a very particular smell she remembered from the scarce weekends Sam came home from training, field dust and army barracks. Engine oil and rain.

Her shaking hand lighted on folded fatigues, sleeve cuffs still dingy with wear. Several uniforms lay beneath. A hat. A canvas bag of old toiletries and his razor set. Three books, one she'd given him for Christmas the year before he died.

Inside a khaki canvas cap lay a few smaller things: two circles of metal stamped with his name and number, strung on a piece of cord; a creased photograph of a pretty young girl Aida had never seen; and a folded Western Union form.

She carefully opened it and scanned the yellowed paper. Sam's name. A date: the day before he died.

Then on the recipient line, Aida's name. The Lanes' old address in Baltimore.

It was a telegram request. He'd filled it out, but the payment hadn't been tallied by the clerk. A telegram that was never sent.

She read his hastily penciled words in the box designated for the message:

*Have some big news for you. Sit down because you will not believe. I met a local girl named Susan. You will like her. I asked her to marry me and she said yes. I know. A shock. Do not tell Aunt and Uncle yet. Will tell you more in a letter later.*

*Much love, Sammy*

A strangled sob escaped Aida's lips. Through bleary eyes, she looked at the photograph again and flipped it over, seeing the name Susan inscribed on the back.

Her brother, who eschewed all sentiment and warned her time and time again about the pitfalls of love and marriage . . .

Sam fell in love.

Her world tilted sideways. "How can this be?" she mumbled.

"Winter hunted down Mr. Lane."

"What's that?" She looked up to see Jonte standing behind her.

"Emmett Lane, I believe."

"How?"

"He lives in the city. Winter was upset about something you lost in the fire, so he tracked down your brother's things."

She picked up the dog tags and squeezed the cool metal inside her fist as she stared at the footlocker in disbelief. "He did this for me?"

"Yes."

Sniffling, she folded the telegram form and sandwiched the photograph inside, then with Jonte's help, stood on weak legs. "Does he want me to go?" she asked, blinking up at him.

The driver gave her a patient smile. "I think you already know the answer to that."


Pink and gold streaks of morning sun lit up the fog covering Union Square. Wrung out and exhausted, Winter could barely keep his eyes open. He climbed in the backseat and Bo sped away from Shreve and Company.

They'd left the ship more than an hour ago. Most of the liquor had been recovered. Paulina's coffin had been hauled away and was on a boat back to Oakland. The tong leaders had seen to the rest. The San Francisco police department would take control of it now; it cost him a small fortune in bribes, but his name would not be connected with the gruesome scene.

Now he just wanted to go home. An even bigger fight

than Yip and his demented logic might lie before him there, and he only had a couple of hours to win it.

"If I ever need a good deal, I'll remember to show up in bloody clothes and bang on the door before the shop's even open," Bo quipped from the front seat.

Winter chuckled for the first time in days. "I think he was seconds away from giving it to me for free as long as we left him alone."

"You're making the right decision," Bo said in a quiet voice.

"I know," he answered. But whether it was too late was another matter.

He dozed off during the ride home but got a second wind when they pulled in the driveway. Leaving Bo to pay the guards, he marched into the house with purpose. It was quiet. *As it should be*, he thought. No gunshots, no telephone ringing with bad news. He breezed through the side hallway and into the foyer.

He stopped.

The luggage was gone.

Panic fired through his sleep-deprived brain. Her train didn't leave for hours—where were her things? She couldn't have gone. *No, no, no . . .*

He called out for Greta but got no answer. He didn't waste time trying to locate his housekeeper, just ran up the main staircase two steps at a time and bounded down the third-floor hallway. He stuck his head in the door of his study. Empty. Something clattered across the hall.

Heart in his throat, he strode to his bedroom and nearly stumbled over something just inside the doorway.

Luggage.

Aida's steamer trunk stood open nearby. And standing in her stockinged feet a couple of yards away was Aida, straightening a dress on a hanger.

He stood still, breathing heavily as she stared at him. She was in his room. She was unpacking. He repeated these facts inside his head, a simple math problem even a child would understand but he couldn't quite calculate. His brain was still stuck in *fight* mode.

"Aida—"

"No." She pointed a finger his way and spoke in a roughened voice. "*You* listen to me. I'm not leaving, and that's final. And since you claim I'm after your money, then I'll damn well take it. I'm not living like some kept mistress across town, waiting for you to call on me when it suits you."

"I—"

She raised her voice. "You'll let me live inside your home, and you'll protect me, because being connected to you is far more dangerous than me moving around the country unchaperoned. And on top of that, I'll need money to start my séance business, because I can't work at Gris-Gris any longer. I got booed offstage because of you."

"Me?"

"Because of our fight in the kitchen, dammit." She threw up a hand and tossed the dress on the bed.

"I see."

"Do you?" she challenged, something between anger and desperation tightening her face.

"Yes." He stepped over the luggage and rummaged in his suit pocket. "And while we're making demands, you should know that I just went to the jewelers and bought you this god-awful expensive ring, and you will wear it, and you will not spend another night outside of my bed."

He plucked out the square Asscher-cut diamond ring and tossed the box on the floor. Then he grabbed Aida's hand and slipped it on her freckled finger. The band was a bit loose, and he could only imagine how thrilled the frightened jeweler would be to have to size the damn thing, but it didn't matter. Nothing mattered but this.

She stared at the ring, lips parted. She didn't say anything.

"Do you like it?" he finally asked. He hadn't let go of her hand. He was a little afraid if he did, he might lose her again.

"Yes," she said softly. "I like it quite a bit. Is this a proposal?"

"I suppose it is."

"Ah, well, it's probably a good thing," she said, as if she were contemplating an everyday matter with practical intent. "Because even though I *could* live without you, I don't really want to. I think that means I might love you."

Her words melted the last of the ice around his wounded heart. He felt as woozy as a Victorian virgin crushed inside a corset in August. He snaked an arm around Aida's back and pulled her close. "Say it again."

She grasped his necktie with both hands, much like she did that first afternoon in his study. Her eyes were glossy with unshed tears. "I love you, dammit."

He leaned down and captured her mouth with his, kissing her firmly. Too firmly, probably, but he couldn't control himself. He was drunk with joy. "Again."

"I love you."

Winter's past, present, and future collided in one singular moment. And he was finally ready to live in it. "I love you, too," he said. "And that's final."

# EPILOGUE

———— ❧ ————

AIDA ACCEPTED THE BOX OF ALMOND COOKIES WITH A WEAK PRO-
test. "I think you're trying to fatten me up like a Christmas
goose, Mrs. Lin."

Her former landlady clucked her tongue. "A little fat is
good, that's what my mother always believed."

"Well, I appreciate them. Mr. Magnusson ate the entire
last batch you brought, so maybe I'll hide this from him."
She set the box on the mahogany desk that separated the
front of the narrow room from the cozy sitting area in the
back, where settees and wingback chairs were gathered
around a fireplace. She'd already banked the once-cheery
fire that had been burning there earlier in the day, in prepa-
ration for leaving sharply at three P.M.

Mrs. Lin glanced down at Aida's desk. A leather appointment book sat open, her last channeling checked off half an
hour ago.

"If you need to speak to your mother urgently, I can do
a quick channeling," Aida said. "But if it can wait until

tomorrow, I'd be happy to stop by Golden Lotus. It's just that—"

Mrs. Lin shook her head. "Once a month is enough. No, I was looking at the sign, here."

The printer had dropped it by earlier. Just something Aida could affix to the inside of the glass door. It announced that she was temporarily open by appointment only, and provided the telephone number to call.

"You're closing the shop?" Mrs. Lin asked.

"Just for a little while. I was going to let you know— Winter and I just made the decision yesterday."

"But why? I thought this was very fulfilling for you. A big success."

"It is." Too successful. She adored her small storefront. It was located between a tourist-friendly tea shop and a dry goods store on the opposite end of Grant from where Golden Lotus sat. She was only a few blocks from Union Square, but still within the invisible Chinatown border—and staunchly in Ju's territory.

Gold and black lettering painted on the front window announced her services:

AIDA MAGNUSSON
TRANCE SPIRIT MEDIUM
CHANNELING—SÉANCES—EXORCISMS
—SPIRITUALISM ADVICE

She'd been performing in-home séances every weekend since the wedding, and was solidly booked with private sessions at the shop on weekdays. Admittedly, a few of them were pro bono, as she'd somehow ended up taking on half of Ju's prostitutes as clients. First it was only Sook-Yin, with whom Aida had come to share a friendly, if not odd, relationship, then came others. They paid collaboratively in custom dresses. Not a bad deal, actually.

But between them and all the customers Mrs. Lin sent her way from Golden Lotus, and the ones Velma sent her way from Gris-Gris, Aida stayed busy. Exhaustion was taking its toll. She'd retired the lancet after that horrible night on Doctor Yip's docked ship, which was a relief. Yet funnily enough, getting a business up and running was turning out to be more stressful at times than performing onstage.

Concerned about recent changes in her health, Winter finally put his foot down.

"The holidays were stressful," she told Mrs. Lin, "and I have a lot of things to manage at home until the spring." It wasn't entirely untrue.

"Spring? Why so long?"

She would actually be on hiatus until summer, but she wasn't ready to give Mrs. Lin the details yet. "Mr. Magnusson's brother is coming back from Egypt today, and—"

"Oh, the archaeologist, very exciting. You will meet him for the first time."

"Yes. I'm a little nervous about that."

Mrs. Lin gave a dismissive wave of her hand. "He should be nervous to meet *you*. But I understand"—she narrowed her eyes suspiciously—"I *think*."

"You have the phone number at the house and pier. Call me anytime you need me. And if Winter gives you any grief, tell him it's an emergency."

Mrs. Lin laughed. "All right. And you tell Bo Yeung the girls at the restaurant are missing his charming smile."

"And his big tips, I'm sure." Bo hadn't spent much time at the apartment he kept in Chinatown since the fire in her room; lately, Winter had been keeping him busy at the pier. "I'll tell him when I get home."

With a smile, Mrs. Lin patted her hand, then bid her goodbye as she left.

Not a minute later, right on time, a silver Packard pulled up by the curb. Aida watched two boys go out of their way to walk around the big man who exited the driver's door, and chuckled to herself as they looked over their shoulders to study him from a safe distance.

Winter strode to the door, pausing to tip his hat to the

owner of a neighboring tea shop, where mah-jongg tiles clicked for hours every afternoon.

The bell above the door jingled when he stepped inside. Aida's stomach fluttered at the sight of his giant body. Wearing a new falcon gray suit with a claret tie and his best winter day coat, he glanced down at the shop's security protection as he wiped his feet on the doormat.

"How's my good boy?" He bent to scratch the glossy brindle coat of a mastiff that spent days in her shop and nights curled up in front of the fire in their bedroom. The great dog had shown up one night at the pier with an injured eye. Though he'd never admit it, this won the dog Winter's instant empathy, and after he nursed it back to health, he gave it to her with the promise that he'd dismiss the man he'd hired to watch the shop.

Not that she needed protection of any kind, really. After the brutal onslaught Winter led that night on Doctor Yip's ship, not a soul in the city from Chinatown to the Presidio would think about touching one hair on her head.

He stood and gave her a beautiful smile. "Hello, Mrs. Magnusson."

"Hello, Mr. Magnusson."

"I don't see your sign." He nodded his head toward the door.

She held it up. "I need tape. I meant to walk up to Woolworths at lunch, but it became too hectic to get away."

He sauntered around her desk, looking her up and down with an approving gaze. "How are you feeling?"

"A little tired, but good."

His gloved hand spanned her ballooning stomach. Three months pregnant, she'd only barely started showing a week ago, and the black shift dress she wore covered the small bump, but it wouldn't for long.

"You look very handsome today," she said. Enough to make her pulse speed, especially when he was standing so close.

"Mmm," he replied, preoccupied. "Your breasts are getting bigger."

She looked down. "They are not."

"Cheetah, there are few things I know with absolute certainty," he said, sliding his hand up to cup one breast in his palm. "And one of them is the exact size, weight, and feel of your breasts." He gave the one he was holding a gentle squeeze.

"Stop that," she chastised. "People can see us from the sidewalk."

"My property, my wife. They can look all they like."

"*My* property," she corrected. The shop had been purchased with money from Emmett Lane's check, in fact. "And if you're going to tease me, don't be selfish. Hurry up and give the other one attention."

He grinned down at her and fondled both breasts at once, sending a pleasant warmth through her. She shuddered appreciatively, then captured his hands and pulled them away as she stood on tiptoes to request a kiss. He chuckled against her mouth and obliged.

"Maybe we should shut the blinds and lock the door," she said when he pulled away. "Take advantage of privacy while we have it. I'm not happy about your brother's room being right below ours. I hope he's a heavy sleeper."

"That house is built like a rock. He won't hear anything." He kissed her bangs and gave her a playful swat on her backside. "And as much as I'd like to take you up on that offer, we need to get going. The station called to say that the train's running early. It's scheduled to arrive in an hour, and we need to pick up Astrid from school on the way." For the first time since his accident, Winter had been driving on occasion, and Astrid was no longer banned from learning how to drive. She claimed Winter shouted too much when she made mistakes, so she insisted that Bo do most of the teaching.

"All right. Grab those cookies Mrs. Lin left, would you?" She retrieved her handbag from a locked drawer in her desk and grabbed her coat and hat from the nearby coatrack, then turned off the lights.

Winter held the door open as she took down the leash hanging on the wall and whistled to the mastiff.

"Come on, Sam," she told the dog. "It's time to meet the rest of the family."

TURN THE PAGE FOR A PREVIEW OF JENN BENNETT'S NEXT
ROARING TWENTIES NOVEL

# GRIM SHADOWS

COMING SOON FROM BERKLEY SENSATION!

LOWE MAGNUSSON SCANNED THE DESOLATE UNION PACIFIC STA-
tion lobby. A young couple he recognized from the train
was spending the brief early-evening stop flipping through
magazines at the newsstand. A handful of other travelers
loitered on benches. No sign of the two thugs, but it was
only a matter of time. Easier to kill him in a dark corner of
a rural station than in the middle of a crowded smoking car.

Satisfied he was temporarily safe, Lowe slid a bill
through the ticket booth window. Not a large bill, but large
enough to sway a hayseed Salt Lake City ticket agent. Surely.

"Look," he said in a much calmer voice. "You and I both
know you have first-class tickets left on the second train
bound for San Francisco. It departs at eight. If we wait for
your manager to return from his dinner break, I'll have
missed it. It's not like I'm asking for a new ticket. I just want
to be moved from one train to another."

The young attendant exhaled heavily. "I'm sorry, sir. Like
I said, I don't have authorization to exchange tickets. Why

can't you just wait for your current train to depart? An hour really isn't that much of a difference in the long run. It might even leave sooner if they get the supplies loaded quickly, and aside from a couple of extra stops, they're both going to same place."

Yes, but the other train didn't have thugs with guns on it.

When he first noticed the men shadowing him, he thought sleep deprivation was screwing with his mind. After all, he hadn't had a decent night's sleep since Cairo. Food poisoning made the usually tolerable Mediterranean crossing from Alexandria to Athens a waking nightmare. But just when he thought he was out of the woods, he spent the storm-cursed weeklong voyage from England to Baltimore hugging both the toilet and his pillow in turns, praying for death.

But God wasn't done punishing him, apparently. Now that he'd endured three nights of restless sleep on the worst train trip of his life and was less than a day's ride away from home, armed men were stalking him.

Where the hell had all his good luck gone?

Right now, all he wanted was to kiss solid ground in San Francisco, fall into his ridiculously luxurious featherbed—courtesy of his brother's ever-increasing bootlegging fortune—and sleep for a week. Some clam chowder would be nice. A two-hour hot bath. Maybe a small harem of nubile women to warm his sheets—dream big, he always said. But if he could manage to avoid getting shot and robbed during the last hours of this hellish trip home, he'd settle for ten hours of uninterrupted sleep and a home-cooked meal.

The attendant eyed Lowe's loosened necktie and three-day-old whiskers. "We wouldn't even have time to find your luggage and transfer it before departure, sir."

"Just forward it to my San Francisco address." Lowe begrudgingly placed another bill atop the first. Dammit. Only forty dollars left in his wallet. Ludicrous, really. A priceless artifact in the satchel hanging across his chest, guarded with his damned life for the last two months, and all he had was forty dollars to his name.

Not to mention the massive debt hanging over his head after the botched deal with Monk.

The attendant shook his head. "I'm not supposed to accept tips, sir."

Lowe changed tactics, lowering his voice as he leaned on the counter. "Can I tell you something, just between you and me? I'm on a very important, very *secret* government assignment." He wasn't. "League of Nations business. Health committee," Lowe elaborated nonsensically.

"Health committee," the attendant repeated dryly. He couldn't have cared less.

"I wasn't aware the U.S. had joined the League," a voice called out.

Lowe looked up from the window to find the voice's owner, a woman, standing a few yards away. She was long and thin, wearing a black dress with a black coat draped over one arm. Black gloves. Black shoes. Black hair bobbed below her chin. *So much black.* A walking funeral home, blocking his view of the platform entrance.

And she was staring at him with the intensity of a one-person firing squad.

"I *did* say it was a secret assignment," he called back. "In case you missed that part of my private conversation."

"Yes, I heard," she said in an upper-crust transatlantic accent, as if it were perfectly polite and normal for her to comment. No remorse whatsoever for butting into his business.

"Excuse me." *And please leave me alone*, he thought as he turned back to the ticket window. Concocting a believable story on no sleep wasn't the easiest task.

But she wasn't done. "Can I have a word in private, Mr. Magnusson?"

Had she heard him giving his name to the agent, too? Ears of an owl, apparently.

"Sir?"

Lowe's attention snapped back to the agent. "Look, just get me the ticket before the train leaves. Have the porter deliver my steamer trunk to my address. I'll be back in a minute."

He stepped away from the counter and strode toward the woman.

"Mr. Magnusson."

"Yes," he said irritably. "We've established you know who I am."

Her brow tightened. "You were to meet me." When he gave her a blank stare, she added, "My father cabled you when you arrived in New York."

Shit.

In his haste to change trains, he'd forgotten about meeting up with Archibald Bacall's daughter: the oddball museum curator. Not that she was unappealing, now that he was seeing her up close. Not plain, either. To complement her owl-sharp hearing, she had an angular face that reminded him of a bird of prey. A lot of bones with long, sweeping lines. Long face, long arms, and nice, long legs. Tall for a woman; the top of her narrow-brimmed hat might fit under his chin, so he guessed her height to be five foot ten. But her boyish, slender body made her seem smaller.

And the all-black widow's weeds buttoned up to her throat didn't do her any favors.

"Hadley Bacall." She stuck out a hand sheathed in a leather glove trimmed in black fur. More fur around the collar of the coat draped on her arm. The Bacalls had money. Old San Francisco money, from the Gold Rush days—her deceased mother's fortune, if he wasn't mistaken. The Bacalls also had significant influence in the art museum at Golden Gate Park. Her father ran the Egyptian Antiquities wing and sat on the board of trustees; he'd been a field archaeologist when he was younger.

Not that Lowe had ever hobnobbed with the man. Without the amulet carefully tucked in Lowe's satchel, Dr. Archibald Bacall and his daughter would not be extending high-class handshakes in Lowe's direction. Hell, they wouldn't even give him the time of day.

"Yes, of course," he said. "Hadley, that's right."

Her grip was surprisingly evasive for someone whose arm was propping up a thousand dollars' worth of fur and an aloof attitude to match. She tried to end the handshake as quickly as she'd offered it, but he held on. Just for a second. She glanced down at his hand, as if it were a misbehaving child. He reluctantly let go.

"You did get my father's telegram, did you not?" she asked.

"Sure." He received a lot of telegrams from the man after the photograph of Lowe and his uncle standing in front of the Philae excavation site circulated in newspapers on both sides of the Atlantic—a photograph that had been reprinted a month later in *National Geographic*.

"Why were you lying to the ticket agent?" she asked.

He coughed into his fist. "Ah, well. It's a long story, and one I'm afraid I don't have time to share. I'm switching trains, you see. So I won't be able to meet with you after all."

One slim brow arched. She was almost attractive when she was frustrated, very glacial and austere. The corners of her eyes tilted up in an appealing manner, and her gaze didn't waver. He liked that.

"You didn't come all the way out here just to meet me, I hope."

She shook her head. "I was giving a seminar on Middle Kingdom animal mummification at the University of Utah."

Fitting for a woman who specialized in funerary archaeology, he supposed. If he wasn't so goddamn tired, he might've been interested in hearing her theories, but his travel-weary gaze was wandering to her breasts. Nothing much to speak of, but that didn't stop him from looking.

"I'm on my way back to San Francisco," she said, diverting his attention back to her eyes. "But when my father found out you'd be coming in on this train, he thought it might be wise for me to book a ticket so I could speak before you arrived. We aren't the only ones interested in your discovery. I'm not sure if you know what you're getting into by bringing the *djed* amulet here."

Oh, he knew, all right. He barely got the damned thing

out of Egypt. While his uncle battled the Egyptian Ministry of State, Lowe defended their dig site from looters. He'd been shot at, stoned, stabbed—twice—and had engaged in a fair number of fistfights.

And though he'd briefly considered the possibility that the hired thugs on the train tonight might be after him because of his debt to Monk Morales, if Monk wanted to kill him, he'd wait until Lowe got home. No, these thugs were definitely after the *djed*.

"I've already received offers from a few collectors."

Her smile was tight. "My father is prepared to give you the best price. That's why I'm to speak with you now. I'd like to inspect the amulet. If it's truly the mythical Backbone of Osiris—"

"Christ, keep your voice down, would you?" Lowe quickly surveyed the lobby again. "I'm trying not to advertise, if you don't mind. Besides, all the artifacts from the excavation were shipped on another boat. They'll arrive next month. So I don't have it on me."

A hurried porter walked past them, wheeling a luggage cart. She kept quiet until the man was out of earshot. "You're lying."

"Excuse me?"

Her gaze dropped to his leather satchel. "From the way you're gripping that bag, I'd say it's inside. But whether it's there or in your jacket pocket, I can *feel* it."

The bizarre accusation hung between them for a long moment. If he hadn't "felt" the cursed object himself, he might've laughed in her face. But truth be told, the amulet emitted some sort of unexplainable current. His uncle hadn't felt it, but some of their hired Egyptian workers did. A fair number of them deserted their camp the night he'd brought it up from the half-flooded sinkhole. The artifact scared the hell out of him, frankly. And the way she was looking at him, all matter-of-factly and unblinking, well, that scared him a little, too.

"Mr. Magnusson," she said in a lower voice as her eyes darted toward something behind his right shoulder. "Are you traveling with bodyguards?"

He stilled. "No."

"Don't turn around," she warned.

"Are there two of them? Black coats. Built like brick shithouses, pardon my French."

"No need to apologize. I prefer frank language. And if you are trying to ask if they are large men, then yes. They've been watching you for several minutes. One has slipped through a corridor behind the ticket windows and the other is approaching us."

A clammy panic slipped across Lowe's skin. His hand went to the Arabian curved dagger strapped to his belt and hidden under his coat over his left hip: a *janbiya*. In Egypt, he'd become accustomed to using it for protection. But after he'd left, he'd continued to wear it for peace of mind, more or less. Just in case.

Looked like he might be needing it now.

"Don't stare at the man approaching us," he instructed her. "Just pick up your luggage and follow me out to the platform. Quickly, but stay calm."

She didn't panic or question him. And thanks to those long legs of hers, their strides fell into a smart, matching rhythm. He caught the crisp scent of lilies drifting from her clothes as they strode past the newsstand, where neat rows of *Good Housekeeping* and *Collier's Weekly* blurred in his peripheral vision.

"Listen to me," he said as he placed an open palm at the small of her back. "Those men are armed with guns. They've been shadowing me on the train all day. I don't know for certain, but I've got a funny feeling they're after the amulet. It probably wasn't wise of you to talk to me, because now they'll think we're friendly, and that makes you a target, too."

"What do you plan to do about it?" she said calmly. Even in the panic of the moment, he had to admire her grit.

"You have a ticket for the 127?"

"Yes."

"Go ahead and board your train. Tell the porter suspicious men are following you."

"A porter's not going to shield me from gunfire."

"Lock yourself in your stateroom."

"I'll do no such thing."

Oh, she wouldn't, would she? He prodded her onto the shadowed train platform, where other travelers were waiting for their departure time to come, saying their good-byes to family members and loved ones. The chilly night air didn't stop a tickling bead of sweat from winding its way down his back.

"If they shoot you and take the amulet, I'll have failed my father," she said logically, as if she were making a decision about dinner plans. "So I'm sticking with you."

"Fine, see if I care if you get yourself killed. You're already dressed for a open-casket memorial service."

"And you're dressed like a Barbary Coast drunkard!"

"Is that so? Well, I'll have you know, I'm—"

Startled cries bounced around the platform. Right in front of them, exiting a door marked EMPLOYEES ONLY, was the second thug—the one who'd disappeared behind the ticket windows. He barreled onto the platform with a polished revolver leveled at Lowe's chest.